A BROKEN PROMISE

THE FRECKLED FATE TRILOGY
BOOK 1

TETYANA WALKER

A Broken Promise is book one in a slow burn, enemies-to-lovers, dark fantasy-romance trilogy, *The Freckled Fate*.

Authors note: Please note this book contains mature content and is best suited for 18+.

For trigger warnings please visit www.Bakumovka.com

Published by Bakumovka Publishing Company

Cover by Mibliart

Edited by Emi Janisch

❀ Created with Vellum

THE FRECKLED FATE SERIES
BOOK ONE

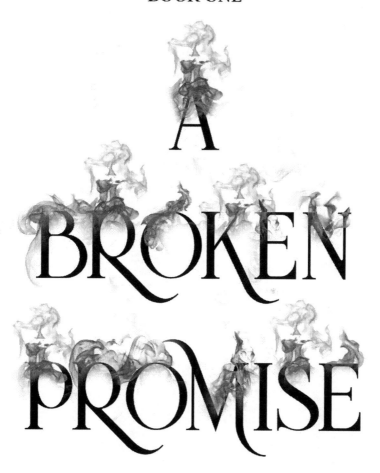

A BROKEN PROMISE

TETYANA WALKER

C
U
L

ROCK
QUARRIES

PORT
CITY

KINDER
RIVE

ESNOX

KINDERBY RIVER
EAST HOLD FORTRESS
TONE LE
HERN EP
DESOLATE DESERT
ELF LAND

PART I

ABYSS

1

"Line up!" The guard's loud voice echoed off the cold, stone walls of our cave. I quickly stood up. Chains clunked in a wave down the long tunnel, rattling in my ears. Viyak was already standing motionless by my side. We were both utterly exhausted, yet alive— better off than many of the slaves tonight.

I took a long breath; the stale air was thick with unease.

"What's going on?" I carefully whispered.

"I don't know. But there are a lot of guards," Viyak replied, his voice anxious.

I could feel his nervousness from the way his body locked, his shoulders squared. He was only in his early thirties, though the ruthless sun and slavery had aged him tremendously.

Viyak and I had been chained together since my very first breath in the Rock Quarries. He was the reason I was still alive. His bright, blue eyes kept my despair at bay. His blond, bearded smile was the only source of solace in my life.

Viyak was the longest survivor here, with over three years of slavery behind him. To me this meant two things: first, he knew all the guards and the intricate details of surviving in the quarry, and he kept me safe because of that. Second, it meant that there was no escape. At first, I couldn't fathom that fact, and yet, day after day I opened my eyes to this new reality. Three hundred and ninety-six days of luke-warm hell.

I thought about escaping at first. My mind created one scenario after another, desperately trying to solve this impossible puzzle. But even if you somehow unshackled yourself from your partner and avoided the guards and their hounds, there was only one large bridge leading out of the Rock Quarries and then, there was the large Rocky Mountain descent. Those snowcapped mountains held the highest peak in Esnox, and we were deep within their core.

There was no escape.

But that wasn't the worst part.

No.

The worst part was watching the slow deaths of the attempters. They were always brought back half dead, tied up to metal poles in the center of the Quarry, and whipped until there was little flesh left on their bones. Then they were left to rot with no food or water under the high-altitude sun, eaten alive by swarms of bugs and flies.

If Fate was on your side, you'd last only a few hours, maybe a day, but if not—a week. Then your body was left to decompose in the hot sun for another week to remind us all of what our luck would be should we think to flee.

I couldn't forget them even if I tried.

It was never the soul scarring screaming as they were whipped that rang in my ears each night. It was the begging after. The desperate, agony-filled pleading for a sip of water or the soul churning hallucina-tions as they welcomed Death. The rotting smell of the human flesh haunted me with each breath I took.

I never believed in human gods. Growing up with my two-hundred-year-old elf maid—the only family I'd ever had—even the concept of them was foreign to me. But in those moments, I prayed to them. I begged whatever gods there were to spare the agony-filled, poor souls and grant them relief.

Because the rest of us were helpless.

The few slaves that tried helping those in torment die, carried their own deep scars from lashings as the result.

That is, if they survived the whipping…

"Kahors," Viyak said with terror in his voice. Hairs on the back of my neck stood up as the meaning of his words settled in me. A shiver went through my body. Suddenly, the large main chain that linked all the slaves for the night got pulled. One by one, we were dragged out into the darkness.

My lungs welcomed the fresh summer night breeze, yet I couldn't take a full breath. My chest tightened with uncertainty.

I was facing Viyak's tall, bony back, unable to see anything. Hushed whispers fluttered around me as unrest rose. Exhaustion completely vanished when my eyes caught a glimpse of them.

Kahors.

I wasn't sure if they were men, women, or something else entirely. Whatever they were, they wore long, silvered robes with a deep hood on top, covering most of their face except for the mouth and chin. Elongated sleeves covered their arms, the ends of them extending down to the floors.

They oozed with rot and decay. I fought the urge to gag as their stench made me nauseous.

Wide in frame and yet so unnaturally thin, the Kahors' figures floated soundlessly just a couple of inches above the ground. One of them stopped straight across from a girl no more than a few years younger than me. I had seen her a few times around the Quarry. She was new, but a hard worker. I respected that.

Even covered in dust and sunburnt skin, she was beautiful. Striking. Big, plush lips and dark, hazel eyes. Her chestnut brown hair was pulled back in a large thick braid.

She whimpered as a big, curved, animal-like claw appeared through the silver robe. The Kahor slowly slid it down her delicate throat, hard enough to draw blood. Large, crimson drops pooled on their nail. I watched in horror as they slowly brought it to their demon-like mouth and licked it off.

The lipless mouth stretched in a cruel smile. *"This,"* they hissed. The sound, high in frequency, though low in pitch, gave me an immediate pounding headache. The guards quickly unshackled the young girl from the long chain and tightened a rope around her wrists and neck.

I flinched at the sound of her quiet begging to the guards, to the slaves around her.

My heart ached as the tears slid down her cheek and despair filled the air.

But begging never worked.

I bit down on my cheek hard enough to stop tears from my own watery eyes as I watched the guards pull her away from us. I didn't know her name; didn't talk to her once, but my soul filled with sorrow for her.

There was only one reason a Kahor—a creature of darkness and abyss—would be delighted like that.

They tasted magic in her veins.

It also meant that she was now sentenced to death.

Unknown death.

Sacrificed by Royals?

Or tortured and killed for sport by Destroyers?

Or sent off to the Queen Insanaria, known as the Mad Queen, for her to split your soul from your body and rip it into a million pieces to exist in torment forever?

At least in the Rock Quarries, if you were a good slave, never causing trouble, never making eye contact and working hard, you could look forward to one day just not waking up from your sleep. A peaceful end for the exhausted soul and body. And if Fate was on our side, Viyak and I would die together, cuddled in each other's arms just like we went to sleep each night.

A sense of doom ran through my mind as they moved slowly to another boy from the line, also just as striking as the girl. Even now, his underfed body was muscular and strong. His light brown hair was down to his chest. His eyes and nose razor sharp.

Another drop of blood, another hiss making my ears bleed. He tried to flee as they unshackled him. The boy punched the guards and was about to hit a Kahor, but their long, deep claws grabbed his throat in a tight grip, pooling blood at his neck. He went completely limp as the creature sunk their long canines into his blood-covered flesh.

I knew I shouldn't look, but I glared at them, letting a glimpse of anger flicker while they licked off the last droplets of the precious blood and wiped their bloodied-up chin and hands with a swift motion.

I couldn't see their eyes but, at that moment, I knew.

I *knew* they stared back. I could feel their dark being slithering. Instant regret flooded me down to my core. Not because I put myself on the line, but because I endangered Viyak. He was always so prudent about keeping our eyes on the ground, always being meek and obedient.

I turned my eyes straight to the dusty ground. Too late. The creature slowly floated towards me. My heart thudded in my chest, my fists clenching tight, but I willed the rising panic to calm.

I wasn't a Magic Wielder. Though, there were plenty of times in my twenty-two years of life when I wished I was one. Through bits and pieces of secret tales, I'd heard of the great Creators, Seers, and Healers. Of them who walked the continent helping people thrive before the Great Betrayal. Long before they were exterminated by the Destroyers.

Mages were everything I aspired to be at one point. Hopeful, selfless, inspiring, loving, kind.

But I wasn't a Magic Wielder.

Neither had I lived up to any of my childhood aspirations.

The Kahor floated above the ground just a few inches away from my face.

I stopped mid-breath. Their smell overwhelmed me to the point of my eyes darkening.

Something deep inside me stirred in wrath and boldness against their presence. But I didn't dare move. Viyak was just as rigid as me, looking down as a cloaked hand rose close to my neck and a large claw appeared. I winced from the sting as they sliced through the tender anterior of my neck.

Though my face was tranquil, I hoped the creature would choke on my blood.

Notes of panic ripped my well-built walls of calm to shreds, as minutes passed and the Kahor stood stagnant in front of me.

There is no magic in my blood. I chanted to myself to chill my heating blood. The creature dipped their nail one more time into the tiny pool of blood between my neck and collar bone.

At last, I raised my treacherous eyes to their hooded face just as they hissed.

"This."

My brain short-circuited.

"There is a mistake," I muttered, as the tightrope slid around my throat, almost choking me.

"Kahors are never wrong, *freak*," the guard unshackling me sneered as he jerked my body out of the line.

"Please, take me. Let her stay!" A loud desperate scream erupted.

From Viyak, tears forming in his eyes.

My heart broke in a million pieces at that look.

My mind was in haze while panic ransacked my thoughts like a violent robber.

I grabbed Viyak's callused hands as tight as I could.

"Please live, Vi, I will find my way back to you. *I promise.*"

A strong smell of pine trees enveloped us as we traveled in complete silence away from the Rock Quarries. The prison wagon resembled a large box and was made from thick, black metal with an underlying purple hue. There was a small door that we had to almost crawl through and only a few very small slits in the ceiling, barely large enough for the air to flow.

The metal was ice cold, even as the sun burned bright above us. At least this cold was refreshing amidst the summer heat.

A positive outlook. A solid attempt to combat the bleak and haunted mind of mine that was flash flooded with thoughts.

There were two tsunamis hitting my mind at once. One: Kahors thought they had tasted magic in my blood. And two: whether they were wrong or right, I was surely heading to face an unknown death.

I glanced at the two people in the wagon with me. The boy was still unconscious and bleeding, but the girl was staring back at me, her beautiful eyes full of terror and defeat.

"What are your powers?" I asked her, with subtle hope that maybe she had a plan to escape.

"I am a lower tier Creator. I can change the colors and sometimes shapes of things," she replied, her voice shaking. "You?" Her eyes lowered to the floor.

I wasn't sure what to say.

"I don't have any." There was no point in hiding the truth. "I didn't think I had any magic in my blood at all until a few hours ago."

"Even if you had all the powers in the world, this prison wagon is so thickly laced with magnesium that unfortunately, we are all useless," she said, her voice filled with sorrow.

"Well, joke's on them, because they've been lacing our food in the Rock Quarries with it anyway." My mouth stretched into an uneven smile, but it fell flat as she lowered her head and sobbed.

There wasn't anything I could say or do to comfort her. I slowly exhaled and rested my head against the wall. The cold was now reaching my bones.

Viyak.

Another wave of thoughts slammed into my soul.

We were a team. Even if we didn't talk much, we somehow knew each other, understood each other, just from a single blink. We survived together, and now I was gone, and he was left behind.

"Do you know what he is?" I questioned the girl again.

I wasn't sure if she felt like answering questions right now, but it was a better alternative than to sit still and drown in my thoughts, accompanied by her heartbreaking sobs.

"I am not sure. But from the looks of it, I'd guess he's a Creator too." She looked at the limp body in the corner. Creators were the most common Magic Wielders. They also were the most beautiful; their magic not only beautified the world, but its wielders too.

"Is your blood red?" she questioned.

"What?" My brows bunched in confusion.

"Does your blood run red?" she repeated in between her sniffles.

"Yes," I answered, raising my eyebrows in question.

"If it helps, you are not a Seer. Their blood runs blue," she explained, adjusting her legs to let her knees rest against the wall.

"It does help." I nodded. It really did. "Thank you," I quickly added. Though Tuluma educated me well, being an Elf, she herself knew very little of the mages and their magic and refused to educate me on the human world.

Well, not a Seer. I guess I knew that now. I highly doubted I was a Creator considering my looks. I was barely 5'3" with a starved, boyish-looking figure. My ashy blond hair was down to my waist, but it was heavily matted and unkempt. My face was round, covered in large, dark freckles that made me look diseased with some wicked kind of pox or sometimes, just outright dirty. My deep green eyes were paired up with dark brown, bushy brows. My lips weren't plump and nice like hers, but instead were weirdly unmatched, with the bottom lip bigger than the top, and constantly cracked and crusty from my terrible habit of picking at them. The only feature I liked about myself was my small nose. Overall, I could barely pass as an average-looking human. In no way was I remotely stunning enough to pass as a Creator.

No beauty, no blue blood. A Healer perhaps?

"What about Healers? Do you know much about them?" I asked, raising my eyes to her.

"Healers are rare. Not as rare as Seers, but not as common as Creators. Unlike the other Magic Wielders, the gift of healing is passed on through generations. Did you know your parents?" Her voice shook less, I realized, though occasional sniffs still interrupted her sentences.

"No. Mother died in childbirth. Father unknown. At least, my mother's maid didn't know who he was."

"Do you have the *light*?" She continued after realizing my confusion. "It's a gold-like, shimmery thread that contains the healing magic. Healers usually have it within their bodies and can tug on it to heal. The stronger the Healer, the thicker their thread. Some legends tell of the powerful Healers with Light so potent and thick that it would glow from underneath their skin, running through them thicker than their arteries."

I couldn't heal. I knew that.

"How did you know you were a Magic Wielder?" The carriage shook yet again, banging our heads against the harsh metal.

Maybe my questions were direct or intrusive.

Perhaps a little desperate.

But she softly replied.

"I grew up knowing. My aunts were human so they each took a kid as my parents ran. Separated, we had a better chance of survival after my dad was killed. I was the youngest. Each of my siblings were Creators but had different levels of magic in them. When puberty hit, I knew what to look for, I guess. Unlike my siblings, my powers never became stronger past the shifter stage." She swallowed. "The less power you have, the less chance of getting discovered." She paused again. This time, a heavy silence laid between us as she said, "None of my siblings made it past thirty."

"I am sorry." I couldn't imagine what it's like to have siblings, family, aunts. But I knew the pain and grief of losing one. I recognized the familiar flicker of anguish. An invisible scar that we both carried.

A small tear rolled over her cheek. "Somehow I foolishly hoped that with the smallest amount of magic and being the youngest, I would at least live until thirty, unlike my siblings." I flinched as she broke into quiet sobs again.

I didn't know how to reply. There was no hope I could give. No hope left.

We rode in silence well into the night.

Even my mind quieted.

The openings in the ceiling were too small to let in the bleak light of the moon, leaving us in familiar darkness.

The previously welcoming smell of the fresh pine trees was long gone, taken over by the acidic smell of stale urine.

My stomach grumbled with hunger, but I welcomed the feeling. We were fed in the Rock Quarries twice a day. Always the same porridge. Always the same size scoop.

But the cooks liked Viyak.

Everyone liked him.

They would sometimes add salt just for him, and he would switch me plates, or share with me his slightly larger portions.

Abruptly, the wagon stopped. I widened my eyes, attempting to see anything in the pitch black. My ears were aware of each noise, each breath. Gravel rattled outside under heavy but slow steps. My heart paused.

Not Kahors. They were silent. Must be the guards.

Moonlight poured into the small box, reflecting little shimmers of deep purple as the small door was opened wide.

"How many you got?" a crackling male voice sounded, not too far away.

"Three. Two girls and a boy," the guard casually responded.

"Hell, I ain't paying you for three," the man angrily protested. "Just grab a girl, the younger the better, and take her in," the same man barked at the guard. I recognized the loud thump of bagged coins against the gravel a second later.

The girl and I quickly glanced at each other. Tears didn't seem to stop pouring from her horrified eyes. She scooted a little further away, shaking her head. I blinked at her in understanding.

I would go first.

A quick nod.

A quick goodbye to a stranger.

The guard's hand peeked through the open door, pointing at us as he shouted, "One of you. Out. Now."

Without looking back, I obediently crawled through the door.

3

Two guards in dark burgundy uniforms grabbed the end of the rope leading to my neck. Some level of Royals, I realized, based on their large crown insignia.

The full moon now hid behind the long, heavy clouds, as if she too closed her eyes, ignoring the downfall of humanity.

Like a dog on a leash, they dragged me to a large manor down the road.

The Royal house was surrounded by tall, ancient pines. The building was made from dark rock supported with large wooden beams in between. I recognized that stone immediately. I still had torn up bloody calluses on my hands from mining it.

There was so much of it. The path, the large fence, the steps leading to the house, the square porch. The gray stone went on and on; stables, fountains, statues.

My eyes narrowed in anger.

How many slaves have died carving these rocks?

I glimpsed back just once. The small prison box was long gone in the night; an empty horizon now lined with shadows of the Rocky Mountains. Sorrow churned in my heart. My thoughts floated far behind them, to a dark, cold cave within the Peaks. To Viyak.

One of the taller guards yanked on my leash, almost choking me. Walk faster.

I was an animal; a dog to them.

No.

I was glad it was me and not a dog on this leash. No animal deserved to be treated with such vile.

We passed the tall fence. The green grass was perfectly cut, and freshly watered too, I realized, as the small droplets covered my bare feet. Waist tall braziers filled with small, red coals irradiated little heat and light as we walked down our path. I cast my eyes past the house. Large stables filled with sleeping horses were left notable unattended.

If I could get there, I could get a horse and then run, I thought to myself.

Run where? My mind followed.

Somewhere far.

Somewhere away.

But I had nowhere to run. Nowhere to hide. I had nothing and no one.

My only friend, Viyak, was chained up deep in the cave right now. I shut my mind from the cruel despair taunting me within. No, I wouldn't let it in. Not yet.

A short, round figure was ambling ahead of us. His walk was heavy with a limp, a cane in his right hand to balance him. Each step was accompanied with a huff and a grunt. He didn't stop to look at us.

We followed him to the main entrance. It was a large, wooden door with intricate carvings and a huge, golden door knocker in the middle, the faded red paint chipped in chunks around its edges.

The air was pleasantly warm inside. The dark hall looked like a throne room. Though "throne" was quite an overstatement for the large chair on a pedestal. Bear, deer and tiger skins were thrown around on the stone floor. The room's ceilings went up three stories; a grand chandelier made out of elkhorns was the only source of light in the dim space. Big, wooden beams framed the stone walls with the occasional tapestry quieting the echoing of our steps.

"Geez, Dimitrii, keep the filth off the carpets," the guard behind me scoffed. Dimitrii tugged on my leash to force me to move further away from the plush furs. I didn't blame them though. The silky fur carpets looked very nice, and I was covered in my own piss and dirt from the Quarries.

Dimitrii yanked on the leash again, pulling me closer to him. "Lord Inadios paid more for these skins than for you," he whispered, just loud enough for me to hear, flashing a small, crooked grin at me. I wanted to spit in his repulsive face, but I chilled that defiance.

One day, I would let it roam free, but not today. Not right now.

I heard much worse too. After all, I was a human child with an elf for a mother-maid, existing in a place where elves were not tolerated, but hated and despised. I had learned about human cruelty before I could understand their tongue.

Lord Inadios appeared from the dim shadows.

"Oh hell, she reeks even from across the room." His puffy face filled with disgust. He took a few weighty steps closer to me. As he approached, Dimitrii shoved me down to my knees and I didn't fight him as I landed on the cold floor, scraping my dry knees.

Viyak's words rumbled in my head as I bowed down to the floor.

"You might not like it, but obedience and meekness will help you survive more than that stubbornness and defiance will." Though my face was down, I made a conscious effort to relax my jaw, to still my body. I knew Viyak was right after the third brutal beating I received from the slave watchers for looking them in the eyes. As my bruises and torn flesh were healing, I had made a mental note to *always* listen to Viyak's advice.

I wasn't sure what their plan was for me yet, but I knew if I obeyed and showed zero resistance, I would have a better chance to find an alliance; a better chance to survive.

I was a slave, after all. And nobody liked a stubborn slave.

Long scars on my back served as a constant reminder of that.

I closed my eyes, letting darkness soothe me as the fat figure of Lord Inadios hovered over me.

"What are you, girl?" he snarled.

"A Creator, my Lord," I lied, shifting my voice to be as soft and gentle as possible.

Up until this moment, I had debated.

I debated whether to tell them that I was no Magic Wielder at all, that the Kahors were wrong. But in that precise moment, I decided. Truth could cost too high of a price, and I was in no position to pay.

Though I was most definitely looking forward to seeing his gnarly face when he found out that he wasted his money on nothing. That he wasted his money on me.

Lord Inadios's sweaty sausage fingers grabbed my matted hair and yanked my head straight up. Grimacing from pain, I willed myself to keep my eyes down.

I stayed silent even as I could feel my hair almost peeling off my skull from his harsh grip. He ogled down at my freckled face.

"I knew they were going extinct, but hell, this is the ugliest Creator I've seen." He huffed with displeasure. My head almost hit the floor as he threw me down. I clenched my jaw, anger gnawing on the thick doors within me. I closed my eyes. It was better in the darkness. Tranquil. "What's your level, girl?" He nudged me with his foot.

"I am a low tier Creator, my Lord. My abilities never went past the shifter stage, my Lord." I meekly repeated the words I had heard just hours before.

"Show me," he angrily demanded. My heart plunged at his request. Kahors might have tasted my blood and Lord Inadios might have paid a high price for a Magic Wielder, but I could barely function as a human, less so perform any magic.

"I would, my Lord, gladly. But forgive me, my Lord, for I cannot. Magnesium still deeply flows through my veins… my Lord." I spun a half-truth and braced myself, hoping that it would work or at least buy me enough time to figure out a way out of this.

He grouchily huffed again. I counted seconds.

It was that second breath of his—that longer than a second pause—that let my heart ease.

It worked.

He barked at the guards.

"Take her to the maids, have them get her ready for him. Get her fed and cleaned up for his arrival tomorrow." Lord Inadios then turned to me and angrily rumbled.

"Let's pray, girl, for you and for me, that you are able to put on a show for *him* tomorrow."

4

D imitrii hastily pulled me down a poorly lit hall. Small torches on the walls were now no more than charcoals. I still didn't dare to fully raise my eyes, only chancing small, hidden glimpses to count the doors and stairs, watch the pathways and listen to the stomping of guards' boots.

I took a long breath as we finally stopped; the air was heavy and humid. Two maids stood by, close to the wall. One was about my age, tall and slender. Her neatly made bun looked so pristine and clean. Right next to her stood an older lady. Her hair was cut short, down just slightly past her ears. Wrinkles and a cold look covered her face. They both wore the same uniform, with a small, white headband tying it together.

We had arrived at a bathing chamber, I realized, as I noticed a towel in their hands.

We were just a few more steps away from the maids when Dimitrii grabbed my arm painfully tight and whispered into my ear, "Don't worry, bitch. I'll come see you later tonight and have you moaning 'yes, *my Lord*' to me." His mouth stretched into a wicked sneer.

Blood left my face at those words. I glared at him, but he was only delighted at the fear in my eyes. I yanked my arm, but he just held on to it tighter. A rush of adrenaline made my knees shake.

Once. I allowed the wave of panic to run through me for once.

I survived this far, and I will survive more, I assured myself a second later.

How?

I had no answer to that.

I might not be a Magic Wielder, but I had time and I would think of something. I would figure it out. Maybe the maids would help me.

Viyak always said that sometimes support comes from the most unexpected places and I had to believe that now, because I was alone.

So completely alone.

I took a low breath—almost a snarl—and stared at his eyes again. This time, refusing to let fear come to the surface.

Even if Fate decided against me today, even if it deemed me worthy of the punishment. Even then, I would endure.

At the request of the maids, he unshackled the heavy chains around my ankles. I recoiled at his possessive, lingering touch. Thoughts of Dimitrii forcing himself on me, and the impending doom of the night approaching, made me want to puke.

I took a small step and almost fell. For the first time in three-hundred-ninety-six days, I was free of rusty shackles on my feet and wrists. I took another step, this time more confidently. My feet were too light. I felt so unbalanced. My arms flopped around in an odd manner without the heavy weight of iron. The younger maid insisted on taking off the rope from my neck as well, though Dimitrii hesitated at first.

I was immediately grateful for her.

This bathing chamber was different from what I expected. It was on the bottom level of the Rock Manor, with just two small windows. Dim lighting was provided from bronze braziers and a large fireplace. Two bulky, circular tubs stood right next to each other. Clouds of steam piled above one of them and all manner of oils and salts were lined up on the small stool right next to them.

"I hope you don't have any attachment to these rags you are wearing, because I am throwing them in the fire," the old maid gently said, pulling my clothes off. I nodded my head in agreement. I knew I shouldn't, yet as I watched her throw my clothes into the small fire pit not too far from me, my lip trembled as I fought back the tears.

No, I knew the grimy, stiff-from-dirt scraps that I called clothing couldn't be saved. They weren't even actual clothes, only two linen cloths tied together in a makeshift dress. It served as the unofficial uniform of the Rock Quarries' slaves. Stripped upon arrival of all their possessions, slaves were given a pair of thin gray pants and a shirt. After only weeks of working, the clothes ripped, leaving the slave's bodies at the mercy of the harsh elements. With no other clothes available, we were allowed to take old linen sacks used to transport the slop we ate. Year after year, the slaves wore that. I wore that. Viyak wore that. The harsh linen was rough against the skin, but it was thick and kept our bodies protected.

I swallowed a lump in my throat as I realized that those burning threads were the one and only thing I had left connecting me to Viyak; to the last year of my life. I never had many possessions. In fact, I only ever cared about two: a large necklace with the eye-shaped green stone from Tuluma, and the very first copper coin I ever earned myself. It was a mere penny, but it was everything to me. The first money I had ever had. The first feeling of control. I kept it for good luck and as a reminder that I could do something with my life.

Though looking back, clearly the coin was a sham of a Goodluck charm, because it was probably rotting in the pocket of my clothes left back in the Quarries. The necklace was ripped off my chest by a so-called friend right before he chucked me into the slave wagon.

I watched the last of the clothes dissolve into ashes. Warm flames reflected in my moist eyes. Another part of my life burned, destroyed by fire.

Maybe it was for the best, I decided. There was no point in keeping anything, since it all would be taken anyway from me at one point or another.

I wiped away my tears discreetly, but the younger maid still noticed. Her face filled with sadness.

"Oh, dear. I am so sorry. I wish the world wasn't such a cruel place," she gently whispered as she gestured to the steamy tub. I didn't care enough to nod my head to agree.

My heart beat rapidly and tiny beads of sweat pooled up on my face as I obediently followed the maid's gesture into the tub. My body submerged in almost *too* hot of a bath. I paused for a minute, letting my body adjust as I slowly sat down.

Each sore muscle eased in the warm water. The delicious smell of oils and soaps now kissed my skin. I could fall asleep so easily right now; close my eyes and dive into the pure abyss.

The exhaustion weighed heavy on my eyes, soothing my racing mind. *Close your eyes just for a minute*, it purred to me. But each time I closed my eyes, each time I attempted to give in to that call, the terror of the upcoming unknown brutalized me.

"My name is Brita," the young maid softly said as she scrubbed my back with some salts. I didn't need to see her face as she paused by my scars, only brushing over them softly. I knew they were gnarly scars; I had seen the same scars on backs of many dead bodies at the Rock Quarry, the torn-out flesh eaten by gruesome infection.

"I am Finnleah," I quietly replied.

"That's an odd name." Brita chuckled. I put on a strenuous smile. I might have hated my name growing up, but not anymore. Not ever again.

I was going to say that it was Elvish. It meant "blonde and courageous." I often joked to myself that my Elf maid had a weird sense of humor, giving me an Elf name while living in human lands. But instead, I just shrugged back.

"I never had anyone wash me before," I spat out. Not even sure why. I think I just hated the heavy silence more right now.

"Oh," Brita awkwardly said, pausing for a moment, scrubbing my hands almost raw. The dirt and the calluses were now a part of me, just as much as those scars.

The old maid came up and pulled my freshly washed hair out of the water. It was so heavy that my neck almost snapped in half.

"We will have to cut this louse infested rats' nest," she grumbled, putting the hair back into the water. My head followed the pull until I rested it against the edge. I didn't mind. Shave it all off, I almost said but paused. The maid chopped off my hair piece by piece until it was just slightly below my jaw.

The old maid took another look at my face and my gangly body. I braved a look back at her but didn't meet her eyes. Meek and obedient. Still, the maid seemed to be more annoyed than concerned.

"Make sure you trim her nails very short so she can't scratch, Brita," she directed.

"Yes, ma'am," Brita said, nodding. For a second, I contemplated asking her who I would be able to scratch, but I had lived long enough to understand that sometimes ignorance was bliss. Soon enough I'd know, but right now, I wouldn't spoil the only and potentially last moment of peace.

Brita motioned for me to stand up. I rose, looking at the filthy black water left from bathing me. Notes of disgust and shame played within me. Even after living in filth—being filth—you never quite get used to it.

Wrapped in a plush, white towel, I followed Brita to a room just a few steps down the hall.

"This is going to be your room for the night." She paused, avoiding looking at me as she added, "Until tomorrow."

The nice, warm feeling wore off me immediately. I was ignorant long enough, I decided. Already regretting the words coming out of my mouth, I asked,

"Lord Inadios talked about someone coming tomorrow. Who is he?"

"Oh, my dear, you really don't know?" She sorrowfully looked at me. I shook my head. "You are being gifted to the Destroyer General tomorrow," Brita replied, almost wincing at a mention of his name.

My heart stopped and my body froze.

Destroyer General.

Destroyer.

General.

Destroyer.

Fate had a twisted sense of humor.

I had hidden and ran away from Destroyers for my entire life, only to be served on a silver platter to their General?

Gifted to the Destroyer General...to be tortured and killed; I finished the unspoken words.

Nobody considered Destroyers part of the Magic Wielders. No, they were brutal, merciless, bloodthirsty warriors, wielding the *Cleansing Fire*—the never ending flame that destroyed everything in its way.

Flames that burned souls.

Though not a flick of fire was in sight, I could still feel the burning ashes in my lungs, the screams of the villagers loud in my ears, Tuluma's lifeless body and complete and utter despair.

I might have survived their massacre, but they destroyed a part of me that day.

Brita continued, adjusting pillows on the bunk beds.

"I am so sorry dear, I thought you realized that. Every time he comes, Lord Inadios tries to win him over by gifting him mages. Usually though, he sends over much younger girls and boys."

My mouth went dry at those words.

No, don't say it. Don't say it, Brita, my heart begged as she continued.

"We've almost always prepped little children for him to take." She shrank at her own words.

I held onto the towel tighter, my knuckles turning white as I glanced at the room a second time.

The reality crushed me like a tiny bug.

A small, worn-out teddy bear lay on the neatly made bunk beds, a little carved horse right next to it. The narrow beds and the small blankets...

It was all for kids.

Children.

My blood heated like molten lava. Mages didn't even get their powers until puberty.

They were innocent.

They were pure children, cursed by blood tinged with magic.

I stopped mid breath as the old maid's request to cut my nails short to stop from scratching replayed within me.

There was no salvation for whoever he was.

I took another look at Brita, my eyes not hiding the shock, begging her to say this was all a lie. But she didn't return my stare.

No, damn them all. They stood there, complicit, as *children* were tortured and destroyed? I closed my eyes, summoning the calmness and letting that anger, that hatred, simmer deep in my soul.

Tears didn't come. They wouldn't come, because the atrocities didn't *scare* me.

They *scarred* me.

I opened my eyes a second later, replacing shock with determination. In that single blink, I promised myself, the universe, the gods above, and the cruel Lady Fate that I would kill him.

I wasn't sure how or when, but I would kill the Destroyer General.

5
_____

I didn't speak with Brita for the rest of the night. She left shortly after dressing me, locking the door after her.

Everything suddenly seemed so mortal and vain. My brain drowned in boiling anger and rage. I sat motionless on the round, wooden stool by the tiny vanity. I hadn't seen my reflection in well over a year and I looked more hideous than ever. My constantly sunburned skin was covered in large freckles and sunspots. My over-grown eyebrows that were now perfectly waxed, looked out of place on my worn-out face. My cheekbones poked out noticeably. Previously full cheeks were sunken, making my round face look deformed. Even with Brita giving me the balm for my lips, they were still cracked, and that one new large freckle on my bottom lip made them look diseased. I ran my thumb down the smile lines. I had aged so much, I realized, as the small wrinkles were now permanently embedded on my cheeks and my forehead. I might have been only twenty-two, but I looked far older than that.

Life had a way of leaving its mark.

I harshly smiled. A worn-out shell for a broken soul. A fitting union.

My eyes trailed to the distorted-looking moon in the small window.

Guards. Dimitrii. Destroyer General. Children. Viyak.

Was the Moon Goddess ever aware of the sheer hell this world has become? Were any of the gods aware? Or did they just not care anymore?

The guards and I would have the keys, Brita mentioned before she left.

Dimitrii had the key.

My thoughts clattered against each other, a panicking, uncontrollable crowd. I pushed through them all. I wouldn't give in. I wouldn't let my mind snare me into overwhelming panic.

First, survive the night, I commanded myself. *Deal with Dimitrii. Then, we will deal with tomorrow.*

One problem at a time.

It dawned on me that I was on borrowed time. The last candle barely flickered in the dark. The room was small, and the windows even smaller. I knew escape was not an option, yet naively, I still jerked the handle. It didn't give. Locked tight in place.

Fight, it is then.

I analyzed each part of the bedroom for something I could use as a weapon. The room was simple; bunk beds by the door, vanity across from it with the bucket to the right. So far, my best option was to hit him with a wooden toy horse. "Better than anything else," I whispered to myself, grabbing the toy.

I climbed to the upper bunk; that way, he'd have to drag me down and I'd have the upper hand. He was strong enough to do it, but it would be more difficult for him.

I sat on top of the bunk bed with the thoughts still racing through my head. *Breathe,* I willed myself. *Breathe.* I could risk breaking a window to use a piece of glass. But then if he didn't show up, they'd assume I was trying to escape and shackle me again. And I really enjoyed even this ounce of freedom.

I thought about ripping my nightgown and creating a strip long enough to choke him, but I saw a man being choked to death once. It required significantly more strength than I had, especially against a large, well-fed Royal guard. A mirror shard was the most lethal available option to me at the moment but shattering a mirror would be loud and obvious.

I threw scenarios at myself, one after another after another. Again and again, what if that, what if this. All of them landed at the same conclusion.

I was a sheep about to be slaughtered.

I sat still in my upper bunk, holding tight to the smooth, carved toy. The bed was so soft and nice compared to the barren caves I was used to sleeping in. And yet, I would gladly trade it for the stone walls if it meant that I could listen to Viyak's heartbeat against his chest as he cradled me.

Please live, I'll find my way back to you. I promise.

I.

Promise.

I cringed as those words swung across my thoughts.

How selfish!

How utterly selfish of me to ask him to live, to wait for me, while I would never make it back to him. For him to spend his days enduring each for me. Foolish. So, so foolish.

"Screw it," I said out loud as I climbed down my bed and shattered the mirror with the wooden horse. It was loud and took more tries than I had hoped.

But victoriously, I picked the sharpest piece and ripped a strip off my long night gown to wrap around it. I hadn't even finished wrapping it all up as a loud click sounded straight behind my back and a second later, my door soundlessly opened.

As if operating on some ancient instinct, I silently moved behind the door. My candle was already out, and the room was filled with a pure moonlight glimmer. A tall figure appeared in the frame.

"Wakey-wakey, little bitch, your Lord is here," Dimitrii whispered. I didn't see his face but felt the bile in his words. He was still dressed in the same leathers from earlier. I clenched my jaw as my heart pounded. Shit. This was going to be much harder to break through with my makeshift knife. *Eyes it is, then.*

I watched him check the bottom bed first and then the top. Just when he realized I wasn't there, he rapidly turned back to the door. I lunged at him as fast as I could, a long shard of glass aimed at his eyes.

"You bitch!" he shrieked as I stabbed and sliced his cheek wide. Not. Fast. Enough.

So close to the eye, yet I missed. Too quickly, he punched my eye so hard I trembled down to the ground. Still holding on to my only weapon, I stabbed his foot.

He squealed. Pissed off, he kicked me hard with his other foot.

Get up. Damn it. Get up! I screamed at myself; at my limp, frozen limbs.

No, the fight was already over. Dimitrii kicked me hard a few more times until the shard of the mirror scattered across the room from me. I felt the oh so familiar feeling of heat spilling inside my body—broken ribs—but the kicking didn't stop. He kicked me again and again. I tensed my body, shielding my head as much as I could.

Maybe if I piss him off enough, he'd just beat me to death. I smirked at the thought of that as I took another hit.

Useless human filth. Get up and fight. Do something!!! I smiled at the angry voice of my elf-maid sounding in my head. For a second I was back in the bushes, barely seven years old, being beaten up by the village kids for having an elf as my family.

Dimitrii stopped kicking me, taking a breath for himself. Then he grabbed my short hair and painfully pulled my head until our eyes met. My lips stretched in a bloody smile.

"You little cunt," he sneered as he spit in my face. I just stared at his bloodied-up, fileted cheek. He would have a scar.

No matter what happened to me, he would forever have a scar. I smiled wider at him, taking a small, agonizing breath.

And then I screamed.

I screamed as loud as I ever screamed, as loud as I could, ignoring the excruciating pain in my lungs.

"FIRE!!! FIRE!!! FIRE!!!!"

Even Dimitrii startled and turned around just to double check.

"You dumb bitch!" he roared in my face as the realization came through. But it was too late. I heard the rushing steps already loud in the hall.

Dimitrii froze. They were so close but with my door shut... His hand covered my mouth, choking me. I listened as the rushing steps went by my door.

I bit his hand, taking off a chunk of his calluses. He gasped, letting go of me just long enough for me to scream again, spitting flesh and blood out of my mouth, gagging as I screamed.

"FIRE in here!!! FIRE!"

He pushed his bloody hand harder against my lips, his blood choking me. But my heart eased as my door suddenly opened wide and a guard stormed in.

"What the FUCK Dimitrii?!" he shouted as he saw us, his torch lighting up the room. "Are you out of your mind??? She is for *him*!!!!" He ran a hand through his hair. "Oh, you fucked up Dimitrii...you fucking fucked up." The guard took another look at the room, at the broken mirror, at the ripped nightgown, and my broken body.

Dimitrii threw me to the ground. His face seemed to clear up from rage to regret, but not regret of coming here. No, he would do it again. His regret was only of being caught. "Relax, Nhey, I'll keep her face clean. The rest they don't need to know. For all we know, she came from the Rock Quarries like that. Plus, nothing that I am doing right now is anything he wouldn't do, so I am just preparing the bitch for him. He will probably thank me for it." Dimitrii wiped the dripping blood, a smug look filling his face as he saw the other guard considering.

I raised my eyes to Nhey, pleading with everything I had.

"You can fuck around when it's your shift, but I am not putting my neck on the line for you to get your dick wet. She is for *him and him only.* You know what he did the last time we didn't follow that. So go and clean up," Nhey ordered. Dimitrii hesitated, growling as he looked at me. But Nhey repeated, "Leave Dimitrii," as he motioned for him to go.

I watched Dimitrii angrily storm off. As soon as his tall figure disappeared in the dark hall, my body began shaking. Uncontrollably shaking. And then I sobbed.

I didn't care that the other guard was still there. I didn't care that each cry hurt. I wept.

"Go to sleep, girl. I'll stand watch nearby," was all Nhey said as he closed the door, leaving me alone with the darkness.

I was lost in the storm, emotions flooding my mind until I drowned in my own tears. Until finally, my swollen eyes closed shut surrendering to a deep sleep.

6

A muffled voice sounded from behind the door, immediately erasing any kind of peace I might have felt.

"Good morning, dear, it's Brita." She slowly unlocked the wooden door.

I tried to stand up from the stone floor I slept on, but flinched at the sharp pain in my side, immediately remembering the broken ribs.

I tried to ignore the pain; the ache of each muscle and the body shivers that came back as I made just enough effort to sit up on the floor.

The loud gasp that escaped Brita's mouth and the dropped dress she had been carrying told me that she didn't know what happened last night. She ran towards my limp body against the wall. My blood stained and ripped nightgown was bunched up at my bruised, bony thighs.

"Oh dear, what happened to you?!" she exclaimed, touching my pale forehead.

My eyes were still closed. My head throbbed with pain, making me nauseous even at the thought of conjuring a solid sentence.

"Dimitrii," was all I could summon myself to reply with my parched mouth.

"Oh no. I am so sorry. I should've known, dear. He is such a nasty man," she said, her voice full of pity.

I was frankly too tired and too beat up to deal with her constant apologies and pity for me.

"Let's get you cleaned up, dear," she softly said, trying to peel the blood-dried hairs away from my face.

I should've been more grateful for her; should have appreciated her kindness. But the truth was that all that kindness and sympathy didn't change the fact that she was still preparing me for slaughter.

I refused to open my eyes, pretty sure I'd puke if I did, so I just sat motionless as she gently patted away at my face with a wet washcloth.

"The dress will be a little tricky since it has a corset in it, my dear," Brita said as she touched my bruised stomach.

I opened my eyes at that, sharp and feral. She nodded in understanding.

"Well, on second thought, maybe we can find you a different dress for today." Her soft smile was interrupted by my stomach loudly gurgling. "Maybe I can get you a snack as well from the kitchens," she replied, walking out of the room.

I sat still, allowing myself only shallow breaths to avoid the sharp pain. After a while, Brita came back with a small broom, a new dress, and a plate full of food.

My mouth watered, though the queasiness wouldn't budge.

The plate was loaded to the brim. Some things I had only seen in pictures, and some things I never even knew existed, yet the smell and flavor floating in the air made my mouth water so much it almost drowned me.

I was in dire need of more nourishment and strength.

Think about dying later. First, eat and fully gorge in this delicious-ness, I told myself as I hungrily took a second look at the food—so much of it.

"Here is the best breakfast of the year for you." Brita smiled widely. "Lord Inadios always throws the biggest feast for the Destroyer General, no matter the time of the year he comes. Once he came to visit during the deep of the winter and famine, and Lord Inadios sent servants all the way across Esnox to the Desolate Desert to bring the most unique and exquisite treats. Servants are never invited or included in the feasts, but we always get leftovers." She extended her hand to help me get up. I held on tight, grinding my teeth as I stood up. "And usually, there is plenty because unlike you—" She paused and giggled a little as I unapologetically stuffed my face a second later. "The Destroyer General is extremely picky and will only eat the best of the best."

I raised my eyebrows just slightly. My eyes looked at Brita with surprise that this might not be *the best of the best*? It couldn't have been, because this... All this food, this was heaven. I didn't have time for words. I was going to puke, I realized. I knew it, but I just couldn't stop. My stomach hurt so much but I shoved another creampuff into my mouth, another bite of ham. At some point, I was pretty sure I stopped chewing and just started swallowing the food whole. It was too good. If I'd died right in this second, I would be okay with it, I decided. My brain was high on the flavors and sugars, and if I ignored the world for just a little bit, I could swear I felt pure joy.

Panting and sweating, I finished up my plate. Brita stood by me the entire time, just snacking on a few purple grapes. When I finally paused and took a deep breath, she turned to me, looking slightly concerned.

"You look like you are going to throw up, my dear." I simply nodded. Maybe. In fact, I was thinking the same thing, but talking or even opening my mouth might provoke the food to come back, so I just slightly nodded. Jitters slowly eased with the sugars flowing back in my veins, and the mind haze was clearing up.

"You need to slow down, or you'll choke." She smiled. "After you are done with that, we will get you dressed and then..." Brita paused, lowering her eyes. Hesitant.

The grim reality slithered through me as we both thought about the rest of the day. I wanted to be dramatic and call it my very last day, but that felt more like gambling with Fate.

No, I knew for a fact I was going to die.

But I was not naïve enough to think I would die today. Or die fast.

I heard enough rumors; I had experienced the destruction they bring.

The uncertainty was never more certain I was going to die a slow, torturous death.

I rubbed a small scar on my wrist, asking myself if I was wrong about the choice I had made some many moons ago.

There was never going to be a peaceful end for me.

Something in me ached at the thought of that.

Maybe I'd used all my luck as a kid, for not dying from the rampant diseases or not freezing in the dead of the night in the fall, or getting a small bump instead of breaking my neck that one time I fell off a tree. I guess I had been running out of my good fortune for a while now, and the time has come to pay up.

I looked outside the dusty, small window in my room and finished what Brita was too afraid to admit. "And then I am sent off to be tortured by the Destroyer General."

"I am so sorry, my dear. I wish things would be different," Brita almost whispered. Again, so much pity in her voice.

It irked me. Anger, as if a dragon within me, stirred, breathing clouds of smoke.

Is that what she tells those small children before putting bows on them and handing them off to a fire breathing monster?

What was the point of her kindness if other people had to pay the price? It was more arrogance then, not kindness, to be able to show you pity and sorrow, and choose not to do anything about it.

I cooled my anger, taking another look at her. She was young, perhaps barely eighteen, working as a maid at a Royal's house. Not a slave, but still a servant. I knew better than to judge a person by their looks. Some scars went unseen, running much deeper than the surface.

Brita carefully helped me put on a dress, her hands warm and soft, each touch gentle and caring. The deep emerald fabric perfectly matched my green eyes, calling out the darker hues in them. Even though it was the heat of the summer, the dress was long sleeved. Smart of Brita to cover all my scars and bruises. Though framed to the body, it was loose; so damn loose on me. It was made to show some

CHAPTER 6

enticing cleavage, but the square cut neckline looked dismal with my chest bones poking through the thin skin. I watched her do a few final touches on my hair and make-up on my face and I wondered then how exactly she knew Dimitrii was a nasty man.

All dressed, Brita took a good look at me, putting on a smile.

"Look at you now, looking like a proper lady."

I raised my eyes at her, questioning the sanity of that statement considering the small black eye that make-up was covering, but I didn't argue.

"Well dear, it's time to head upstairs."

Brita held my elbow as I walked away from the room, helping me make each step. Walking up the stairs was hard; my ribs were on fire, and my stomach twisted and turned in pain. The nausea was back stronger than before. I needed to be operative, aware, but my pounding headache and aching muscles were almost blinding me.

Brita kept up her pace until we arrived by the tall, dark, wooden doors. They were exquisitely carved with thorns and roses and a large crown in place of the door knocker. Two guards stood by them with large spears at their sides. Just like the guards from the night before, they were dressed in burgundy leathers with the crown mark over their heart.

She nodded her head to them in a semi-bow, welcoming them with a smile. They didn't bow back; didn't even greet her. I narrowed my eyes in annoyance. Guards, servants—same people, different uniforms. She didn't deserve the hostility. But I kept my mouth shut.

Brita turned to me and smiled tenderly, the corners of her eyes creating tiny wrinkles.

"I am sorry, but this is where we part," she said. "The guards will take you to the throne hall where you'll await his arrival." As if sensing my question, she continued. "We are not sure when exactly he is coming today or how long he is going to stay with us, but if I don't see you again, I wish you good luck, Finnleah."

"Thanks for the food, Brita. It was the best I've ever had." I didn't bother smiling or offering fake pleasantries, but I was grateful for that. It was sincere gratitude, though my voice was dull and lifeless. Brita stood still with her hands deep in the white apron pockets, watching guards put the large rope around my neck to leash me and tie my hands once more.

Unnecessary, really. I could barely walk, less so fight or even try to object. And if I had any strength left, I would save it for my last hurrah to take the Destroyer General with me if Lady Fate was benevolent enough to grant me that chance.

Lately though, it seemed that she ultimately didn't care.

7

The guards opened the heavy doors and led me into another hall. I was thankful it wasn't Dimitrii. I didn't think I could've handled him right now. Not when my mind, mixed with agony and strength, barely stayed afloat.

The guards were quiet and distant and so was I. They were much less patient with me than Brita, almost racing across yet another hall. Tripping a few steps, I winced at the piercing pain in my side as I quickly caught myself.

The throne room was much brighter than I remembered. Now, in the daylight, large stained-glass windows, stretching high up the walls, lit up the large room in bright colors. Walls and ceilings melted together into the large dome above. Great wooden beams lined the gray stone walls. Tapestries on the walls depicted beautiful hunting scenes, engraved in ornate, golden frames.

The large table in the center of the room was now decorated with skulls of large animals, serving as vases for full blooming flowers. The contrast of the mighty dark table with white skulls and gorgeous colors of the flowers imprinted in my brain. Soft, yet harsh, and so beautiful. Most chairs were gone, leaving only two, placed opposite of each other. My eyes paused as they ran over two large, ivory plates on each end of the tables. *Only two.*

I took another deep breath as we stopped. I didn't remember seeing them yesterday but there were small lounge couches spread across the room, just big enough for two people to sit on them. They were covered in luxurious red velvet with small pillows on top of them, embroidered with gold threads. The soft furs thrown across the floor pleasantly tickled my feet.

But no décor could change the heavy air in the room. The anticipation of waiting for the Lord of Death to arrive.

Lord Inadios stood still, ignoring my arrival and admiring one of the oil paintings. His sausage-like hands gripped tight his carved cane. It seemed like his neck was nonexistent with his face melting into his chest. His hair was thinning out with a large bald spot on the top of his head, yet he brushed over the remaining hair to try and cover it up. The hair itself was yellow, greasy, and laying in thin strands just past his ears. He wore a tight suit with pants that looked too short and exposed his hairy ankles. His dark brown vest was unbuttoned, showing the mustard color shirt stretched tight underneath.

In such a room of luxury and contrasting beauty, he stood out like a thorn.

But so did I.

He turned around, his cane squeaking under the heavy weight of his body as he made a few steps towards me. The guards tightened their hold on my leash.

"So, girl, do you have magic yet?" he growled, glaring over me.

In all my thoughts and plans of survival, I forgot they thought of me as a Creator.

As a lower tier Creator, I should be able to change colors and shapes, but I couldn't even stand right now, much less try to perform magic I didn't have.

"I am so sorry my Lord, but I am still bound by the Magnesium in my blood." I bowed deeply again, tugging on my leash just a bit. I didn't drop on my knees for him this time, aware that I wouldn't be able to get up. My eyes stayed on the ground, breaths shallow and small.

Meek and obedient and a good slave. A slave. That's who I am, I reminded myself, though images of ripping out my leash and choking them all with my rope flashed through my mind.

"Hell on you, girl." He scoffed and took a large sip from his golden goblet. His fingers were covered in large heirloom rings. His wine-laced breath reached me as he huffed again and muttered something I couldn't hear.

The loud knock this time came from the door across from us. I straightened up, keeping my face still as Dimitrii walked in. He angrily glanced over me; my eyes narrowed as I looked back straight at him. My large mark across his cheek was covered up with a bandage. He hid it too well for anyone to notice—anyone but me—as he walked with an almost unnoticeable limp. I forced my mouth still, fighting the corners of my mouth from spreading into a wicked grin at each of his steps. Good, his foot hurt too.

Dimitrii approached Lord Inadios and quickly bowed.

"My Lord, scouts confirm he is approaching with his battalion."

"How far now?" Lord Inadios didn't even look at him as he took another sip of his wine.

"He should be here within the hour."

"I want your best guards stationed in here at all times and send someone into town for the whores for his soldiers. Double down the guards by his room, too. I want to know everything he does and says to anyone." He barked the orders at Dimitrii.

"Yes, my Lord," Dimitrii quickly replied and promptly walked out of the room. Lord Inadios unevenly walked up to the pedestal and loudly thumped into the wooden throne. The wine in his cup spilled a little on the bright white fur at his feet, though he didn't even notice.

"And now we sit and wait for the Lord of the Death to arrive."

The hour went long, each passing minute harder than the last. My legs felt like they'd filled with lead, and my arms and neck itched at the coarse, tight rope around them.

But that was nothing.

My mind produced its own kind of torture. Thoughts about everything quickly overwhelmed me to the point that it was easier to not think of anything at all; to shut the steel doors in my head. To try and keep the flood of thoughts from drowning me and leaving me in sheer panic. So, I just stood there, motionless, watching specks of dust floating through the air.

My heart ached for the tall, blond man left to survive alone in those steep mountains on the horizon. I needed him more than anything else right now. Involuntarily, my eyes filled up with extra moisture. I swallowed and blinked rapidly. I wouldn't let myself cry. Not here. Not now. I had to shut Viyak out completely. Forget his kind smile and the messy beard. Forget the veiny, thin forearms that kept me warm at night. Forget the never-ending hopefulness that followed him. I had to forget it all because if I allowed one more thought of him, one more memory of him, I would not be able to endure anymore. I would fall apart.

I bit the inner bottom of my lip hard enough to leave a mark. Pain was grounding me to now, to this stuffy room, to the painful deep breaths.

My heart skipped a beat as the large doors across the room suddenly opened with a loud thud. Lord Inadios's snoring abruptly stopped and he rapidly stood up.

Like crackling thunder after lighting, nine men marched into the throne room. Their steps—a destructive melody—beat in unison. A deathly march.

Destroyer soldiers wore dark gray, almost black armor, covering them from head to toe. Large swords weighted them down around their hips with round shields behind their backs. Their heads were covered with the same armor as their bodies, helms of dark gray molded together to outline and protect their jaws and noses yet opening their faces for clear vision.

As one, they stopped without a single breath, their presence filling up the room. Four men up front followed by four behind, and between them all was *him*.

The Destroyer General.

As if commanded by a thought, they took a perimeter formation, making way for the Destroyer General to walk past them. Unlike his soldiers, his armor was obsidian black. Darkness so abysmal, it consumed the light around it. Tungsten so rare that only a Destroyer's raw fire could forge it.

He didn't have a shield; instead, two huge sword hilts peeked out from behind his back. Made from platinum, they shimmered in the morning rays of sun; a shimmer mixed with red glow from the dark, diamond-shaped rubies that topped the sword pommels. The gems' sharp ends pointed outwards, creating a bloody halo. As if the God of Death himself arrived amidst measly mortals. His long, midnight black cape flowed behind him like a shadow as he approached Lord Inadios.

Blood chilled in my veins and I could feel the entirety of my soul tremble in his presence. The breath itself caught in my lungs, unwilling to let go.

Lord Inadios nervously fidgeted with his fingers and feet, knocking over the wine goblet. The gold metal made a few loud clicks against the stone floor as the cup rolled down the stone pedestal to the Destroyer General's feet. Lord Inadios chokingly coughed.

Piercing eyes of the General slowly moved from the goblet to Lord Inadios.

A reaper that has come to collect.

"Lord Destroyer General, welcome!" Lord Inadios bowed as low as his round waist allowed him, his voice trembling. There was nothing left of the cocky, pompous Lord from the night before. It was as if he had completely evaporated; now a mere rat, cornered by a mighty snow leopard.

"Lord Inadios," the General replied, his voice husk, commanding; so crisp that I could feel it slicing my bones down to the marrow. He didn't bother to dismiss the still-bowing Lord.

"We are so pleased you have honored us with your visit, great Lord Destroyer General," Inadios whined back, his face turning bright red from all the blood pooling up as he still bowed.

"Even miserable rats like you, Inadios, need a visit once in a while." The Destroyer General waved his armored hand, releasing Inadios from his bow.

"My Lord Destroyer General, we are truly blessed in your presence," Inadios screeched again. The Destroyer General ignored him as he sat on one of the small couches not too far from the pedestal, his large, armored figure filling the seat made for two. His soldiers remained standing so still that I wasn't sure they were breathing.

"Sit, Inadios, before your disgusting face hits the floor," he ordered.

"Yes, Great General. Thank you, my Lord," Inadios replied as he sunk into his chair. He looked so small and so miserable right now that somewhere deep in my heart, I felt bad for him.

"I see you've cleaned up the place since the last time I visited," the General nonchalantly mentioned as he took a slow scan of the room.

"Oh yes, my Lord, I have taken your advice and made sure the manor is up to your standards."

The Destroyer General chuckled. So callous. Hairs on my neck stood up, as if life itself dwindled at the sound.

"You are a funny man, Inadios, to assume this shithole is ever going to be up to my standards." He paused; his eyes glanced over the white skulls on the carved table. Inadios froze. I could almost smell his panic, his fear, as the General continued. "Maybe you should try again but this time start fresh... after I turn this hideous rock to ashes." The Destroyer General paused, his words echoing through the room, as a small white and silver flame appeared at the sway of his fingers.

The Cleansing Fire.

My heart stopped. Fully stopped. So did time. I could see the small specks of dust freeze in the air, as if sensing it too. The little droplets of sweat on the Inadios's face pooled in horror. I didn't dare look at the General, but my blood churned at the presence of that silver flame. I could feel it burning me even far across the room.

A blink. My heart resumed beating, now racing so fast that it was hard to breathe. The loose dress, even with the low cut and no corset, felt suffocating.

I needed to breathe, to calm myself, but I couldn't.

"My Lord, Destroyer General…" Inadios began after a brief pause but didn't get to finish as I dropped to my knees panting and gasping for air. My head was spinning. The guard jerked on my leash, forcing me to rise. The rope asphyxiated me even more.

I needed air, needed my lungs to work. I felt the tight reins of the self-control I held my mind with completely disappear as I spiraled down into the abyss.

There was one rule, and one rule only that Tuluma made me follow, that I had memorized before I even knew my name: to stay away from Destroyers; to run even at the slight flicker of their flames, their presence.

Like a frightened animal, I pushed the guard with everything I had and lunged towards the door, ignoring all instincts but one.

Run.

I wasn't sure where or what, but I had to run.

Without even reaching the door, my rope got caught and yanked back so hard that I crashed all the way to the stone floor, brutally falling on my back. Warm liquid trickled down my head. The loud ringing in my ears joined blurred vision.

Breathe.

Breathe.

I willed myself, reaching for those reigns. Control. I need to control my rancid mind.

Two guards dragged me across the floor to Lord Inadios's pedestal. They held me up tightly by my arms as I thrashed in their grasp, ignoring the mind shattering pain rolling through me with each move.

My mind locked on one thing.

Run.

Run.

Run.

"Care to explain yourself, Inadios?" The General's firm voice now sounded closer; each cell in my body could feel his approach.

"Oh, my d-d-dear Lord D-d-destroyer General. Forgive your humble servant. I—I wanted to deliver a gift to you. This girl-this girl is a Creator, my Lord." Inadios paused, looking for even the slightest hint of approval from the General, only to find stone cold loathing displayed on his face.

Inadios rapidly continued. "I know you prefer them much younger, my Lord, and I deeply apologize and regret I couldn't find something more to your taste. But I beg for your forgiveness and plead with you to accept this Magic Wielder as a gift from me." Lord Inadios motioned the guards to drag my trembling body closer to the General.

The musty air burned my lungs. Shoved by the guards, my broken body hit the floor a second later, my nose now inches from the armored boot of the General.

Breathe, I commanded to myself.

Just breathe…. Please. I pleaded, but I was locked out.

My mind, my body, my control was gone. As if a fire, pure panic burned everything within me.

I *couldn't* breathe. I forced myself to open my mouth, gaping like a fish out of the water.

Large, callused hands roughly grabbed my face. The armor covering his hands was so cold, yet felt scorching against my skin. I winced, feeling the ghost of the Cleansing flame on his hand.

I closed my eyes shut as he jerked my head up, darkness soothing my soul.

"A Creator you say?" He stared at me. I could feel him piercing my soul with his eyes.

"I know she is quite displeasing to look at my Lord, I apologize. She doesn't quite fit the type, but it was confirmed by the Kahors. She is indeed a Creator."

"So, an unsuitable old Creator? Is that really what your gift to your master, Lord Destroyer General, is, Inadios? I find it a bit…insulting." He still gripped my cheeks tight between his fingers. My eyelids quivered but righteously remained shut, even as I heard a loud thump. Inadios landed on his knees.

"Forgive me, my Master…" Inadios trembled. "Magic Wielders are so scarce these days, and especially children. They…seem to be finally going extinct. But I should've known better. Forgive me, thy unwise servant. I will dispose of the girl myself and will not trouble you. I might not have any Magic Wielders in my lands left, but I will find you the most beautiful children to your taste, even if it's the last thing I do." The General's grip loosed on my face slowly and he let my head slump down yet again. My short hair covered my pale face. I opened my eyes just briefly to see his boots turn silently to face Inadios.

"All I hear are excuses, Inadios, and you know how I feel about them. Or do I need to add another limp as a reminder?"

Inadios whimpered.

Bile burned my throat, turning my face shades of pale green. My lungs were still spasming, only letting gulps of air in.

I watched the armored boots as they marched away from me towards the wooden door, pausing near the threshold. His soldiers were still standing motionless across the room.

The General's razor-sharp voice rumbled through the room as he decreed.

"I'll accept the *so-called* Creator this time, but do not disappoint me again, Inadios...Orest and Broderick, bring her to my quarters." He quickly glanced over the Royal guards by the door, trembling under his gaze and added, "Keep your useless dogs away, Inadios."

My heart sank as two soldiers quickly approached me. I was so, so nauseous and the pain...gods, the pain was so unbearable. My mind was wrapped in a thick fog. They didn't bother making me stand up as one of them threw me over their shoulder like a large flour sack and followed the Destroyer General out of the hall room.

This was too much.

All too much.

8

I slowly opened my eyes. The bright summer sun almost blinded me immediately. I didn't have a chance to even blink twice, as nauseating dread rolled through me. Panicking, I raced my eyes to the wall-length windows and then back to my damaged body. It was still daytime, and I was still dressed in the same clothes.

Good.

I couldn't have been out that long. The rope was gone from my neck, but it brought little relief as I realized that my wrists were tightly wrapped and anchored around one of the four large bed posts with rope just long enough to move my arms.

Alive. I was alive. Though, still a slave, now to the worst kind of monster. I took a second look around. It was a very spacious room, furnished with taste and luxury. The ceilings were high with an exquisite golden chandelier. The hardwood floors matched the color of the wooden beams through the ceiling. Right across the bed I was laying on was a large couch made from the albino tiger fur with a magnificent glass and metal coffee table in front. Tree-like plants in the large, painted pots were neatly trimmed and stood in two of the corners. The statues, the one-of-a-kind art on the textile-like walls, were much more luxurious than in the throne hall or anywhere else in the manor.

My eyes paused on two doors in the room. I didn't have to question which was which as one abruptly opened, and the Destroyer General walked in.

His muscled body was steaming, and I could swear glowing, as small droplets of water rolled down his naked, smooth chest. He wore nothing but a wrapped white towel around the low of his waist. He ran his fingers through the still-wet hair, neatly trimmed on the sides and ruffled on top, and walked towards the dresser across the room.

At the sight of him, I jolted on the bed. His fierce, dark brown eyes turned on me.

A vulture and his prey.

"You are awake," he stated, his eyes sliding down my body, assessing. My heart raced, yet my figure froze, gulp stuck mid throat.

A second later, like I wasn't even there, he turned back and walked towards the dresser.

I bunched my knees to my chest, tugging my twisted dress skirt lower to cover my bare legs. He casually pulled a few items of clothing out of the black armoire.

Get away. Run.

But the initial panic settled in and though my heart begged me, I understood well enough that even if I was one of the Magic Wielders there was nothing—*nothing*—I could do right now to stop the Destroyer General from melting my skin away; from burning me until I was nothing but ash.

There was *nothing* I could do to even try to run.

I was wounded and hurt, tied and locked in a large manor, deep in the woods.

Alone. There was no one that would come and save me.

Nobody that could help.

I could do nothing, and I had no one.

Hopelessness was a poison that simmered through my veins. Deep anger and rage heated up inside of me, boiling, as if it were molten lava, spilling to the very ends of my limbs.

Commanding me to survive. Ordering me to take charge—to live.

I would survive or die trying.

Defiantly, I raised my eyes from underneath my bunched-up brows and stared at him. My eyes hit the back of his head. He was still facing the dresser, lazily putting clothes on. A white tunic now covered his defined back. Within a breath, the towel dropped, exposing his round and firm backside just for a second as he pulled his black leather pants up. I didn't look away, even as my heart raced at an unknown speed. Being a slave didn't quite grant you privacy.

He turned to me, as if feeling my stare, slowly rolling his sleeves up his tan, muscled forearms.

I tensed my jaw, fighting the panic within me. He was in his late twenties, perhaps older, though oddly young for a general. A *feared* general. Lord of Death, Inadios called him.

I wouldn't let myself be tricked by his handsome features. True monsters were always hiding underneath a pretty mask.

He sauntered across the room carelessly, until he reached the bed and rested against one of the bed posts across from me. Folding his arms, he looked down at me.

"So, a Creator girl. What's your name?" His dark brown eyes flashed with curiosity. His face was mature, and those eyes seemed ancient. A shiver went through my body.

For a split second I thought to lie—come up with a name and a story fitted for a Creator. But a part of me wanted him to know my name so if... No, when.

When I kill him, or he kills me, it would haunt him for the rest of his miserable existence.

"Finn," I sharply said without backing down my stare. My eyes watered but I refused to blink. We stared at each other for what felt like an eternity. His face was expressionless, but I hid none of the hate in mine.

He finally unfolded his arms and put his hands in his pockets.

"You know, my father used to incinerate people if they looked at him without his permission. How the times have changed," he said, his eyes narrowing while the corners of his mouth tugged upwards, his voice sinful.

I wanted to kill him then. It was my life, my existence, and for him, it was all a joke…

"What are you going to do with me?" I asked and immediately regretted it.

He straightened up and stared out of the window, ignoring me.

I could feel the anger burning me from within.

Perhaps, Fate never gifted me magic because she knew that if I had even an ounce of it, I would slowly make him choke on the air he was wasting and have his own ash fill up his lungs.

"You need to change," he finally said without answering my question. My body trembled from pain or anger—I wasn't sure. He continued, "You are filthy and covered in vomit and blood."

I smelled the dried vomit on my sleeves the moment I woke up and could feel my hair crusty with blood, but that was fitting, considering my circumstances. I didn't even remember throwing up, but that must have happened when I passed out. Either way, I wasn't going to just play a pretty dress up doll for him.

"No," I rebelliously said, glaring back at him. Though my voice was quiet and missing the intended bite to it, it didn't shake, and I was proud of that.

I watched his face carefully and clenched my jaw tighter, seeing a slight flicker of amusement in his face.

My large, scratchy ropes evaporated into nothing but specks of ash as silver flames appeared out of thin air and ran through them. Scrambling, I shut my eyes and stopped breathing, preparing for the encompassing pain of the Destroyer's fire. Yet when the pain didn't come, I opened my eyes just to see my wrists free and silver flames gone.

I sharply looked back at him, my eyes full of hate and terror. He returned the stare, though, casual. Like nothing ever happened.

"A few rules, *Finn…*" He paused, tilting his head to the side just a bit. I willed my eyes to keep his stare, though my whole existence begged me to look away. "You do *what* I say *when* I say and *how* I say it. You do not run away, or even think about running away, unless you want to end up dead. You do not use your magic unless I tell you so. You will address me as the Lord Master or Lord Destroyer General. Now, do we have an understanding?"

I didn't reply, staying completely silent. Something inside of me stirred furiously at just his presence.

Child torturer.

Child defiler.

A monster.

Monster of all monsters.

Defiance will be the death of me, Viyak once told me, and I was pretty sure he was right as I murmured.

"Go. To. Hell."

His eyes widened in bafflement, but he quickly corrected that slip up.

"The dress is in the washroom. Go clean up," he ordered as he swiftly strode out of the door.

The room filled up with heavy silence. The defiant façade I was keeping up crumbled down faster than a sandcastle against the large ocean wave. Tears started dropping down my cheeks. *No, not yet,* I told myself as I bit down my inner lip again, but even that didn't help as emotions overcame me.

"*One minute,*" I whispered to myself. One minute is all I was going to take to pity myself and cry. And then I would get dressed and I would listen.

I would be obedient and meek.

I had to play that role many times and I could do it once more.

The bathroom was breathtaking; nothing compared to the one I bathed in just the night before. It was a spacious room with walls and floors made from pure white marble and delicate gold fixtures on the bathtub and sinks. There was a huge mirror spread above the tall, marble counter with cut in sinks. On the opposite side from the door was a semicircle giant window. It was a stained-glass mosaic. Colors of purple, red and blue mixed with green and yellow danced everywhere in the room, bringing life to the cold white of the walls. A large bath on golden, curved legs stood right in front of it.

You could bathe in rainbows, I thought to myself as I took another slow breath of the pinewood aroma coming from shampoos and oils laid out on a small stool near the tub.

The General never told me when he was coming back, I realized, and I supposed it didn't matter. I wasn't going to allow myself to lounge in the bubbly bath and risk anyone catching me off guard. I grinded my teeth and clenched my jaw, putting on the large, baby pink dress. The long skirt was made from layers of sheer pink tule. The top was made from a darker flushed shade, connected to the skirt just above my waist. Small but puffy, short sleeves stuck out like oversized pom poms on my bony shoulders. At least the top looked less baggy on my starved bust.

A few painful grunts came out of me as I attempted to tie the top of my dress in the back. Attempted, but didn't succeed, leaving my back half exposed.

The wet, white towel turned crimson red as I ran it through my wet hair, dried blood slowly soaking off in pieces. I stared at myself, gradually moving the comb through my poorly chopped hair. All the makeup that Brita so religiously put on me this morning was ruined, leaving running streaks of mascara. Whatever powders she used were now streaked from tears and caked in creases like dirt. At least, the small black eye and the large purple and blue bruises covering my arms worked as an accessory to the pink fluffy dress.

I forced my mouth to stretch in a wide, glowing smile. I would smile until I felt the claws of darkness ease their grip from my soul. Smile through tears, smile until the muscles of my jaw would hurt. I would smile until I would convince myself that the happy image I see is what I am.

Yet the lump in my throat grew heavier, almost choking me.

"Stop, damn it," I muttered to myself as I wiped snot with the back of my hand that was dribbling down past my lips now. Still shrugging with internal sobs, I squinted my eyes tight to stop the tears.

You are truly pathetic.

Get it together, Finnleah.

The anger, like my righteous protector, was ready to barge in to raise the crumbling walls back up. Like a switch, I blinked and let the anger flow in.

I stared at myself again. *I am strong and I* will *survive.*

I rinsed my red face in the cold, almost icy water, tiny droplets almost evaporating at the touch of my skin.

I felt hot. I was hot. Feverish.

My mind might be able to climb any mountain, yet my body was weak. Broken.

I sighed in defeat, though some level of relief came with it. I was grateful that my body carried me this far, and if I must rot from within to meet my Death, so be it.

Better that, than by the hands of the Destroyer.

9

I was half asleep when a loud knock woke me up. I quickly sat up, hissing, as a wave of pain rolled over me. The bright sky outside was now turning soft coral and the shadows thickened. A tall soldier walked in. It was the same man that carried me here. Orest.

He was still dressed in full armor, though his helm was off, exposing a full head of messy, dark burgundy curls reaching just the tips of his ears. Though he was large in stature, his face was young. He was young, more of a boy than a man.

"You are expected in the throne hall." He nodded slightly in greeting. His voice was deep, yet youthful and soothing. I gasped as I took a wrong step and tumbled. He quickly closed the distance between the door and my fallen body. His well-built arms gently raised me on my feet, stepping away from me a second later.

"Your dress is undone," he noted.

Though I was back on my two feet, I felt as low as the ground I was just laying on a minute ago. I muttered through my teeth.

"I can't...reach it."

"May I help you?" he asked without making a single move. I narrowed my eyes on him. But he had *asked*, and I nodded defeatedly. He quickly tied up the rest of the dress, though I could see him pausing as he saw the scars. Something about this soldier was different. He was a Destroyer, no doubt, yet he radiated comfort and care that for a second there, felt good. I felt secure. A part of me was grateful for that kindness, yet I didn't thank him, nor did I take the hand he offered to walk me down the stairs.

"This way." He opened the already familiar large doors for me and let me in.

The walls of the throne room were already lit up with large torches, the chandelier lighting up the rest of the room in the mid evening light. Small oil lamps stood between the skull vases. The large, wooden table was now covered with all manner of dishes. A lone violinist was playing softly in the background some sad tune.

A few of the Destroyer soldiers were positioned along the perimeter of the room. Lord Inadios and the Destroyer General were deep in conversation, sitting in the only two chairs by the table. Both glanced over me as I walked in, though the General's eyes lingered on me for too long. As I lowered my own eyes away, he swiftly turned back to Inadios a second later.

"Rumors of the Rebel forces are growing even this far West, my Lord Master," Lord Inadios said, sounding concerned. "I have had to send additional forces to the villages to monitor and clean out any traitorous scum who spread such atrocious rumors."

"And what do you do with those Rebel sympathizers then?" the Destroyer General asked, putting another grape in his mouth.

"Some of them are sent to the Rock Quarries, some of them are executed immediately. Based on how useful they are with providing any information," Lord Inadios said, putting on a determined smile. He was clearly pleased to see the Destroyer General interested in what he had to offer.

"Hmm," Destroyer replied, motioning him to continue.

"Well, we've come to find out, General, that Rebels are gathering in the North."

"Do you have a specific location?" he asked matter-of-factly.

Lord Inadios screeched a little before quickly mumbling.

"I am sorry, my Lord Destroyer General, but not yet. So far, we have yet to catch an actual Rebel. Just sympathizers, and they run on limited information."

"How unsurprising, yet still deeply disappointing, Inadios. Again, you're offering me a gift but giving me only the wrapping," the General lazily said as his eyes slid back to me, pausing on my bruised arms.

He turned back to the puffed-up, sweaty Lord sitting across from him. "Unlike you, Inadios, we operate based on actual information and not skimpy rumors. But, I applaud your pathetic efforts to keep Rebels at bay. They are indeed pests we must not tolerate."

"Much appreciated, my Great Lord," Inadios whimpered, slightly nodding.

"As you do get more solid information, I will await your full report." The General paused, taking a sip out of his gold goblet. Like an eagle and his prey, his eyes clawed to me. Lord Inadios turned nervously to me too. "What do you know of the Rebels, mage?" the Destroyer inquired.

With my head still lowered and eyes firmly on the floor, I replied as softly and pleasantly as possible, "Nothing, my Lord."

He scoffed.

"He is no Lord to you, you senseless, stupid girl. He is the great Lord Destroyer General, you filthy scum!" Inadios barked at me.

The General's face lit up with a wicked smirk. He gestured to Inadios, silencing him, as if a dog.

"Forgive me, my Lord Destroyer General," I replied and nodded low, flinching from sharp pain in my side.

The rage inside of me filled up to the brim, like a fuel ready to spark in flames with a single match. Anger within me overflowed the longer I stood there, motionless. Helpless. But I stood there still. For Viyak. For my promise. For me.

What's the point of the dragon inside, if you keep it on the chain? My mind raged but I kept it still. Restrained.

Lord Inadios fidgeted, trying to ease the tension.

"My high Lord, not sure how long you are staying with us this visit —" One look at the Destroyer's raised eyebrows and Inadios jumbled over his words to continue. "Oh no, my Lord Master, we are the utmost blessed to have your presence among us and will be delighted to host you and your soldiers as long as you wish! Forgive me, my Lord, for my words sometimes come out all wrong. All I meant was to invite your high presence to visit the Crystal Bridge over the Dniar river. It's not quite finished but you'll be delighted to see much progress since your last visit."

"Perhaps. Given your history of disappointments, Inadios, I doubt I'll be *delighted* from this visit after all. But I shall accept your invitation. We will head out tomorrow then."

"How blessed! We are forever grateful, my Lord Master. Perhaps a day after tomorrow? My High Lord, local royalty and devoted servants of the Queen have awaited long to meet their most valued Destroyer General and Queen's great protector! Plus, it would give us enough time for preparations since the Crystal Bridge is a long journey from here."

The Destroyer General took another sip of wine. His expression was cold as ice and yet his dark brown eyes burned bright.

"Inadios, do you know that Destroyer's raw fire can turn things to ashes in a blink of an eye?" he said while swirling wine in his big goblet and looking at the painting on the wall.

Inadios nervously wiped droplets of sweat off his forehead.

"Oh, my great Lord, I have heard wonderous things about the Cleansing Fire!" Inadios exclaimed.

The General, ignoring him, continued.

"And yet, Destroyers are taught to reel that fire in during their training, to simmer it down. Do you know why?"

Inadios blinked, tripping over his words, not finding an answer. His knuckles turned white as he clenched his fists stressed.

Because swift death is mercy, and Destroyers are merciless.

I spat out in my mind. As if reading my thoughts, the General's prying eyes went back to me. I bowed my head low until my neck cramped, but an invisible hand grabbed my chin and jerked my head up until our eyes met. I instinctively moved my eyes down.

Meek and obedient. But then I saw the fire-like hands holding my jaw. My eyes widened. Frozen mid-breath, I attempted to reel in the sheer panic rising in my chest. The fire hands jerked my head up again, tightening the grip until my eyes met his. Something primal in my body roared and clawed at the sight of fire on my skin. It didn't burn, yet I could feel the heat of my anger lighting up, my blood on fire.

My heart pounded against my chest faster. *Breathe*, I willed myself again.

Breathe.

Inhale.

Exhale.

The General stared at me oddly. My mind was rancid.

Breathe, I cried out, though my chest closed off, unwilling to let the air flow.

Like a swine, Inadios squeaked back, bowing his head a bit.

"Sorry, my Lord, but your humble servant doesn't know the answer."

A low chuckle came out from the Destroyer General. That sound alone raised hairs on my arms.

"It is because, Inadios, we have to be taught restraint young, so the world doesn't burn at our sight." His eyes sharply slid down my neck, to my bony chest, to my bruised arms, fire intensifying around my face as he continued, "Yet some days, even the most patient of us are unable to resist."

Dead silence fell in the stuffy room. Even the violin paused. My muscles locked, not able to move even an inch. Terror settled in me as the white flames circled around my waist in a thick tight loop.

"Sit," was all he said, and with a swift motion of his hand, the fire loop now enthralled me in a cocoon of fire. I screamed, but no sound came out. It took my mind a minute to realize that the fire didn't burn my skin. Painless, yet I could feel each ember of white and silver flames prickling my skin like a thousand needles.

I was trembling, my heart pounding loud, hands thrashing against the cold fire encircling me. I gasped for air with no luck. My vision darkened. Passing out was a mercy before my lungs collapsed, the air sucked right out of them. With another swift motion, the fire sphere moved and within seconds, disappeared completely as it dropped me straight on the throne.

Through my teeth I swallowed the loud screams that wanted to rip from me. I clenched my jaw and bit my inner lip until it painfully bled, but it did nothing to stop the traitorous tears rolling down my cheeks. I tried to get up as Inadios angrily huffed.

"Sit," the General repeated. "What do you think, Inadios?" The General jerked his chin to the fuming Lord. "Doesn't she look like a proper Queen?" He mocked him.

Inadios was seemingly upset by this. A slave, a Magic Wielder, sitting on *his* throne. His face turned almost purple at the sight of me.

I ignored it all. The fire was gone, yet the tears wouldn't stop. My body shook uncontrollably as if those sobs I stifled poured through my limbs. I sunk my teeth even deeper, biting my inner lip, focusing on the iron taste in my mouth.

"My Lord Great Master, this throne has been in my Royal family for generations." the Lord started, steam almost coming out from his ears. Before he could finish, the General sharply cut him off.

"And now there is Creator scum sitting on it. Isn't it rather fitting?" The General stood up. His entire focus was now completely on me as he strolled past Inadios and walked up to me. His calloused hands gripped both sides of the throne chair. His large body bent close enough that I smelled his pine and smoky ash scent. I could feel his cool, steady breaths on my burning skin. I closed my eyes, trying to calm down the quiet sobs that went through my body with each breath. His large body towered over me even as he lowered his hand to tuck a strand of my hair behind my ear, to slowly wipe away my tears with his thumb.

He lowered his head all the way down to me until his lips were almost touching my ear.

My vision turned to haze, my body was shutting down, from fever or fear —I wasn't sure. But fighting the haze, I sharply opened my eyes, seeing his exposed neck so close to my mouth, so close to my teeth.

I might look meek and broken, but I would not be his prey.

I didn't have a chance to think, but the tears stopped rolling down my cheeks. He opened his mouth to whisper something in my ear but within a second, I sunk my teeth as hard as I could into his neck.

The overwhelming taste of his blood—almost bitter, so different from the regular iron taste—made me instantly sick.

Fire ropes tied me tight to the chair, this time exuberating heat from them, melting my flesh raw.

With a flip of a switch, pure anger took over my panicking brain. Deep inside I knew there was no turning back. No act of meekness and kindness would redeem me from what I had done.

I sentenced myself to death.

Truth was, I was doomed from the start.

At least now I knew for myself how it would end.

In a complete act of defiance, I raised my eyes to face him, snarling, his blood dripping down my chin. Sheer astonishment flashed on his face, but it was quickly replaced with a stone-cold look. Icy fire played in the irises of his dark eyes. Rage or anger or shock? I wasn't sure. I hoped that he would incinerate me before I had to find out.

"You will have to try harder to get rid of me, *Creator*." Like a cold knife, his voice sliced through me. The dark red blood from my bite trickled down his neck, down his white shirt.

"In this life or the other, I will kill you; I *promise*." I scowled at him. My fevered brain was clawing in a desperate attempt to survive.

Inadios was in complete shock with his mouth wide open, trembling.

"My Lord. My Great Destroyer General..." he pleaded, dropping to his knees.

"Quiet," the Destroyer General snarled at Inadios, his eyes on me, and that smirk. Gods, I wish I could cut it out with a dull knife.

"Please, my great Lord, please..." Inadios begged almost quietly behind his back.

"I said *quiet!*" the General snapped at him and a large flame, like a gag, wrapped around Inadios's slimy head.

I glared at the General, at the abyss of hell in his eyes.

"Do it." *Kill me now*, I demanded, still tasting his blood on my tongue. Desperate panic, like quicksand, was pulling me in.

"*No*," he sternly said, regaining his composure. With a snap of his fingers, two of his soldiers appeared right next to me.

Fire ropes now scorched me, the skin on my wrists melting as if ice. My body locked in pure agony. I couldn't think straight, my mind so close to shattering.

I couldn't hear anything anymore. A high-pitched noise now filled up my ears, vaguely remembering as they grabbed me. I might have thrashed and kicked, might have been screaming. But the fiery ropes were gone… and pure darkness embraced me.

10

I woke up to a freezing touch on my wrist. Instinctively, I jerked my hands away.

"It's ok, my dear," Brita whispered. She sat on the edge of the bed with a cold washcloth and ointment, cleaning and lubricating my burns. My heart pressed in relief.

"Brita." My tense voice eased.

"Oh dear, I'm so sorry," she whispered but refused to look at me. Instead, she rinsed a washcloth in ice cold water and put it back on my wrists. I flinched, but immediately felt relief as it touched my burning skin.

I scanned the room quickly. Large windows were now covered with heavy curtains pooling on the floor. Exquisite chandeliers were the only source of light, leaving the room dim.

Covered in their dark armor from head to toe, two Destroyer soldiers stood still by the door. Orest and Broderick. Orest nodded briefly to me when he caught my eyes on him.

Features on his face were softer, exuberating kindness each time he smiled. I knew he was a Destroyer, a soldier in the Destroyer General's army, yet something deep inside of me knew for certain that he wouldn't hurt me; that I could trust him. It didn't help that he wasn't just caring, but also good looking with perfect lips. A little bit of blush came to my skin as I pulled my eyes away from his smile.

*He is a Destroyer...*I gave myself a mental slap. A Destroyer and trust? A Destroyer and kindness? Whatever infection I was fighting was making me mental.

I looked toward Brita, who was still avoiding my stare. Anxiety tugged my heart. Brita was always so full of pity, yet this time she wasn't even willing to look at my face. Thoughts about the handsome soldier by my door went out of the window as I quietly, yet sternly, asked her a question.

"Brita. Tell me. What's going on?"

"It's okay, Finnleah, dear. I am here to help." She put more ointment on my arms.

"Brita. Just tell me." I kept my voice down yet placed my hand on her.

She finally looked up at me with the saddest eyes.

"Lord Inadios sent me here to *prepare* you for the night." My heart dropped. Tingles went through my body. I shouldn't have asked. I should've been dead.

I would *rather* be dead than defiled by the Destroyer. Yet it seemed that Fate had long stopped caring about my opinions.

I tried to keep my face neutral but couldn't keep my lips from thinning and brows angrily bunching together, glaring at Brita.

"Your dress is ruined anyway, so we must change that. Can't have you looking like an old chimney sweep, my dear." She tugged on the burned pieces of tulle.

I looked down. The dress was indeed ruined, charcoaled from within. The lump in my throat got bigger as Brita grabbed what was supposed to be my night gown—a tiny piece of sheer fabric with small straps, not even long enough to fully cover my backside.

My eyes met Brita's, silently begging her.

"Now come, miss, we need to get you changed." Brita chose to ignore my pleas. I eyed the two soldiers still standing by the door, both looking at us. "The Lord Destroyer General commanded that they are not to leave your sight at *any time, with* no *exceptions*."

I reached for that familiar, comforting anger, yet even the anger well felt empty. Only sadness and pity lay there now, echoing what used to be the mighty rage. The world was cruel and unfair. I didn't do anything to deserve this or cause this, yet here I was. Alone. In pain. Lost and forgotten. And now… left to survive *this*.

I didn't dare say the right word.

But if it wasn't me, then it would've been some other unfortunate soul, born at a wrong time and in the wrong place, left to endure this life. And if I had to pick me or someone else to endure this fate? I'd always pick myself, because something deep inside of me was always certain that no matter what happens, I would endure it.

Still, I shot an angry look toward the soldiers before twisting my back to Brita, letting her untie the rest of my dress.

Her hands were gentle and surprisingly warm. She slowly went through all the ties, stopping each time I flinched. Soon enough, I slipped out of my dress completely. My undergarments were gone next.

Ignoring the harsh reality, I barricaded myself deep in the flood of thoughts and memories. Hiding behind the small bushes I used to hide from Tuluma, or to the little streams where she and I fished. Or the elvish chess that we played each night for hours, or the wild dances that we did for Nymphs, or the ballads that Tuluma sang late at night as we watched the Starfall.

Brita pulled down the small, sheer nightgown on my body. The silky straps rested awkwardly on my scrawny shoulders. She brushed my hair gently and bandaged up my wrists.

"Okay dear, my job here is done," Brita said as she cupped my face with her warm hands. Her eyes silently wished me luck as she scooped up the ruined pink dress with one hand, holding the bowl and ointment in the other, and walked out quickly, glancing at me just once more before shutting the door behind her.

I pulled the heavy blankets up to my shoulders and waited. Each time steps sounded in the hallway, my muscles tensed, each noise setting me off.

Waiting for minutes at first, and then hours.

Hours had passed, and yet the Destroyer General was nowhere to be found. Broderick soon left the room, leaving only Orest standing by the door, still just occasionally glancing over me.

I looked to the side, avoiding his gaze. Something about his presence was so soothing, yet I was quite aware that while he looked gentle, he was just as deadly as any of them.

"I need to use the bathroom," I said, glancing over my bandages, wondering what kind of scars those burns would leave.

"It's all yours." He gestured with his hand to the door right next to him leading to the bathroom. I tried to move as gracefully and pridefully as I could, but my broken body humbled me with each step as nausea rode up and my vision blurred. I finally reached the bathroom door, only a step away from the soldier.

Only up this close did I notice his eyes. They were deep gray with a purple hue around his iris. So unique, so beautiful. His eyes dropped below my neck. Though my body was exposed, it wasn't the look of a lusting man; his face still irradiated all-encompassing comfort. I almost made it to the bathroom as his strong hand grabbed my forearm.

"Who did this to you?" he firmly asked.

"Your General," I bitterly said. Rather ironic, I thought of him to ask. He still didn't let go. Irritably, I looked at him from underneath my brows.

"No, I mean the bruises and your scars?" He pointed with his eyes to my exposed midsection and legs covered in large dark bruises.

"Does it matter?" I jerked my hand out of his grip.

"It's not an answer, Finn," was all he said without letting me go. "Who?"

"Life," I replied, jolting my arm again. He didn't let go.

"I will let go once you tell me," he insisted.

"Not that it matters, but one of the Royal guards. Dimitrii," I said. "Now can I go, or should I relieve myself right here?" My body tensed but with an apologetic nod, he released my arm.

I stepped into the bathroom.

"Door needs to stay open," he said, his voice calm. And maybe it was the compassion in his voice or the bare and broken reflection of me in the mirror, but I was crumbling, disappearing with each breath, replaced by hopeless burn out.

Breaking down, I walked back to the blankets. The bed was still warm when I came back. Wrapped like a cocoon, I stared at the ceiling. Loud silence was the only lullaby for me, time becoming obsolete.

After a while I finally broke the quietness.

"What is your name?"

"Orest," he replied. But I already knew that.

"That's an odd name," I dryly said.

"Thanks," he replied with a gentle smile. I chuckled to myself. I was so utterly tired. Unable to fight the exhaustion, I opened my mouth in a large yawn.

"You should sleep, Finn," Orest said.

I was going to object, to tell him that I wouldn't let the General catch me off guard, that I could never fall asleep knowing whose bed I was in tonight. But those thoughts dissolved into nothingness as Orest dimmed the lights further until darkness took over the room.

"Sleep," he whispered, extinguishing the last light and letting the darkness drift me deep into slumber.

11

The large river was tranquil, calm, reflecting a bright full moon and shimmering stars above. Viyak's tall figure treaded ahead of me through the silver bluegrass while tiny campfires flickered on the horizon.

I knew it was a dream, but I still had hoped that he would turn around just once. For me to see his face once more.

Stupid delusions.

As if a ghost, my dreams haunted me my entire life. A shadow twin that followed me each step. Tuluma asked me about them regularly. She always had an explanation for them too. A scary monster: just my imagination adding some details to a dark cloud I saw earlier. A red-eyed devil: a mix of poppies I collected that day and that grumpy farmer's lady that yelled at me. She could always connect the dots between reality and the vivid dreams. It was our game; who could make a more reasonable connection? Like the one I had today was clearly because I missed Viyak, fires because of the Destroyer, and night because I stared at the moon too much last night.

A peaceful image of Viyak and I in a beautiful place together: a desperate shot of my subconsciousness for any kind of sense of hope.

CHAPTER 11

Maybe a part of me really needed it. To see us free, to feel free, to be at peace.

Life was too chaotic for me to linger on my dreams, but a part of me was grateful for this little glimpse of another world. Maybe in a different universe, Finn and Viyak were happy.

But in this?

Not him.

And not me.

12

Heavy curtains were pushed to the side, exposing the bright day sun, letting the little rays dance with specks of dust in the air. I rubbed my eyes harshly, waking up from what had felt like my most restful night in years.

My mind was clear, thoughts well organized. A refreshing change given the last few days. Though I was acutely aware of my current circumstances, my despair was somehow replaced with fortitude.

New soldiers in their dark silver armor were stationed by my door, their emotionless figures cold, missing the comforting warmth of Orest. I pulled off one of the smaller blankets and wrapped it around myself. There was no need to flash more soldiers with my sheer night-gown. With a dress in one hand and a makeshift blanket robe in the other, I slowly made it to the bathroom.

The dress was simple yet elegant; soft, lilac satin with small shoulder straps and a square neckline. The skirts went all the way down to the floor with a knee-high slit on both sides. I ran my hand against the lovely fabric.

Somehow, I always imagined my first nice dress would be a wedding one.

It seemed an eternity ago when Oliver...when *my Ollie* and I would talk about our upcoming marriage, cuddled up against a mossy tree. We spent so many late summer nights daydreaming about our future together. Even Tuluma, who hated all humans, secretly saved coin for our wedding.

We are meant to be, Ollie once said to me, and I wholeheartedly believed him. Yet in one day, I lost them both. My family, my past, and my future all turned to ash, leaving only small glimpses of memories left behind.

Now, covered in the richest silks and satins, with tulle and laces, I was a slave, not a bride. So far off from the life the seventeen-year-old me yearned for.

The small rainbows from the stained-glass window covered my skin in a wave-like pattern. I should've been ecstatic that I spent the night securely asleep and not brutally tortured by the General. I should've been glad. Fate granted me a gift.

But I fully knew that to Fate, this was all a game, and I was just a simple pawn.

THE MANOR WAS WELCOMING IN THE MORNING LIGHT. ESCORTED BY the soldiers, I walked towards the large garden. Trees and flower beds with metal benches around them created a large sitting area. Enormous marble vases full of blooming flowers were lining the stone path from the garden to the tables, covered with ivory tablecloths. Ice sculptures of dragons breathing fire and water nymphs served as decorations between the never-ending rows of fine dishes and eatery. Neatly dressed servants carried massive trays with all manner of drinks. A string quartet was deep into another classical melody.

Gathered in small groups, all kinds of ladies and gentlemen conversed, only occasionally passing glances toward me. They were all clearly Royals. Familial connections or friends, they were here to pay their respect and dues to the Mad Queen and her well known vicious General.

It didn't take long for me to find him in the crowd. In the sea of colors and outrageous dresses and outfits, he chose to wear a well-fitted black suit with a black silk shirt underneath. He stood tall, surrounded by Royal ladies of all ages grinning up at him, shamelessly flashing their half bare busts covered in a myriad of precious metals and stones. My simple satin dress looked more like a nightgown compared to their gowns.

Yet the embarrassment didn't come from not being dressed to code. No, the source of my embarrassment was a loud cry coming from an elderly woman not too far from me. Her eyes were locked on my back, finger pointing. My jaw clenched involuntarily as I took a long breath, realizing where her finger was pointing—my scars. My fucking scars were exposed, thanks to the low cut back of the dress. My now-chopped hair did nothing to hide them.

I took a second longer to open my eyes from a blink. The entirety of the crowd was now looking at me. I wasn't sure if they were more shocked or scared. Granted, I didn't care either way. I doubted any of them ever saw a survivor from the Rock Quarries before, or even ever thought about the possibility of one surviving. Or maybe if they did, they never thought I would stand in their presence, participating in their social hour.

However, that embarrassment didn't last long as it was replaced by the growing anticipation of *why*.

He wanted me here. Given the dress, and the scars... the timing.

Loud bells chimed in my mind, sounding the alert.

Why bring me here now?

I had no doubt the General had a plan for everything.

Yesterday, I served as a tool to degrade Lord Inadios. And today...

I quickly raked in all the possibilities. There weren't that many, but all lay on a scale from magic shows to public execution. I swallowed hard, trying to weather the brewing storm in my mind.

There were a lot more Destroyer soldiers stationed all over the garden and around the manor. The Royal guards stationed in small groups seemed so harmless in their burgundy leather uniforms against the dark armor of the Destroyers.

My eyes paused when I saw Dimitrii walking a step behind Lord

Inadios. He didn't have a limp anymore, though smaller bandages were still on his face. Even long after I am gone, that scar would forever serve as a reminder to him of the slave girl who fought back.

Shock in the crowd was quickly replaced by intrigue. As if a shadow, the Destroyer General silently approached me from behind. Small whispers and not so subtle glances towards us rolled in a wave. My body tensed in his presence, breaths becoming so shallow, I almost panted. I closed my eyes only to remember Viyak's tall figure from my dream.

Meek and obedient.

I willed myself as I turned to face him.

"My Master High Lord General Commander." I bent my body in half, bowing so low it hurt. I wasn't sure if the nausea came back from the sharp pain in my abdomen or the fact that I was bowing to a child murderer.

My blood boiled at that thought.

This was low, even for me. I might have been a slave, bound and naked; I might have been homeless and lost, but I always fought for what was right, stood up to the oppressors. Yet at some point, surviving broke me, because here I was now, bowing to the monster.

Were righteous morals a worthy cause to die and break promises already made?

"Rise," he ordered. A little shiver went through me. His voice was so unsettling, like smoke slithering through my skin, deep in my soul to haunt me. I rose but didn't dare meet his eyes. Instead, I eyed a small red mark on his neck.

A bite mark.

My bite mark.

He was almost flaunting it with the unbuttoned collar of his crisp shirt. I would've been embarrassed if I were him. Yet he was not bothered by it at all.

Such a great General bit by a rabid slave?

I pushed the concerning confusion out of the way and let myself dwell on the fact that there were not one but *two* male pricks in this gathering with fresh scars thanks to my defiance. A small detail, though still a win.

"Walk with me," he commanded. The two soldiers that escorted me quickly found new positions to take.

Cocky of him to let the soldiers go so easily, when the wounds from my attack were still fresh on his skin. But without any objection, I walked alongside him until we reached tables full of food.

"Get some food." Another command.

It seemed that nausea was now a constant part of my life, so it wasn't hard to ignore it as I shoved small bites of food on my plate. With an over-filled plate, I followed him to a small metal bench. Another command, and I sat while he stood ahead of me, observing the crowd in front, occasionally nodding in acknowledgement to the patrons passing by.

A few bites of sugared pastries and I dared to look up. The General was exchanging a few words with another Lord, his calloused hands gripping together behind his back, as if taunting me, reminding me that at one motion of his fingertips, Cleansing Fire would be blazing through me.

I squeezed the small dessert fork in my hand. If I was fast enough, I could stab him in the heart, perhaps? The silver fork probably wasn't long enough to go through layers of his thick muscles, but I could jam it hard enough for him to have another scar from me.

I raised my brow, considering it. A plan, though not a very good one.

Commotion spread through the gathering when I finally saw Orest and Broderick and to my concern, a smug Dimitrii marching towards us. The two Destroyer soldiers walked casually, expressionless. Dimitrii seemed arrogant—though a bit annoyed as he saw me.

I anxiously watched them make their way through the crowd to us. To me...

My muscles tensed and I held on to my fork.

A familiar tingling feeling inside of me awoke and begged to run, yelled to get away now. But I couldn't. I wished I could listen to its warning plea for once.

"You have all gathered here to pay heeds to my armies and my soldiers, to give gratitude to the Order, and to plead your allegiance to the Queen. Royals have long been reaping the benefits of our Great Rule." The General's voice was quite blatant; the crowd went incredibly silent, even my uneven breathing seemed to be too loud.

He paused, observing the crowd. "Yet yesterday, I was attacked in this house." Loud gasps and murmurs now sounded through the crowd.

The edges of the fork cut hard into my hand. *Public execution it is, then.*

I should stab him right now. Stab him before he says another word. But frozen as a sheep at the slaughter, I sat motionless.

Pathetic.

"By Destroyer laws, I have the right to incinerate this entire house, for such an assault that happened on your lands, under your rule." His eyes went to Inadios as the crowd surrounding him took a few steps away from him, leaving him stranded.

I could smell fear on him, his face turning bright red, fidgeting with his sausage-like fingers as he opened his mouth, but the General continued.

"But I hope today serves as a reminder to all of you that Destroyers are always just and kind, and value loyalty of those who obey. That our patience and restraint are never ending."

Dimitrii huffed, earning a sharp, irritated look from Orest.

"The punishment by death will be placed on the one responsible for the attack," the General carried on.

I swallowed hard and closed my eyes. My life didn't flash before me, I hadn't lived long enough for that. My soul didn't tremble from fear, but from the broken truth of longing for the end. Longing for those who I love, who have long crossed this line, though drops of regret, as if dye in the water, tinted my soul. Regret, that I had never lived up to the promise I made so many summers ago amidst the burning trees.

To live a better life.

Shame.

It was shame masked as sorrow as I took my last breath.

Loud screams abruptly interrupted my tangled thoughts. I opened my eyes to see the crowd panicking and screaming. Some were frozen in terror. Some were hastily attempting to jump out of the garden area because it was now surrounded by a ring of white flames.

Surrounded, Destroyer soldiers stood guard without letting anyone out, as if herding prey.

My mouth dropped open in complete shock when I saw Dimitrii. His skin was untouched, yet silver flames came out from his mouth, his eyes, his ears. His face twisted with pure agony as Cleansing Fire burned him from the inside out, turning his blood to liquid fire. Orest and Broderick held him up as the Destroyer General nonchalantly crossed the distance between them. Unable to make a sound, Dimitrii's body was frantically convulsing in pain.

"This is what happens when you touch what's mine," the General said, cold hatred radiating from him. He watched Dimitrii burn for another minute, then with a single flick of his fingers, the entirety of Dimitrii's body immediately turned to nothingness—small specks of white ash, withered in the summer breeze, never to be seen again.

I gasped for oxygen, but as if those ashes poisoned the air, painfully, I suffocated. My lungs burned as my heart raced at impossible speeds. The bright flames of Dimitrii's eyes flashed behind my eyes with each blink, adrenaline making my brain cloudy and my vision blackening.

Orest's fluorescent gray eyes seized mine. *Breathe,* he silently willed. My lungs, as if on command, slowly opened. *Breathe in and out.* My chest expanded unevenly, letting the cool air in, heart beating intensely.

Breathe in and out.

"She is having another panic attack," Orest muttered to the General. "Probably going to pass out again."

The General rubbed his temples and then yawned. They were completely unphased by what had just happened, their voices calm and calculating. He turned to watch the rapidly fleeing crowd, no longer surrounded by the soldiers or the ring of fire.

"I still have a few more things to take care of but we will leave tomorrow. For now, take her back in and keep watch." Orest quickly nodded and approached me.

"Come with me." He extended his hand, but I didn't move. My eyes lingered on the towering figure of the General departing away from us. The remaining Royalty all bowed as he walked past them. He sat down amidst a group of few Lords that, unlike the crowd, were calm though clearly intrigued. So casually he picked up the conversation, as if nothing had happened, as if he didn't turn a man—a whole man and his soul—into ash.

"Can you walk?" Orest must have asked me this twice because before I could answer, he already had me picked up and put me over his shoulder. Refocusing, I quickly blurted out.

"I'll walk...Yes, I can walk."

Surprisingly, he hastily set me back on the ground.

"Sorry, you didn't look like you could at the moment," he said. I adjusted my twisted skirts. "Just don't pass out on me this time. Deal?" Orest smiled and offered his arm for support, but I refused.

We walked as fast as my body allowed. However, broken bones and burns were of little concern to me now. My mind was stuck in perpetual hell, I realized. As if an animal in a cage—aware, yet unable to do anything about it.

But Orest's welcoming earthy scent of oak and lavender calmed me, almost putting me to sleep by the time we made it to the room.

I laid on the couch. Orest stood by the door only a few steps away from it. Heavy silence filled the room as I lost myself to the deep pit of never-ending thoughts.

"Why do you work for *him*?" I finally mumbled.

I couldn't stop myself from wondering about that. Orest was unlike any other Destroyer I had met, yet still somehow one of them.

His shoulders stiffened and he awkwardly scratched the back of his head, rustling the burgundy curls. His dark armor shimmered against the afternoon rays peeking through the slightly curtained windows.

"Because it is my privilege and honor as a Destroyer to be a soldier and to follow the greatest general and leader there is," he replied.

I wasn't sure what I was expecting, but his reply stung a bit. The *greatest* General and leader. The *greatest* murderer. The *greatest* monster. The *greatest* torturer. A part of me wanted to debate him, to argue and fight, but I was so utterly exhausted—completely drained—that I just let out a long sigh. Orest's lips curved up. "Not the answer you were hoping for?"

"No," I said, taking another look at him. He rested his hands on the tilt of the sheathed sword at his side. "Do you ever get tired of just standing there?"

He raised his eyebrows in question, amused.

"What? I am guessing that armor isn't light," I said, tugging on the ends of my bandages.

Orest chuckled.

"No. But you do get used to it. Though at times, my back does get stiff, guarding duties are usually not a thing that I do."

This time I chuckled at this little truth between us.

"Will I die?" I asked calmly. My voice didn't tremble, and my brain didn't run panicking as the realization of the question settled in.

"I wouldn't put it past you, considering you bit the General yesterday," he softly teased. I turned to face him, letting him see the little embers of coal still flickering in my eyes with craving for life.

He added, "We all die, Finn. Some are just meant to pave the way."

I didn't ask any questions after.

13

Yellow tassels at the top of the large curtains lazily swayed from the touch of the night breeze creeping in from a slightly opened window. Occasional owls' hoots and crickets' melody came from the miles of dark forests below. The night seemed so peaceful.

I laid still in my bed, pretending to be asleep. Orest was long gone, replaced by Broderick and another soldier. Brita didn't visit either and neither did the General. Unfinished, now cold, left-over dinner in a silver tray was still on the large coffee table by the couch. The day went by too quickly and now under the cover of the darkness, my thoughts raced faster than ever. This time I didn't fight them. I didn't try to calm them down. I let the fury rise.

The words of the Destroyer General were branded in my mind.

Tomorrow.

We will leave tomorrow.

For better or for worse, my circumstances were going to change tomorrow.

As if my own torture, Dimitrii's agonizing death played nonstop in my mind. His face twisted in pain, his convulsing body and ashes as if just small specks of dust scattered in the wind.

He deserved his death. I should feel relieved that there was one less prick in the world, but where I hoped relief and satisfaction would come, now gushed more uncertainty and anguish.

That could've been me. Should have been me. And yet I was fine. Alive, and now wrapped underneath my heavy covers. My wounds quickly healing, scars and burns itching as new layers of skin formed.

Maybe it was Fate or maybe it was just pure luck, it didn't matter to me. I hated the anticipation, the lack of control over my existence.

Kill me now or let me be free.

And maybe it was the exquisite food or the day full of rest and sleep, but I was tired of waiting. I was done bargaining with Fate.

Whether gods wanted it or not, *tomorrow, things were going to change,* and I would make sure of it.

14

We were deep in the Evergreen Forest. The summer air was cool, filled with thick mist. Tall peaks of pine trees gently brushed the passing clouds. The Destroyer General rode on a large black mare ahead of us, Inadios following him on his wide draft horse. Behind us, perfect lines of soldiers silently marched on.

I was grateful to get a horse—more grateful than I was willing to admit—and yet when Orest hopped on right behind me, my stomach twisted, making me a little queasy. I had no desire to share a horse with anyone, let alone a Destroyer soldier. Though, that dreadful feeling quickly went away, replaced by a surprising wave of comfort as his large arms wrapped around me to grab the reins.

I had to fight a small smile when he whispered close to my ear, "If you promise not to bite, I'll promise not to knock you off the horse."

At first, I resisted the urge to rest my back against his stiff armor, but after hours of horses climbing the rocky path, I gave in, resting my sore body against his. He didn't say anything, and I wasn't going to participate in small talk. Instead, I eyed the long, black cape of the General. Small gusts of wind occasionally lifted the edges, exposing two large swords, crisscrossed on his back.

I hadn't seen the General since the garden incident. He hadn't visited me in the room, or even said a word this morning as he eyed me getting on the horse.

It bothered me. Whatever game he was playing, whatever his plan was... he was winning. And while Fate was benevolent enough to keep him out of my bed at night, I was nowhere closer to figuring out why he was waiting.

After riding all day, we were finally approaching the Crystal bridge. The clicks of the hooves and almost silent march of the soldiers was now completely replaced by the sound of the gushing waters. With a quick whistle, the group came to a complete stop, soldiers halting with one large step. Orest got down first, before helping me to the ground.

The view was breathtaking. Two tall peaks of the Rocky Mountains were cut sharp by the mighty Dniar river. There were two majestic waterfalls, one above the bridge and one below it, connected by a short section of bursting water. Right in that section was a half-finished bridge made from pure crystal.

Only when my eyes inspected the curved bridge did I realize that it was indeed made of untainted glass—Destroyer melted glass. So pure and so stiff that it was almost impossible to damage. All matter of workers and guards bowed, some even dropping all the way to their knees, kissing the ground as the General walked by to the riverbank.

The bridge was unfinished, yet already so magnificent. Small droplets of water from the gushing waters underneath turned it into a walking rainbow, each piece of crystal reflecting large rays of the sun.

I took a few steps away from the soldiers and the worker camp, eyeing the Dniar river. Glacier runoff, strong and unyielding, rushed past us in an unstopping beat. I couldn't see the lower waterfall, only that it led off the large cliff, exposing the rest of the valley to view. That view alone left me speechless. I had never seen it like that. All small villages and larger towns spread out across the long, green valley with large hills and snug mountains surrounding them, all weaving around the expansive river. Small wheat fields radiated gold, even from miles away.

There were free people there, living their life, working this very second, so unaware of the deadly Destroyer army amidst them or a small slave girl looking upon them all.

I walked closer to the bridge, feeling the cold mist kiss my warm flesh. The riverbank was covered in mossy rocks. The constant gushing of the water was never ending. With each breath, the ferocious flow slammed against the rocks, wearing them down one by one until they became nothing more than smooth pebbles.

I stared at the pathway by my feet. Mixed with summer burnt grass, there were millions of small rocks. Each of them unlike the others. I squatted to pick up a perfectly round and smooth black rock. It was little, smaller than a silver coin.

Between the sea of dust, grass, and multitude of gray rocks, this one stood out the most to my eye. It didn't belong here.

Neither did I.

Was it a new low for me to relate to a rock? Tuluma would have made fun of me for this. Ollie would have probably laughed. I should laugh at this too.

Finnleah, Daughter of the Dead and the little black rock against the world. I smiled, squeezing the rock in my hand.

"Found anything of value?" the General curiously asked, looking at my clenched fist.

Caught in surprise, I hastily turned to see the Destroyer General near me. Orest was long gone, and the feeling of dread now choked me.

I bowed just a bit and took a deep and slow breath.

"No... my Lord, Great Master."

"You are not a very good liar." He reached and grabbed my hand. I refused to open my fist, but the General squeezed my hand tighter until I winced from pain and opened my hand. He eyed a small black rock, now wet from my sweaty palm.

"A little black rock? And they say creativity is dead in Magic Wielders," he grumbled, completely unfazed as he let go of my hand, letting the rock tumble onto the ground.

No, they say all Magic Wielders are soon to be dead... thanks to you, I wanted to say, but I remained silent.

It was just a rock. Yet why did it feel like he just tore into my soul?

Even after he let go, I could still feel the impression of his ice-cold black armor against my skin.

Rage. So much rage was building up inside of me that my skin boiled.

"Thinking of turning it into a murder weapon, *mage*?" There was no fear or annoyance in his tone, almost as if boredom slipped past his put together look.

The General quickly glanced over me, pausing only slightly at my still-bandaged wrists.

"Not very chatty today, I see," he said, taking a deep breath. "Come." He motioned with his hand to the bridge. I listened.

Workers made way for us to approach the sparkling glass.

"Do you like it?" he asked, looking at the million rainbows shining around.

"Yes." There was no point of denying the pure beauty of it.

"It's quite fascinating, don't you think?" He spoke as we continued walking up the bridge all the way up until we stopped only steps away from the large gaps of the unfinished part.

Even with the bridge being high, the chill, cool water drops splashing across the bridge foundation dribbled on my feet. "That our fire can take something dull like sand and turn it into pure diamonds."

"Lord Destroyer General..." Inadios called out for something but was muffled by the loud sound of gushing water beneath us. The General turned to look at him, taking a couple of steps away from me.

I looked down below. The river was fast and deep, covered with rocks of all manner in its path to the mighty waterfall. This was my chance, I realized.

It was a very crappy chance, but a chance, nonetheless.

I knew how to swim; not very well, but I knew how to stay above the water when it mattered.

The heavy, velvet green dress would try to keep me down, that is, if I didn't bash my head against the rocks upon impact. Then I'd have to be able to swim or at least float far and quick enough in the cold water without the freezing temperatures seizing my body first.

I made a step closer to the edge. A cold breeze of wind went up my skirt, caressing my skin. At least I was wearing new leather boots. Jumping legs first would be my best option, I concluded. I closed my eyes and took a step into the air.

Painfully, I was jerked back by a rough yet familiar touch.

The General.

"Not so fast," he angrily said as he gripped my hand awfully tight.

No! No! No!

This was it. My only chance. I jerked my hand back, but he held on tight. There was no point in leashing my hatred, no point of shoving down my rage. No point in pausing to think, to plan. The sleeping dragon within me was awake, roaring hungrily for retribution.

"You. Sick. Bastard! Let go of me!" I shouted at him. I could feel all the dams that I had carefully built up through the years inside of me to reel in my utter rage breaking up with one big gush.

His jaw tightened, but he was cool and collected.

"Let's go," the General barked at me. Orest and a few soldiers, noticing the commotion, were making their way to the bridge. I had to get away *now*. My eyes locked with his. I could see the silver flames reflecting, growing within that darkness.

My heart pounded in my chest so fast until it stopped.

"Burn in Hell," I yelled as I let my fury take over me, blinding me as I threw all my strength at him as I yanked my hand out of his grip.

Shocked, he abruptly let go.

Unbalanced, I fell through the crisp summer air down to the ice water, my back taking the brutal hit of the stone-cold surface.

15

I didn't have a chance to think as severe underwater currents sucked me in deep. Air was still in my lungs. Good.

It might have been the freezing waters, but my heart slowed down to a nonexistent beat. I had to get away before the General blasted this river into nothing but boiling mist. I didn't have to try hard to swim away as the rapid current carried me.

I just had to not drown.

Air was now alarmingly low in my lungs. My eyes were completely useless against the murky waters. Tossed around like a leaf on a windy day, my body bruised against the river bottom. The icy water caused my limbs to go completely numb. I slammed against a large rock, clenching my teeth as the pain riddled through me, but it briefly anchored me against the rushing river. Refusing to let go, I clawed against the rock until my face broke the surface. Fresh air cut through my lungs like knives.

I glanced back; the crystal bridge was still in my view, though now smaller and less distinctive. Blurred vision or not, I could still see his large black cape wavering on the edge of the bridge. Soldiers and Royal Guards ran down the side of the river.

I felt his haunting eyes on me. It didn't make any sense how, but I could feel it. My heart confirmed it by racing against my chest faster.

Something was off, but I didn't have the time to think about it as I took a big breath and jumped back into the water.

I knew it was coming, yet fear roared inside of me as the river pulled me to the cliff. The waterfall. Loud and murderous. I wasn't going to go back, but even if I changed my mind, there was no going back now. I took another large breath and dove.

Nothing could've prepared me for it, as I free-fell alongside the large body of water, my body awkwardly trying to grasp onto something. In the last seconds, I managed to fight the gravity with enough strength to have my legs hit the water first. My body slammed against the water like concrete and plummeted deep below. Legs first might have been a great idea if it wasn't for the long dress I was in.

Wrapped around my upper body, heavy fabric disoriented me completely, dragging me further down into the deep. Flopping with my arms tangled up in the skirts, I swam to the surface.

I gasped for air, finally breaking out of the cold water. This part of the river was much wider than the top, expanding out like a wide lake. The current was now more of steady flow than a rancid stream. The large, rocky cliffs on both sides of the waterfall served as a reassurance —unless they jumped straight into the water right after me, it would take them a while to hike down to find me. Still, I wasn't going to stay and wait for them to find me.

Deep in Lord Inadios's territory, it wasn't safe to wander in the forest, but the growing dull ache in my ribs reminded me I couldn't run far. Wincing, I kicked my legs faster, pushing my body through the water. My teeth chattered nonstop; it was only a matter of time before the frigid cold completely stopped my heart.

I had no belongings, no food, or shelter, and while the sun was still shining brightly, it was just mere hours away from hiding behind the horizon. That dreadful reality pulled me down just as much as my heavy dress. I incinerated those thoughts with each stroke, pushed and fought the brooding gloom.

I made it.

For the first time in well over a year, I was free.

I let that thought ground me.

Free.

Away from Destroyers, away from the Quarries. I was *free.* That was all that mattered. It was now up to me to make the rest.

My body was shaking, but I disregarded it. Doubt tried to creep up in my mind, but I did not yield. I wouldn't let it take this victory away from me.

I had been completely alone before. I had gone hungry before. I lived against all odds in the Rock Quarries. Gods, I bit a ruthless Destroyer General and fought a Royal Guard.

I will make it. I will survive.

Sometimes I just had to remind myself of that.

I swam through the river until the current became almost nonexistent. Maybe it was hypothermia, but the water was feeling warm, welcoming. My legs painfully cramped, and I went under, choking on gulps of water.

I had to get out right now.

My muscles were leaden. Each stroke requiring tremendous concentration as I made my way to the opposite bank of the river from where I jumped. Tears mixed with fresh water clung to my lashes when my feet finally touched the slippery, rocky bottom of the river.

Alive and free.

I smiled at the fluorescent sky.

Free.

I dropped to my knees, crouching between the large green shrubs surrounding the riverbank. Now that I was splattered against the hard, warm earth, overtiredness tugged on my body, demanding to be addressed.

I just needed a minute to lay still, to feel the sun on my skin, to feel my limbs again.

After fighting with the buttons, I finally clawed myself out of the soaked fabric. Splattered in a small grassy spot, I let the warm afternoon sun wash over me, thawing my frozen body.

I had to keep moving, had to go as far as I could, but after swimming for over an hour, my body refused to move.

Just ten minutes in this warmth and I will venture...My eyes closed shut before I could even finish that thought.

PART II

ASSASSIN

16

"You look rather wrecked."

I sharply opened my eyes to a curvy female figure standing directly above me. Any previous resemblance of sleep quickly abandoned me. She took a few steps back until her back leaned against a small water ivy across from me.

"I don't know what rathole you've come from but considering the damage..." She scanned my exposed body covered in large bruises and burns. "I am guessing you weren't here for a great swimming lesson, were you now?" She sneered, though her voice was sultry and low. Her eyes wandered off to my still wet dress.

"No, I wasn't," I replied, quickly getting up to my feet. I grabbed my soaking dress and started pulling it back on my body.

"Oh, for the cry of all holy." A long sigh came out of her. "Here." She pulled a silky tunic out of her bag and threw it at me. "Are you a slave?" she asked with intrigue.

I held the fine fabric and looked cautiously at her. She was drop dead gorgeous. Her features were attractive; dark, tanned skin perfectly smooth without a single imperfection. Her black, thick lashes long and curly. Her full, round lips soft pink. A thick, long braid dropping down to her navel, with just a few strands of large chestnut curls free. She was dressed in extremely well-fitted brown leathers, extenuating her flawless, hourglass shape and rich curves.

She was striking.

"If you stare too much your eyes will fall out," she snarkily replied. I couldn't quite get where her accent was from; it was unlike any other I had heard before. Every word from her sounded like music, a sensual melody. "I asked, are you a slave?" she repeated, raising a perfectly trimmed brow in question.

"Not anymore." A calculated risk.

I pulled on her dry tunic over my body.

"Rock Quarriers or Royals?" she asked, tilting her head just a bit.

"Does it really matter?" I said, shaking off the sand in my hair, taking a quick look at my surroundings. My head throbbed with a lingering headache, mind in a fog as if someone was roughly shuffling between my thoughts, my memories, my feelings.

I needed food and proper rest.

I needed a plan.

"Thanks for the tunic, but I have to go." I gathered my wet boots in my hand and took a few steps, not failing to notice the well-hidden, elongated daggers strapped to her thighs and short knives at her hips. She was armed to the teeth, yet each piece of armory was almost undetectable, sheaths smoothly woven into the leathers.

It was time for me to go.

"You are not going to get far in these lands, Freckles."

I watched her hand caress the dagger's hilt, though her eyes were still on me.

"So, what do you suggest I do?" I was aware of the clear display of my desperation.

"You could come with me," she offered, straightening up and throwing her braid behind her. "I am in dire need of a servant girl."

I narrowed my eyes at her, clenching the wet boots tighter to my body.

"So, trade one slavery for another? And who am I to trust a stranger deep in these Royal lands?"

She wholeheartedly laughed. Her laugh was rich and seamless.

"Smart. I like you, girl. You can stay with me for the night and then leave if you wish. But if you do end up wanting to work for me, I would pay you." The stranger walked past me, giving me a teasing glance.

Half-naked, hurt, and hungry, I didn't have many options. And whoever she was, she clearly knew that.

"Fine. But only one night," I replied with a sigh. No longer a slave, yet still chained by my circumstances.

She loudly clicked her tongue and grinned with her perfect white teeth.

"Deal."

The stranger strolled further away; so feline, like a black panther on the prowl. I watched her hips sway in motion. She was absolutely gorgeous, yet there was something sinister, deadly about her.

"Leave that gnarly dress in the river, Freckles. No need for the Destroyer soldiers to come looking for you here."

I wasn't sure how she knew, but somehow, she knew. There was no point denying it.

Apprehensively, I let the dark green dress float down the river, away from this shore. Away from me.

"Gods, are you done yet? I am starving," the beautiful stranger called out while dramatically rolling her eyes.

* * *

WE APPROACHED A SMALL VILLAGE, SIMILAR TO THE ONE WHERE Tuluma and I used to sell herbs to humans. There weren't a lot of people walking the dirt streets, yet the ones that were stared at the two females so clearly out of place. But my newly acquainted stranger didn't care. Her walk emanated pure arrogance, each step flaunting her sensual curves.

She slammed the large wooden doors open, stepping into a local tavern. The strong smell of moonshine and roasted meats burned my nose. It seemed like the whole village was gathered here. Chatter and poorly played music pounded on my ear drums.

She snapped her fingers to the old, bearded man sitting not too far from the bartender and like a dog, he ran to her quickly.

"What can I do to be of service, miss?" He bowed to her.

"She'll be staying with me so bring an extra bed to my room," she demanded. "Also, I want your cooks to make some good food and make sure to include a dessert this time."

The man nodded and rushed away.

Quickly, I followed her to our room on the top floor. The room was spacious and well kept. It was furnished simply. Each item was clean, though slightly worn. There was a large four-post-bed, a small couch, and a tall dresser. Just two windows lined the walls with wooden shutters and a full-size oval mirror. The wooden floors were covered with a thin, threaded rug.

The girl opened the top of the dresser and threw a pair of well-made pants at me.

"Put them on. Those toothpick legs of yours are hurting my eyes." She scoffed.

I didn't argue with her as I pulled thick, light brown pants on my scrawny legs. They were embarrassingly loose on me. I tied them with a rope she handed to me a second later.

After I was dressed, she looked over at me again with a devilish smirk.

"Hell, are you sure you are even a girl? Because you look like a feral twelve-year-old boy."

I should've laughed at her teasing. I would have laughed, if I had even an ounce of objection to her statement. Long gone were any ounce of my youthful female shape. The small though well-shaped breasts, strong thighs and soft skin were now replaced with only saggy skin and a poorly shaped skeleton underneath, with gangly limbs and sun-scarred skin.

A hesitant knock on the door had her opening it promptly, letting in a few large men with a new mattress and a few of the maids carrying bedding and large trays with food.

Both of us stared at them as they set things up quickly and left just as promptly as they had arrived.

"Lock the door," she said, and I followed her command, locking the door with a swift motion of the key.

"What's your name?" I asked, sitting down on the edge of my floor mattress.

"You can call me Priya."

"I am Finn."

"Yeah-yeah, I don't care. Here, come unzip me," she ordered, pulling down her heeled boots.

I hastily came up to help. Her soft scent of jasmine and cinnamon pleasantly kissed my nose. I slowly pulled the well-made zipper down until she could reach it. Priya finished unzipping it and completely removed the top. I wondered if her skin was mixed with glitter at the shine of it. Her large, brown braid fell down her exposed back, well past her waist.

I was so wrong to stare. I really was. She turned around with her full, round breasts completely exposed, her small, perky buds of rosy nipples staring at me. I almost dropped my jaw wide open. Being a slave in the Rock Quarries, I'd seen many shapes of female busts; droopy, perky, large and small, round, triangle.

I thought I had seen them all. But these—no, these were perfect.

I blushed a little, moving my eyes down to my dusty feet. Gods, I was no better than a lusty man thinking of this girl, this woman, this way. So shameful.

"It's so fucking hot today." Priya slowly walked to prop the window wide open. I raised my brows in surprise. Quite a brave move by her, considering they faced the town square. She turned her back to the window, exposing it to the evening breeze.

Noticing color in my cheeks and my shameful stare, Priya proudly smirked.

"Relax. I know my boobs are magnificent." She then squished them together with her hands, kneading them slowly, seductively winking at me while running her tongue across her plump lips. My heart traitorously raced faster. I froze in my seat, unsure of what to do.

When I didn't laugh or even smile, she dropped her hands down and rolled her eyes. "Never took a slave girl to be a prude."

"I am not a prude," I replied, fighting myself from nervously fidgeting in my seat.

I really wasn't. In fact, most of the time I didn't care about other nakedness. After all, it was just a human body.

"I was taken by surprise. Never seen breasts like yours before," I retorted.

Pleased by the compliment, Priya chuckled. "Well, I am one of a kind, what can I say?"

Her laugh eased the heated tension in the room. I rested my clammy hands on my knees. She rested her hands on her tight waist. Only then did I notice a scar, though well healed and almost unnoticeable in the bleak lighting of the room, it was the size of an apple, right above her belly button. A burn mark. A large letter S. As if a brand on an animal.

Noticing where my eyes have lingered, she twisted.

"Never seen a scar either, Freckles?" she snarled, her features quickly changing from relaxed and sultry to cutthroat and angry. The air in the room dangerously shifted. My eyes, without hesitation, found trays of food on the bed. A well needed distraction.

"Can I have some food?" I meekly asked, falling into a familiar tone.

"Go for it."

Priya went to pull another shirt from the dresser to put on. Her nipples perked up at a light touch of the cotton fabric. When I involuntarily gazed across them, she stuffed a big roll in her mouth and murmured, "Bras are for pussies, and we let titties roam free here, so you better get used to it."

Almost choking on my own roll, I smiled. Maybe it was the food, or the comforting warmth of the blankets, or the realization that I was finally free, but my heart filled with relief because at that moment I wasn't sure who she was, but I knew I could get along with her.

We silently finished our dinner. Priya was already propped up on her bed with square pillows, flicking a large ring in the air like a coin.

"So..." I was unsure how to ask the question.

"So what?" she said, still eyeing her large ring.

"Who are you?" I blurted out. There wasn't a good way to ask this. She would either answer it or wouldn't, no matter how well I could word it.

"Does it really matter?" She repeated my own words from earlier today, her copper eyes following the ring in the air.

"If I am to accept your offer of employment, I'd like to know," I countered.

She caught the ring and sat up crossing her legs.

"So, I flash a pair of nice boobs at you, feed you once and you are ready to be my bitch?" She grinned wide and then added, "Do you pee standing up too?"

Flash of embarrassment ran through me, but I continued.

"I didn't realize being 'your bitch' was part of my employment offer, but that's good to know," I threw back, pulling the blankets over me.

"Oh, slaves are so sensitive these days," Priya teasingly laughed.

I was not a slave. Not anymore. I locked my jaw, ignoring her jab.

She clicked her tongue and took a loud breath but answered.

"You can say I am an entrepreneur."

Fair enough. No answer then.

I wasn't mad at her, I was grateful, though I didn't appreciate the constant jabs and never-ending teasing.

But we were mere strangers, and she had already shown me more kindness than most people I had ever met. That leather suit of hers with daggers and knives strapped all over her body was a loud enough indication that she had her own secrets to hide. I had enough of mine, no need to keep hers too.

Ignorance was bliss after all.

"What were you doing by the river? Why so many daggers?" It was another question that bothered me.

"So. Many. Questions. Agh." She scoffed. "Blah blah blah. Who? What? Where?" Her hair was completely unbound now, long, large curls covering her body. She held a few pins in her hands. Some of them looked like small vials with liquid in them and some of them looked like tiny darts and daggers. I didn't even realize they were in her hair.

"One thing that is a complete drag is laundry and cleaning. Like who has time for that?!" She dramatically sighed. "Anyway, so my job offer is quite simple. You clean and do my laundry and I will pay you."

Clear enough.

"Do you live here?"

"This dump? Hell no." She pretended to gag. "Gods, please murder me immediately if I ever end up living in this shithole. I was here for much more exciting stuff than this worn-out furniture." She twisted the large ring in her hand.

"Just your laundry then?" I asked again, though aware that deep inside I already made the decision.

"Precisely."

"And you will *actually* pay me?"

"Be careful there, Freckles, that sounds a lot like an insult. I always keep my word." A jab and a threat.

"What's the catch?" I suspiciously asked.

"Oh, wouldn't you love to know?" She smiled, narrowing her eyes. I tensed up. She ran her fingers through her loose waves. "Gods, Freckles, relax. There is no catch." She paused. "As long as you don't ruin my precious silks. If you do, I cannot guarantee you will walk away alive." I swallowed and clenched my jaws. "Geez, girl. Seriously? So tense, loosen up, I am not going to chain you or sell you. Have a sense of humor." She grumped and rolled over in bed. "I am leaving this dump tomorrow, so you have the night to decide."

"Where are we going?" I asked.

She chucked at the clearly intended "we."

"*We* are going to the City of Svitar."

My eyes grew wide as a little thread of excitement went through me.

The city of Svitar. The capital of the Royal Lands. The largest city in all of the Esnox. The most beautiful and extravagant place. The most ancient too.

You could find anything in Svitar. *You could be anyone there.*

At least, that's what I had always heard. Tuluma was extra careful to keep me away from any major human settlements, especially cities like Svitar. But she was gone now, and I was going to Svitar.

My present course seemed to be much different from the past path.

I laid back on the large pillow and tucked myself tight under the sheets. My bones ached, my head throbbed, and my muscles were utterly sore, but for once in a very long time, I genuinely smiled to myself.

This was going to be good.

17

We had been traveling almost two weeks now, only stopping occasionally to switch carriages until we arrived at the Port City, waiting to board the steamboat to take us to Svitar. Our travel was uneventful, and I appreciated that. Often, we stopped for the night in a tavern or a hotel, sometimes staying for a day or two. During those days, I diligently cleaned and washed all the laundry, eager to prove myself. I needed this job, but even more so, I needed this opportunity to make it to Svitar. The rest of the time I spent absorbing the picturesque views through the carriage windows, admiring the beauty of nature.

It was easy to get along with Priya. The small jabs, the never-ending sarcasm and the constant rolling of her eyes, was growing on me; becoming a new norm. In the long carriage rides and slow evenings, we spent our days talking about everything and nothing at the same time. I learned fast that Priya seemed to have a strong opinion about everything. She also would rather murder me than let me win in tic-tac-toe. Luckily, I didn't mind throwing the games for her; it made me content knowing that she was happy. I knew her favorite color and that she loved to eat desserts, and that she got stung by a bee in her right butt cheek a couple of years back.

Priya already told me that if I was smart, I'd save my wages for a Svitar surgeon, who she knows very well, to get new boobs. At my raised brows, she replied, "What? It's not like you have any." I genuinely laughed at that because truthfully, I couldn't argue with that.

In our short time, I had also learned that Priya loved nudity. There was no privacy with her. She walked around naked anytime she felt like it. Even after two weeks, I was still in awe of her perfect figure and full hourglass shape, but I'd gotten better with my staring.

Occasionally, she'd disappear in her leathers only to come back hours and hours later. Even though curiosity was killing me, I pretended to ignore that part of her life. Whatever it was. She never asked any questions about mine and I respected that. A fair trade. But one thing was certain: Priya spared no expense for her own comfort.

* * *

WE FINALLY ARRIVED AT THE LARGE PORT TOWN ON THE BANKS OF THE Kinderby River. Small lanterns on the streets were being lit up, shining as if little fireflies lit the mist. The sky was now stretched with gray clouds, hiding the lovely sunset. The Kinderby River was large and voluminous. A thin line of another shore on the horizon served as the only reminder that this wasn't, in fact, a never-ending sea.

I climbed out of the carriage last. My bruises were faded but my bones still occasionally reminded me of the damage, though now pain was more of a ghost; nothing more than a memory, one that I tried to forget. I could feel my body getting stronger each day, my mind blossoming at the access to food and rest, and just eagerness of life.

Excited.

I was very excited.

It was a beautiful afternoon, and the pier was crowded with different vendors trying to win each customer's last coin. I inhaled full lungs of the misty river air. Green moss covered snugly-fit, gray stone buildings; the same little dabs of stone were on the long cobble streets along the riverbank. All kinds of steam ships, sail ships, and even regular fishing boats were peacefully anchored for the day.

"Ugh, gods, I hate this town!" Priya's voice sounded right next to me.

"You do?" I asked, surprised.

"Yes, it smells like rotten fish and disease." She huffed, walking up the steps to an antique-looking townhome. "Are you going to stand there and stare?" she snarked.

"Um, sorry, coming." I pulled my eyes away from the beautiful pier, the rushing crowds and the ever-still water. We walked in a poorly lit room. A skinny young man, barely fourteen years old at most, approached us to take in our luggage.

"Welcome, miss Priya." He slightly bowed.

"Ronald, you talk too much, you ugly shit," she jabbed but still smiled, walking to the counter. By now, I was used to Priya bossing everyone around and by the looks of it, Ronald was too. He just beamed and nodded.

"Where is that old hag? Hello?" Priya banged on the dark cherry counter.

An old sweet lady walked out from the curtained door. "Oh, miss Priya, so glad to see you back so soon." She bowed as well.

"Yeah-yeah, here is the thing." Priya dismissed her and started spitting out her demands. "I want you to draw a big bubble bath, none of that lavender grass shit, an actual nice bubble bath." She paused, glaring at the nice lady as if to see if she understood. The lady nodded in agreement. Satisfied, Priya continued. "I also want a chocolate cheesecake and you know full well how I feel if anyone cooks or so much brings a fish to this house."

"Yes, my lady." The old woman bowed again as Priya handed her a small copper key.

We walked up the large, wide staircase leading up to the second floor, passing a few rooms that seemed to be empty.

"What is this place?" I asked.

"Think of it as my personal bed and breakfast," Priya casually said, as if it was nothing.

It seemed a little odd that we were the only ones here considering the perfect location of this place. As if reading my thoughts, she spat,

"I'd be damned if after all the travels, I have to share a room with one of them." Her face grimaced with disgust and her chin jerked to the large windows in the atrium, pointing at the pier full of people.

"This is yours for the night." She pointed to one of the rooms on my left. "I'll be right there," Priya continued, pointing to the large double doors across the hall. "Our ship departs late night tomorrow, don't sleep in," she teased, showing her tongue and marching on to her room.

Right before entering her room, she turned and threw me a small bag filled with coins.

"Here are your wages, Freckles. Don't spend it all in one night and for the love of all holy, save some for the boobs, I am begging you." She winked at me and before I could say a word, she shut the door.

I quickly poured out the contents on the floor. I counted them once, then twice, then thrice.

There were too many coins.

Gold coins.

Priya never mentioned the amount she was going to pay, and I was desperate enough to accept work even just for food and shelter, so I never bothered to ask.

This, however, was the most amount of money I had ever had. No, I had ever seen!

This was too much. With this money I could easily feed and shelter a family of ten for at least two months. Maybe it was a mistake. No servant would ever get paid this much for two weeks' worth of work.

I thought for a minute and still felt uneasy. I didn't need this much, much less deserved it.

I knocked on Priya's door. She didn't reply.

"Priya?" I said, opening the door.

"Better be important, Freckles." Priya was already naked, sitting on the edge of the quickly filling up bath, pouring a glass of wine.

"You've paid me too much." I didn't beat around the bush, holding the money in my hand.

"No, I paid you correctly," she replied, climbing into her bath.

Doubt crept in. Gods, she wasn't illiterate, right?

Or was she?

It would explain the never-ending money throwing. I never paid attention if she was good with math, and I had not seen her read or write anything either.

She sighed and as if reading my mind and blurted out.

"Oh gods, I know how to count, and I've paid you correctly. I will pay you again in two weeks the same sum." Priya took another sip from her glass. I wasn't sure what to say but she continued. "Unless you insist on interrupting my relaxing time, then I'll take it all." She growled, lowering her body into the water.

"This is very generous of you, Priya. Thank you!" I genuinely beamed with gratitude.

She waved me off.

"Go buy yourself something nice and leave me alone."

I nodded and quickly left the room, right before her fingers slipped between her legs.

It was already too dark to venture out to the pier. All the street vendors packed up their carts and by now there was nothing but quiet docks lit up by the full bright moon. I laid still on my bed pondering. My thoughts swirled with Viyak, the tall walls of Rock Quarries suffocating me. Was he still alive? Was he holding on to the pointless promise of mine? Viyak's kindred glance shifted in my tired mind into a faceless hood covered figure. *Kahors.* Anger rose in my mind at the memory, hate simmered within me, though I wouldn't let it boil.

No, my hate was saved for *him*. As if on command, the General's figure appeared behind my closed lids. Standing so still on that bridge, his black cape wavering in the wind. Chills went through my body. My rage was begging to let loose.

Not yet, I reminded it.

Not yet.

I rolled to my other side, pinching the ends of my blankets until they were wrapped tight around my shoulders. Laying still amidst the darkness, I whispered the same words I said each night since the day on that cursed bridge; that I, Finnleah, Daughter of the Dead, was free.

18

The fresh morning air filled my lungs. The pier was crowded. Even early in the morning, the streets were filled with people. Some travelers were carrying their bags and boarding large ships docked at the port. Street vendors shouted out their daily deals or waved products in the air, trying to attract more customers. Already far on the horizon, new ships were approaching the lively city.

I anxiously ruffled a few gold coins in my pocket and excitedly walked to the docks. After seeing all manner of vendors and other things and exploring the town for what felt like a whole day, I finally settled on a small bench alongside the pier, away from the crowded docks.

A large black raven landed just a few feet away, hungrily staring at me with its obsidian eyes.

"Starving?" I asked. The raven just tilted her head curiously. I softly smiled. "I understand. I would be too with all these seagulls ganging up on me."

I bit off a small piece of the apple I was snacking on and threw it in her direction.

The raven crowed in gratitude as she nibbled the small piece. Then crowed again as she jumped closer, asking for more.

"I like apples too." I chuckled as I threw another piece. Then another. Now the bird skipped so close I could pet it without stretching out my hand.

"Brave one I see?" I smiled, fighting the urge to pet her. But something about this bird being desperate for food enough to trust a human tugged at the forgotten strings in my chest.

Life was hard for everyone.

Suddenly spooked, the raven flew away. I twisted around to face a sailor dressed in his Royal uniform, his shadow lurking over me. His face was clean shaven and tan. He was fit and must had been well into his thirties.

I was caught off guard as he smiled at me and spoke.

"Annoying little pests, aren't they?"

No, they are anything but annoying. They are smart and beautiful and unless you were blind, that raven wasn't little.

"Um..." was all that came out of me instead.

He chuckled, his mouth stretching in a satisfied grin.

"I have to give it to them. They always find the most sparkly thing around." He winked at me, and my stomach twisted with unease. Before I could object, he plastered himself right next to me on a small bench. The smell of his strong cologne ran like acid through my nose.

Too close. He was too damn close. I inched a little closer to the edge.

"Couldn't help but notice you today on the pier in your sultry dress. First time in town?"

The red polka dot dress was definitely not sultry, and neither was I.

It was time for me to go.

"Yes." I wrapped up the rest of my apple, shoving it in my bag.

"Traveling for pleasure or business?" he asked, still grinning while extending his arm over the bench as if to wrap around my shoulders.

My body ricocheted against his not-so-subtle brush against my back.

"Oh, just visiting my uncle. He is the town's constable," I quickly lied. I knew it was a terrible lie, but I didn't have time to come up with anything else.

"Oh really?" He was surprised and taken back a bit. Good.

"Yes. Well anyway, nice meeting you but I have to go, my aunt will worry sick if I don't get her scones soon. Bye."

I stood up, picking up two large boxes filled with my newly purchased leather boots and some clothes.

"No need to hurry. It's still light outside." He stood up right behind me, following me. *Following. Me.*

"Oh, but I do have to go. I insist. My uncle takes tardiness quite seriously." I politely chuckled, though my face didn't show amusement and my steps hurried. But in a few long strides he caught up with me. Though my heart was racing, I forced myself to take a few deep breaths not letting panic slip through.

"I'll walk you home. I was going that direction anyway. It wouldn't make me a good gentleman if I let a damsel like you get lost in the city," he murmured, just inches away from me. But I didn't turn to look at him.

Crowds were thinning out in the late afternoon, yet we were still surrounded by many people.

It's going to be fine, I tried convincing myself as I rushed past a large road into oncoming traffic of carriages and buggies. Carrying flimsy boxes made my escape harder but I ran as fast as I could, mingling with the little crowd still out, switching paths. Only once I turned back to see his blue and white tassels flayed on the wind far behind. My heart eased a bit.

Thank Gods.

I had to get back to the townhome, find Priya and get on that ship to take us to Svitar tonight. Late afternoon was now turning to early evening with a soft river sunset. I finally made it to the right street. It was quieter, emptier. Twilight reminded me of the upcoming night, as if urging me to hurry.

"Just right around the corner. Easy," I whispered out loud, trying to calm my throbbing heart. I was only a block away from the blue door leading to safety. Familiar brick and moss mixed townhomes lined in neat rows. I walked through a cobblestone alley. A shortcut, or so I thought. Until a shadow of a man appeared in front of me.

"You are quite an escape artist, I have to say," he seethed, his chest rising in paced breaths after what must have been a run. I recognized him immediately. The Royal sailor. Thoughts flooded my brain. No, I can't panic now.

Play it nice. Maybe he will let you go, I tried to convince myself. Meek and kindness. *Meek and kindness.*

"Oh, you startled me." I fake laughed, trying to justify a few back steps I took.

"Going somewhere?" He crossed the distance between us in his few quick steps.

"Just going home," I replied, eyeing the lightless alley.

"You are a little liar." He came close. *Too* close.

Run.

You need to run now. My instincts shouted at me. I threw the boxes at him and ran.

The alley wasn't long, I could make it at least until the next door. But after a couple of strides, his tight grasp on my arm yanked me back.

"You little bitch. Is this how you show gratitude to a Royal sailor?"

I thrashed against his touch and screamed, but it seems the streets went silent, and it was just us against the murky, gloomy, star-filled sky.

"I'll teach you to not *ever* disrespect a Royal Sailor," he angrily spat, pulling my thrashing body closer. He was so much stronger than me. I tried kicking and screaming, yet he shoved me against the wet brick wall, his body pressing hard against mine. I could hear it then; the belt buckle clicking as it was being undone, the slide of the zipper.

Gods please, I cried as tears pooled over my face. *Please.* I screamed to Fate, locked between the wall and his body in a tight grip. Panic completely overtaking me.

"Freckles, don't you know the gods won't do *shit*." A mocking female voice came from the shadows. The sailor froze in surprise, yet still held me tight against the stone.

"Priya!" I cried out in relief, still fighting against his tense grasp.

Suddenly, he completely froze with his hand still on his crotch, and fell straight on the gray stones as if a statue.

Priya's figure slowly emerged from the shadows in her leather suit with her two braids swaying with each step. She held an intricate blow-gun, no longer than her finger.

"Is he dead?" I asked her, wiping away the fresh tears of my red cheeks, letting the anger anchor my obscure mind.

"Oh, not yet, Freckles. He may wish for it soon, but not yet. He is completely paralyzed though." Excitement filled her face, thrill playing in her copper eyes. A cat playing with a trapped mouse.

Priya quickly glanced over my shaken-up body.

"Oh, lighten up, Freckles, you are fine," she said, rolling her eyes nonchalantly while staring at my terror-filled eyes.

"I am okay," I repeated. More of an assurance to myself than anything.

Priya pulled a sharp knife out of an unseen leather sheath. She squatted right next to the sailor's unmoving face. I then saw the small, long, silver needle poking out of his neck, straight into his pulsating artery.

She moved a knife across his cheek, slicing it, dipping it in his blood as if it was a paint brush. Tears poured out of his eyes, but he couldn't even blink, much less scream.

"Ugh." Priya dramatically growled. "This is kind of irritating," she said, looking at his face with primal craving. "You see, my dear sailor friend..." She continued while now running the knife down his chest and stomach, scraping his skin until small beads of blood appeared.

"You've put me in such a predicament." She huffed in disappoint-ment. "How am I going to filet your skin little by little while you are still alive if I must get on a ship soon? Perhaps, I'll just have to let you go." She twirled her dagger a little deeper. "Tsk tsk tsk. Such a shame though. I think I would rather enjoy seeing you bleed out drop by drop."

I watched her silently, feeling unsure.

"It is a pickle. Don't you agree?" She tugged on his cheek playfully. Pure enjoyment was bursting on Priya's face in the same way his blood was pouring out of his wounds.

A killer whale tossing the helpless seal.

I finally moved, picking up my thrown boxes, eager to go, away from him, from this alley, from this town. Eager to leave. I wasn't sure how long the paralytic was going to work but I also wasn't going to interrupt Priya with questions in what clearly was an exciting moment for her.

She stood up, but not before wiping off the blood of her knife against his white uniform.

"But you know what, my sailor friend? I appreciate your service. You've turned out to be quite the soldier, so I think I have just enough time to do this though." She drew one of her daggers and threw it straight at his crotch. Like butter, the dagger sliced through his frozen hand into his cock.

Something inside of me twisted. This was justice. Cruel, evil and brute justice.

"Oh darn, sorry, I think my dagger might have slipped. So silly of me." Priya theatrically shrugged and crouched above him. "I'll be more careful with this though, I promise." She pulled the dagger out, slicing off his limp exposed manhood. "We wouldn't want you to get hungry," Priya said, smiling as she tugged his mouth slightly open and shoved the chopped off tip of his cock in. Blood quickly pooled underneath him, trickling down the pavement as if a black ink.

I stood frozen, unsure what to say or even how to feel. My thoughts raced so fast that I couldn't find a coherent one.

Later. I will deal with this later.

"Freckles, time to go." Priya motioned for me to start walking and I did.

"We are just going to leave him there like that?" I asked, peeking over my shoulder at his helpless bloodied carcass.

Royals might have closed their eyes on slavery but murdering a Royal Soldier was still punishable by death. "What if he recognizes us?"

Priya laughed, as if I said the most hilarious thing she had ever heard. I frowned, slightly unsure.

"What now?" I impatiently asked.

"You got attacked and that's your first concern? Shouldn't he be worried that you'd testify against him?"

I was not naïve enough to believe that law was equal for everyone. It definitely didn't apply to those in power but it sure as hell applied to me though, a runaway slave.

"I am serious, Priya. *This* is serious."

Priya cackled. "Look at you, so worried. Then go kill him yourself."

I stopped in my tracks. My eyes met hers, asking if she was indeed serious.

I had never taken a life before.

But at that moment, I knew I would do it. Even if it haunted me for the rest of my life.

If that was the price I had to pay for my freedom, I would do it. Priya's mouth stretched in a wide grin. Noting my growing unrest, she finally countered.

"Relax, Freckles, he has about thirty more seconds of life left in him before his heart completely stops from the poison." At my concerned look she added, "I like to give them a little hope before the light goes out." She loudly patted me on my back and led the way to the dock.

19

The large steam ship carried us well into the night. Priya was nicely settled on the bottom bunk of the small, though luxurious, chamber. She made an excuse about needing to pee every five minutes. I didn't object, climbing onto the top one.

We stayed in silence for hours now. Words seemed trivial; thoughts lost in the abyss. The low humming of the engines blocked out the never-ending rustling of wrappers as Priya pillaged the stash of strongly packaged snacks.

Finally, resting on my elbows, I propped up my body.

"What is it about me that just screams I am an easy victim, Priya?" I finally had the courage to say out loud what had been ravaging my mind ever since the alley.

I needed to know. Why me?

What. Was. Wrong. With. *Me*?

Priya sat up in her bed, shaking off the crumbs on the floor.

"Because you have a vagina?" she said indifferently. "But also, it might be because you look pathetic and weak, who knows? Men are really not that picky; even dead you are not hundred percent safe." She scratched her nose, still loudly chewing. "But if you want my opinion, your eyes are desperate for belonging and yet you've given up on it.

Like a sad little kitten on the street that might puff up and hiss but in reality, completely harmless." She went through her wrappers, trying to find any last hidden candy there. She squealed and chucked another treat in her mouth, smacking her lips obnoxiously. "Truthfully, you are the type of person that chooses forgiveness over justice and that really shows," Priya added, taking a long sip of water.

Perhaps I was wrong to ask an important question to a stranger that I only met a little over two weeks ago. A stranger, that too, made some questionable choices.

But that rising annoyance and anger within me was a cover for hurt. Because everything she said was right and everything hurt.

Though, I couldn't shake off the feeling as if she blamed me for it. As if I was at fault for the choices of the sailor. Resentment tinted my mind.

As if reading my thoughts, she continued.

"No, it wasn't your fault. It's never your fault, Freckles. Men are shit. It's as simple as that." Her voice softened. It was good she didn't see my angry face. Priya threw a giant pile of wrappers on the floor. "Life is cruel and unfair. We don't get to pick and choose what it throws at us. Humans are also nasty creatures. Monsters lurking underneath our skin, prettied up by nice conversations and good food, just waiting to come out."

"But you saved me." A simple truth.

"A nice convenience, not going to lie. I have enjoyed my fresh laundry in the past weeks. Good thing too. It would have been such a hassle trying to find another half drowned, runaway slave."

My heart eased and I smiled. A hassle indeed.

"Sometimes I wish things were different, the life, the world," I said, laying back down on my pillow, staring at the white ceiling. "Do you?" I asked, my voice becoming somber.

"Nah. I can't spend my life wishing for a different life only to realize I wasted this one."

"Do you ever dream?"

"Of what?"

"Of happiness?"

CHAPTER 19

"Happiness and innocence go hand and hand. And I lost both a very long time ago." Her voice for once was more serious and tender. "But excitement, thrill and pure pleasure. That, I can have any day. No need to dream, Freckles."

"So, what are you? Some assassin of sorts?" I doubted she was going to tell me, but tonight seemed to be painfully honest.

"An assassin...? That sounds so official." Priya chuckled. The room was now filled with gentle warmth. "I guess you could call me that."

"Who do you work for?"

"I don't work for anyone."

"Do you kill for money?" I had a feeling it was more than that.

"I never work for hire, if that's what you are asking but I do get... payments." She ruffled sheets, cozying up in her bed.

"How did you become an assassin?

"Do you ever stop with the questions, Freckles?"

That was her limit then, but I pushed anyway.

"How many have you killed?" I mentally added up the days she was gone in her suit in the last few weeks. Often, I realized. She was gone quite often.

"Ugh. Go to bed. I am tired now." She grumpily dismissed me.

I smiled. That sugar rush of hers must have finally came crashing down.

"I could train you; you know." Priya rolled over again, loudly yawning.

"Train me?"

"Yes, to be a badass *assassin* like me. " She mimicked her accent to match mine.

I wasn't sure what becoming an assassin entailed, but I was done feeling weak and useless.

"I'd like that...I'd like that very much."

20

The deck was almost empty, with just a few occasional workers walking by. Large pillars of steam rose high into the dark sky. It was surprisingly warm for the night. The Kinderby River, almost stagnant, stretched far and wide.

My entire body ached from the brutal exercise and feeding regime Priya instilled. She was ruthless; from dawn until late night, we spent training. I was her first ever apprentice and she'd proclaimed that she "doesn't deal in failure," so I had no choice but "to step it up," because truly, I was weak. Even if my mind was eager, my stomach wasn't; I wretched my guts after almost each workout. Priya, though filled with utmost disgust, sent encouragement from a healthy distance away from my spilled intestines.

"Lighten up, Freckles," she said. "It might not be better tomorrow. But I promise you, it will be in time."

And I believed that. Relying on that simple truth, I pushed myself past the embarrassment because for the first time in years, I had a clear goal.

Exhausted, I spent the last few nights completely unconscious, but today I couldn't sleep. Overtaken by the nightmares, one after another, loud clangs of armor and metal, blood and fire consumed my mind.

CHAPTER 20

Screams of unfamiliar people still rung deep in my ears. I knew it was a dream, probably brought up by exhaustion thanks to Priya's daily gruesome training, and yet my whole body still quivered each time I closed my eyes.

I would eventually let go of the soul-crushing sounds, forget the screams, the falling ash from never ending fire—but it would take time.

Time seemed to be the only currency life took.

21

"See you tomorrow!" I waved to the large lady behind the counter. Nadine was one of my favorite vendors, always friendly and helpful; the owner of a well-known butcher shop in Svitar. I wrapped my sack across my shoulders, and I finally strolled back home.

It'd been a month since we arrived in Svitar, walking its white cobblestone streets daily. Smells of fresh laundry and blooming flowers ran through the streets, petting my nose.

The City of Light, Svitar was built on a spacious hill, with the Royal Castle and its golden roof shining at the very top. Limestone townhomes and condos filled the never-ending streets. It took me a few days just to adjust to the sheer brightness of the city. All of the buildings were either made of the white stone or painted white, contrasting with the black doors and window frames, as if the whole city was uniformed. Flower beds lining up their porches and window wells were the only bits of color to the monochromatic palette.

People in Svitar were different too, so unbothered by the realities of the lands behind the city wall. The world was exciting in Svitar.

And I loved it.

I loved visiting the Fashion Corner just to see the outrageous outfits of the fashionistas and the store galleries airing the most dare some clothing. I loved going down to the Wing Market, where you could find any manner of small trinkets and unique objects; to the Artists Hill, where night and day, various artists sat with their brushes and their paints making small strokes on their large canvases, painting the gorgeous view of the city; or the Library of Light that was so quiet yet filled with never ending books; and there was so much more.

I was in love with it all.

I walked up the short steps leading to the bulky golden gates. Sizeable carriages were driving up and down the road. Golden Quarters was the most beautiful part of city; I knew it from the moment I took my first step there.

Priya enjoyed luxury so it wasn't surprising that she lived in this neighborhood. Unlike the rest of the town made from limestone, the Golden Quarters' roads were made from pure white marble, scuffed and buffed daily. Narrow townhouses became brilliant manors with large columns and statues, golden fences and exquisite gardens, guards and lackeys always standing watch. Staired sidewalks were perfectly clean, with nicely trimmed trees providing shade from the soft fall sun.

Priya's manor shimmered past the golden gate. It was made with fluorescent opal material, making it sparkle as if a diamond against the rays of sun. The large columns and wide stairs decorated the front façade. Enormous gargoyle statues guarded the huge, dark, wood double doors.

It was not the largest house on the street, but it had the most land. Perfectly green lawns with precision cut bushes, and full blooming flowers, bird baths and a large fountain welcomed me back. A piece of paradise.

"I'm back!" I shouted, walking in the house and closing the door behind me.

Priya was lounging on a round, bright red couch. Her head on the pillow and legs resting above. Her large, silk robe with peacock feathers wide open, exposing her lacy underwear and skintight cropped shirt. Priya's long, chestnut locks dangled onto the floor. Instead of sitting up, she just flipped her head upside-down and yelled across the open hall at me.

"Did you get it?" she asked, looking at my sack.

I nodded, taking the sack off my shoulder.

"Oh good! This trashy neighborhood is going to be so jealous. In fact, I am going to send a postcard to that bitch Clara just to let her know." Priya smirked. Nadine was famous for her tender, marbled, cubed steaks—a delicacy even for the rich.

I was pretty sure that Priya spent an outrageous amount of money bidding on the steaks before the calf was even killed so that her neighbors wouldn't get them. I had come to learn that Priya highly disliked her neighbors. She highly disliked people in general, but especially the *"rich pricks"* living in these Quarters. Though quite an ironic view, considering she was most definitely rich and also living in these Quarters.

Ratika, an older lady, peaked through the small door leading to the kitchen.

"I heard you got something for me?" she whispered quietly, poking just her head through the door.

"Oh, yes." I turned to her and handed off the satchel. She nodded in gratitude and disappeared right away.

I liked Ratika; she was extremely quiet, almost like a ghost, but cooked food like a god.

Unlike everyone else in the neighborhood, Priya had extremely limited staff living on site: just Ratika and I. Occasionally she had Ovaya, and a couple of her girls come do the cleaning, and Diego and his crew maintaining the gardens. Yet in this huge manor filled with never ending rooms, all kinds of luxury tapestry, statues and artifacts, it was just the three of us.

"Training room in ten." Priya finally got up and started walking up the broad staircase, carved out of pure brown marbled stone, covered with thick, plush carpet down the middle. At the top, it split in half, leading to another two sets of the same staircase going up to two wings of the house.

I walked down the stairs leading to the basement. Even though Priya called it a training *room*, it was so much more than that. A large gymnasium, filled with all manner of equipment, a fighting ring, an armory and its adjoining weapons training area, and even a large dance floor with a ballet bar. The entire left wall of the pavilion was covered in mirrors going all the way to the ceilings. Even though there were no windows, the entire place was well lit by sizable lamps attached to the large wooden fans, slowly cutting through air.

At first, training hurt—pained me to the point of giving up—but day after day, I kept going. Priya pushed me to utter exhaustion each time. But truthfully, I started to enjoy it, curious to see that line, that edge, pushed further and further with each day. I was stronger than I had ever been, more capable and trained. And it felt good. It felt empowering. It felt so damn right.

I smiled, eyeing the sparring mats in the middle, reminiscing on the many times I fell asleep on those mats after deciding it was not worth the climb over three flights of stairs to my room.

We trained here for hours, multiple times a day. Occasionally, Priya would take a day of rest, but on those days I trained alone. There was something primal in me, awakened from the years of slumber. A part of me that was always there but never nourished, never nurtured...not until now. In the moments—when the breaths became shallow and sweat covered my body and each muscle trembled on the edge of collapsing—in those moments, I felt alive.

My body was becoming a well-oiled machine.

My soul might be cracked in pieces, but my body was now my armor.

I looked in the mirror across from me, staring at a figure of a woman so different from how I remembered myself; so different from the previously starved, slave girl. My face was much rounder, my previously sharp cheekbones now smooth and soft; my thin arms were now thicker with a solid layer of fat and muscle going through them—no more bony arms and shoulders poking through my shirt. My legs and hips now were muscled and curved. My no-longer-slim figure now had a hint of femininity to it.

Priya entered dressed in her work-out clothes a minute later, her hair styled neatly in two thick braids with curls poking out on the ends.

"Ready?" she asked, winking at me. I chuckled. It was never a good sign that Priya was deviously smiling at me before sparring. She was going to kick my butt and she was excited for it. But I taunted her back.

"Bring it on."

We sparred for a while, Priya correcting my moves, knocking the breath out of me with each of her steps. She moved so gracefully. Each move was a calculated motion with a deliberate goal behind it. Even if I managed to throw a move past her guard, she always managed to get me back.

"You miss because you are gloating half the time," she said while we were getting a drink. "You need to stop being so surprised each time you land a blow."

She took another sip.

"You need to be more confident. Feel entitled to it."

"Entitled to break someone's nose?" I raised my brows at her in amusement.

"Yes, Freckles, entitled to break their nose, smash their balls or tits and make their life a crying hell until they quit it. You are entitled to all of that, so act like it," she grudged back.

I never felt entitled to anything in my life. Tuluma made it perfectly clear that it was by the grace of gods I was still alive and since I was *human filth,* I was nothing—entitled to nothing. As a kid, I might have tried to defy that, but Fate had a way to show the truth of that statement.

"It's hard for me to feel that way." I laid the truth barren.

"Well, figure that stuff out, Freckles. Life will keep taking from you until you stop giving to it. You will never succeed if you don't think you deserve it." She took another sip of water. "So, when you smash my guts next time, remember you earned it, you deserve it, and you keep going until I am dead." She wiped a few drops of sweat off her brow, both of us burning red from the heat. "You are entitled to feel good in this life, to enjoy it fully. To say, fuck you Fate, I am in charge now."

That primal, wild part of me roared in agreement with her. I had given up so much with nothing in return, small slivers of happiness and joy ripped from me after only a glimpse.

But how could I ever feel content and happy knowing that while I lounged and ate my weight in divine food each day, slaves were dying, and people were starving?

In the twisted works of Fate, I was here and not with Viyak. I was alive and well, even after I encountered and escaped the Destroyers, the Royals, the Kahors; and I was now training to become an assassin.

I was grateful and humbled to be lucky enough to be free; to be able to run in the mornings and never stop; to be able to sleep in comfort and never worry where my next meal would be; to be able to stroll down to the market and shops and spend money that I now had.

I couldn't say fuck you all. Not when I believed that most of it was not from my well doing but a twist of luck—a generous gift of Fate.

"Ugh, you are getting lost in your depressing thoughts again," Priya whined, rolling her eyes. "Let me know when you are done 'pondering' and ready to actually do shit."

She walked down to the large table in the armory. Walls surrounding it were covered in all manner of weapons, starting with small daggers and knives, cross bows of all kinds, axes, swords, bows, and arrows. The armory had it all.

Across the large table was the target wall, covered with a very thick material, in all matter of scars, damaged from so many ruthless practices.

"I wasn't lost," I countered. "I was just thinking that I can't say 'Fuck you, Fate' when it was her that brought me to you," I said, picking up a medium-sized crossbow and loading it with thick arrows.

"You are giving a dead Goddess too much credit," Priya said, throwing a knife straight into the bullseye.

"But..." I started, but Priya didn't let me finish.

"The way I remember it, it was you who planned the escape, you who fought the soldier, you who were swimming in the cold river. It was you who survived slavery. I don't remember Fate doing anything there to help."

"Yes, but..."

"Let's also not forget that Fate was the one who put you in slavery to begin with." I frowned. She chucked another knife into the male mannequin used as a practice target, launching it straight into his balls. "You are so eager to give Fate all the credit for the good, and yet pin anything bad as your fault. It's really stupid."

"It's not that simple," I opposed.

"Yes, it is, Freckles. You are just an ignorant, self-loathing, weak minded, average human. It's not that hard. You either give all the credit to the gods—the bad and the good—and float like a leaf down the river hoping you won't drown. Or you can get your shit together, stop relying on gods or luck or whatever you want to call it. Accept that you do have a say in this life, even in shitty situations and take control of your life. Don't let the gods define you." Priya threw another knife at a fake bird target far on the ceiling. "You can wait for Gods to do their justice, or you can become Justice itself. The decision is on you."

"You are right," I said to her, aiming for the head of the mannequin.

"I always am, Freckles." Priya smiled and threw her last dagger.

I took my aim. Shot. Bullseye.

"Finally. It's about time you start making your shots." Priya smirked.

I laughed. My aim was never terrible, but I usually took too long to aim, to concentrate. Not like the swift and thoughtless movements that Priya had.

"You might be better suited for the shitty snipers in the Royal army since you clearly have to take five hours to make a shot."

I showed her my tongue and she flipped me off.

Practice went on for hours. I worked on throwing knives and daggers and sparred with swords. Priya also added an obligatory blowgun practice and by the end of it poor Julio, the mannequin, was left without a single spot unwounded.

Drenched in sweat, we made it to the dining room. The savory, delicious smells made my mouth water. Ratika already had soups and breads, all perfectly lined up, ready to serve. She wasn't in the room, but I could bet the small cook was behind that tall door, ready to answer any question or demands.

I tried finding some time to come down to the kitchens to help. Ratika never spoke much, even after a month. I wasn't sure who she was or where she was from, yet I knew she took pride in her cooking. Priya knew that too.

"Food looks delicious, Ratika," she yelled to the closed door.

"It's amazing, Ratika!" I added, loading up my plate and heading to the table.

The enormous stone table was decorated with golden statues of Pegasus and ancient warriors.

"Do you ever invite her to the table?" I asked Priya, sitting down at one of the wide, upholstered chairs.

"No," Priya answered by digging her fork in her dessert first.

"Why not?"

"Why would I? She is a cook." *Obviously.*

"Yes, but it's only us in the house, don't you think she gets lonely eating by herself all the time?"

"She is a servant. That's what they do."

"So, am I," I earnestly replied. While Priya might have given me a room upstairs, the large piles of laundry and daily chores reminded me that I was, in fact, one of the servants.

I didn't mind it. Most of the time I enjoyed a chance to work, to earn an honest living. A given purpose. Yet at times, it felt unfair and awkward knowing Ratika never got the same treatment.

"If she wanted to, she would ask," Priya reasoned.

"I never did."

"Oh, my gods, Freckles, just get to the damn point."

"Maybe you should invite Ratika to dine with us one of these times. I think she would enjoy being included. She must get lonely being all by herself each day."

"Well, I simply don't care. I for once, want to enjoy peace and quiet while eating my cake. Can I not?"

I nodded, quietly finishing my lunch and made a mental note to check on Ratika again today to see if she would enjoy more company. Priya clearly didn't. In fact, for the entirety of my living here, we rarely crossed our paths outside training and meals. Even then, I was sure Priya was here just to observe my eating habits to make sure I was still putting on weight.

Priya was content with solitude. A part of me wished I could do that, to be left alone with my thoughts without feeling like I was being swallowed by the never-ending darkness. Without feeling broken with no chance of recovery.

No, for me, solitude was painful.

My body might have been becoming an assassin machine, my mind sharp and clear, but my soul?

No.

No amount of food or sleep or training could ever fix that.

22

Large waves crashed against the dark rock. So loud and powerful. The horizon was so clear as the endless waters met the blue sky. The afternoon sun was covered in sheer clouds. A tall, large figure stood near the edge. I ran my hand through the tall grass, walking towards it, watching a large raven coast against the strong current of the ocean airstream. The salt filled air kissed my lungs, welcoming me to the edge of the world.

The tall figure now turned to me. His dark eyes staring at me. Not *at* me, *through* me. Straight to my shivering soul, as if he could see me.

All of me.

Abruptly, I woke up to the static darkness in my room. My heart beat faster and faster while my lungs became leaden.

"It was just a dream. Just a freaky dream," I repeated to myself out loud, trying to calm myself down, turning on the unique oil lamp on my carved nightstand, lighting up the large bedroom.

Just a dream.

I ran a hand over my forehead, rubbing my face, tugging on my cheeks to ground myself.

I could never forget that face.

Those dark, haunted eyes.

The eyes of the *Destroyer General.*

A drink. I needed a drink.

I moved away the heavy warm blankets and made it across the room to the washroom, my bare feet loving the feeling of the deep, plush, cream-colored carpets. I could feel cold water washing down my throat, cooling me off.

Some nights the dreams never stopped, and I enjoyed seeing a glimpse of the depth of my imagination, but I would rather never sleep than see *him* in my dreams again.

There was no point in trying to fall back asleep. Not when that dream made me feel so open, so violated. A small shiver ran through me like a little lightning bolt.

I could still feel the salty air in my lungs, the silky grass at my fingertips.

It all felt so real. That look. Those eyes. Ripping my scars wide open. Encroaching

into my soul.

I fought the traitorous thoughts in my brain. As much as I wished to be able to be in complete control of my feelings, of my dreams, I still wasn't.

Angry and defeated, I grabbed a thick book off my nightstand and flipped it open.

If I wasn't strong enough to erase my dreams, then maybe "Plants and Poisons around the world" would.

23

M y fingers were still wrinkly from being in water too long. Newly washed laundry was now hanging up in the laundry room, a large wall fan blowing the air was slowly drying them.

Laundry was my kind of therapy. Warm and cold water kept my overstimulated thoughts anchored to the present. The stretching and the rubbing and the twisting of fabric let the feelings out; the chemical smell of soaps and salts stung my eyes, burning the tears out.

I worked until my mind was just as fresh and crisp as the fabric neatly pinned on the laundry lines.

Priya was already in her large greenhouse, her hair up in a messy bun with large, dangly earrings sophisticating her otherwise simple look. Garden beds and pots were stationed everywhere, filled with all manner of vegetation.

She didn't look at me as she dug a small hole in the moist dirt and planted one of the small green plants into the ruffled sod.

"Rough night?" She pointed to the small pot by my foot. "That one."

I quickly passed it on to her.

"Couldn't sleep much." I shrugged.

She planted another herb in.

"The good news though," I continued. "I read Plants and Poisons for hours until I fell back asleep."

"Gods, I fucking love that book," Priya exclaimed.

I chuckled. Plants and Poisons was a kid's book. A kid's encyclopedia, to be exact, filled with pictures and names of all kinds of plants, their purposes, and where they came from. Very informative, but also fun. Who knew there were fifteen types of mint, all ranging from bitter to sweet, from purple to light yellow; or that you could make an immune boosting soup from plantain leaves?

"I did learn how to make a calming tea out of dried dandelions, and even practiced grass whistles." I snickered, passing on another small pot to her.

"You laugh, but grass whistles are wonderful. I bet you couldn't do a proper one even if you tried."

"I probably couldn't." I smiled. Grass whistles seemed so bizarre compared to the training happening in the basement, but everything was always slightly bizarre with Priya.

"You think you are ready?" she asked, glancing over at me with demise.

I wasn't sure what Priya's test entailed.

"I think so?" I raised my brows in question.

"Gods, such confidence, such grace." She rolled her eyes, finally standing up, shaking off the dirt from her skintight black pants.

We walked away from the enormous greenhouse, down the path leading to a lab.

This was Priya's world. Unlike the rest of the perfectly pristine house, the workroom was filled with clutter. Or at least it seemed so, until you looked closer. Cabinets with small, never-ending drawers, shelves filled with different glass jars and containers, some of them empty, some full, other shelves filled with small glass tanks with crawling creatures in them. Spiders, bugs, and occasional snakes. Thin laundry lines hung across the room with plants in their different stages of dryness. A musky sage smell encompassed the room. Unlike the rest of the counter space, the top of the large island was completely empty, a few metal barstools near it.

One by one, Priya showed me a leaf or a whole plant, either full of life or completely dried, asking me what kind it was and what its purpose was. I answered each question with confidence.

Recognizing plants and their attributes was almost second nature to me. Growing up, I often tagged along with Tuluma, collecting herbs to make potions and teas to sell to the struggling humans, desperate enough to pay a coin for a salvation in a bottle from an elf.

Priya was pleased as I answered all her questions correctly. Her mouth parted in a large, feline smile.

"Good," she spoke. "Now, let's talk about murdering people." She pulled out a large tray with all manner of vials, some full, some empty.

Priya talked for over two hours, educating me, mixing and grinding small plants into powder, then liquid. She pointed to the now-mixed black liquid and the bowl with now-wilted green powder.

"A little dry rub of this herb will help you with pain, a speck of it on your tongue and it will numb it completely, a good thing to use when people talk too much." She smirked and I returned the smile.

She mixed it with salt water.

"Now get this straight into the bloodstream and you will get your heart to stop faster than you'll realize what happened to you."

I quietly listened, taking notes in my large notebook. Priya was in her element. Each little movement, each precise pipette drops of liquid —this was her home. This was her comfort zone.

She looked so relaxed explaining each step, bringing more and more glass jars or vials until there was barely any space left. Multiple copper and gold scales were spread out across the counter.

"Why do you make poisons?" I asked curiously. Why was this her world? Priya was a skilled assassin. I had seen her movements, her precision and talent. She could eliminate anyone she wanted just with her knife throwing skills alone.

"That is the dumbest question you have ever asked. I just showed you literally how to extract burning acid from a merrow root and you are asking why poisons?" She scrunched her eyebrows and lips together.

"Sorry, it just seems like a lot of work. Meticulous work too. I mean you must plant or find the plants first, which some of them are extremely rare or take ten years to mature... Then make sure you harvest them at the right times, then make sure you prep or dry them correctly, then some still need mixing or stuff done. All that work just to result in a small drop of poison and even then, you have to store them right so they would work?" I shifted on my tall barstool a little bit. "It seems rather complicated."

"It is *complicated AND extremely* time consuming. But when you are a woman, Freckles, you don't get a chance to be sloppy and just bullshit your way in life like men do. Even if you are a skilled assassin."

"I guess that's true." I tapped my pen on the paper.

"You *guess*?!" Priya angrily closed a jar. "It's all fun and jokes until you come across four-hundred-pound Jimmy over there who is trying to strangle you and *can* single-handedly knock you out with one punch and—" She thinned her lips and narrowed her eyes at me. "And considering that your speed to action is somewhat similar to that of a dying snail, I'd say making Jimmy paralyzed first, or quite frankly dead, before he smashes that pretty nose of yours is quite helpful, even if it does take a while to make the poisons."

"Are there a lot of women assassins?" I was genuinely curious.

"How the fuck would I know?" She looked at me annoyed while checking on some plants drying on the walls.

"I don't know, maybe because you are an assassin and murder people for a living?" I threw that sarcastic tone back at her.

"Gods, first, I *live* to murder people, not murder people for a living. A big fucking difference. And second, I told you, I am not an official assassin, but even if I was, it's not like you just go sign up and join a queen's tea party of female Royal assassins where we discuss the new trends of slicing someone's throat and current fashion takes on updos." She shook her head, displeased.

I knew Priya was being sarcastic but a part of me really liked that idea.

Just imagine the power and the brilliance if all the badass women united. The world would be a different place.

Priya now fished out a few live crickets and dropped them into the terrariums filled with all kinds of creatures. "But my guess is, there aren't many, considering most women spend their time trying to please society." She dropped a few more. "When in reality, they'd have much better luck murdering it."

I nodded in agreement.

24

GIDEON

"*G*IDEON!*" I grimaced as I heard Zora's voice before she stormed in. "Are you out of your fucking mind?!"

I ran a hand down my face. I knew this was coming from the moment I made the choice to leave. And to come back.

What I had done was reckless. Stupid. Irresponsible. And the worst part—it was futile. Because yet again, I came back here alone.

Zora's jaw was about to snap from the force she clenched it with.

"Zora..." I calmly started after taking a long breath.

"You are such an idiot. Risking it all for *a girl*? I need armies, Gideon, not a girl!"

She was furious. Understandably so.

"She needs our help, Zora." I leaned back in my chair.

"*You* fucking need help," Zora spat, pacing across the room.

I couldn't argue with that.

"You have people relying on you, you have responsibilities, gods dammit it, you have our lives in your hands! You can't just fucking disappear by yourself to look for someone you think *might* have the same power as you."

I unwrapped the bandages, gazing at my healing hand.

CHAPTER 24

Her fury didn't scare me, though I'd prefer to get yelled at less. But that was the thing with Zora. She cared. More than anyone else I knew. Though she would never let anyone see it. But I recognized that anger, that ferocity, for what it really was worry…And maybe a bit of anger issues.

"See, Zora, that's where you and I disagree... For once, I have absolutely no doubt about what she can do." I closed and opened my wounded hand, watching the tight scars stretch in motion.

"I'll believe it when I see it." She folded her arms tight, her voice taunt, though no longer yelling.

"It would be quite hard to do so, if she is not here to show it to you." I half smiled but Zora didn't appreciate my amusement.

"You need to promise me you won't go out looking for her again." She stopped pacing and glared at me.

"While I appreciate the concern, Zora, I will do no such thing," I said, wrapping bandages back up. My hand was almost healed, though the gnarly scars would stay there forever. A constant reminder of my shortcomings.

"UGH! You are insufferable!" Zora yelled and stormed out.

Xentar's face peeked through the tent door in delight.

"I see someone is excited to see you again." Both of us watched as Zora marched through the camp. "Welcome back, brother." He chuckled as he took a seat in a chair across from me. "I take it another big nothing?"

"Nope. Not even a single clue. Like she just disappeared into thin air." I ran my other hand through my hair, bottling the increasing frustration.

"I am assuming you will continue to keep looking for her?" Xentar said, petting Liriya, a large, black raven sitting next to him.

I nodded. Wherever she was…. I had to find her.

"I must admit, I am rather curious to meet her. Granted, I am less curious of her powers, more so of her ability to make the Great Gideon Bellator into a brooding teenager."

Liriya cawed as if joining Xentar in his mocking.

"You two need to get a life," I said, ignoring his teasing smirk.

Though a part of me couldn't deny that she had caught my interest long before I knew about her power.

25

FINNLEAH

The straw mattress was prickly and stiff, even against my black leather suit. Still, this bed was a much better alternative to the half-rotten hammocks we slept on the past three days while traveling on a one-man boat down the river to this gods forgotten village.

Priya seemed to share the sentiment as she twisted and turned on her mattress relentlessly.

Even in the middle of the night, the first floor of the tavern we were staying in was still full of people. Most of them were so drunk that they couldn't find their way home, but considered themselves sober enough to gamble away their life possessions. The bar owner was a smart man to take a cut from all the gambling, especially since he was the one providing the booze. Though he clearly had poor taste, considering the state of this room. Priya was annoyed at the lack of luxury, but not enough to turn down the half-blind cook's dinner concoction that we devoured a little while back.

"Ugh, if they don't shut up, I will murder them all right now," Priya grumbled from under her blanket as the crowd bellowed another huge roar of laughter on the floor beneath us.

"I think they are celebrating," I supposed.

I'd been laying still, listening to the chatter and the sounds for a while now. It was too far and too noisy to differentiate individual words, but I had heard a couple of toasts and shouts. "I think it's Laze Day."

Priya's lips thinned. "Like they deserved one. Useless pricks."

"I don't know much about human holidays, since my elven maid and I never celebrated them, but from the sound of it, it seems to be a big deal."

"You didn't miss much, Freckles. Gathering is about to start tomorrow and so today they are supposed to rest and save their strength for the next several weeks of harvest." She tried twisting again, this time to her side, to try and get more comfortable. "So, Elven maid? How did that happen?"

"I wish I knew." I adjusted my braid and hairs away from my face. "Somehow twenty-two years ago, according to Tuluma's point of view, my mother *conveniently* died during child labor, making Tuluma swear to protect and care for her newborn baby. The how and why she was in a life debt to my late mother, or what she was even doing in the mortal part of the world, considering Elves' standing with humans, always remained a secret from me."

"Is she dead?"

"Yes." My eyes darkened from the memories of Tuluma's death. My body twitched, remembering the acid burn of her ashes on my body from the Destroyer's fire.

"If it makes you feel any better, my parents were murdered too." Priya offered a simple truth.

"I am sorry."

Priya just casually shrugged.

"I had a sister too. She didn't make it either. So now it's just me." Another truth.

For the first time in months of knowing Priya, I saw a small glimpse of sorrow that went through her face as quick as a lightning— there and gone a second later.

"Do you speak elven?" Priya asked, changing the subject, getting away from that painful silence.

"Yes, I do. I used to even have an accent. Little village kids bullied me for years because of it." I chuckled, remembering those innocent days when mean names and words were the biggest concern of my life. "Tuluma would beat the soul out of me if I ever spoke in human tongue to her and since she was the only person I had, I spoke primarily elven my entire life."

"Say something in elven," Priya eagerly demanded.

I paused.

I hadn't spoken elvish in years, only occasionally reliving my memories or reading my thoughts.

But I hadn't said a single thing out loud since the day Tuluma died, sealing those memories.

My mind was tripping over thoughts as they somersaulted from one tongue to the other. A few coarse words came out of my mouth, and it felt comforting. As if I had a glimpse of *home.*

Priya now propped her chin on her hands and curiously looked at me.

"That sounded so ferocious. What does that mean?"

"It means, *I taught you better than that, you human filth.*"

"Weird choice of words, but okay." I laughed at Priya's sarcastic confusion.

"It was my maid's favorite thing to say to me." Something nostalgic churned inside of me. I could almost hear Tuluma's voice near me, angrily hissing. That voice, though harsh at times, was now something I wish I could hear just one more time.

"Well, she sounds like a charming lady."

I chuckled at that. Tuluma was closer to a feral animal than a proper human lady.

"She sure was."

The crowd below roared yet again.

"I want to know more," Priya yawned.

"Well, she was very beautiful, even with her sharp pointy ears and elongated canines. Over two hundred years old, though she looked not a day older than us, and her turquoise eyes were so mesmerizing against her pitch-black hair and porcelain skin that as a kid, I often just stared at them to imagine wild oceans."

But it wasn't her beauty that I remembered the most. It was the slow spring tracks between small villages that we walked, filled with peaceful quietness. It was the long nights spent listening to Tuluma's tales of the lost, forgotten elven lands, filled with mystical creatures. It was us celebrating Leuflun, Tuluma's favorite elven holiday. It was how we danced to worship the Dryads or the songs we sang to Nymphs or the elven chess we played on long summer days, or the elven riddles I spent nights guessing, just for her to smack my head and tell me to try harder. Or the shivering winters we spent cuddled together far in the south to survive.

I told Priya of her.

And of me. Of whom I was before. Before life took my fiery free spirit and molded it, suffocated it with destruction until there were nothing but clumps of coal left.

My voice turned into a whisper. Priya's eyes were already closed shut, her breathing slowed, and the twisting stopped. I smiled seeing her sleep. Who would have thought a cold-blooded assassin would look so peaceful?

I stared at the low ceiling, still listening to the drunken serenades coming from below, realizing that for once, the memories didn't hurt so much.

26

The moldy tavern was now long gone, replaced by never ending horizons of ripe fields. Priya was already in a foul mood, and I stayed quiet, though a list of unanswered questions knocked in my mind wanting to barge in.

There were only two things Priya told me before setting off on this journey.

One, the person I was about to kill was a man, and two, he very well deserved to be dead.

The rocks on the gravel path were thinning out, turning our walk even more silent than before. Dust covered our boots all the way to our knees. The occasional breeze and shimmering of cottonwood trees breaking up the fields were the only source of relief against the warm fall sun and heated dark leathers we wore.

The small, nondescript cabin stood at the end of the straight path. Unobtrusively, we approached the crooked door.

This was it. Though my palms were sweaty, my heart beat strong.

I had never killed a man.

Especially not in cold blood.

I wasn't worried that I wouldn't be able to do it.

Because I would.

But I was anxious about the life after. Would his face forever stay in my mind? Would I enjoy it or hate it?

The unknown scared me. I willed myself to stay still, to relax my muscles. I was ready. I had lived long enough as a victim; now it was time to learn to be the executioner too.

My thoughts were abruptly interrupted when Priya knocked very loudly on the door. A coarse male voice sounded deep in the cabin.

"Comin'."

My heightened senses could hear each step of the man approaching the door, each step like thunder. Did he ever think today would be his last day? Did he realize these were the last steps he'd take? Last breaths to breathe?

Priya didn't seem to care.

A man in his early fifties opened the door. He was average build; his clothes worn out and a few days-old gray stubble on his pale face.

His eyes widened with fear, yet there was no shock or surprise. Only acceptance of defeat.

"Priya." He recognized her.

"Hello, baker," she purred, slipping into a hungry predator voice.

He didn't have a chance to blink as she blew the dark purple powder she was holding in her fist straight into his face.

Our faces were already wrapped with bandanas.

The purple powder covered his entire face. A single cough. Priya stood still, carefully waiting until his body hit the floor a second later.

I knew the powder. It came from the Bellaroot mushrooms, usually used in sleeping tonics, yet in this form mixed with Ionna flower pollen, it worked like a sleeping charm. A little could distract, but if the person inhaled enough of it, it sent them off to a deep sleep.

We acted fast and yet I could feel each minute lasting too long. Each second, as we dragged his body to one of the chairs in his two-bedroom log cabin; each second, we took to tie him up, his legs, his wrinkled arms.

I was waiting for the cue. An order from Priya to take his life. But she just watched him cautiously, as if he was a prized statue in one of the Svitar's museums. Something inside of me stirred anxiously, almost craving the destruction, the power—yet another part of me stilled and hesitated.

A life would be lost today because of me, by *me*. A red line for me to cross and never come back.

"I want him to be awake for this," Priya said, her face full of power and high on excitement.

She pulled another chair away from the round table. Turning it around, she sat across it, resting her arms on the back of the chair, twisting a long, curved dagger in her hand.

I leaned against the wall, occasionally glancing out the window. There was nothing but nature. The birds were singing their cheerful melody, so unaware of the death settling around them.

Priya growled, the only sign that she'd just ran out of patience. It'd been less than ten minutes since we knocked. She lasted longer than I expected.

Impatiently, she kicked his leg without getting up from her chair.

Groaning, a few minutes later, he finally opened his heavy eyelids. Bright green eyes shone through them. He didn't tug at the ropes, just looked at us, at me. I saw the dread in those eyes, the defeat and the silent request.

"Long time no see, Jonah. Missed me?" Priya purred at him while picking her nails with her dagger. "I must admit, you were quite a hassle to locate, so I have to give you credit for that."

"I knew it was always going to be you, wasn't it? Mel, sent me a letter saying you were gone, and I've been waiting since then." His voice was full of regret. A voice of a person who had given up.

"Oh, sweet old Mel. She was so quick to send out warnings and yet so slow to die." Priya rolled her eyes dramatically.

This was a show for her. A performance.

That unquenchable monster within her was out, yet so casually dressed in cheerful tone and movements so human, except for those eyes. Her copper eyes were like windows to hell—open and ready to devour him.

"It was a different life, Priya, you must understand that. I wish...I wish I could change things."

"Oh Jonah... But I don't." Priya paused picking her nails and finally she looked at him. "See, I don't wish to change a single thing." A verdict.

He didn't cry, he didn't beg. She ran the dagger across his chest, pausing occasionally. I watched them silently, unable to put the pieces together. Priya never mentioned him or Mel. She never mentioned her past or who she was. In that moment, I realized I knew more of Nadine the Butcher than of her. But just a few glances at them and an undeniable past was laid in front of me, though completely unreadable.

A past. This was as close as Priya would let me be a part of her life.

Priya pulled out a hair-thin pin, longer than a needle. He flinched as she stabbed him in his neck, precisely in the large vein pumping his blood tirelessly.

"I do have my procedure to follow, as you might have heard. This will paralyze you to the point that you won't be able to even blink *or scream.* A luxury I wish I had so many years ago. But don't worry, I will keep you alive until I am done. But she—" Priya pointed at me with her dagger, grinning in satisfaction. "She will do the killing for me today."

Molten adrenaline caressed my veins as if lava, yet my body was still, my mind was perfectly clear.

"You are going to be her first kill, you know. I hope you appreciate that. You never got to be first." His eyes widened a little, and Priya's smile got bigger. "Oh yes, I remember. Take it as my gift to you. After all, we are friends, aren't we?" She patted his cheek.

Priya's face lit up with a deathly thrill as she ripped the buttons off his shirt, exposing his chest wide.

"To remember me by even after you die," she whispered into his ear. His eyes still wide open, unable to blink, were tearing up with large, murky tears dripping down his cheeks.

Small strips of skin fell off as Priya fileted his chest until a large S appeared. Blood trickled down his stomach, catching in between his gray body hair.

The image of the similar scar flashed in my mind. Priya's. Her burned scar in the shape of an S on her stomach. It was the only connection I could make from all of this.

She pointed her dagger up, holding up a freshly sliced piece of his skin. Priya looked at it with the same devouring look, as if she craved it; as if she would eat it right now to satisfy that hunger that ran wild through her. The drops of blood ran down the blade in slow motion.

"You know what comes next now, don't you?" She heinously smiled at him. Her eyes filled with wicked happiness. I wasn't shocked or scared, no, what I felt was more a feeling of reverence. Priya was a force of nature. A tsunami wave; powerful, wild and so free. A shiver went through my body. Destructive. Yet each of her movements were filled with a hunter's thrill and determination.

She slowly unbuckled his belt and tugged his pants down just low enough to fully expose his manhood.

"You know, years after years, and I have yet to find one that looks decent or even remotely appealing. I seriously don't know what women find attractive about *this*?" Priya spoke to me, as her dagger sliced through that most sacred part of a man in one fluid motion.

There was no screaming, no twitching or twisting. Even his breath now slowed down to almost nonexistent. Blood pooled quickly under him, dripping down to the worn-out rug.

Priya turned to me with a satisfactory grin on her face.

"Your turn, Freckles."

Every night I'd been thinking of this moment; since my training began, since Priya told me she was taking me on my first kill. I spent hours pondering what I would feel, what it would be like to take someone's life. Would I take it slow or be one and done? Would I want to say a few words or just be silent?

I thought about this pristine moment so many times before.

And yet now, my mind was empty. The ever-flowing sea of thoughts dried up. The room was quiet. There was no chirping from the previously loud birds, no heavy breaths shared. There was just deep, utter calmness. The depth of it felt so unfamiliar, and yet so welcoming.

I didn't say anything as I pulled my crossbow, loading it with a short arrow. My mind and body turned into a well-oiled machine, precise and careless.

His heart or his head? That was the only question that mattered to me then.

Arrow to the head was the most practical, I decided. I wanted to see the strength of my crossbow; the quickness of the arrow's blade as it pierced through the bone and flesh deep into his gray matter.

I didn't take a pause to breathe as I pulled the trigger.

His eyes finally blinked from the impact as my arrow sunk deep into his head, leaving just the metal tip poking through the other side.

I lowered my empty crossbow. My eyes trailed the dark red stream of blood running down his face.

A line crossed. A life gone. Taken by me. His blood to forever stain my soul.

But the truth was, my soul was ruined long before this click of the trigger. It was born tarnished. Created by Death. It was stained with my very first breath. With my utter existence, I brought death.

The line might have been crossed today. But his blood? That was just a drop in the ocean.

"Nice shot, Freckles!" Priya smiled as she took a closer look at the arrow. His head now slumped back, exposing his neck. "Here." She handed me her bloodied dagger. "You should try to cut his skin too. With a good knife it feels just like slicing warmed butter."

I set my crossbow down on the table and took her blade into my hands. The handle felt so warm from her hands against my cool skin. Without blinking, I ran the blade against his opened chest. Small trickles of blood came out one by one. His skin turned ghost pale as more blood pooled underneath his chair.

I twisted the dagger deeper. The blade went through with no hesitation, no resistance. It was too easy. The human flesh was so vulnerable, so defenseless against the sharp blade.

Priya observed each move, each blink and breath.

"Good," was all she repeatedly said as I dug her dagger deeper and deeper until it pierced his heart completely. "You feel that?" she asked with anticipation and ecstasy in her voice.

But I didn't feel anything at all, except calmness like the dark, still waters in the midst of a moon eclipse.

I didn't reply to Priya. She was ecstatic, full of energy and life.

"This is what it's like to feel powerful. To run the course of other people's lives. To decide who lives and who dies. To deliver justice. To *be* vengeance. No other feeling in the world feels like that. Their fear, their pure terror; no drug in the world could replace that."

I pulled the dagger out and handed it back to her, my eyes still on the limp body of the unfamiliar middle-aged man. Priya wiped the blood off her dagger against his ripped shirt.

"So, what do you do next?" I asked her.

"I find myself a trophy. Something to remember this by."

"A trophy?"

"Well usually, I take all their gold and jewelry, but I also like to take something personal of theirs." Priya glanced around the small cabin. "But since this guy was as poor as the church rat, I doubt we will find anything of value."

I had no desire for a trophy, no desire for someone's possessions. I stayed by the body still, while Priya made her way to his bedroom, rustling his sheets and his dressers looking for something of value to her. A souvenir.

Even with the sheer calmness, my stomach ached. Pain seemed to worsen since this morning. Nausea and the headache were to be expected, as I skipped breakfast today, but the pain seemed to now distract me.

I felt it then. Like a bucket of ice water, the sticky wetness and the feeling of a slithering blob landing between my legs, washing away any calmness I had felt.

"I need a washroom," I yelled to Priya.

"What?" she yelled back at me, through the loud screeching of the moving furniture against the wooden floor.

"I need to use the bathroom."

"Well hell, go then."

The crooked outhouse, filled with buzzing flies and mosquitoes,

stood not too far from the house. The definitive stench didn't help my
now panicking thoughts.

Please don't be it. Please not now. I opened the door to a hole in
the dirt, filled with shit and piss, and gagged. The hot, burning sun was
not helping today. With the stench burning my lungs, I rushed away
from the hole. The outside would do.

"Oh, please not it," I begged out with my closed eyes, pleading the
gods and spirits above to have mercy on me. But deep inside I already
knew the answer. My underwear was soaked with blood as I pulled the
leather pants down.

"Oh, fuck fuck fuck, utter holy fuck," I muttered under my breath,
with my butt exposed to the world as the realization of what was
happening to me came.

It'd been years since I had my period, and even before I was just a
child, never steady, never full. But now... I should've known. I
should've guessed. Now that my body was well nourished, the dreadful
reminder of womanhood came back with it too.

I hissed. A cruel Fate. Laughing at me. Blood for blood was quite
literal to her, it seemed.

Priya finally popped out of the cabin with a satisfactory look on her
face. She was carrying a small, carved figurine in her hand. Pausing just
a few steps out of the cabin, she bunched her eyebrows in amusement.

"Want to tell me why are you stripping down? Shining your sparkly
white ass to the world?" Priya's lips stretched in a large smile.

"My period came," I said pulling my pants up.

"Oh fuck. I forgot you could have those."

"What do you mean you forgot about those? Don't you have them
too?"

"Oh, hell no, Freckles. No offense but fuck no. I cut my birthing
machine out a long time ago."

"Wait what?" I asked, surprised.

"Oh yeah, the moment I found a doctor competent enough to do it.
I had them cut it out completely. No mess and pain, just pleasure for
my lady parts." She rubbed the lower bottom of her stomach, smirking.

"But why?" I asked, rubbing my forehead. This day was getting too long.

"Meh, something about blood coming from down there just brought too many unwanted memories. Plus, look at you…it's such a hassle and inconvenience to deal with it every. Single. Month."

I agreed with her there. My stomach twisted in pain. I grunted in frustration. At that moment, cutting out my treacherous uterus seemed like a reasonable idea.

Priya was still amused. She chuckled.

"Don't look so heartbroken, Freckles. Being a woman sucks at times, but would you rather have a dick? Like, heaven's no. Disgusting," she said, laughing. I chuckled back. "We will get you supplies before we leave."

The cold wetness of bloodied underwear against my smooth skin sent an ick down my spine. I was ambushed. Thoroughly ambushed by Fate.

Priya, unlike me, was in a fantastic mood.

"Aww, it's okay, Freckles. Look at the bright side. At least now we know for sure you are not a boy." I scowled at her.

We started walking back. Priya played with the small carving of a bear.

"Did you find what you were hoping for?" I asked her.

"Yes, and I got you something too."

She pulled another carving like hers, but of a bird. Though small, the carving felt heavy in my hand.

"You can fly now on your own, Freckles. You are *free*." She smirked.

But I didn't feel free. In fact, I didn't know what to feel at all.

All my feelings were still quieted down deep inside of me. Like they were too lost, sunk deep in the ocean. Always so loud, they were now muted, hiding in the darkness, scared to come out.

But the truth was, I didn't need to feel in order to function.

27

We walked on foot past the long fields of golden wheat. Rows of people with their large sickles, working nonstop until the dark of the night. Harvesting.

We still had a few hours of walking until we reached the small dock Priya secured the boat at. The purple sky now stretched bright on the horizon. Loud crickets chirped away in the grass along our dirt path.

Priya was snacking on an apple with another loaf of recently bought bread.

"You are awfully quiet today," she said, taking another loud bite of her pink apple.

I was indeed quiet today. Not sure what to say. Not sure what to ask. Not even sure of my own thoughts, but instead grounded to my surroundings, keenly aware of the end of my ponytail caressing the top of my now-cleaned crossbow.

"I guess I am not sure what to talk about or what to ask." I offered her the truth.

"Well, staring on the horizon like that is kind of weird and frankly annoying. Spill it."

CHAPTER 27

"I didn't feel anything." The truth came rushing out faster than I could think of it.

"What do you mean?" Priya murmured, eating that apple so loudly.

"I just didn't feel anything." I *don't* feel anything, would have been more correct.

"I heard what you said. I just don't understand," Priya annoyingly replied.

"I took a man's life in cold blood, and I felt *nothing*. I should have felt bad, terrible, maybe even scared or at least overwhelmed, but I didn't feel any of it. I felt nothing at all. Like an empty pickle jar."

Priya just kept on chewing. Minutes after minutes of us just walking, that truth hanging up in the air. She finally paused.

"And this is a problem because…?"

"Something is wrong with me. I killed a man, Priya. I ended someone's life for no other reason than you said so. A stranger to me that lived his life and I cut it short for no reason. I should feel something. Why am I not feeling anything?" That question nagged on me ever since I walked away from that cabin two days ago. My feelings were so quiet, as if veiled; still there, but now I only saw them through a fog.

Priya halted our walk; I stopped a few steps away from her.

"First of all, that man that *just* lived his life was a complete piece of trash, so believe me when I say the world is not going to miss him. Second, I have no clue why you are so screwed up like that?"

I slightly frowned. The familiar feeling of loneliness was waking up in me. Alone. I was in this alone, then.

"Oh, get over yourself." Priya scowled at me. "You make such a big deal of it. So big whoop, turns out you are more of a sociopath than I am. Whooptee-doopty-fucking-doo. You learn new things about yourself every day, things that you like and things that you might not like. If you are going to let one little fucking detail derail you like that than what is the point of you trying something new?" Priya's angry voice rumbled. She was clearly disappointed I didn't share the same feeling she had during our kill, but she still added, "So, you've never killed a man, and now you have. And nothing has changed for you? Take a win when you can, damn it, Finn."

"I guess you are right. It was just not what I expected. I was hoping to feel something grand. Something powerful. And all I have felt is just the calmness of a machine. Like a stupid steamboat." I agreed with her, easing the tension between us.

Priya chucked the left-over apple core far into the field, her thick braid swaying with the motion.

"At least you are a steamboat and not a fucking dryer fan." We both smiled at the idea of that. Priya threw another apple in my hands.

"Eat something first, miss bloody pants. Steamboats don't run on empty fuel." She winked and we continued walking.

28

I threw the pen and paper on the bed, rustling the sheets as I got out of the bed. Hours. At this point it had been days. I spent too many days working on it. The still empty paper glared back at me. Making fun of me.

The loud drops of rain knocked on my window relentlessly. Already in my comfy pajamas, I opened the window just enough to smell the rain mixed air, inhale the smell of wet stone, to feel a few droplets of the cold rain against my skin. It felt so refreshing.

It'd been more than a month now since my first kill, and just a couple of weeks since my second. The calmness and the numbness were now more like an emotional support pet. Most of the time, playful and laid back, but always there when it mattered the most.

I turned back, staring at my bed. The stupid paper looked so big. Gods, why didn't I grab a smaller piece? I rubbed my small golden studs in the new ear piercings that I got. They were still slightly sore, but now felt a part of me just as much as my own freckles.

I was surprised when Priya brought me to the piercing parlor, just a week after we came back to Svitar. It was her version of making me *feel* something after the kill, though quite manually. But I didn't mind it. I never had my ears pierced. Always wanted it, yet Tuluma said there was no point since we could never afford any jewelry anyway.

But unlike my elven maid, Priya declared that I would be getting piercings after every kill I do, so I "could feel the pain and remorse I was so desperate to find." To my reply that eventually I'd run out of places to pierce, she laughed saying, "I didn't know little Freckles over here had such a long murdering list."

But truthfully, I had the skills and resources now, and there were enough bad people in the world, so I wasn't planning on stopping now.

She gasped then. Loud enough that people turned and glared at us as Priya flipped them off.

"Write a hit list. I want you to go kill off your people. Maybe you are not feeling the satisfaction because you are killing for sport, but you need to do it for retribution first. Revenge is always the best feeling," she said, licking off a drip of French pastry cream on her palm.

So here I was, making a list. Priya gave me today as a deadline, otherwise she promised to make me kill every single day until I gave her the names. And as much as I had come to accept the feeling of numbness within me, the clear calm taking over me each time I pulled the trigger or slid my knife across someone's throat, I had no desire to go on a murdering rampage in the city I lived in.

I sat back down on the bed. Priya was many things, but she always did what she put her mind to. So, it had to be a name on this paper or a death of some innocent person tonight.

I tapped the pen against the paper anxiously. I didn't know that many people, and the ones I knew were already dead. Having no friends had its perks. It meant I had no enemies either.

There was that one merchant who kicked Tuluma and I out of the village once. Maybe him? Or there were those girls that threw swine food at me once for speaking elvish, but that seemed so trivial and pitiful. I felt sorry for them, not angry so as to avenge it in death.

Clock sounded the last midnight ring. Shit. I had to go now. Maybe it was the hesitation, the unwillingness to relive those memories, but there were two people that deep inside I wanted dead. I craved it. I promised to kill them, in fact.

Bornea Miteno. The man that sold me in slavery.

And the man I despised the most: the "great" Destroyer General.

I scribbled those names on the yellow paper. Each line of ink almost felt like a black thread connecting my soul to those promises, writing out our destinies.

I ran barefoot across the large hall to the other side of the manor, down to the double sided, large, white doors, staring at the letters on the paper. Bornea Miteno, Destroyer General. Destroyer General, Bornea Miteno. Something powerful stirred at the thought of them being dead. Killed by me.

I took a few steps in before finally raising my eyes from the paper.

"Pri—" I swallowed hard halfway through my word as my face filled with all shades of pink. The soft sound of moaning and light giggles filled the room.

Priya's full naked body was on a complete display as she laid wide open on her crimson silk sheets. She was slightly propped up by a large pillow under her neck, oh so slightly relaxed back and her curls spread on top of the pillow.

There were five other women there, each one more gorgeous than the next. Each a goddess in their own right. Most completely naked, some wearing nothing but a small piece of sheer fabric. *All* devoted to pleasuring Priya.

"Got your list? Finally?" Priya raised her arm in the air, summoning me. The lovely women around her didn't pause even for a second, as their luscious lips sucked and licked those large round breasts of hers, their hands teasing and stroking what their mouths couldn't take.

"Um, yes," I said, unsure where to guide my traitorous eyes as I walked towards her. I stretched out my arm to hand off my list just as a beautiful blonde slid her tongue deep in the apex of Priya's thighs, her body twitching just slightly at the touch, releasing a soft moan. The redhead was the only one now watching me, meeting my flushed gaze as she laid near the blonde, kissing and scraping her teeth on Priya's thighs. She watched me curiously, attentively, as she slid her slender finger in-between Priya's full exposed bottom.

Bright, lush carpets were now feeling so stiff, and I shifted on my feet, forcing my gaze towards a painting. It was a painting of Priya, gods, a giant painting of half-naked Priya on a large wall. I slid my gaze further to the left, willing myself to completely ignore the loud swallowing and paced licking and those sultry, feminine purrs.

Priya grabbed my list, taking a quick look at it.

"I don't fuck with Destroyers. But whoever this...Bornea guy is, it's a start." She handed the list back to me.

The fifth girl now was spread out right above her, kissing and nibbling her neck and then her ear.

"Okay," I mustered to say, not exactly remembering what Priya said.

"Freckles?"

"Um, yes?" My hand was already on the door, rushing out.

"Beatrice would be happy to take care of you too, you know?" The redhead paused, smiling seductively at me.

"Anything your heart desires," she purred. Her dark, periwinkle eyes locked in with mine again. It felt almost wrong to say no to her. But I heard myself speak.

"Um...I am okay for now. But um, thank you... Beatrice."

She winked with her foxlike eyes, still not letting go of her gaze on me as she lowered her plump lips back on the tanned skin of Priya.

"Well suit yourself then." Priya waved with her hand, dismissing me.

I walked down the hall. My mind was still racing, trying to process everything my eyes devoured. The chill air was prickling my heated skin as I turned off the lights and plummeted into the bed.

I tried not to think of what was happening across the house; tried not to think of the pure pleasure and ecstasy I so craved at times. It'd been well over five years since I felt it. Ollie was my first, and the only guy I had ever been with. We were just kids when we crossed that line on a mossy floor, deep in the forest.

So awkward and yet so natural, the flow of our bodies uniting as one.

I closed my eyes.

I promised I would never forget his face, and yet his soft features were now a blur in my memories, his scent of cedar now just a mere ghost in my mind.

Fuck, maybe I was lonely. I never really cared for women, not in that way at least. I admired their beauty and goodness; and I'd be lying to myself if I didn't admit that some days I really *really* wished I cared about the touch of a female as much as a male. Men were gross and filthy, yet Ollie was able to stir up a storm in me with just a simple touch, light up my world with single thrust. He could make my heart explode with just a touch of his lips.

I slid my hand between my legs. It'd been so long. Too long. The fingers were met with already welcoming warmth and wetness. I slowly slid them up then down. My mind lit up like stars in the night, remembering the utter pleasure so long forgotten. I sped up my pace. Gods, damn them all. Just a little more. My full hand was now at work. My legs tensed and my back slightly arched while I found the exploding release. My body shuddered. I didn't realize just how much I needed it until now. Gods, it was so good.

I didn't even realize that the rain had already stopped, and now just the utter quietness of the late autumn night rocked me to sleep. Maybe I was pathetic to pleasure myself at the thought of my dead lover, but I was too tired to care as I closed my eyes and fell deep into my sleep.

29

I ran my fingers down his strong, muscled back. There were so many scars. I never noticed those scars before. I pressed my fingers deeper into his sun-kissed skin, massaging my way up. He released a soft groan and I bit on my lip, my insides melting at the sound. I raised my eyes to the back of his head. The dark brown hair was perfectly cut on the sides, thick and slightly ruffled on the top. I stiffened at the need to run my fingers through his hair, to lower my lips down to his now exposed strong back. Oh gods, and that smell of him. The scent of the fresh pine and smoke. So familiar, so beckoning. Gods, to hell with them all. I should let go of the restraints that I had been holding onto forever. Forget it all, for a small taste of him. I tucked my loose, long strand of hair behind my ear as I inched closer, until my lips were just a breath away from the curve of his neck. My hands paused as I lowered my lips, gently caressing them against his warm skin, one and then another and another. Our breathing heavily intertwined, bodies heating up with undeniable desire.

"Finn..." That voice...*his* voice.

I silently gasped, waking up completely disturbed, desperate for air. My eyes were wide open. Dawn was creeping in through the window.

CHAPTER 29

I immediately sat up, my breathing uneven, my body still shaking at the voice of the Destroyer General echoing deep in my mind.

His voice.

My name.

Finn.

I rubbed my face with both of my hands. A twisted and cruel nightmare. I forced my thoughts to look for a reason, an explanation to the twisted way my conscience turned on me.

"It's a stupid dream. This is what I get for making a murder list and finding release the same night," I said out loud, trying to sound convincing.

Yet the lingering feeling of his voice, his scent, the taste of his skin on my lips sent my body into complete overdrive.

"Hell. This is an utter piece of hell," I muttered to myself as I washed my face in the cold water. The cold water on my face was of no help to my frenzied body. Fine, cold bath it is, then.

If these dreams don't stop, I am going to have to knock myself out with one of Priya's potions, I decided.

30

The warm, late autumn sun was welcoming the ever-rushing city residents. The still, chill air was the only reminder of last night's pouring rain. The smell of pastries and coffee greeted us as we walked past the small shops of Svitar.

"Gods, these beignets are going to be the death of me," Priya moaned as she threw another piece of fried pastry in her mouth. It wasn't long into our walk before she pulled out the snacks Ratika had packed for her.

I should've known better than to think Priya would wait even an extra day, even an extra hour, before heading out far into the Royal lands to kill Bornea Miteno.

"It could be weeks' worth of journey though," I said to her when she'd barged in bright and early that morning. With winter quickly approaching, I wasn't sure Priya was aware how far deep in the gods' forgotten lands we were going. It could take us months to find him. To which she snarkily commented, "That's why I am bringing my laundry girl with me."

Now packed, we were walking on the busy streets of Svitar. My eyes were still glued to the utmost beauty and luxury of the city. It would never stop to amaze me. Every day I was out, each ancient street

I walked, it imprinted forever in my mind. The intricate details, the neatness of architecture and contrast, the never-ending variety of colors perched up in small pots and flower beds along the walking path. It was breathtaking.

"Shit," Priya swore. I turned my head to her and burst out laughing. Powdered sugar from her accidently dropped pastry now spattered on her dark brown suit, landing straight onto her crotch and leaving a bright white, round mark on it. "You laugh all you want, but let's just hope you know how to get powdered sugar out of these leathers," she sneered as she tried to shake off the remaining sugar from her suit and fingers.

I laughed while sneaking one of the beignets for me as well.

"Where are we going anyway?" I said as we were approaching the oldest part of the city, the Motra's Square.

"I have to talk to some people before we head out."

We approached a grand building straight across from a giant fountain portraying Destroyers on horses, with their swords and burning arrows pointed forward. Water droplets now turned like glitter, covering the sculpture. Though made from real gold, I secretly wished it would rust.

"This way." She motioned to the small alley leading to the back. My heart sank in slight disappointment as we stepped into a poorly lit alley instead of the main entrance to the grand building. Even in the morning daylight, the shadows covered our steps and the temperature dropped noticeably thanks to the icy rock.

Without knocking, Priya walked in through a smaller black door. The carved stone steps were slightly more worn out as I took each step down the curved, sharp angled staircase.

A large open room welcomed us. A restaurant of sorts, I thought at first, with round tables and nice dark chairs, yet further down, a spacious platform surrounded by gold lounge couches. A stage.

Even with large chandeliers hanging from the ceiling, the room's lighting was dimmed. I followed Priya to the long, dark, cherry wood bar.

"We are closed," a smooth male voice shouted from the shadows.

"Oh, go suck one, Florian," Priya shouted back and dramatically rolled her eyes.

"Priya!" the tall slender man with long auburn hair behind the bar cheerfully called out. "Long time no see." Florian smiled wide. He put a towel on his sharp shoulder and pulled out two shot glasses. "Always good to see my favorite partner looking alive and well." He grinned with satisfaction seeing the irritation on Priya's face. His teeth were perfectly white against his slightly tanned skin. His long, straight hair was neatly tied in a low half ponytail in the back.

"So nice of you to bring me a gift." He mischievously smirked at me, taking my hand and landing a soft kiss on it. Priya impatiently growled near me, and he held my hand a second longer. Whoever he was, he got under her skin like nobody else could and he enjoyed that. "So, who is the new eye candy with you today?" He pointed with his sharp chin towards me and winked with his bright hazel eyes. "New girlfriend of yours?"

Priya smirked as if remembering last night.

"No, but she really wishes."

Baffled, I opened my mouth to object, but Florian continued.

"So, she *is* on the market then. Interesting." He now stared at me, his eyes intriguingly poking and probing me already. I bit on my lip, just slightly fighting the urge to smile back yet the corners of my lips still curved up as he ran his thumb down his chin, those eyes teasing me.

"Did you run out of whores here that you're getting so desperate, Florian?" Priya shot back a snarky smile and took a quick shot of whatever drink he poured into her glass.

"What can I say, whores are fun, but I am a sucker for a diamond in the rough." He winked and I stifled a small, girly laugh. Though, by the look of his eyes, he knew that.

He poured another shot.

"My new creation. We call it the Devouring Destroyer. Becoming quite popular these days," he said as he lit up the clear liquid and a bright silver flame sparked in the cup. Priya rolled her eyes hard and quickly drank hers. I froze. My eyes pinned on the flames.

He must have noticed my unmoving body and the dread stirring up in my eyes.

"It won't burn, I promise," he said, his voice comforting as he ran his hand through the flames quickly.

"Hmm." Priya's eyes were now on me, as I fought the utter panic crawling up from within.

"It's okay, beautiful," Florian said as he took the shot and drank it whole. I finally exhaled, shoving down memories that those silver flames called back in. "Not your cup of tea and that's okay. Just wait until you try this. And this time, no fire needed." He gently smiled as he turned to the bar and poured in a few cocktails in a tall cup.

"How is the business?" Priya asked, getting up from the chair.

"It's been doing great, especially since people are still so tense after that Rebel bust a few weeks back. It has been quieter here, but demand on deliveries has been through the roof," Florian said, squeezing a small piece of lemon. "Pesky little pests or not, those Rebels are good for business."

"Rebels my ass, I told you that new stuff is good shit." Priya smiled like a cat, content with whatever Florian reported.

"What can I say, you are never wrong." He winked at her.

Priya smiled but flipped him off with both hands. Though she was completely and utterly annoyed, I had never seen her as relaxed and comfortable with any man as she was with Florian.

"I am off to see the old man and convince him to chop your head off." Priya took a few steps down the hall. Florian chuckled but nodded.

I stood up, unsure if I were to follow.

"Try to keep your panties on while I am gone." Priya looked at me and waved goodbye with her hand before I could say a thing.

"Not if I have anything to do with it," Florian shouted at Priya's back.

"You know I am not mute, right?" I rolled my eyes at him, smiling. Florian was charming and he very well knew what his presence and his flirtatious looks could do to a woman. He truly enjoyed seeing the light blush on my cheeks. I sat on the barstool, tucking in my hands under my thighs.

"So, she does speak after all." He grinned.

Florian leaned towards me on the counter. His long sleeve, white, button up shirt was crisp, top buttons completely unbuttoned showing just a peek of the large floral tattoo across his smooth chest. "What are we going to do with you today?" he purred.

I eyed the bright pink drink in a fancy glass he now set in front of me, pretending to ignore his not so stealthy stare.

"So, what is this place? What do you do here?" I finally dared up to look at his seductive smile. His thick brows raised in amusement.

"She is a player after all... and here I thought we were just merely exchanging smiles." He smirked even wider. "Good move, gorgeous, good move."

Confused and somehow feeling slightly embarrassed, unaware of what just happened, I awkwardly took a few sips of the bright drink.

"Wait, you really don't know, do you now..." He opened his mouth wide, almost stifling a laugh. His long fingers ran along the edge of the cherry wood counter slowly. "Aww precious, which rock did you crawl out from?" He drew out his words, speaking to me like a child. I clenched my jaw in annoyance. For a second there, I flashed back to being an embarrassed six-year-old seeing a tavern for the first time, being confused and laughed at by the other kids when I asked if it was the church.

"So, are you going to answer my question or is stupid flirting all you are good for?" I asked, sipping on my juicy drink.

He chuckled and leaned back on the counter, tugging on the towel on his shoulder.

"So, you are aware we are flirting then?" He smiled from ear to ear. "This is the Queen's Palace, beautiful, the most famous and desirable place in the whole lands of Esnox...Upstairs." He pointed to the ceiling. "Is where most of the formal stuff happens, where the Royals come for their events and gossip and here," he gestured to the space behind me, "is where all of the actual fun happens, and I just simply work here."

Something about him saying "simply work here" with that devious look on his face told me it was more complicated than that, but before I could ask another question, he continued.

"I'd ask if you were satisfied, but then you keep wiggling on that chair like that with your hands there and those tight leathers, and I am guessing you haven't been satisfied in a long time." He smiled wickedly, knowing exactly what he was implying. "More questions, little thing?"

I froze, even stopped breathing, so as to not make another move on this stupid chair. A tint of flush and a little bit of that embarrassing heat ran through me. I tried not to smile but failed. I suddenly related to Priya's urge to flip him off, as he bit his lip just slightly.

"Well, I guess now we know that flirting is *the only* thing you are good for after all," I shot back, but also stood up, refusing to sit in any chairs anytime soon.

"Forgive me, my lady." He bowed melodramatically and then grinned wide as he looked from underneath his eyes. "My tongue is usually much more useful doing other more *pleasurable* things than talking."

I chuckled, biting my lip just a bit. Florian had no shame. Absolutely none. He slowly licked his lips without breaking eye contact.

"And what if I am already in a relationship?" I teased him back, narrowing my eyes. Fine, two can play this game.

He smiled wide. That wicked, cruel, teasing smile of his. "And who says I am against sharing?"

I couldn't take it anymore and just laughed. This man was totally out of control.

"Oh, my gods, you really never quit, do you?" Only a second after his face turned even more devilish, I realized what came out of my mouth.

"That's what they always say," he added, laughing.

"I'll give you that one. I deserved it." I smiled but my eyes went back to the long hall where Priya disappeared.

"She is okay, and she will be back soon," he gently said, turning his face to the hall.

"Is it that obvious?" I said, leaning against that chair.

"You keep looking down that hall every other second so yes, it is, but I promise she will be back anytime now."

"Thanks." I nodded, relaxing my face.

"Thanks for what?" His face turned gentle, soft.

"This is the second time you've tried to calm down my nerves and I appreciate it."

"Oh, so I *am* good at more than flirting, after all?" He teasingly smiled. His eyes creating small wrinkles in the corners.

"I wouldn't go that far." I rolled my eyes.

"So, you are new to Svitar then?"

"You could say so, yes."

I had been in Svitar for a while now, but the city was grand, and I still hadn't explored even a half of it.

"I must show you around. As amazing as this place is, there is so much more to this city that will absolutely blow your mind in *all* senses of the word."

I laughed, gods, my cheeks were starting to hurt from smiling too much.

"I—"

"Hide your cock if you want it still attached to you, Florian!" Priya's loud voice roared down the hallway. My heart jumped in surprise.

"All hidden now," he shouted back, without breaking his eyes away from me.

Priya's figure emerged from the dimmed hallway.

"Ready?" she asked, running her eyes up and down me, as if checking if anything was out of place.

"Um, yes," I said, glancing over to Florian in silent goodbye.

We were almost by the door.

"Wait, I didn't get your name," Florian asked from behind the bar.

Priya rolled her eyes, stopping just for a minute and turning her head to him.

"Gods, Florian you are honestly a dumbass, you didn't even ask her name? Hell, and Heavens above, It's Finn. Her name is Finn, like a fish *fin.*"

I fought a laugh. I wasn't sure which of Priya's nicknames I preferred more, Freckles or Fish Finn. Florian ignored Priya's remarks.

"When you come back, me and you, fish *Finn,* are going out!"

I didn't know what changed in my heart in the moment, but I turned my face to him as I spoke confidently.

"Okay."

"Then it's a date." He smiled and ran the towel down the bar.

31

Tall aspen trees were lined in a neat row, glimmering brightly even through the foggy glass of the small carriage we were in. It'd been three weeks of nonstop journeying, deep into the Royal lands. Long gone were the mighty buildings of Svitar, or the moss-covered brick of Port City, replaced by gloomy, cabin-like houses and tiny villages. Hotels and taverns were getting poorer and dirtier the further we traveled. Soon, even the carriages wouldn't make the trip that far into the gods' forsaken lands. Even the weather seemed to match the lack of life in these lands. It was cold and gloomy, with only occasional yellow and orange leaves stranded in the sea of grays.

The carriage abruptly stopped. Half asleep, Priya raised her head to the corner.

"Why are we stopping here? For gods' sake!" she grumped, rubbing her face angrily.

The old man with large, white sideburns opened the carriage.

"The bridge is under construction, miss; the carriage can't pass."

"Then what am I paying you for, old man?" she argued, getting out of the carriage. I followed. The cold, autumn air wrapped my body immediately. The dark rain clouds were now constantly covering the skies, as a reminder of never-ending gloom.

"I could take you back and try again in a week or so," he offered.

"Oh, and spend a whole week in that rat infested motel? I'd rather die." Priya dramatically growled in frustration. The old man just shrugged, climbing back on his high seat.

"On foot it is then," Priya irritably said, chucking a silver coin to him.

I grabbed our bags and slid one across the shoulder, passing another one to Priya. There was no point in arguing. Not when I had to save whatever remaining bravery I had to find the one man that had altered my life. Plus, I wasn't that eager to return to that nasty motel either, and if we were fast enough, we could make it to the next village before sundown.

Tall grass ran up to my shins, my boots now covered in moisture. The grass was muted green in anticipation, before it slowly rots underneath the layers of soon to come snow.

"Let's play marry, fuck, kill?" I asked. I had heard the village girls play that game a few times growing up, but I was never included.

"Oh gods. Are we five?" Priya rolled her eyes as we crossed the small makeshift bridge across the lazy river, but nodded her head in agreement.

"Florian, Beatrice, Ronald?"

"Obviously kill Florian. Kill Ronald too. Fuck Beatrice, that's easy."

I laughed. A Priya-fitting answer. "It doesn't work like that; you have to pick one to marry."

"I'd rather kill myself and they all can go fuck and marry together. Beatrice would probably enjoy it too."

"So predictable. Boring." I yawned.

"Fine, smartass, your turn."

"I mean, not that I've thought about it but marry Beatrice because I am sure she would be the best. Fuck Florian for obvious reasons, and kill Ronald." I eyed the sky and whispered, "Sorry, Ronald."

Priya chuckled, pulling out another treat from her bag. At this point I got used to the fact that Priya mostly packed food for her trips and not clothes.

"Ronald deserves it," Priya sneered. "And Beatrice would make a terrible wife, are you kidding me? In fact, Florian would be a better wife than her, granted she talks less and fucks better than him, so I guess I could see it."

A little shadow crept over my thoughts. I tried to be subtle about it.

"Wait, are you saying you and Florian....?" I paused, anxiously waiting.

"OH FUCK NO. Gods, NO. Bleawh..." Priya just continued making vomiting noises for about five minutes. I chuckled, rolling my eyes.

"I take it as a no then."

"This might be the most offensive thing you've ever said to me. Oh, Freckles, fuck no!" Priya kept on fake vomiting. "Such atrocity. How do you even dare? Like, I chop dicks for a living. I am not putting one near me unless it's to cut it off."

I smiled, though slightly embarrassed that I had asked that question to begin with.

"Florian and I met a long time ago," Priya said, slightly warming up to the conversation I had been leading to and hoping to have for a while now. "I met him shortly after I moved to Svitar. His grandfather and I have mutually beneficial investments and since Florian is the named heir, I have to get along with him once in a while for the money to roll in."

I slapped another mosquito on my arm. Gods, there were swarms of them now coming at us.

"Named heir for what?"

"Does the name Casteol mean anything to you?" Priya said with her mouth full of dried biscuits.

"No? Should it?" I warily asked. Priya rolled her eyes as if I was the most ignorant creature on earth, but I tried to fight that. "You forget that I spent most of my life in places like this, living cast out with the elven maid." I motioned my arms to the gloomy nothingness around us. "And after being forced into slavery, we didn't quite get the morning gossip of Svitar." My words were sharp, but I smoothed my tone. *Incompetent, unaware, clueless.* It always irked me. That feeling like I didn't know something but should have.

"Oh please, yes, be so dramatic, slave girl." Priya clicked her tongue at me. "Relax. Casteols are drug Lords, but not just drug Lords, they are *the* emperors in the drug world. Their family has been running the drug cartel in Esnox for generations now. Florian's dad was murdered, his mom is some singer, performing day shows at the Queen's Palace. And his grandfather, two years ago, announced Florian as his sole heir to the Casteol Empire."

"And when exactly were you going to tell me any of that?"

"Are you not going to go out with him now?"

I opened my mouth to object but paused. Yes, I would still go. Drug empire heir or not, Florian was fun. He was such a ray of sunshine in the dark gloomy days.

"Yeah, that's what I thought. So, if it doesn't change anything, why would it matter?" Now it was Priya's turn as she smacked a few mosquitos off her thighs.

"So, you are an assassin and a drug Lord?" I asked casually. It didn't surprise me at all. Not anymore.

"Me, a drug Lord? Oh please, those men are pure savages with no class."

"Well, there is *some* class." I smirked, my thoughts drifting to that slightly unbuttoned, ironed shirt on that summer tanned skin.

"A. Super gross." Priya rolled her eyes. "B. Poisons are not the only useful thing you can make out of plants. C. When you make extremely potent opium, there are people, very rich people, that are willing to pay for it. So, as I said, it's an investment. I like to diversify my portfolio. Who knows, maybe one day if I get bored and Florian pisses me off, maybe I'll murder them and take over the empire. Who knows, life is full of possibilities." She slapped another darn mosquito.

At my stern glance, she continued.

"What? I didn't say I'll do it for sure, I just mean I would like to keep it as an option." She smacked a mosquito on my shoulder.

"So, besides the fact that you are thinking of murdering him, what else should I know of Florian Casteol?" I curiously asked.

"That you will probably get an STD just by standing too close to him."

"Very funny," I sarcastically said and stuck my tongue out.

She flipped me off with both of her fingers.

* * *

THE NEVER-ENDING BARREN FIELDS WERE NOW GETTING BROKEN UP BY occasional cabins. Finally, we were approaching the village.

The tall grassy road turned into half-dried mud. The village was small, with just a few barely noticeable smoke streaks coming from the mud-covered chimneys.

A handful of young women passed in their patched up, worn-out cloaks, eyeing us with concern and interest.

I adjusted the crossbow on my back, my cloak covering most of it.

"This stench. Gods. Would it kill them to plant a flower or two or pick up this shit once in a while?" Priya cursed as she had to dodge, yet again, another large pile of cow shit. I was too deep in my flooded memories to tell her that planting flowers or cleaning up shit would be the least of their concerns when they were simply trying to survive each day. It was easier to adjust to the smell of wet cow shit than to find the strength to clean it up.

I knew that because I too had to survive that.

Not that long ago, I was in a village just like this, covered in mud and shit, laying on the frozen ground, completely numb from pain. I was barely eighteen, kicked out without being paid yet again, with nowhere to go, no money to my name, and nobody. Not a single soul in the whole wide world to care. My mind drunken, blurred with grief, unable to cope with the loss of the only family I had ever had, loss of the future, loss of hope.

It was so oddly chilling to be back now, when I was well dressed, my belly full of food and my pockets full of coins. I was a different person now; my body strong, my mind, though scarred, craving life more than death.

But familiar notes of grief played within my soul as mud spattered across my winter boots. Yes, I was a different person, but that aching, soul crushing grief had never really gone away. It had torched my soul leaving just ashes in the previously flourishing Eden.

You don't survive grief. You don't overcome it. You get used to it. Just like you get used to the wet cow shit smell. One day, you just wake up not feeling it. Its mark had never left, you just have adjusted to it.

I pulled my brand-new cloak tighter, reminding myself that though I was broken, I was no longer floundering in an abyss of pain anymore.

My boots were splattered in dust and drips of nasty mud, but my feet were warm and cozy, the boots fulfilling their purpose, doing what they were meant to do. I kept my eyes on the mud below my feet.

What was my purpose, really? That question had nagged me for a while now, though I masterfully ignored it. When my energy was spent keeping haunted memories at bay, that thought consumed me.

Why was I here?

I was here to kill.

I killed before, and I would surely kill again. That didn't bother me. It mattered to Priya for it to be specifically Bornean Miteno. In some way it probably mattered to me too.

But why was I here? Fate or no Fate. *Why was I here?*

What was my purpose?

The quiet numbness stirred in me, purring, calming the rising storm within.

My eyes trailed off the mud, up to the horizon. I halted. My mouth dried out completely as I saw the pile of dismembered, half-burned bodies thrown together in a heap.

I didn't move. I wasn't sure if I could. Even the tiny mosquitoes plastered on my forehead and neck stopped sucking my blood. The world paused for a minute, sorrow and anger flooding my thoughts, like pent-up water through a broken dam.

The charcoaled, clenched fingers and half-burned faces were forever frozen in agony, in their never-ending scream.

No, the world was silent in the moment, but I could hear them still. Just like I did years ago. Those soul wrenching screams.

The heap of bodies was cold, not even an ember of fire, yet I could still smell it; the human burnt hair, the burnt smell of blood and flesh. There were no ashes floating in the air, no smoke suffocating me, though my lungs burned.

Breathe. I needed to breathe. But how could I?

"You look pale," Priya nonchalantly said as if she didn't see those bodies. I didn't reply. My eyes were unmovable from the lives forever lost. Gods, a couple of them must have been less than ten years old, their small, half-burnt feet now forever exposed to cold, never to run through the green fields again, never to laugh or to smile. The world darkened around me.

Breathe. I willed myself. *Breathe.*

"Gods, Freckles, if you are going to pass out, at least move your perfectly braided hair away from that pile of horseshit because I am not braiding horseshit hair ever. Like ever."

That was her command, but I didn't move. Priya took a few more steps away from me, closer to the bodies.

Bright lightning lit up the sky and loud thunder crackled seconds later. Large drops of rain landed on my skin. I blinked. My lungs expanded in the desperate breath again and then once more. *Breathe.* I stood still, letting the cold-water burn against my skin like acid.

"Come on, Freckles, let's go." She motioned to the small saloon a few houses down, quickly walking away.

My eyes were still glued to the bodies, now being washed and cleaned with pouring rain, soon to be drenched in moisture just like me. Except I was alive and breathing and they were gone, never to live again.

A soft hand jerked my arm and pulled me forward. Priya.

"For fuck's sake," she grumped. "If you want to stare at the half-burnt corpses all night, be my guest, but do it through a window in the saloon. I haven't gotten these nice leathers for you to just let them rot like that."

Priya didn't let go of my arm until we walked into the saloon. A couple of the gruff men scoffed and growled at our arrival. Priya jerked me to the chair.

"Sit," she ordered, and I obliged. There was no point of fighting, not with her eyes throwing knives at me.

But was there a point to any of it all?

I should've been dead. Should've been dead a long time ago. A little tear bit my cheek when the most painful truth had sounded clear in my mind. A truth that I had been fighting my entire life.

I should have never been born to begin with.

That was the most painful truth, because I full heartedly believed it.

Priya went to the big, bearded man carving slices off a large lamb leg. I couldn't hear her as she argued with the man, but even if I did, it wouldn't matter.

She shortly came back and sat on the chair, mumbling some profanities as she scraped off the caked-on mud on the edge of the table leg.

"Who were they?" I asked.

"He is the prick owner that will be bringing us the best meal he has ever made because frankly if he doesn't, I will be murdering everyone here." Priya was in a foul mood.

"No, who are *they*?" I repeated, slightly tilting my head to the fogged-up window with nothing but the small droplets on the other side.

"Hell, if I know," Priya said, dropping her bag on the table and rustling through her belongings. "And I am out of chocolates? Oh, fucking fuckers hell..."

"I want to know who they were," I stated calmly.

"This day is seriously getting on my nerves." Priya rattled her bag again before dropping it on the other chair at our table. She paused, looking at me for once. My question still stuck in the air, unanswered. I watched as servers put a large batch of freshly baked bread on a dirty cloth.

"How the fuck would I know? Not my fucking problem." She scowled at me.

Fine.

I would find out myself then. Another flash, another loud roar of thunder; so loud I could feel the tremor in my bones. Even the gruff men splattered all over the corners paused their loud chewing and drunken arguing for a moment.

The owner brought a small plate filled with nicely sliced cheeses and breads and some jam.

"Your starter, ma'am" He nudged the plate to Priya.

"Do I look like I am fucking fifty? I am a fucking miss to you, bastard!" Priya spat out quickly, already taking a bite from the fresh rye bread.

The owner scoffed from disrespect but didn't say anything, taking a few steps back to his kitchen.

"Who were they?" I stood up taking a step towards him.

He turned back and faced me. I looked at the dull blue eyes against his red face.

"Those bodies outside. Who were they?" I asked again, when he didn't answer.

He paused, wiping his hands on the stained apron, hesitating to answer. "That is what's left of Rebel sympathizers."

But I already knew that; had guessed it from the moment I saw those fire marks on them. "No, who were they?" His gray eyebrows bunched up in confusion. I repeated my question again. "Who were those people? What were their names?"

"I am not sure," he replied defensively. "I don't deal with Rebel sympathizers."

"But did you know of any of them? Did you ever see those kids running down this street?" My voice was heavy though steady, there was so much anger within.

"Um ma'am...um miss," he corrected himself immediately as Priya growled. "I didn't know any of them, and even if I did, it would be of no good to ask these questions or answer *any* regarding the sympathizers here." He slightly bowed again and walked away as Priya waved him off.

I rested my back against the chair, my arms folded tight. A storm much larger than the one outside was brewing deep in my thoughts.

"Eat," Priya commanded, pushing the plate with food closer to me.

"I am not hungry," I replied, my eyes pinned on the back of the owner as he chatted with his help and added a few logs to the fire.

"The fuck you are not. You haven't eaten since the morning. Get over yourself and eat," she barked at me again.

"I will, when I am hungry," I firmly replied. A line in the sand.

"Oh, so this is how it's going to be today." Priya's lips turned into a thin line. "Why are you so obsessed over half a dozen rotten corpses?"

"Why aren't you?" I shot back.

"Some people live, some people die. Thus is life." Priya dramatically gestured with her butter knife as she plastered red jam on her bread. So trivial.

"Then what's the point of life then? You suffer then you die suffering?" I said as calmly as I could.

"That is precisely the point, Freckles. You live and then you die. Just as simple as that. There is no point. So might as well live your fucking miserable life to the fullest." She gave me a skittish smile and took another bite.

"Why not just die now, if it truly doesn't matter?" I countered.

"You are so dramatic." Priya rolled her eyes again. I ignored her jab. "I mean sure you can go die now, or later. I personally am in no rush, considering gods are boring pricks and the afterlife is going to be such a bore." I watched her take another bite out of the buttered bread.

Is everything really that pointless? Live or die, who cares?

"And if that's not enough for me? If I want more out of life than just to simply exist?"

"Freckles, let me be *very* clear...*you are nothing*, but a speck of dust in this world. Simply existing is already more than you could ever wish for."

I stayed silent, watching a young man approach us with two bowls full of whatever hot liquid it was. Priya ignored him as he placed the soup and quickly returned to the large prep table in the corner.

"If you really must have a mission," Priya's voice softened as if she realized the sting of those sharp words. "Why don't you just stop overthinking and enjoy your life for once? Make that your *purpose*. Have fun. Murder some people. Go see a show or a circus. Get laid for once. Maybe even get plastered drunk. Hell, get a girlfriend maybe?" She winked at me. I didn't smile back. "Geez fine, I could even try and accept a boyfriend but only if approved by me though." She pushed the bowl of soup towards me. "And maybe you could start by just eating some food for once before I force feed you in front of everyone."

I looked out the window and pulled the bowl closer to me. I'd eat right now. One spoonful after another, letting that liquid burn my throat. My cheeks heated, turning red. Between the steaming pots, the small chimney and large men producing body heat with each of their breaths, the saloon was getting warm. Too warm.

My eyes stayed on the small, crooked window. Another sip and another. My bowl was now empty. The darkness of the evening hid the silver drops of the never-ending rain.

"We are sleeping here by the way." Priya broke the silence after a while. "This stupid rotten village has the fucking Rebel sympathizers, but not a decent bed and breakfast?! Cook said that we could walk around the town and ask if anyone has an extra bed, but I am not doing that in this weather. Plus, gods, I don't want to repeat that whole louse situation from two years ago. So, we are sleeping here."

I nodded in acknowledgment.

Hours went by. My soul and mind slowly twined with dark threads of fog. Most men were now gone, just a couple of drunks left resting on the spit-covered floors. Priya didn't talk much, only occasionally complaining about one thing or the other. After a while, she stacked a few chairs together and plumped her bag, using it as a pillow.

Sleep. I should get some sleep.

Though my eyes were heavy, my soul was weary.

I watched the small golden and red embers of fire of the giant stove slowly wither away with each breath, the only color now left in the dreary, dark room. The cold draft of wind from the large gap beneath the front door embraced me, taking away the last chance of settling my rancid mind down.

Have a better life. Tuluma's dying wish for me. *My* promise to her. Was it a better life now?

Have I been surviving for so long that a part of me forgot what I was living for?

The small, half-burnt feet flashed in front of my eyes with each blink.

Maybe I was just a piece of dust, a little speck of nothing, useless and foolish with nothing to offer, but if we all were to die in the end, I would rather die knowing I stood up for something good, than wasting my entire life wishing I had.

32

I wiped my knife clean against his limp shoulder. Blood soaked his black linen shirt. Knife to the heart. Quick and easy. I had gotten much better at aiming and my draw to action speed had increased significantly. Though each time, it still surprised me how human flesh, usually so resilient, was nothing against the sharpness of a blade.

"You never said that he was a SulnGod priest," Priya said from the adjoining room of the small house-turned-church. She was finishing up her carving of the letter S on the dead priest's wife.

Bornea Miteno didn't have a chance to run as I shot him with a crossbow arrow the moment he opened his door. I had no speech for him, nothing to say to his familiar face.

Just pure justice. Maybe not even justice, considering I was still alive, and he was not. His dead body now left forever to rot.

Karma was a bitch.

"I never took you for a religious one," I shouted back to Priya. She laughed.

Miteno was a priest, but he and his wife were more rotten than the demons of Hell itself.

It was easy to find him once we got to the village. His wooden church with a brick step was the only building with the circle at the peak. Worshipers of SulnGod.

He didn't even recognize me. But then again, I didn't give him a chance.

The whole day walking down here, to this village, I thought about what was I going to say to him. Would I ask him why? But the truth was I stopped caring about why a long time ago.

So, when I saw his face, I dove into the familiar numbness. Shot, punch, slice. His wife only had a chance to scream once before Priya claimed her life as well.

"I am just curious, why him though?" she shouted back from the room.

"He sold me into slavery. He took me in at my lowest, I opened up to him, trusted him, and then when I questioned him about receiving wages, he sold me off." I sheathed the knife. My face filled with revulsion as I took another look at Miteno's body. Even now, the deep wrinkles on his face made him look so comforting and welcoming. A wolf hiding in sheep's skin. No more.

"Remind me to never sell you into slavery." Priya's laugh echoed as she came out from the room, but I didn't share the sentiment. I should have felt relief, victory. I made it out of slavery, despite the odds, and came back to take his life. A sweet revenge. But there were no celebrations held, because deep inside, a part of me was just as lost as the day I showed up on Miteno's porch asking for work and shelter.

"We should've buried them," I finally said, verbalizing the thought that had been truly on my mind all day.

"What?" Priya asked, confused, going through their drawers and shaking out the books in search of her trophy.

"We should've buried those bodies." I paused. "Those Rebel sympathizers," I clarified.

"Oh hell, Freckles, is that why you've been so quiet today? It's a pile of dead bodies. Above the ground, under the ground, they will all rot and turn into dirt eventually."

I should've buried them. I should've, but I didn't. It took all my strength to just glance one more time at the frozen, tangled arms and legs, hands and feet exposed forever to the elements, and walk away. I had a million valid reasons not to bury them. I didn't know them, I could've been easily killed for helping Rebel sympathizers, plus the ground was frozen rock solid by the morning, and hell, I didn't even have a shovel.

But valid reasons don't clear up a guilty conscious.

I should have clawed the frozen ground with my bare hands, ripping my nails apart. I should have buried them.

Should have.

But I didn't.

"Who knows how many more this prick sold into slavery, and now thanks all to you, he is no longer. If it makes you feel any better, you can count this kill as your contribution to the Rebel cause, if it so inclines your bleeding heart."

My mind froze as I saw what Priya held in her hand.

"Where did you find that?" I asked, my face lit up in shock.

"Um, that dead bitch was wearing it. Pretty, isn't it?" Priya said, dangling a necklace. A large, emerald stone, shaped and carved like an eye, hung down on a meticulously made platinum chain.

"That is the eye of the Troiyan," I said, almost disbelieving what was in front of my eyes.

"And?" Priya ignorantly whirled the long necklace around her finger.

"And....it was Tuluma's, *my Tuluma's. Her* talisman." I didn't believe the words coming out of my mouth. "She gave it to me on the night she died. Miteno ripped it off my neck when he shoved me into the prison wagon. I thought it was gone forever." All manner of emotions flooded my mind, heartache, anger, sorrow, joy, relief, gratitude.

"Well, I like it," Priya said. "I never had anything elven in my collection."

"I need it, Priya. Please take anything else you want." Priya's face changed into slick satisfaction. I was never below begging. I knew that. I was also too aware of the hold Priya had on me. And for this—for this small piece of my past—I would do anything.

"Please, just let me have it, Priya. Anything else but this. It is the only thing I have of her."

Her eyes lit up in a wicked smile.

"I will give it to you, but only if you drop this Rebel idea...*forever*," she demanded, aware of the lofty cost.

For once, I had absolutely no regret in becoming a liar and a traitor.

"Okay," I answered without hesitation. The platinum chain and the cold, eye-shaped, green stone now swung around my neck. I gently placed it underneath my leathers, still in incredulity that this was the actual talisman. My chest tightened as the peculiar chain ran deep until the rock settled not too far from my heart.

A piece of my home.

33

"Ouch," I whimpered as Priya's swift kick to my ribs sent me back a few steps.

"Whiny, whiny, whiny," Priya replied as another kick and blow came my way. This time I was fast enough to block it. One more step closer. Another block, and another. A second later, a zinging slap across my cheek angered me.

"Keep your hands down like that and your cheek is going to bleed by the end of it." Priya smirked while blocking my move. She was good, predicting each move of mine. I made a step forward, attempting a swing at her. She ducked and with a swift motion, knocked me on the soft, padded floor of the training room.

A frustrated "ugh" came out of me as I laid my head down on the floor. Priya can kick me to death, but I needed a break. It's been hours since we've been training, again and again. I was exhausted. So wholly exhausted.

"Oh, get up." Priya grabbed a small face towel and threw it on my bright red face. Even though my hair was now long enough to stay in a decent braid, small pieces were glued all over my face with sweat.

"I am pretty sure my legs will give out if I do," I said, wiping sweat from my face with the white towel. "Are you ever going to let me win?" I asked, smiling like a predator. Finally finding the strength to rest on my elbows, I slightly lifted myself up. Priya was resting against the wall, gulping down some water.

"Let you win? Who do you think I am? A charity case over here?" She smirked. "The real question is, will your skinny ass ever get to beat me?" Her face stretched into a large grin. I grinned back.

Soon enough, I wanted to say but didn't.

"Hey, my ass is no longer skinny." I shoved my tongue out. "Just be ready Priya." I paused for a moment. "Wait, what is your last name?"

"I don't have one," Priya casually said while chucking me the water bottle.

"You don't?" I was taken a bit aback.

"No. Do you?" she shot back defensively.

"I mean yes, but I guess technically, no. But that's because I grew up differently. Elves have a different way of naming things."

"Who says I didn't grow up differently either?"

"I mean, clearly you did." I smirked giving a look around the enormous training room with work out gear, fighting pads, armory, and the target practice area.

It was nothing but a clear red flag for "different."

"What is your last name then?" Priya asked, her eyebrows bunched up.

"It's not a last name per se. Elves give you a name and then call you daughter or son of whoever you were son/daughter of... Tuluma was very creative with mine," I sarcastically said. "She called me Finnleah, Daughter of the Dead, since my parents died and I was born on the day of the Dead. She used to say it was meant to be since we were constantly running away from Death too." I paused. Tuluma would get a good laugh at how accurate that name has become. "Honestly, now that I think of it, it is rather fitting, considering my occupation."

Death seemed to be the only constant in my life.

"Oh, I think it's rather shit." Priya chuckled from the corner.

"Well thanks for that." I grimaced at her. "Would you want one?"

"A last name?" she asked. I quickly nodded, taking a sip of water. Gods, even my neck was sore. "Fuck no, it's exciting. I am to be nameless, just Priya the queen of everything."

"Or nothing." I teased her.

"A lot to say for a girl that can't land her punches fast enough," she said smugly.

"For now," I added, smiling.

"Would you?" she asked me back.

"Get a last name? Oh, most definitely, yes, always wanted one. I think it's quite romantic to take a man's name in marriage. A notion that I am forever to be his. For everyone to know that we are a husband and wife. A single unit. Forever united. And for our kids to carry *our* family name. It's very cute. Plus, it's not like I have one I'd like to keep." I chuckled.

"Gods, Freckles, so many wrong things one after another. Marry? Bleh. Man's name? More bleh. A child? A living breathing child AND *your OWN*? I think I am for sure going to throw up." Priya theatrically gagged a few times. I rolled my eyes and chuckled but continued.

"I mean, not now but one day. I've always wanted to have a family. We'd live in some dreamy cottage and have a garden. A big barn too and a horse, maybe two. A dog and for sure a cat. Gods, I always wanted a big fluffy dog and a big, red barn cat. Maybe even a few goats. For sure, chickens. We'd paint our small fence together while our kids played tug of war with a dog and laugh, and then I'd bake one of those delicious pies and then we'd all cuddle into the night on our small little swing with lots of blankets and watch the sunsets together while snuggling our small, sleepy babies." I closed my eyes for a second.

My little dream. I had once been so close to that. Once. I could've had that with Ollie. In my previous dreams, Tuluma was always there with us too, chasing after the kids and telling us to never make more, yet spoiling them rotten with anything they'd ask for.

I craved that life for so many years. A place for her and me to feel at home, to never be cast out again, to live the remainder of our lives together. Tuluma was supposed to outlive me. She always said that she'd tell my great-great grandkids just how difficult I was. We would have a family, a nice warm house, a place of happiness and peace.

Every night for years I dreamed of that; imagined my future life. Every night, until I lost it all. I grieved that life for me too. There would be no Tuluma there, and it wouldn't be Ollie swinging on the swing with me. That little cottage and those sunsets would never be the same without them. The little drops of sorrow clouded my mind as the dark rainy clouds on the summer day.

"Are you high?" Priya's face was filled with laughter. "Did I kick you too hard this time? Or did you go sniffing stuff in my lab?"

"Oh, whatever," I sneered, finally getting up on my feet. A little flush of embarrassment ran through my face. It was foolish of me to share that part of me. It was also dangerous of me to even consider a world where I could have a family. My own loving family, my own kids that I would take care of. My family that I would love more than anything in the world.

Perhaps I was delusional indeed.

No, I knew better than giving myself a false sense of hope.

"Don't you ever dream?" I asked curiously, walking past Priya's curvy figure, getting more water.

"Oh, I dream, alright." Priya's luscious lips stretched in a wide, wicked smile. "Except my dreams are a lot more entertaining than your pathetic housewife ideas."

"You say that, but really, what is your wildest, craziest dream?" I squinted my eyes in determination. Priya was an enigma when it came to her thoughts.

"I don't have one. My life is perfect as it is. Why dream of anything when you can already have anything you want?"

"You must have something you truly dream of," I insisted.

"Nope. Nothing at all."

"Oh, come on," I contended.

"Fine. If I could do anything and dream of anything, I would want to travel through time," Priya snarked.

"Who is delusional now?" I raised my brows and cackled.

"At least time travel sounds a lot more reasonable than your 'being a wimpy mom and housewife in some gods forgotten village' dream."

I opened my mouth to object, but Priya continued.

"And then I could take you to the future you and then you'd see just how depressing your dream is, cottage and all. And when the little soul eating suckers scream all day, your so called 'loving husband' beats and cheats on you and you are left running the dump all day with no way out. Then you'd be back to me, begging for my time traveling abilities to take you back."

I rolled my eyes, annoyedly.

Priya took another sip of her water. "Yeah, now that I think about it, that is my new dream."

"At least my dreams are happy," I quietly shot back. Priya snarled.

"You forget, Freckles, that I AM happy."

"Are you though? Or do you just keep telling yourself that?"

"I think you have no idea what you are talking about," Priya growled back.

"Maybe, but—"

A soft knock on the door interrupted our heated discussion and a small head popped in. Ratika.

"Miss?" Her voice was always so soft and gentle. My spiked-up anger eased just at the sound of it.

"What do you need?" Priya irritatingly asked, her eyes still on me.

"There is a gentleman here asking for you two." Ratika's eyes stopped on me.

"Tell him to go away," Priya barked.

"I told him you weren't home, but he said that he will just have to stay here until you were."

There was only one man cocky enough to do that.

"Florian," Priya and I said in unison. My heart skipped a beat. Whatever notes of defiance and anger I had before were now completely replaced with a tiny bit of excitement.

I bit my lip and smiled.

Florian.

"I am going to murder him," Priya yelled with rage, racing past Ratika.

"Sorry," I mumbled to Ratika stumbling past her up the stairs to keep up with Priya.

34

"Better hope you said your prayers, Florian, because you are about to meet your gods." Priya's loud voice echoed through the hall to the tall figure facing the large tapestry on the wall.

"Priya. The most welcoming hostess. How fortunate that you made it back home to see me." Florian's smile widened as he turned to face us. He wore a similar white shirt, slightly unbuttoned, and crisp black pants. His long, auburn hair was unbound and tucked behind one of his ears.

I smiled back as he winked at me.

Florian.

"You have two seconds, Florian," Priya hissed.

"Is it not good enough for me to want to visit my favorite business partner?" Florian tugged on his exquisite cufflinks.

He ducked to the side just as a sharp knife nearly grazed his ear, landing straight into the picture behind him.

"Priya!" I loudly gasped. "Seriously?"

Florian, though, was unfazed. He turned to look at the small knife sunk deep into the painting.

"It's a shame. The picture was quite pretty."

"I won't miss next time, Florian. Last chance. What are you doing here?" Priya's mouth turned into a thin line.

"Fine. If you must ruin my fun. We need a new batch of the opium in two days for the Royal ball."

"I was already aware of that. There is such thing called messengers." Priya already pulled another dagger out of her thin sheath. Unsure, I pulled out mine.

"I also came to check up on my friend." Florian jerked his chin towards me. "She hasn't stopped by, and I believe we have some unfinished business." He smirked.

"She's been busy," Priya dryly replied. "And if you ever step inside my house uninvited one more time you will never see her again."

My face frowned at that remark, though I stayed quiet. If Florian was irritated by it, he didn't show it. Slowly, he turned to pull the knife out of the picture.

"Always so violent. Come on, Priya, aren't we friends?" He took a few steps towards her. She clenched her jaw.

"I'd suggest you go take a walk, but dead men have a hard time walking," Priya angrily spat, but Florian simply chuckled.

"I'll have to tattoo that wisdom on my chest next time." He slid his hand into his slick pocket, pulling out a letter. "Too bad dead men can't deliver this to you either."

Priya violently grabbed the envelope from his hands and viciously ripped it open. I watched as she read and reread the contents again and again. Florian's eyes were going back and forth between her and I.

After too long of a silence, he finally spoke.

"Don't go ahead and thank me all at once. I mean it's not like it cost me an arm and leg and some questionable choices." He smirked, slowly folding his arms.

"The Royals Queen's ball..." Priya's tone changed to low, calculating, as if she completely forgot the death threats thrown against Florian only a minute ago. Her dark copper eyes glanced over to the gardeners outside, raking up whatever was left of the burgundy leaves. She then turned to Florian. "Short notice, but I'll make it work." She glared at him.

"Oh, but wait, there's more." Florian's frivolous lips stretched in a wicked smile.

"The Baroness is going to be there too," Priya quietly mumbled. Not a question, but a statement. Her face was now expressionless, lost deep in her thoughts.

Florian nodded.

I quietly observed their silent exchange, stilling my body and folding my arms, hiding any of the irritation I was feeling. I had absolutely no idea why any of this was important. Whatever it was though, it overshadowed Florian's little stunt, so it was big enough to ignore Priya's number one rule of no males in the house. But I didn't know the meaning of any part of that conversation. Lost, as a child between adults conversing. Secluded, as if I was an outsider.

"Anyone care to explain what's going on?" I finally barged in.

Florian looked at Priya, giving her a chance to explain when she didn't, he spoke.

"Well, you and I are going to the ball, gorgeous." He smiled.

"The Royals Queen's ball?" I asked, not even sure what that entailed.

"Yes, the grandest ball of the year for the Death Day Celebration."

"Death Day?" I tried hiding the sudden surprise in my voice. Has it really been a year already?

"Yes." Florian smiled. "Only the most rich and famous made the list and I just got you two invitations. So, you are welcome."

"Death Day?" I asked again.

Florian was slightly concerned at the appalling look on my face. "It's a holiday people celebrate to remember their dead and to celebrate their life. You know, longest night of the year? Please tell me you know of Death Day?"

"Um yes...yes, of course," I muttered under my breath. It was more than that, though. A simple holiday for some, but for me... Death Day was my birthday. But it wasn't a birth that made that day special for me. It was Death. It was the day my parents died. A ridiculous holiday to celebrate nothing but grief. I already had to live with constant guilt, much less needed a holiday to remind me of what I had lost.

"Of course, beautiful, you are my date and Priya, well..." He took another glance at Priya, still lost in her thoughts. "I guess Priya will do what she does best, meaning, whatever the hell she wants."

"Okay," I mumbled in return. I didn't even realize until my tongue tasted the irony tang of my bitten inner lip.

"I mean, I always leave my ladies speechless but honestly, I don't know why you two are like this. I thought this was supposed to be good news?" Florian confusingly gestured with his hands. "I, for one, am excited. You don't get many chances to go to the Royal Castle."

"Yes, that's where the ball is." Priya abruptly cut back in, folding the paper back in half. "I still stand by the statement of murdering you, Florian. But we have a ball to prepare for, it seems, so I shall wait...for now." Her voice was cold, calculating. There was no anger or her usual sarcastic playfulness.

"How considerate of you." Florian smiled as he comically bowed. A brave move considering the knife mark still fresh right behind him. "I will be picking her up. Do you want me to send a carriage for you too?" I opened my mouth to say something but instead shoved the words further down. It irked me that they talked about me with me right in front of them, as if I was nothing but some possession, discussed and "managed," without any regard for my opinion. Though I wouldn't mind going with him. I enjoyed Florian's company and accompanying him to the ball sounded enticing if I chose to ignore the occasion, but for once, it would be nice to be considered, asked, or even just be heard.

"I will find my own transport," Priya said, already moving up the stairs. I stayed still. My thoughts focused on the looming Death Day.

"Are you sure? Mine are mobile carriages. Top of the line. Only a few of the Royals have them." He moved his eyebrows at me as if hinting at something sinister. I rolled my eyes at him but smiled.

"Fuck off, Florian," Priya shouted from the top of the stairs in response. She would've flipped him off for sure, if she wasn't still clenching the paper.

"She really has a thing for me, doesn't she?" Florian smiled wide, walking towards the front door. I watched his slender but not frail frame pause, turning back around. He was tall and I was sure his back was always just a tiny bit slouched.

"So, long time no see, gorgeous. Did you enjoy your little murder spree?" he teased, resting his shoulder against the door frame. His hands slid into his ironed-out pockets.

"You came here," I said, slightly curious. Still trying to make sense of everything.

"You didn't come to the bar, and I never got a reply to any of my messages, so I figured it was time to stop by."

"Messages? You mean the child drawings you've been sending here for weeks?" I asked mockingly.

"Child drawings?" He gasped dramatically. "It's called art, Finn. Gods. I've poured my soul and heart into them, and you just go and offend me like that." He put his hand over his chest. "I shall forever stay heartbroken."

"Oh, forgive me, my Lord, the ill-educated person, I shall cherish your stick figure crayon art forever as my most prized possession." I rolled my eyes at him but didn't hide the smile.

Florian had indeed been sending letters, or drawings, to be exact. He had been sending them through gardeners or some other messengers, never for Priya to know, and I for once didn't feel like indulging her in it either.

I enjoyed them; the silly drawings of what looked like an excited eight-year-old with crayons. Florian's drawings were always so colorful, filled with silly, dramatic portraits of him seeing me with the hearts in his eyes, or him eating a cake waiting for me to reply, or him topless with way, way too many muscles, telling me that he works out. Sometimes he sent only one, sometimes it was a whole story, but I had come to look forward to those little messages each day. They always made me smile.

"That's right. That's the recognition a true artist deserves." He pulled another paper out of his pocket. The man loved attention. My eyes narrowed in on the piece of paper and he handed it to me. "Just for you, beautiful."

I quickly unwrapped the paper. It was a drawing; this time of him in his suit and me in a very bright pink dress, with lots of other stick figures behind. My face lit up in amusement.

"My official date invitation for you. I had to buy extra crayons just for that pink color. So, I hope you appreciate that brightness."

"Oh, I love it!" I laughed. "The shoes are a nice touch too." The heels were drawn so tall and large that they took half the picture.

"Well, I figured since you are short and I am oh so, so tall and we obviously would have to kiss at one point, those heels would only make sense."

"Obviously." I took another look at his ludicrous picture, avoiding his stare. "Your parents must be proud." I cringed almost immediately as the realization of what I said came in.

I knew his dad was long dead and his mom was not a huge part of his life. This was tone deaf of me to make such an insensitive joke. Gods, why would I say something like that? His beaming smile slightly softened.

"Oh yeah, my dad is rolling in his grave, regretting not discovering this talent of mine earlier so he could cash in on it. My mom is just jealous I am better at art than she is. She is so jealous; she spends her days drinking because of it. I mean, I would be too if I had known my son was so much more talented than me. Honestly, being this talented is a curse." He sighed theatrically but his smile was still slightly dull.

"I am sorry," I quietly said. I very well knew that even behind laughs and jokes and the silliest little things, sometimes hid the forever unhealed wounds.

"It's all good, gorgeous. Parents sometimes are shit. What can you do?" He shrugged and slid his hands into his pockets again.

"Freckles!" Priya's impatient yell roared through the house. I sharply turned my head towards the top of the stairs.

"I guess I better go," I said, folding the drawing and stashing it under my bra.

"Is that where you are keeping them?! Ah, I am going to need some copies back. Or you know what? Why don't I just inspect those galleries myself, just to make sure my art is being properly stored." His eyebrows twitched in amusement, so proud of himself.

"You are seriously ridiculous." I shook my head, but I'd be lying if I said I didn't chuckle inside either.

"I'll see you soon, gorgeous." Florian bid farewell by saluting me like a soldier and walked out of the front door.

I shot up the stairs, remembering how exhausted my legs were, sweat all dried and crusty around my face. I needed a good shower and a nap, and maybe a lunch or two.

35

"In here," Priya yelled again. I took a few more quick steps to her quarters. Priya's office door was wide open. The room was spacious, just like every other room in the house. The large, wooden beams ran through the tilted ceiling, and the carved antler and wood chandelier sat high in the well-lit room. The wall high windows behind the dramatically large desk were slightly curtained by the deep burgundy fabric, the silver tassels running loose along the heavy carpeted floor.

Grand bookshelves were filled with all manner of texts and books, tiny to large bronze and silver statues decorated the space in between. Priya sat on her large, out-of-place purple chair. Even in sweat-covered workout clothes and ruffled, messy hair, she looked like a damn queen on a throne. I stopped by the desk. Priya sat still, staring at the display of all manner of rings in the black velvet box. There had to be over fifty of them, each so unique with many different stones and designs. All exquisite.

"What are those?" I asked. I had never seen Priya wear them.

"These are the Royal rings I've collected so far," Priya drew out, her eyes on the empty spot between them all.

I sat down on one of the chairs, not too far from her desk. "These are your trophies, you mean." One look at Priya's eyes, her predator's gaze, the possessiveness and obsessiveness were very clear. Priya was a collector. She never left a kill empty handed. Always a thing, always something of value to her.

"There is one missing. That's why we are going to the ball, isn't it?"

"Look at you, being clever," Priya said, running her finger over some of the rings, slowly, as if reliving each one of those executions. "It's missing two actually. One of them, the kill was already done, yet I never got my ring." Her eyes slightly narrowed, stopping on that small empty space.

"Why Royals?" I asked intently.

"Why not? You'd think, you as a Rebel lover would be excited for the death of another rotten Royal, you know."

Though I wasn't excited for yet another death, I wouldn't object to it.

"I am not some *Rebel lover*." I scowled, aware of the implication of Priya's words.

"You can say whatever you want but I know you've been sneaking behind my back, collecting their rotten propaganda." Priya narrowed her eyes on me. I stared back in those shimmery, copper eyes, determined.

I would not be intimidated. Though, there was no point in hiding it.

"It's not propaganda, it's called history books, Priya. Just because they are forbidden or restricted doesn't mean that it changes history or the truth, it only means we are not aware of what has been happening all along."

"And you think *you* will figure it out after reading a few so-called *history* books? You give yourself too much credit, Freckles." Priya huffed, putting on one of the rings.

"I might not figure it out, but I'll be damned if I had a chance to learn and I *chose* to ignore it."

Ever since the death of Bornea Miteno, I had spent all my free time searching. Countless hours at the best of Svitar libraries, scavenging gods-forgotten antique shops and any kind of markets offering even something remotely ancient. There was so much to learn of the past, of magic. Of the history that was being so well rewritten.

Maybe I was getting obsessed and lost, but what else would I be doing with my life since I still had yet to discover an actual Rebel group.

"Whatever you say, Freckles. Whatever you say. I do hope you drop it soon…considering I'd have to take that precious necklace you wear around your neck back."

My hand twitched, eager to clamp the eye-shaped stone pendant hanging by my heart, but I stilled it.

"You brought up the Rebels, not me." I shrugged, pasting a soft smirk on my face. I'd have to be better. Sneakier, more cunning.

I had no intention of dropping it.

Priya adjusted a few rings before covering them with the large black lid.

"You are feisty today," Priya noted, openly annoyed.

I calmed my heart, letting myself see her; really-really see her. Whatever her past was, whatever secrets she was hiding, I could look past it. Whatever it was, it was important to her. Valuable enough to put everything on the line.

I knew the risks. I also knew it had to be someone high in the Royal tree—could be the damn King himself—and it mattered to her, and I would look past it all and be there for her because truthfully, I wish someone could've been there for me.

She needed me here more than I needed to be heard.

"I guess I am still sore after losing our sparring today," I casually said, placing a comforting smile on my face.

"Rebel lover and a sore loser? Well, you'd fit right in with them, I guess." Priya cackled as she stood up from her desk. My eyes twitched as I chose to ignore her jab, a foul joke about the sympathizer that was loudly preaching at the town square about liberating humans and joining the Magic Wielders and yet when he was captured and sentenced to death he screamed and cried, begging for forgiveness. He'd taken it all back, denying his own words. I was there for his speech and his execution. A sad cry, a pathetic way to die, yet my heart broke in many pieces for him, and still ached even days after.

At times, I forgot just how daunting Death could be for people, even so quick as an ax to their necks. They never wanted to leave, clung with any chance they had to still exist, to fight for survival.

Death always walked alongside me. The only constant. Always there, just a step away from me, yet never willing to fully embrace me, to finally walk me across to the other side of the veil.

"I don't have a dress for the ball," I mentioned nonchalantly. It was better to switch topics completely.

"Good thing I know a place."

36

The previously wide limestone cobble streets of Svitar were now narrowed down to nothing more than a small walking path. The buildings resembling more bright grey than the original white stone. The regular, beautiful flower arrangements were long replaced by unkempt moss of all kinds growing at the base of the leaning condos. The welcoming pine and cranberry wreaths, which hung all over Svitar in preparation of the Death Day, were nonexistent here.

Here in the Slums, the empty flowerpots were left with nothing but frozen dirt. No cheerful holiday decorations, just half empty window displays and faded paint on doors.

I had been here twice. Once by accident and one time looking for something I had never found. People stayed away from the Slums. Here, the laws of nature ruled the streets and though I never came here without my belt loaded with knives and crossbow locked in, I couldn't stop thinking that this was still nicer than some of the rundown villages I had been too. Whores, standing with one foot against the walls, still had most of their teeth, and even occasionally got paid. The shops and houses still had windows and roofs, and rats… rats were still scared of the people.

Priya hated the Slums, but even here, she walked pridefully, staring in the eyes of every drunk passing by, as if looking for trouble. I trailed right next to her, calm and aware of each sudden move within our radius.

Finally, we approached a decent sized shop, "Silken Arrow." Priya opened the small door, and the trivial bells chimed, signaling our arrival.

The immediate warmth of the shop heated up my ice-cold skin. I took a quick look around. One side of the chipped wall was covered in large rolls of plain fabric with only a few color variations. There were shelves covered with pins and needles for sale, and a few sewing kits. The other wall was filled with bows, quivers and arrows of all manner, with occasional knives laid out on display.

"Silks and Arrows, quite literally, huh?" I said out loud, turning my head above me as a small piece of candle wax dripped on my arm from the low chandelier.

"You'd be surprised, miss, just how often those two go together," a scratchy voice sounded from behind the counter. A man appeared a second later. He was covered in gnarly scars and only a few feet tall. His arms and legs were short, yet painfully curved, as if in a half circle. His hands were just as badly scarred as the rest of his body. He was missing a few fingers, but it was the yellow, long claws he had that grabbed my attention. The left side of his scalp was completely exposed, all the way to the bone, while his right side still had small brown patches of hair coming through. One of his eyes was completely blind, lazily rotating on its own, as if a watchful ghost lived inside of him. The white of his other eye was completely bloodshot, with only a black pupil to swim in the ocean of red.

"Laviticus." Priya nodded at him.

"Miss Priya, welcome. It is always a pleasure." He bowed slightly to Priya. He then looked at me, almost smiling, though his look was heavy, assessing. "I am glad those leathers fit your guest nicely."

"Your work never fails," Priya said in return, her voice soft and appreciative.

I never met the person who made my leathers, yet for some reason I imagined it was one of those large sewing buildings I walked past often in the Fashion Corner, filled with gold threads and rows of seam-stress sewing by the windows for pedestrians to look at, to awe at their skills and speed, then to look at their perfected works a few steps further as the large gowns of all kinds were spread out on the full window displays with live models, only occasionally changing their poses.

Somehow, I had not imagined this.

"Come," Laviticus said as we followed him up the tiny stairs with a ceiling so low that even I had to bend my neck lower to avoid bumping into it.

Upstairs was one big, cozy room. The roof and ceiling, being weathered, were letting in a draft thanks to the small gaps above. Yet a tiny hearth in the room kept that air warm, and the strong smell of myrrh and burning sage filled my nose. There wasn't much around. A large rug covered most of the worn-out slabs of wood serving as floor-ing. A couple of windows provided generous lighting, even on darker days like today. He had a small desk in the corner with a few sewing machines on it and large shelves with huge, glass doors filled with various tools. He climbed onto the big chair with the help of a small wooden stool.

"So," he said, laying his hands on his desk. "What can I do today for my favorite client?"

Priya pulled out a large sack filled with gold; pure gold, not even shaped as coins.

"This is short notice but we both need to be dressed for the Royal Death Day Ball."

"Oh." Laviticus's eye filled with vile excitement. He wiggled on his chair, his small legs dangling in the air from anticipation. "I've waited a long time for this day to come. A gown created by *me* for the Royal Ball." He chuckled, taking a second look at me. "And now I get to make two. What a good day today is."

"I do have a few requests, though," Priya said, standing up to pass on the payment.

"Your wish is my command." He bowed, accepting the payment and quickly opening the sack. Priya paid generously. I knew that. But a hint of surprise still ran through my eyes as he poured out the contents of the sack and pure gold bars fell out. With that sum, she could easily have bought his whole house and the entire street as well.

"As much as I know you wish to create a masterpiece...I need to be able to blend in, since I am going for a job."

"Oh, putting restraints on me like that already? What is the point of having wings if you never get to fly?" he said with just a few notes of frustration. Yet when a second passed, he smiled again as he put away the gold-filled sack and pulled out a thick sketch book with a white writing feather. "But it will be done."

"Come, friend." He motioned with his sharp claws to me. I obediently came up to him. "You remind me of the bright moon and stars if the colors were inverted." He said, taking a deeper look at my face. "As if you were a galaxy and those freckles were the stars, lighting up the path to the forever unknown." He scribbled on his paper some notes, I quickly glanced to see a sketch not of my gown but of me, my face. "I shall create you a gown of silvers and deep purples."

"She will be carrying that night also," Priya added from the couch.

"I shall make accommodations for that as well."

"For you, Priya, yours will be a dress called Death's Kiss. With such deep blacks that you will absorb the darkness of the night with each of your steps."

"Sounds good, Laviticus, but remember I need it practical; this is a big night for me, if you remember."

"I shall never forget, my dear," he said, exchanging a deep glance with her.

He pulled out the small measuring tape and motioned me to come closer to the round mirror in the corner. He carried his stool and started measuring me from head to toe.

I stretched out my arms and stood still. Priya sat quietly on the small couch, staring out the window across from me. For being in the Slums, Laviticus had a gorgeous view of the Kinderby River. Large steam ships were sending their last hurrah as they departed down the water path.

"What are those?" I asked, pointing with my chin to the three large black arrows hanging on the wall above where Priya sat.

"Those are Basalt Glass Arrows."

"Glass arrows? That seems rather impractical." I smiled, trying to make small talk.

Laviticus chuckled at me, his thick claws scraping just a tad as they dragged the measuring tape against my back.

"Very impractical indeed, especially if you ignore their practical ability of stopping the Cleansing Fire."

"They stop what?" I sharply turned to face him.

"One shot with those, and the poor Destroyer bastards cannot summon their powers until that glass is out of them."

I paused.

I wanted to know more. I *needed* to know more.

"Why have I never heard of this? Why is this not common knowledge?" I asked, conflicted.

He chuckled as he motioned to put my arms down.

"Why would it be? Why would the Mad Queen and Royals want us, the regular folk, to know that there is a cure to the Great Rot that the Destroyers have become? Why would they let us know when we are so easily controlled by fear?" His bloodshot eye narrowed on me. I understood that stare. I had seen it in my own eyes; that anguish, the defeat, the disappointment.

"Where can I find Basalt Glass?" I asked. My thoughts were now churning and twisting like an awakened dragon preparing to unleash its fire.

"You won't," Priya objected from the couch; her face filled with clear impatience.

But Laviticus continued.

"It's been banned for a long time, and even before the Great Fall, it was almost impossible to find. A rare commodity even then, and with Destroyers in power for years before the Mad Queen, it was a miracle Basalt Glass of any kind survived at all." He grabbed his tape and went back to his desk.

My mind chose to ignore the impossibility, focusing on one truth: it was *rare* but not *gone*.

"Yet here you have not one but *three* arrows," I mumbled, now staring at the long, thick arrows against the chipped beige paint of the mud made walls. "How did you get them?" They were larger than any arrows I had ever shot.

"They were gifted to me by those who no longer exist," Laviticus said, now finished with his sketch and measurements.

"By whom?"

"By the High Lady of the Creators. Raylin the Fair, Blessed Be Her Name." He bowed down as he said her name, moving his hand in a swift motion from forehead to his chin and then round his face.

"I've never heard of her," I stated.

"It's a shame. She was the most beautiful and courageous woman alive." His face filled with grief and subtle sorrow. "That is, until she died."

"What happened to her?" I took a few steps closer to the arrows. The light reflected from the black glass as if it was a mirror.

"Murdered by the Mad Queen, alongside all the other High Ladies and their courts. She gifted me these arrows not long before her death and I've kept them safe until the right moment comes." He paused now, looking at the arrows himself. "It's truly a blessing and a curse to have them, you know. A dream to use them for good, and the reality of knowing *I* could never make a difference. So, I am cursed to see them every day, to always remember their potential and my complete uselessness."

I turned to Priya, trying to keep my voice calm, ignoring the raging heart inside of me. "Why didn't you tell me about this? This—" I motioned with my hand to the arrow. "This could change everything."

Priya's thick lips turned into thin line. "It could, but it *won't.*"

"I could kill him. The Destroyer General. I could kill him once and for all," I uttered. "With this I could kill him and—"

"Not *kill* him, Freckles, but only disable his power for a brief time, until he rips that arrow out and burns you to the ashes," Priya shot back.

"Not if I shoot him straight in the heart," I countered, my thoughts lighting up faster than a dry twig against the forest fire.

"Destroyers heal faster than regular humans, and *you*... you are a terrible shot."

"I can do it. I can kill him. I..." I knew I could.

"Enough!" Priya's raised voice echoed through the room. "I told you once and I will not repeat myself twice. I don't mess with Destroyers, and neither will you."

An impasse. What was previously a small crack in the foundation felt now more like a giant rift.

The dragon within me was ready to roar. But not yet. I calmed it. Not yet.

No, the anger and the rage can stir inside of me. That so-well-built dam that I had been constructing within myself my entire life can stay put a little longer.

I bit in my words, though a sliver of anger slipped past my shields, igniting my core with sparks of defiance and *hope*.

Priya walked towards the door hastily, and I quietly followed.

Patience. I needed more patience. To think, to plan, to figure things out.

There is no point in arguing, I tried to convince myself. *Priya is right,* I said to my heated thoughts, slipping back into a familiar meek and obedient mask.

Even if I found more Basalt Glass, I would still have to find the General, approach him, and get close enough to successfully shoot straight through his rotten heart.

It would be impossible; unreal and probably completely unreasonable. *But...*now there was a chance. The little drops of defiance, not patience, like black ink on white crisp paper, spread slowly out. I hid those thoughts deep in me, behind all my dust-covered memories, behind every plan I ever had.

Be patient, I chanted to myself again and again. Though I could no longer ignore the corrosion on my dragon's leash.

I took a last glance at the three black arrows as I walked down the stairs, following Priya. They were strong and proud, waiting patiently for their fate.

I would find a way.

Laviticus hurried down the stairs behind us.

Priya quickly opened the front door, the small bells chiming loudly at the rough swing.

"You shall hear from me in six days' time," Laviticus said as he bowed in goodbye. Priya didn't reply as she heatedly stormed off in the cold afternoon.

"Thank you," I softly said to Laviticus. "And not just for the dress, but for your kindness and honesty."

Laviticus's damaged hands cupped mine. The brutal scars and claws were so warm. His dark eye met mine.

"Keep your hope, little child. Great things shall come to those who wait."

I smiled at him sadly before rushing off to catch up to the quickly departing Priya.

My heart ached at that word.

Hope.

37

The sound of steaming pots and sharp knives chopping fresh veggies filled the otherwise quiet kitchen. Ratika, as usual, was silent. She chopped and peeled and prepped ten things at the same time across the room from me. The smell of roasted chicken and caramelized onions teased my nose.

"Ouch," I hissed as I knicked a part of my finger and bright red blood seeped through the freshly broken skin. Ratika's only response was a long pause from chopping to glare at me for disrupting her kitchen's symphony.

"Sorry! It's a deep cut," I justified my gasp, now searching for a piece of cloth to wrap my finger.

The large copper bell that usually signaled deliveries rang loud, echoing from the stone walls.

Ratika huffed as she hung the kitchen towel on the rack, checking on her filled-to-the-brim pots.

"It's okay, I got it," I said, holding the rag against my bleeding finger. When Ratika silently questioned my competence for such a task, I motioned to her with my half-wrapped finger. "Let me get the delivery, unless you want blood in your food." I smirked, knowing that she would sooner murder me before letting me ruin one of her masterpieces of a dish with blood, and I would totally agree with her on that.

Pushing past a few doors with my back, I finally made it to the servant's entrance room where most of the deliveries were made. The small shelves and coat hangers were, as usual, empty, the stone-like tile cold and unwelcoming. I jerked the heavy door with one hand, keeping the other bent at the elbow up to keep from bleeding more.

"Hello, Frank." I smiled at the sturdy delivery man holding two large white boxes in his arms. The freezing winter air kissed my kitchen-heated cheeks. Death day was usually the coldest day of the year, and this year was no exception.

"Hello, miss," Frank said, his large mustache stretching in a welcoming smile.

"They are making you do deliveries even on the Death Day, Frank?" I asked, taking the boxes.

"This was such a high priority that I couldn't say no." He fixed his large, fur-laced hood and rubbed his gloved hands together. "After this though, I am going to spend some time with my family. My wife is making her famous goat stew and my sister is bringing my favorite baked apples. It's going to be a great feast!" His face lit up with excitement.

"That sounds nice!" I smiled back. "I am just going to some party with Miss Priya today."

"Well enjoy your holiday Miss Finn, and happy Death Day to you!" Frank replied, walking down the path back to his handcart, now empty of all deliveries.

"Happy Death Day to you too, Frank!" I returned, closing the door fast. Two boxes weighed down my arms, blocking my view as I carried them up the stairs, all the way to Priya's office.

The strong smell of the sweet citrus and spice filled my nose.

"Hiiii Beatrice," I said, even though I couldn't see most of the stunning redhead walking down the hall. She smiled, pausing, slowly putting in her golden hoops.

"You need some help with that?" she asked. I smirked; I could swear she made her voice purposely low just for me.

"I am good, thanks," I replied, still making my way to the office. "How is *the queen* herself doing today?"

"Oh, you know, nothing much out of the ordinary. I'd say she is somewhere between eating a cake and murdering someone later."

"Eating a cake first and only *then* murder someone? Wow! It must be a good day after all then." I cackled. Beatrice giggled and followed me for a few steps.

"Must be the holidays, I guess." She smirked. "You know," She paused, looking further down the hall to the large double doors leading to Priya's room. "If you ever need to talk, just come to me. I've known her for a while now and I know how obsessive she can get and how it's hard to constantly navigate those moods and...anyway, if you ever need to vent just send for me, alright sweet cheeks?"

I nodded, letting the unspoken words settle in between us.

"Happy Death Day, Finn!" She smiled as she landed a kiss on my cheek and pulled her hair from underneath her shirt.

"Happy Death Day, Bea!" I saluted back, though it still felt wrong to say those words each time. *Happy Death Day.* Happy. Death. Except there was nothing happy about Death. Maybe for the dying? To finally be free. But for the living? There was no happiness in knowing that you were left behind to never see them again.

Priya's office was empty. I strolled in and finally dropped the two large boxes on top of her desk.

"Do you ever notice how after you orgasm you get so damn thirsty?" Priya's raspy voice sounded behind me. I turned to see her bare body in an open silk robe.

"Maybe?" My eyebrows rose unsure.

"Perhaps I will put a little drinking fountain by my bed. Like the ones little hamsters have. I could just sip away, staying hydrated while enjoying my orgy." She leaned against the door taking a sip of her water in a wine cup.

"Who am I to be a naysayer? I just ask to see the face of that handy man installing a giant rodent drinking tube by your luxurious bed." I smirked, stepping aside from her desk. Priya walked towards the table. One click. The tiny razor blade appeared from the top of her large ring.

The sharp edge cut through the hand-sewn red ribbons, tightly covering the box.

She threw the lid on the floor, exposing the most gorgeous fabric I had ever seen. Laviticus didn't lie when he said that these kinds of darks would suck the light from the room. She glanced over the small note he included, quickly chucking it, and pulled out her mesmerizing dress.

I leaned back on the desk, resting my hands on the edge.

"This is gorgeous, Priya!" I exclaimed.

Her full lips stretched in contentment. "Laviticus rarely disappoints, am I right?" Priya ran her fingers down the fabric. It was a suit; the most opulent suit, I realized. "I think he dreamed of designing dresses for the High Ladies of the Esnox but got burned and tortured instead. Really, such a shame. Just imagine what he could've done if he wasn't such a little monster?"

I held back my rising quarrel.

"He is no monster, Priya. He is beyond talented, and I don't think his looks have anything to do with that." I wanted to say so much more but I stayed quiet.

"Whatever, Freckles. We leave come sundown, unless your dumbass boyfriend arrives sooner." With that, she dragged on the detachable skirt to trail her suit and walked out of the office, leaving the door wide open.

I waited until she was gone to reach for my box. Anticipation boiled in me. I wanted to rip the box, to tear off those ribbons and finally see, but my anxious hands cut the ribbon with surgical precision.

Dark purple satin intertwined with black mesh, sparkling with glittery silver threads. The heavy fabric jerked my arms down as I pulled the dress out. The top was thick and corseted tight with silver embroidered ornaments and decorated with all kinds of tiny diamonds. The skirt was slick, fraying past my knees into a long tail.

A silver lined galaxy, indeed.

This dress was beyond gorgeous. A masterpiece. How did he create it? The materials and the craftsmanship of this was not even comparable to the most one-of-a-kind boutiques of Svitar.

This was art.

I was in complete awe, yet also filled with intimidation. I would do no justice for this dress. No, this masterpiece would be worthy of only a queen, or even a goddess, to wear, not a runaway slave.

I wasn't sure how long I stared at the dress. Small rainbows danced on the ceiling from the astonishing sparkle of the diamonds. So many thoughts were piling, flooding in my head.

Finally, I lowered my dress, wrapping it over my forearm like a hanger as I lowered it back in the box, pausing just to move the large, white silk it was wrapped in. Suddenly, my heart stopped. My hands froze. I didn't dare blink. Not when I saw it.

Underneath the thick layers of silk was a large, black, glass arrow and a dagger with the obsidian glass blade and a note.

I recognized the arrow immediately.

Ever since I saw it that day on the wall of the Silken Arrow, my dreams were occupied with launching it into the heart of the Destroyer General. At times, those dreams were so vivid that I woke up with my arms stretched in the air, as if holding a bow.

The never-ending dreams with the Destroyer General might have started as nightmares but now that I knew I had a way to kill him... no, they weren't nightmares anymore. Each time we faced each other in my dreams, I was no longer filled with dread but determination, insatiable hunger, and one purpose: to kill him.

It was something I was too afraid to admit to myself; even in those dreams, I was filled with something I had thought I lost long ago. Hope.

Basalt Glass reflected the welcoming rays of sun beaming through the sheer curtains. I reached for it, though my hand stopped midair. I jerked my head to the open door behind me. Priya was so close in the hall. *Too close.*

I quickly shoved the dress back in the box and walked as casually as possible out of the office and down to my room, locking the door. Locks might not stop Priya, but it would give me time.

Rushing to my bed, I set aside the dress, pausing. I took a second look at the Basalt Glass in front of me. The note card was almost empty with just a few words scribbled in perfect handwriting.

"Put them to good use, child. Darkness might wander, but light will always guide."

My eyes ran through the lines a few times. A little shiver went through me, raising the hairs on my arm as I grabbed the large arrow. The glass was cold, and I could feel the humming of my blood against it, as if aware of it, feeling its power. The arrow was heavy, and Priya was right about it being almost impossible to properly shoot from a long distance. I would need a long, sturdy bow and to get as close as possible.

I put the arrow down gently, afraid to even breathe on it as if it would shatter. The dagger was much smaller than the arrow; the razor-sharp, black blade was long, thinning out until the end which was as thin as a needle.

Heart Piercer. The name rang loud in my mind. The silver handle was exquisitely made with flora-like carvings, and on top of it sat a large emerald, the size of a gold coin. Unlike the thick arrow, the dagger was light and easy to maneuver. I pierced the air with it; another move and another, as if I was wounding a real enemy, precise and short, quick bursts. Maybe I wasn't the best shot, but when it came to knife fights, I was *good.*

Priya might have never wanted to admit it, but I was better at it than her.

I paused, listening for any steps. Heart Piercer shone brightly in my hand, demanding the warm blood of the Destroyer on its sharp edges. I could feel it, as if begging me to sink it through even my own flesh. Blood thirsty. I unwrapped the thin cloth covering my cut finger and gently wrapped it around the blade. The dried blood stain on the worn-out cloth rang an unspoken promise. "Soon, Heart Piercer, soon," I said as I slid it under my pillows.

Priya's loud voice rang through the hall.

"Freckles, I fucking give up. Come fix this corset."

"Coming," I sweetly shouted back.

I shoved the box with the arrow deep inside my closet, covering it with newly bought fur cloaks and other recent winter purchases. Not too far from it was also a well-hidden Death Day gift for Priya that I spent weeks searching for.

Even with a low dose of adrenaline running through my blood, I couldn't resist but smile with a slight excitement. Priya yanked the handle. I rushed to the door slamming the closet door shut.

"Locked?" Priya's confused voice rang through the wall. "What the fuck, Freckles?" Her perfectly trimmed eyebrows wrinkled in suspicion as I hastily opened it for her.

"Well, I couldn't let you see your gift now, could I?" I smirked, thinking of the small leather sack hidden well in my closet.

Priya's suspicion was replaced with pleasantry and intrigue. "A gift for me? You got me intrigued, I'm not going to lie. When will I get it?"

"Tonight, after the ball."

"Fine." She dismissed the topic, though kept her smile. A good day indeed. "Well don't expect one from me because I didn't get you one."

I was a-okay with it. I rarely got any gifts and frankly was quite used to it. Maybe a part of me even wanted not to receive any, to pretend that this day was no different than any other holiday. That it wasn't my birthday.

Another year for me. Another waste.

No, I didn't want any more reminders of that.

"This dress is much more than any gift I could possibly get! Look at these threads and rich fabric. Isn't it breathtaking?"

Priya took a few steps to my bed, eyeing the deep, galaxy purple fabrics spread on the bedding.

Shit. Laviticus's note. Shit.

I quieted the tiny fury of a panic, keeping my body still and casual. A normal breath, a simple blink. Priya picked the note up and casually threw it on the floor without reading it. She never cared about semantics and maybe that truly was her downfall.

"It is pretty, indeed. Not quite as practical as mine though. But I guess for Florian's useless sidepiece, it will do for the night." Though a clear jab, I chuckled. Priya might have used it as a reminder of her annoyance at Florian's friendship with me, but I enjoyed that reminder.

We were friends. His lovely caricatures never stopped coming and I even dared to send a few back too. I didn't have piles of multicolored crayons so my drawings were rather simple, basic, with just pencil stick figures, but I knew Florian would get a good chuckle out of them.

In fact, for once I was looking forward to our night of just having fun, where I would let myself be me just for a bit. Priya, Royals, or not.

"Are you going to just stand there or come help?" Priya rolled her eyes as she motioned to her half undone back.

"Sorry, I was just admiring that your dress actually has pants." It was indeed a jumpsuit of sorts.

"Laviticus knows my feelings about never ending skirts." Priya smirked.

I pulled on each string of the metal wires that her corset was constructed of. Each wire wrapped with the velvety fabric, knitted together as if they were nothing but woven threads. It was armor; I realized. A corset at first glance, but deep inside it was the stealthiest carved armor.

I already knew that those new slick, black leather boots she was wearing were full of weapons. I also knew that the large gold choker covering most of her neck with the fist-sized stone in the middle was hollow, filled with powdered smoke to choke out and paralyze any threat. Each hair pin in her well-braided bun also contained deadly darts. And those long, golden earrings were filled with deadly poison, giving the silver stones a black hue. A few strands of her curls were left dangling loose, calculatingly placed there for pretend ease and care-lessness. A predator's trick to lure the naïve prey, unaware of the danger hiding behind the veil of smiles and bouncy, chestnut curls.

A deathly queen indeed.

38

GIDEON

"Last chance to back out." I shook Kaius's hand as he opened the door to the carriage. He laughed as he squeezed my hand back.

"You could only wish." He confidently smiled, buttoning up his brown vest, his invitation hidden well in his pocket. "Tell Ophelia I'll be back by dinner."

"Good luck, my friend." I patted him on his shoulder and watched the carriage depart.

The sky was layered with thick, heavy clouds. Dark and gloomy. Not even a star or a ray of silver moon getting through them but the air —the air was cold and crisp, filled with anticipation. As if it too was aware of what we were planning tonight.

"Xentar didn't disappoint." Zora snuck to me from the shadows of a townhome, also watching as more clouds bunched up together—courtesy of Xentar. Dressed in all black, she was like a shadow herself, moving quickly and undetectable.

"Is everyone ready?" I asked Zora, eyeing as more people joined the crowds striding towards the Royal Castle.

"Yes. Everyone is in their positions, waiting for the signal," Zora whispered, running her fingers up and down the thin black chain linked at her belt—the only sign of her nervousness. I scratched the two-day old stubble on my face. I didn't have a chance to shave today, and it irked me.

Because today I needed everything to go perfect.

"You are distracted, Gideon," Zora sneered. "And if it has something to do with the fact that you wasted another day looking for her, I swear to gods—"

"Perhaps it's because you keep rattling your chain all day." I arched my brow at her, baiting her. She curled her lip in annoyance at me but stopped.

"How many Destroyers are in town?"

"A garrison or two. I'll deal with them."

"You always do." She rolled her eyes at me, and I smirked.

"Try not to get lost in the clouds, cousin."

"Try to come back less charcoaled this time, *cousin*." Zora mimicked my tone and shook her head, before disappearing into the shadows of the night.

In a few quick and silent strides, I joined the flowing mass of people.

39

FINNLEAH

The bright winter sun was well beyond the horizon, leaving only specks of purple hues skidding through the darkening sky. The first couple of stars made their cold appearance, only to be hidden by heavy gray clouds minutes later. I was fully dressed, standing in the living room by the front door, awaiting the light buzzing sound of the steam engines pulling up on the street.

Priya walked down the stairs just as a loud knock rang against the door.

"You look fantastic!" I started beaming with glee. Priya was gorgeous, but that black makeup outlining her eyes and her lips made her look like Death Incarnate herself. She was a Queen, maybe not by title or birth, but she was a queen to be reckoned with and this was her kingdom.

"I *am* fantastic." She winked as she passed me to open the door for Florian.

With no invitation, he walked inside the hall.

His long hair was unbound, resting on his slender shoulders. He wore a dark burgundy tuxedo made from rich velvet. Underneath was a black, crisp shirt with golden buttons, though most of them were left unbuttoned, putting on display that large, eye-catching floral tattoo.

"Oh, gorgeous, you are *stunning*," Florian said in awe as his eyes lingered on me and I couldn't resist but to smile sheepishly.

"You don't look too shabby yourself." I smirked, giving him a welcoming nod.

"Not too shabby? Oh, darling, I look fucking amazing." Florian laughed, taking a few steps closer until he linked our arms and strode to the door.

"Oh gods, I am going to puke," Priya snarled as she looked at us.

His eyes lit in wicked amusement as he extended his hand to Priya.

"As if." She grimaced and walked down the stairs outside until a well-dressed driver bowed and opened the door for her to a slick looking machine.

"I bought a separate one just for you, Priya." Florian and I walked down the steps. "You know, since me and gorgeous over here are planning on staying the whole night...and who knows if things go well enough, maybe we won't be back for another day or two." He clicked his tongue, leaving a fat smile on his face.

Priya flipped him off before the chauffeur shut the door to her vehicle. I chuckled. Sometimes I forgot just how fearless Florian was at pissing her off. She rolled her window down a second later, looking at me.

"Word of advice, Freckles, if you actually want to get good head tonight, don't waste your time with him and find someone who actually knows what they are doing." This time, Florian just rolled his eyes while he viciously ran his tongue across his lips nonstop until Priya closed the window and took off.

My eyes trailed her car quickly departing into the night.

"Well now that the can-do-no-wrong grouch is gone. Let's get this party started." Florian chuckled as he let me in the car and followed behind.

I was pleasantly surprised at the warmth inside the vehicle and the comfort of the cushioned seats. This was definitely like no carriage I had ever been in.

Florian just stared at me with a large grin on his face. I pursed my gloss-covered lips together and squinted my eyes at him.

"You know, staring is rather impolite," I said to him, straightening my dress just a bit.

"Oh, I never bothered to attend etiquette lessons. Rather boring. I only actually attended once. I collected enough frogs to cover half the desks in the class and let them croak and jump while poor Mrs. Eleonore ran in pure panic. So, my manners might be rusty, forgive me, my lady." He bowed his head just low enough to take a good glimpse of my seductively exposed bust. The corset did wonders to my usually boring chest, and I couldn't blame him for taking a quick glance. Even I gawked at that cleavage for a good fifteen minutes, not believing that this was what my body looked like now.

Feminine and even a tad bit seductive.

"You know I won't sleep with you," I teased him. Florian loved to mention sex any chance he got. He might have even been alarmingly obsessed with it, but ever since that very first moment I met him, his eyes and his soft face radiated nothing but comfort and friendship, and a little boyish attitude. At times though, I wondered if he would follow up on the promises he made if I was indeed interested.

Now with this dress on, I had no doubt he most definitely would. Even if it was out of pure physical curiosity. That assurance brought a little bit of satisfaction to my ego.

"Ah." He acted out the dramatic scene of being stabbed in the heart as he slowly slid against the leather chair he was seated on. "You've shattered my heart; o divine angel, I shall never return to live a happy life." He paused, closing his eyes as if dead. "Unless..." He peeked with one eye. "Unless you cure me by showing me your boobs, then I shall come alive again".

He winked and closed his eyes again.

I wholeheartedly laughed. "Who knew a good rack of boobs would be the cure to all broken hearts of men?"

"What can I say, breasts are truly magical," he said, opening his eyes and resting his ankle on top of his knee, his dark brown, leather shoes exposing the small slivers of his skin.

I could see through the layers of his boyish remarks, a charming, well-built Heir of the Drug Empire facade, just him. A life loving boy, now burdened with a soul crushing legacy to uphold. More than anything, he needed a friend.

I understood him.

I needed a friend too.

"So have you ever been to the ball before?" I curiously asked him, breaking the sudden heavy silence.

"Do you insist on insulting me today?" He smiled, raising his eyebrows. "We might not be the *titled* Royals, but Casteols have been the honorary guests for generations now. Ever since the Royals learned that with good opium, their dull lives become so much better. So yeah, I've attended ever since I was old enough. At this point it's more of a tradition for me, but this year, I am spicing things up and bringing you with me."

"Is your grandpa going to be there? And your mother?"

"My grandpa has been at the Royal Castle for two days now. Since all the Royals arrive for this holiday, they usually have a large gathering and discuss all matters of business. Before you ask, yes, I've attended a couple of those before, and honestly, I would rather be tortured by an old snail than spend another hour of my life there unnecessarily. Instead, I get to hear the most important points from their wives later in one way or the other." He winked at me. I knew exactly what other ways he meant. "My mother, on the other hand, does absolutely nothing today, since she gets locked in the apartment." At my eyes raised in question, he continued. "Ever since she got so high that she ran naked across the streets to the palace and fucked a random drunk guy in front of everyone on the palace's front lawn. It made the news. Grandpa was so pissed that she embarrassed him like that; he would murder her for it, but she is his daughter after all, so he instead cut her off any drugs other than alcohol and just left her locked in the house under careful watch, so she has no chance of escaping. She usually gets insanely drunk and spends the day ranging anywhere from being absolutely psychotic to deep asleep."

"That sounds rough. I am sorry." I tried to hide the slight wince at his hidden pain as he casually continued.

"Well believe me, I'd rather have her drunken asleep or even psychotic than trying to pull her naked ass off someone else's cock in front of the Royal crowd when you are thirteen." His lips stretched in a soft smile, but his eyes hid behind a veil of hurt.

At times, I forgot that we were all wounded, in our own ways. In our path, one way or the other, we all fell and scarred ourselves. And those scars never went away. We just got so much better at masking them, even wearing them as if precious jewelry, yet never forgetting the true cost of them.

"Well, I once pretended I was coughing blood when my elven maid questioned the blood on my clothes. She thought I was dying and tried to find any possible cure to heal my lungs until two days later she finally realized it was my first period. She was so mad that I was sure if I wasn't dying before, I would be now. But at one point I was desperate and determined to stick to my lie that I had to put period blood on my face and lips to make my story convincing. So, when it comes to thirteen-year-old embarrassing stories, clearly, I win." I dramatically blinked at him.

"Kinky!" He cackled, his eyebrows raising in sinful questioning. "So, tell me more, did you have to use multiple fingers to check yourself?"

"Ew. You are gross and disgusting." I kicked his leg, and he winced. "Fine, you want something truly kinky? Then..." I pinched my eyebrows together in a snarky grimace. "I raise your stakes for a kinky story."

"Now we are finally getting somewhere." Florian bit his lip in anticipation. He moved his arms until they rested on top of his knees as if preparing for the most intriguing story of his life.

"My first time being on top, I gave my guy the worst splinter-filled, moss carpet burns on his back, like his whole back was bloodied up. The worst part is that he kept quiet the entire time until we were done, and I noticed the blood on his back. He tried to deny it at first but then I spent an hour pulling little pieces of tree bark from scratched up skin. He had to make up a story about how he got hurt but I was so embarrassed."

"Ouch. So ruthless of you... But props to the guy. True gentleman." Florian whole-heartedly laughed.

"He really was. I vowed to never again be on top but quickly broke my promise when he showed up with the horse blankets and leathers and a perfectly raked spot without a single bump." I softly chuckled at the precious little intimate memories running through my mind as a little stream. Ollie. My dark eyed lover, my best friend, my everything.

I painfully smiled.

Gods, I missed him. I missed him so damn much. I missed his forever ruffled hair and those large dimples. I missed his always eager, but at times awkward hugs, his never-ending infectious laugh, that charming smile. I missed his unbroken faith in me and my dreams, his never-ending support even when I had my doubts. Gods of all, I missed how I felt when I was around him. He gave me hope. He gave me a future, and, in the end, he gave his life for me.

Gods, I really fucking missed him.

"Did you love him?" Florian suddenly asked, his gaze strong on my quieted eyes.

"Yes, I did," I said. It was never hard to confess it, even though at times admitting that also meant knowing that love was not all powerful, nor healing or caring. No, for me love would be forever linked with pain and anguish. Because I did. I loved him with everything I had. Even if it was "a child's love," as Tuluma called it, I loved him then and I loved him now, and I was sure a part of me would love him forever.

"He is gone, huh?" Florian carefully asked.

"Yes. Killed by Destroyers." The truth stung each time I thought of it.

"I am sorry, those fiery bastards really need to be put in check." Florian rubbed my knee with his warm long hand. "He does sound pretty fun though."

"He really was." I chuckled, remembering the time I screamed at Ollie for throwing flour at me. Actual flour, that he stole from his father's mill, because he'd found out I'd never seen snow.

"Still, you could never beat my most embarrassing story." Now it was Florian's turn to pull my drifting mind; tugging on a thread, away from that sharp edge leading to the pit filled with grief.

Florian went on, sharing a deeply disturbing yet truly hilarious story until I had to wipe tears from my eyes from laughing. The tears that might have been bottled up for years, stored and preserved for pain and anguish, but now released through pure laughter.

Yes, we were all scarred, yet those imperfections shaped a thing of beauty.

40

The bright, white stone fence was like a fortress wall, thick and tall. Large golden gates opened wide, leading to the most beautiful building in Svitar.

The Royal Castle.

No pictures or postcards could ever do it justice. It was grand, celestial. The rounded towers seemed to be never ending, the carved columns supporting the cut-out bridges leading to the multiple halls and places within the walls.

The long, mahogany carpet lined the way from our car down to the main entrance. There were multitudes of people gathered around, watching the Royalty arrive.

Watching *us* arrive.

Holding Florian's arm tightly, I followed him, slowly making our way to the ballroom. My steps were steady though my heart only sped up at our arrival.

Florian beside me walked confidently, not fazed by the wandering eyes pausing at his presence, even in the crowds. If I didn't know better, I might have taken him for the king himself, considering the amount of people that recognized him or slightly bowed at him. Some of the women were bold enough to give him a lusty smile and a seductive glance as they held the hands of their own husbands.

Perfect, white marble floors, like a mirror, reflected our moving figures inside the ballroom hall. The building was grand. Enormous, Apollon columns stood throughout, supporting the second-floor ring of balconies. Large, ceiling-tall windows were slightly curtained, showing the most gorgeous view of the Svitar and the Kinderby River.

I tried to keep my head still, making a conscious effort to avoid twirling around to see the exotic dancers strung up to the roof with nothing but a cloth line, performing all manner of aerial dances. Far below the sizable stage, a large orchestra played festive melodies, accompanied by the feather light dancers wearing nothing but black feathers and their pointe shoes. I couldn't stop looking at them, moving as if they were nothing but feathers themselves; so elegant, each move so precise, each stroke so effortless.

I didn't notice that we'd stopped until the upbeat voice of Florian snapped me out of my complete infatuation with the dancers.

"Anastacia! What a pleasure to see you!" He smiled, exchanging a couple of kisses on the cheeks of the beautiful dark-haired female.

"Florian, long time no see." She smiled, patting his shoulder with her peacock fan.

"Oh, you know me, always busy with the business. How are things with dear Provost?" he said while wrapping my hands around his arm once again. I couldn't help but notice Anastacia's piercing look at that gesture.

"He is doing his best to stay away from any parties," she said smiling, yet a few notes of frustration made it past her perfect tone. "Who is this gorgeous guest you've brought today?"

My heart slightly fluttered, realizing I had nothing to reply, but Florian continued as if nothing was of less importance than this conversation.

"This is my dear friend, Finn," he said, patting my hand with his.

"Oh, what an interesting name. I don't remember hearing it on any of the Gala Lady Roasters."

"Oh, she is foreign, I am afraid," Florian replied gently, though his eyes already wandered off to another group of beautiful young ladies giggling and waving at him. Anastacia turned to see them, clearly irritated. She took a step closer, blocking them from his view and grabbed my hand in hers. Her hands were so much warmer than mine. Mine were covered in cold sweat, the only proof of my rising anxiety.

"Crowned Lady Anastacia," she introduced herself. "I shall hope we will get to know each other better," she said, smiling at me, yet her eyes never leaving the now uninterested face of Florian.

"My pleasure. I am Finnleah... Daughter of ... The Dead." Florian looked at me slightly amused and surprised as I muttered the words with the so familiar elvish accent. Tuluma's accent. My accent. The one I had hidden so well but never forgot. It felt almost comforting to tweak my tongue just a bit to draw out the words just a notch. Anastacia was slightly taken aback, stumbling, looking for words, but Florian took the opportunity and waved at another lady not too far in the crowd.

"Enjoy the party, Anastacia," he said, bowing so slightly.

"I shall hope to hear from you soon Florian." She smiled and frustratingly bowed back.

But he was already pulling us back into the swelling crowds.

We walked past a dancing crowd and the rushing servants when Florian finally nudged me with his elbow smiling.

"Nice job on that fake accent, gorgeous! And Finnleah, Daughter of the Dead? So much better than Finn like the Fish Finn. Gods, I need to step up my game. Florian Casteol sounds so boring now." Florian smirked while I rolled my eyes.

"For your information, it's always been Finnleah, Daughter of the Dead, and the accent is not fake. I had an elven maid. Before I spoke your language, elvish was my native. It took me years to get rid of that accent."

"Well don't. It's actually pretty hot, not going to lie. Can you say something else so I could remember it better for my fantasies?" he asked, amused.

Discreetly, I elbowed him in the side. Content by his immediate flinch, I continued.

"But really Florian, a crowned princess? Dismissing her, too? I mean how do you even know her?"

Florian heartly laughed.

"Oh, beautiful, I might not have the title, but I am more of a crowned heir than she is. She is like the fifth crowned lady. Royals get obsessed with their presumptuous titles and heirs. Anastacia and I had school together. Come seventh grade, we made out. Once, okay? And before you get defensive, I usually don't kiss and tell, but she was... gods damned awful. Terribly, excruciatingly bad."

He shook his head and frowned dramatically in remembrance of the awfulness.

"Anyway, she has been obsessing over me ever since. Granted, now she is married to a wealthy businessman, Provost. She has the title, he has the money, you know how things are. Women can be very ambitious at times, even at the cost of their own happiness." He nodded to another female, sending a flirtatious smile his way. Before I could say anything, another two ladies stopped by to say hello to Florian, as if he was indeed the crowned Prince himself. One after another, more gorgeous than before. Similarly, each conversation more pointless than before. Yet each girl more eager to land another kiss on his cheek or run her fingers against his arm. After a while, I pretended I was a mute, just smiling and waving.

I learned that I had no interest in wasteful pleasantries and bogus conversations. Instead, I watched, amazed by the dancers or the acrobats spinning in perfect pirouettes and somersaults.

"Gods, you two look utterly disgusting over here mingling with this filth," Priya said, sneaking up behind us while we hid in the shadows of the large column, avoiding the crowds.

"Priya. Would you like a kiss too?" Florian smirked as Priya imitated the kissing that everyone greeted Florian with.

"It is astounding you all are not dead of some serious disease," she grumped.

Florian rolled his eyes while I chuckled. Priya had a point.

"How is the hunting going, Mother Death?" Florian asked as we all stood scanning the ever-moving crowd.

"Not very fruitful," Priya said irritated, her eyes pinning the large woman with an even larger wig surrounded by a few people, including guards. "When do the rest of them arrive?" she asked Florian, stealing a small appetizer off a clueless waiter passing by.

"Right about now," Florian whispered, and if on cue, the loud trumpets sounded through the noisy crowd, making everyone pause and bow as the doors opened wide and the lines of Royal guards walked in, making way for the Royal Queen and King to arrive. They made their way up the pedestal and sat on the large carved thrones. With a swift motion of the King's hand, the crowd rose as one.

"Pricks need to learn how to walk faster," Priya whispered in the back, rubbing her cramped neck. I stifled the smile.

I was about to turn to Priya when the music changed again, and the crowd stayed still as more Royal Lords and Ladies slowly marched, walking up all the way to the throne, personally bowing to the reigning couple.

"Who are they?" I asked, still slightly bowing each time, while yet another Lord strode in. followed by his guards.

"These are all the Royal Lords and Ladies of the Esnox," Florian replied.

"I thought most of the crowd were Royals?" I asked, slightly confused, ignoring the growing ache in my neck.

"They are. In one way or other. But these Lords," he whispered, continuing swiftly, bowing his head once more. "These ones have not only titles and money but *land*. Given by Queen Insanaria herself to rule over."

"Is the Mad Queen going to come as well?" I asked as my skin shivered even thinking of her.

"No, she has been letting Destroyers do all her dirty work. People haven't seen her in years now."

Priya huffed in annoyance, completely uninterested in our conversation, but Florian went on.

"That one is Lord Ferola. Ruler of the Western Isles." The tall man in his late forties walked upright with the young, barely of age lady by his side. I raised my brows at that, Florian's quiet whisper continued.

"He is on his third wife, yet still no heir, people question why. My guess? Might be something to do with the fact that he has a boyfriend, but that's just my opinion." Florian shrugged. "That one, Lord Reinar, ruler of the Greenwich Pastures. During the Great Fall, he murdered his own family and then traded his niece who was a low tier Creator to the Mad Queen for the right to the land."

The crowd bowed again.

"That one is Lady Eanaya. Ruler of the Cursed Lands, or as she renamed them, Forgotten lands." The old lady was quite petite, surrounded by the large number of the guards. She brought the most guards of all the Royals. "She's been super paranoid recently; in my opinion she's been hitting the opium too much. The last time her head maid was in town she said that she painted her mansion in weird symbols and is just losing her mind slowly. It's really a shame. That lady did some crazy shit back in her prime."

Florian continued dropping names and gossip about every Lord and Lady that walked in and every important guest that followed.

"How do you know everyone and everything?" I said as Florian mentioned more head-turning gossip.

"Oh, precious, I am a barman in the most prestigious club." He flicked my nose and pridefully smirked. "You'd be shocked just how little it takes for a person to open up when you give them a listening ear and a kindhearted smile."

"I am sure it has nothing to do with you getting them drunk," I whispered back, even though deep inside, I knew firsthand of Florian's soothing presence.

"I got to make my job interesting somehow." He smiled, fixing a small strand of his hair behind his ear.

"That's my cue," Priya said, slipping out like a shadow towards the now departing Baroness past the crowds, disappearing behind the large doors leading to the rest of the castle.

"Good luck!" I wished her, though sure she wouldn't hear me. Florian didn't heed to her leaving.

"That one, you see, is a prickly bastard. He rules over the largest piece of land and controls the majority of the overseas trade too. He might not look like it but don't be fooled, he is a force to be reckoned with. Especially considering all those rock and salt quarries he runs."

A loud bell rang in my head at those words. I turned sharply to the entrance to see the face I had seen before.

"Lord Inadios," I whispered. My heart froze as I watched that large, familiar figure make his way across the ballroom. That limp, those pig-like features, still imprinted in my mind as if it was yesterday. As if I was still on my scraped knees in front of him.

Florian stumbled slightly in surprise.

"Yes. You know him?"

"I...." I paused, debating. There was nothing of a reason that would explain how or why I knew him. *A truth or a lie?* I asked myself, but the truth was too long to unravel, and I just ran out of time.

A lie it is.

"I don't feel too good. Can we maybe go outside?" I asked. Perhaps more of a truth now that my heart pounded against my chest and the tight leash that kept my anxiety at bay. It was ripping with each step of that man and his guards closer to the crowd. Closer to me.

"Um, sure." Florian's brows bunched up in concern. "Not sure how we are going to leave right now... but..."

The air in the room dropped a few degrees. For a minute, I thought it was just me who noticed the sudden change. A familiar yet unknown slight stench filled the air. Florian turned his head back to the walls, looking for another door leading outside per my request.

But I stopped.

My heart, my mind, my entire soul froze.

The blood in my veins chilled as I saw silver robed figures floating in, just a few inches above the ground. Their heads covered with hoods, exposing a pointy chin from beneath. The tight, almost see-through skin showing dark blue or black veins.

Kahors.

I didn't dare speak, didn't dare breathe. *Kahors* were here.

Kahors.

As if awoken by a spark, my thoughts exploded, flooding with the memories, panic and sheer terror. Still, I stood motionless.

"Ouch." Florian snatched his arm out of my hand that I involuntarily gripped too tight. "What was that for?" he asked, rubbing his hand against his forearm. "Gods, is this blood? Finn, why are you bleeding?" He grabbed my hand. "What is going on?" His forehead wrinkled in perplexity.

My eyes widened as I saw the little drop of blood on his velvet jacket. My innocent small cut from this morning reopened, treacherously letting small drops of bright red roll down my finger.

Blood.

My blood.

It was past the point of return, I realized. There was no time to decide something, to plan. Not when Kahors would smell my blood within the next breath.

I made a mental check of all my securely latched daggers; the poisonous pins still attached well in my hair. The crowd whispered loud at Kahor's arrival, but I didn't pay attention to them.

I had to go right now. *Act then think.*

Act then *think*, I murmured to myself. There was no time for hesitation. I turned my head to the large doors that were still guarded. Lord Inadios and the Kahors were just one look, one glance, away from seeing me.

I started walking in the opposite direction, pushing through the crowd painfully slow, but I couldn't afford to draw in any attention.

"Excuse us. Excuse us," Florian's voice echoed in the back as I made my way closer to the columns by the wall, to the windows. A bad plan; a terrible plan, but a plan, nonetheless. If I couldn't get out of the castle, I would hide behind the curtains, I would break the window. I would run.

I would escape.

"Slow down, Finn. Where are you going?" Florian's voice sounded just a step away from me. The crowd's noise rose, slightly unsettled, but I didn't dare look behind me, slipping closer to those large columns, hoping their shadows would cover at least some of me.

"Gods, can you just stop for a minute and explain what's going on for gods' sake?" Florian finally yanked my hand, pulling me to a complete stop. Our eyes met just for a second,

"It's—"

The large entrance doors slammed open as loud screams erupted in the room.

"REBELS! REBELS ARE HERE!"

41

I blinked so slow. The world itself paused. My lungs burned as heavy stone dust settled deep within them. Loud ringing hijacked my ears. *Breathe. See. Hear.* My mind whispered to me.

A labored slow breath. My chest ached.

My mouth was so dry. Mind blank, just listening to that nonstop flat ringing.

I rubbed my eyes. Stinging pain in my arm woke up my haze filled brain.

It was so silent.

Why was it so quiet?

What happened to the orchestra?

To those singers? To those loud trumpets?

For a second, I thought I was dreaming as the red velvety petals of carnation flowers fell upon me, landing on my body completely covered in dust and rubble. I stretched my hand out as if reaching for the invisible cloud of flowers above me that rained red petals. My arm was surprisingly powdered white, except that large streak of dark red as if paint against the canvas.

Blood.

Gods, it was blood?

The sound hit me only a few seconds later. It was a cry of terror. The loud screaming mixed with complete dead silence of the large crowd.

The rubble, broken stones, and shattered windows were everywhere. The dark, thickly clouded sky appeared where the ceiling was only minutes ago.

The realization of what happened snapped me out of my mist immediately. There was no more crowd. No orchestra or artists singing, just limp bodies covered in dust and rubble from the blown-up roof, with survivors wailing around them.

Florian.

Oh gods, Florian.

I shook the debris off my body, getting up on my legs, thanking Fate that nothing was broken.

"Finn?"

My heart dropped as I heard his voice. I stumbled over rubble to him. He laid on the floor still, just inches away from the large broken piece of a column, remnants of it crumbled behind him.

I took a quick glance at him. The shattered glass pieces were embedded in his skin, his face.

"Gods, Florian." I shoved tears back, though they were still probing their way out.

Not right now. I gritted my teeth. Not now. I shredded the fear away, though my voice still shook just a bit.

"Are you okay?" I cried, pulling the rubble off his body.

"Well, I am pretty sure my leg and arm are broken." He tried scooting an inch closer but immediately stopped, clenching his jaw from pain. "Add to that a rib or two."

I lowered to my knees to help him adjust away from the still crumbling ceiling. Once he was secure, I quickly pulled a few pieces of broken glass out of his face.

"Ouch. Finn, I am starting to realize you just love seeing men bleed. Name the time and place and I'll be down, but so openly in public. Good for you for being so open with your kinks." Florian winced from pain.

I gave him an angry look before yanking on another large shard stuck in his cheek.

"This is not the time nor the place for your stupid jokes Florian," I said as I pulled one of my daggers out and cut my dress in pieces to wrap his wounds.

"It is *always* time for stupid jokes, Finn." He blinked heavily. I flinched as I moved his broken arm into a makeshift sling. Florian's eyes unwillingly rolled for a second.

"Don't you dare pass out on me." I slapped his face. He shuddered from pain but still smirked.

"Gods, if only I knew all it took for you to start ripping your clothes off for me was getting bombed, then I would've done it sooner," he whispered with his eyes still closed shut, taking slow, painful breaths.

I took another look around. The red petals of the carnation flowers, as if blood, covered the whole ballroom floor. People of all kinds were climbing out of the rubble as if dead bodies were rising out of the ground. A few patrons were now up, still shaky and slightly dizzy, they rushed off to cry for help and find their companions, or what was left of their bodies.

Within seconds, new Royal Guards poured in, rows of medics following them.

My head sharply turned to the door several feet away.

"Priya," I gasped. I made a step towards the door but hesitated.

"Go find her, Florian said. "I'll be just fine. I promise not to *walk* away."

"I'll be back," I said as I rushed to the castle doors.

42

Priya. Gods, if she was hurt, or if she was captured... thoughts raced through my mind, fighting the raising panic.

I had to find her.

The guards were long gone, letting me easily sneak past the large doors. The ripped tail of my beautiful dress left on the ground was the only evidence of my presence. I adjusted my holster full of daggers to my thighs, just one quick reach away.

The air in the castle was warmer, heavier; quite a change from the freezing, dust-filled air of the ruined ballroom. There was no breeze, and surprisingly it was so vacant. Not a single guard, not a servant. Empty and dark.

All the guards must have rushed to help and so did the servants, but the lack of light? Not even a single oil lamp lit up in the midst of the castle? That I couldn't explain.

I passed room after room, now coming up the wide, wooden staircase. While the outside of the castle was built out of stone, the inside was made out of the darkest exquisite wood, carved and polished.

I stayed cautious of my moves, aware of each step in the pitch darkness. Each step quieter than the previous, not a single squeak escaped as I made it upstairs. Large, stained-glass windows served as the only source of light. I welcomed it, though shadows bouncing off the nice furniture along the perimeter made me uneasy.

I wandered further down the hall. Only now that my mind was calmed, I realized that this was quite a bad idea.

Clearly, I wasn't thinking straight looking for Priya in a castle I had never been in. I had no clue where I was going, or where she was.

I had a higher chance of getting lost than finding her.

I stifled an angry grunt within me. I should just go back, stay with Florian, and wait for Priya there, instead of uselessly wandering the castle.

I turned sharply to walk back and saw a creeping shadow then.

This time it was not mine.

A quick shiver went through my body and goosebumps rose. Gods, was I really that afraid of the dark?

I noticed then the cherry wood door slightly opened, letting in a little flicker of light and a mingling shadow.

I should go back.

Ignore it.

But instead, I took another step towards the door, dagger out, ready to strike.

I tightened my grip, even though cold sweat covering my hands made it difficult. My whole body stiffened as I willed it to take another step closer to the door until my fingers slightly pushed it further open.

Our eyes met within a second. His were so light blue. He was tall and well built. I quickly sized him up. He glanced over me.

The man was dressed in a suit, yet there was none of the luxury of the ball attendees; the worn-out elbows and patched up knees were a loud indicator of it. The ruffled shirt and unbuttoned vest exposed a few well-made daggers, neatly sheathed in his holster—within his reach.

I didn't dare move my eyes from him. Though out of the corner of my eyes, I could tell I was in a large study, with books and shelves, but more importantly a large desk. The unknown man must have been rummaging through the stacks of papers and drawers, the loose cabinets and half-opened bookcases were left messy in a hurry.

He was clearly an intruder.

But so was I.

Yet if this was some royal scheme, then he could easily blame me for his actions since I was clearly the only witness of his presence here.

Shit.

I was now not only a witness to crime but an accomplice too?

I readied my dagger.

A few seconds. All it took for him to decide that whatever... whoever I was and what I was doing was no threat or concern of his, as he nervously smiled at me first, and then looked back down to the stacks of papers all over the desk and started shoving a few of them in his hidden pockets of his brown jacket.

I saw the little red carnation flower tattooed on his wrist as he moved his hand close to the candles to look over another paper.

A *red* carnation flower.

He realized his mistake too late. As he paused, stilling his wrist, quite aware of his exposed mark.

A Rebel.

His summer eyes filled with desperation, as if a summer storm. But not the desperation that leads to begging. No, it was a look of someone desperate enough to kill, to fight no matter the cost.

I recognized that look because I had seen it in my own eyes.

My eyes narrowed as I adjusted my wrist just so slightly, discreetly aiming my dagger. I watched his shadow covered body take a slow, calculating breath, preparing to make a fatal move.

A quick move. A shadow behind him. He drew his dagger, but it was too late. The clasping fingers of the Kahor were on his neck. The stranger didn't even have the time to gasp as Kahors teeth sunk into his flesh.

My eyes widened in panic or shock or just pure terror. I wasn't sure.

Act then think, I willed myself.

One swift motion. One quiet move and my dagger landed straight into the center of the hooded head of the Kahor. The eyes of the Rebel blinked in horror, but the Kahor just pulled its long teeth out of the bloodied flesh and hissed.

"You. You are the girl from the Rock Quarry." The Kahor let the bloodless Rebel drop onto the floor as he moved swiftly towards me, my dagger still deeply rooted in his brain.

Fuck. Fucking fuck.

I needed to run. But there was no point. Even if I could. They would rip my veins out within seconds, within my single breath.

I rapidly reached for the neatly hidden dagger on my back.

Heart Piercer.

There was no time to aim. There was no *need* to aim as the large, hooded figure was floating in the air just mere steps away. Without a single breath I shoved Heart Piercer deep into its flesh straight to its heart.

The Kahor's body went limp and then loudly fell against the floor. Black, sticky liquid seeping through its cloak. My arm was still out, though empty, Heart Piercer left deep inside the creature.

I didn't dare pull the dagger out even as I pushed the hood off and I saw the nightmare-like face. An eyeless creature, only with holes instead of a nose and a large monster-like mouth filled with those sharp teeth.

I gagged. The increasing reek almost made my guts hurl until I turned my eyes to the desk.

The stranger.

That rebel.

I rushed across the room to the messed-up desk and the body right next to it. He was alive, yet his blood was a constant stream, running from his neck over his hands as he tried to apply pressure to it. I ripped another piece of my dress and wrapped it again and again. The wound was too big. I added more of my cloth, now using both of my hands to apply pressure.

"You are going to bleed out," I told him, but he slowly rose to his feet using his desk to support him.

"We have to go." He used his hands on his neck now. He was so pale. Too pale.

I followed him without a question.

"You killed it?" he asked, pausing just for a second by the dead creature. I stopped too, ignoring the slight notes of surprise in his voice.

"If I pull the dagger out, will he come back?" I asked the stranger.

"I don't know. Usually, you have to behead them completely," he said, walking through the door into the hall. The blood running through his fingers slowed down, almost stopping, though his jacket was thoroughly soaked with it.

I hesitated for a second but then quickly drew another dagger out and severed the Kahor's head, choking as I sliced through the rotten tissue and cartilage until its head rolled away. Only then did I rip out Heart Piercer and rush out of the room. The rebel was already a few strides ahead. I took a step towards him but then hesitated.

I glanced at the two ends of the hall, both dark and empty.

Unsure. I was so damn unsure of which path to take.

"Are you coming?" he finally asked, breaking the silence. His voice echoed through the darkness. I didn't reply and he took another slow step further away. His body dizzy from the movement.

Are you coming? His invitation hung heavy in the air.

Such an easy question to ask and such a difficult one to answer.

Are you joining the cause?

Are you joining the Rebels?

Am I?

I felt that strong *Yes* before my mind could even create a thought. As if Fate herself stood there, pushing me to follow him. To follow a stranger into the dark.

I glanced towards the rebel, now only a mere shadow down the path.

"To hell with reason," I whispered to myself, dismissing my last doubts as I quickly closed the distance between us.

43

He swayed and I wrapped his arm around my shoulder, using myself as a crutch.

"Thank you," he said as he heavily blinked, but continued on walking, without letting go of my shoulder.

"Where are we going?" I whispered as we made our way further into the castle, all of it so poorly lit I could barely make it past the large tapestry and wood carved walls.

"Once we get to the stairs, there is a secret passage under the stairwell behind the sunflower painting. It will lead through the sewers and then there will be a boat waiting for me."

"Okay," I said as he slowed down even more, each step harder than the last.

Stairs, sunflower painting, sewers and a boat. I repeated the directions in my head as if a key to a password.

The man wavered again, almost blacking out.

"Hey." I tugged on his jacket, pulling him back. He shivered but straightened up. He was getting colder by the second.

We had to hurry now.

We had crossed yet another large hall, leaving behind the only lit up space we had. Though completely swallowed by the darkness now, the rebel led us through as if he knew every step like the back of his hand.

He stopped to take a heavy breath.

I stayed quiet, unsure of what to say. He was a stranger and I had saved his life from the Kahor, only for Death to demand it back.

"Almost there," he whispered; more for himself than me.

The loud canine barking sliced my ears. My heart panicked as I quickly drew a dagger, anticipating the inevitable attack.

A second later, a large fluffy animal crashed into us. Yet instead of devouring us, the dog was crying and licking and whacking us with its long tail, unable to stay still.

"Hey Gera. Hey, hey, hey girl." The rebel dropped to his knees, letting go of my arm as he hugged the dog and petted her without a stop. The dog barked again and again as if she was talking to him, complaining, yet her body was unable to stay still, overtaken with excitement and pure joy. He, as if understanding, talked with her.

"Hey, I missed you too, I missed you so much, baby girl. I know. I know."

As if by command, the hall lit up all at once, blinding me wholly. By reflex my eyes closed shut, adjusting.

It cost me a blink, as I opened my eyes and faced two groups of fully armed Royal guards approaching us with their weapons out, surrounding us.

The rebel paused, even as the large dark dog whimpered around him still. He didn't move his hand away from her but made an attempt to stand up.

Tried and failed.

My mind was no longer panicking. No, panic was long gone, replaced by calculating instinct to survive.

The approaching guards circled us.

One man behind us laughed cruelly. His laugh was psychotic, unhinged.

I sharply turned to see him. The rebel next to me didn't.

"Long time no see, Kaius." The head of the guard addressed the rebel, taking a few steps closer to us but still a spear length away.

Kaius, as if completely unaware of the guards or the man behind him continued to pet his dog with whatever strength he had left.

I glanced over to him, trying to understand, trying to plan.

But I saw it then. Gut wrenching defeat. Almost invisible, but a trace of loss on his face.

Utter defeat, as he stayed kneeling down, letting the dog lick his face, his bloodied-up hands.

"You know at first, I was going to murder her. Torture, then skin her alive and use her fur as a rug in the barracks. But then..." the man paused. "Then, I realized that you would come back for her. You never loved anything more than that stupid dog." The head of the guard strode casually around us until he faced us. "Did you know you can retrain any dog, even the most loyal and stubborn to obey every command of yours if you torture them long enough?" He leered.

My eyes went back and forth. Between the lined-up guards, between the so painfully weak and weary Kaius and the happy dog, the head of the guard, his malicious eyes. I watched his face fill with disgust as he looked at the dog.

"Yet even after a couple of years you make a step within these walls and she feels your presence here, as if you never left. Runs for you as if you never abandoned her." Kaius winced at those words, and the head of the guard sneered in amusement from that. "You know, I wouldn't even know you were here if it wasn't for her going completely insane. So, I guess she served her purpose after all. Come Gera." He raised his voice at the unaware dog. She hesitated for a minute, looking straight at Kaius's face, her happy tongue hanging out, the wagging tail pausing in the air, as if asking for permission, waiting for Kaius to give the command. "Come, you stupid dog," Head of the guard shouted again. She paused; her ears slumped down, but she obediently came to her new master.

I watched as he pulled his sword out and with one swift move, he stabbed her deeply in her chest. Kaius flinched so hard, as if a part of him got pierced too.

Gera only had a chance to whimper once. As if her last chance to say goodbye, not to us but to Kaius. As if to tell him that last time, that she was so happy he came back. Her body went limp a second later, her fluffy tail just laying flat, unable to ever wag in excitement again.

The guard pulled his sword out of her lifeless body, letting the dark blood pool around her.

"Now that, that is out of the way. Let's find out who you are?" He looked at me with his bloodlust eyes.

I didn't answer. My eyes still pinned on the motionless body of Gera, rage building up, bubbling so close to the surface as if a magma ready to burst out of a slumbering volcano.

"Is this your new slut?" he asked, taking a step closer to me. I turned my eyes to him, but his were on Kaius. "How does your whore of a wife feel about it?" He laughed again. A few guards chuckled. A few stayed still as if also shocked by the violent death still lingering in the air.

Kaius's eyes narrowed.

"Leave my wife out of this." He left it at that, unable, unwilling, to say a word more.

A truth or a lie. The only weapons I could wield right now.

I took a calming breath and confidently said.

"I am just a lost guest. I've never met this man before. There was an explosion and I got disoriented and clearly lost. When I came to my senses, I saw him in the hall hurt so we've been trying to make our way back, but I think we got even more lost since there was no light. We were looking for help since he is clearly hurt. And now I am not just lost but completely baffled and puzzled."

A sliver of hope glittered in me as I saw that pause. His face changed only for a second, as if believing... no, *considering* my story.

It was a lie, but like any good lies it was mixed with truth.

"A lost guest, you say?" He took another step, taking a hard look at me from head to toe.

"Yes, sir," I said, now nodding my head just a tiny bit, a survivor's costume I was so comfortable wearing. "I don't know this man, and I don't know the reason for this ambush, but I demand to be treated with respect as I am a Royal guest."

He paused, as if surprised at my sudden found voice.

"A Royal guest, huh?" He narrowed his eyes. I swallowed hard as I watched him lower his eyes from the dagger in my hand down to my exposed thighs. Precisely on my visibly secured daggers, just within a reach of my fingertips.

A quick draw and I had a chance of killing him, yet against the twenty soldiers, I was powerless.

"A lady of nobility and yet carrying enough ammunition for an army..." His eyes met with mine. I glared back, unyielding. "One would say this is," he motioned with his hand to my daggers. "More fitting for an assassin... or a *Rebel*."

My heart sank. But I wouldn't fold, not now. Not until the end.

Though I could see my lie crumbling slowly.

"I am deeply offended by what you are insinuating, sir. But given the circumstances of this terrible night I shall be graceful and forgive you for it, and I shall also provide you with the proof. Ask the crowned Lady Anastacia and she will vouch for me."

His face changed slightly at the mention of Lady Anastacia, yet even that was not convincing enough as he barked at his guards.

"Take them both." He pointed at Kaius. "I will question him and her..." I paused, waiting for my own judgment. "Keep her until I figure out what and who she is."

44

The group of guards hurried towards us, dragging us through the castle all the way down to the dungeons below. They didn't bother to bind us or cover our eyes. No, they transported us to the dungeons and locked us behind metal bars in a dark, tall, cave-like cell.

The night was dark; even the moon was hiding behind the thick and heavy clouds. The small round opening in the ceiling, as big as a hand, served as the only source of light or fresh cold air, but none of it mattered.

I didn't try to resist them, all twenty of them walked us down. I didn't fight them as they shoved me roughly, until I tripped and fell down to my knees. Kaius was already there, resting against the cold stone wall, his eyes closed, his legs straightened, his arms hanging down, no longer holding the slow bleeding wound.

The moment the guards' steps sounded far enough, I rushed to him, putting my hand to his bloodied, cold neck, applying as much pressure as I could. I paused only for a minute, trying to rip another part of my dress. My daggers were taken, except for one. I pulled Heart Piercer from behind, hidden well in the sewn sheath in the back of my dress. I cut another large piece of fabric and wrapped it as tight as I possibly could without choking him out, keeping my hand pressed on his wound.

The warm blood kept on leaking, even now.

Gods, it would not clot at all, as if the Kahor's bite was an anticoagulant.

I lowered my head to his chest. His face was so pale. His heart was so quiet that I had to feel his chest expand—the only sign that he was alive.

"Kaius, wake up. Stay awake, Kaius." I moved his shoulders and pinched him hard.

He finally grunted, shrugging a bit.

"Oh, thank gods!" I whispered in relief as he slightly moved.

"I am so thirsty...." he mumbled without opening his eyes.

"What do we do now?" I asked, determined. No panic in my voice, just a simple soldier asking for direction from a commander.

"Nothing..." he said, his tone full of defeat.

I fought my rising frustration.

I ran inventory in my head of my possessions. A few poisoned pins and a dagger. I also had sleeping powder in my ring, yet only enough for one person. Not enough to escape alive.

Short of poisoning myself and stabbing Kaius, my options were quite grim.

I was left with nothing but hope.

Hope that Lady Anastacia would remember me...or that she was at least alive and coherent enough to testify to my alibi.

But then there was the matter of Kaius.

"Who are you?" I finally asked, looking at his still body.

"I used to be Head of the Royal Guard," he whispered, just loud enough for me to hear.

"As in *the* Royal guard?" I asked, not wasting energy to hide the surprise in my tone or my face. "And now you are a Rebel? How did that happen?"

I asked, adjusting my sore arm just a bit to continue holding tight his messed-up neck.

"It's rather ironic if you think..." He took another heavy breath.

"To be back in the same dungeons where it all began. To die here. Fate has her humor, doesn't she?"

I ignored that bit about "dying here." I had no such plans, but I wouldn't argue with him, wouldn't try to prove him wrong. I had been defeated before. No words or stern actions can raise you up from the bottom. Only your own strength, only your own desire.

Nobody can make you want to actually live except yourself.

"You've been here before? How did you escape?"

"I didn't. I was in here, but I was on the other side. My wife was in *here*. I was the Head of the Royal Guard when they captured a group of Magic Wielders and brought them here. She was one of them. I knew she was a Creator. I knew because I was the one locking her up and giving her only a few months before the grand execution. I'd come to see them personally, to laugh at them, to see the monsters they were...But instead of monsters or demons, I met her. She was the most beautiful and smart woman I had ever met. I knew it was wrong, I knew I shouldn't, but I kept coming back every day, at first just under the disguise of security and then before I could admit to anyone, I knew I was done for. There is no magic stronger than love and I was so in love with her. Still am." He painfully smiled as if remembering her. "So, I made a plan. I freed her and her people and told them to run. But she refused to go without me, telling me that she cared for me, breaking me and making me all within one sentence. That's a thing they don't tell you about love. It might be petrifying but it's the most beautiful thing there is. So, I abandoned everything that day and I left with her. We joined the Rebels. I married her shortly after."

His voice shattered just a bit. "Gods, my son." He opened his eyes as if the realization hitting him was more painful than anything he had experienced before. "My son...I won't be able to see my son... Gods, I will never get to meet him." Small tears rolled down his cheeks. "She's only a couple of months away from delivery. Gods, I won't be there for her either."

I blinked a few times, hiding away my watery eyes. There were no heart wrenching sobs or loud screams, just silent tears rolling down our cheeks.

I wasn't sure why I was crying. I knew life was cruel. People died each day; we were just living our lives ignorant of that. A survival mechanism really. Yet stripped of that ignorance, I hurt. My heart broke for his soon to be widow and fatherless son.

Shattered in so many pieces.

I swallowed hard, steadying my voice.

"Why do you do it? Be a Rebel, fight the Royals. Risk your life. Risk everything. Why do any of that?" I asked.

I wanted to know why. I *needed* to know why.

I might have agreed with the Rebels. I had seen, no, I had experienced enough of the horrors brought by the Mad Queen and her Royal lackeys, that I recognized that desire to fight it, to stand up for injustice.

Yet was this cost worth it?

Dying on the cold floor in the dungeons far below the castle. Far away from anyone to even hear your plea? Far away from anyone, left only with a stranger to comfort your last dying breaths. Was *this* worth it?

"Because it is the right thing to do." He shivered now nonstop. "Because I want my son to live free, I want my wife to live free, without a fear of persecution, without the constant threat of death and torture. Because I want the world to be a beautiful thing. A place of comradery and peace, a place of love and unity. And for that I've joined the cause. I might have been born a regular human with no magic and no gifts, but I've lived my life ignorant enough. My wife was my salvation and with her, we've created a new life, our precious son. For that alone, I would live this painful life again and again. For him to live a better life? Yes, all of this was worth it." He clenched his jaw hard, attempting to stop teeth from chattering.

I wished I had a blanket or a jacket or anything to wrap his now frozen body, to warm him up. I didn't have any of that, but I did have my body.

"You are freezing. I am going to give you a tight hug," I stated, as I moved my body closer to him. He didn't object.

We sat in silence. My thoughts, as if given up, calmed too. Gone were all the plans and all the strategies, as the dried salt streaks from tears earlier.

"I am dying," he finally said. "I will be dead soon and... maybe... it's the last gift of Fate to die here and not out there with them. At a place that I called home for so many years." His voice broke just once, and I sniffled again as a new stream of tears flooded me.

Gods, the thoughts were quiet, yes.

But the feelings? No, the feelings were overtaking me.

"Gera will be so happy." He smiled through his silent tears. "We will be reunited so soon."

I bit my lip hard to stop myself from sobbing. Gone was the strong façade I had built up and the cold heart I pretended to have.

Life was just so cruel.

Hell. To hell with all the gods, but let this man live, somehow, please. I begged, desperate. Yet no spirit appeared to save him.

He grabbed my hand tight, a sudden moment of gained clarity, and shoved a few papers in it.

"I need you to take these to the Rebels. *Promise me* to deliver these to them. Our future depends on it." He commanded me in the tone of the commander of the Royal guard. I stumbled in thoughts, in feeling, in words.

"I am not a Rebel." I shook my head. "I don't even know how to get to them. I... I won't even make it out of here," I protested.

I knew this was a Deadman's promise. A promise I couldn't keep.

I had given so many broken promises it made me sick to think of one more.

I couldn't.

"You might not be a Rebel, but you are a fighter. I need you to deliver them, *please. Please, promise me.*"

"I don't even know where to find Rebels. I am a runaway slave, Kaius. I am no soldier," I said, wincing at the truth spoken out loud.

A runaway slave.

A slave.

I never said it out loud, not like that. Not admitting something that constantly nagged in my mind.

I was no Magic Wielder, no soldier, or a fighter. I was a runaway, useless slave. Chains might have been gone, but I still felt like a prisoner.

He shoved the papers back into my hand, our eyes locking in. His bright blue eyes flickered with the silver streaks.

"A *runaway* slave. You've *escaped* slavery, not many people do that. You've survived this far, and you've killed a Kahor, and… you've saved my life. Don't let fears diminish your true capacity." He clasped my hand in his.

"I don't even know where or how to find them?" I countered in desperation. "I spent months looking for them without a single trace." Now tears were a stream running on my cheeks, I wiped them quick.

"Go as far north as you can, and you'll find them. Go past the Cursed Forest. Find Gideon. He will know what to do with these. *Promise* me."

I hated myself for saying it as my mouth slurred the words.

"I *promise.*"

"Thank you." He smiled in relief as if he was finally able to rest.

"Take this ring." Kaius pulled the large family crest ring off his finger and handed it off to me. "When you find the Rebels, give it to my wife and my son. Tell them… tell them that I loved them more than I loved anything else in the world. Tell them that I am sorry. So …so sorry." His voice broke then, small shrugs now interrupting his body convulsions. "I am so sorry…. Tell my Ophelia to never let her light go dull. Tell her that I will see her again. That Gera and I are reunited now, that we will watch over them and we shall see her again one day, on the other side of the veil."

He clenched his jaw, shaking uncontrollably. I held him tighter. A second later he turned completely still, his body now so heavy and limp against mine.

I sobbed then.

The tears poured out of me like a spring river overflowing its banks.

I sobbed until there were no tears left, until my eyes hurt, and my lips cracked.

254

I wasn't sure why I cried so much, but it broke me.

I hadn't cried like this in years. I hadn't cried like this since I was in the charcoaled forest, covered in ash. I hadn't cried like this since the day I lost everything.

It was all too much. So much to cry about. So much to pour out.

But the tears began to stop, the shaky breaths slowed, and I sat in the cold cave, feeling so drained and numb. There was nothing inside of me of substance, just pure emptiness now. I still clung to Kaius's body, not willing to let go of him yet. I rested the back of my head against the cold wall. My arms ached from hugging him, and my legs had long fallen asleep.

As if some cruel joke, my mind ran to an ironic phrase that was so commonly spoken today.

"Happy Death Day, Finn," I said to myself and then added, "Happy birthday, Daughter of the Dead." I bit my bottom lip again; afraid I'd spiral down into the abyss.

I heard the approaching steps from afar. I didn't move, emptily staring at the opening in the ceiling. I could feel Death walking near me, so close, feasting on the souls of those long gone. Even now, she wouldn't leave, still here lingering, still waiting to see if Fate would push me further, as if knowing that I had thought about it, as if knowing that behind those burn marks on my wrists were other scars hidden. The only lingering proof of my broken soul.

I thought about using those poisoned pins on me. I knew it would be painful, but I was patient. I could endure pain. Surely, I had endured enough so far. I could set myself free and forget about all of this. Yet my fingers didn't move to pull the pins. They didn't move to pull the dagger out either.

No, instead I slipped Kaius's ring on my finger, subconsciously realizing a simple truth. I wouldn't do it. I couldn't do it even though I wanted to; though I craved that freedom.

I had made a promise.

A promise to live a better life.

A promise to see Viyak again.

A promise that even as I go down, I would take down the evil Destroyer with me.

A promise to find the Rebels. I would keep the promise; not for them, not for me, but for Kaius, for his son.

I would keep all my promises, I decided then.

Fate or not, I would keep my promises until my last breath, no matter how long it would take.

45

The loud clunk of metal pulled me from my deep thoughts. My heart hardened and my neck stiffened. I quickly shoved the papers deep into my bra under the cover of darkness.

"He is already dead so don't bother," I bitterly said to whatever soldier was here.

"Well don't be so gloomy, Freckles." Priya's sarcastic voice echoed through the dungeons.

"Priya?! Gods, Priya?! What are you doing here?" My chest rose in surprise. I slid Kaius's body to the side, getting up to my feet.

"Saving your sorry ass, Freckles, *clearly,*" Priya said as she unlocked the gate. I rushed to her, throwing my arms around her.

"*Priya,*" I just mumbled as she pushed me away.

"You are filthy," she said, taking a better look at me now that we were close.

"There was an explosion and then I went to look for you and I saw him and I…"

"Yeah, I don't care. We need to go," she said, glancing over the half open door just a few levels above us and already starting her way up. I glanced over the cold body of Kaius, saying my goodbyes, silently promising him again that his sacrifice was not in vain. I twisted his ring on my finger and clenched my fist.

"Freckles, get your fucking ass going *right now*," Priya grumbled as she moved swiftly up the stairs. I followed.

Priya waited for me as I caught up with her after two flights of stairs.

"Ugh, your daggers are gone. Poison?" She looked over my body again now that the open door to the dungeon lit up the stairs.

"Pins are good, powder just for one." I mentally recounted the still well-hidden pins.

"Good," Priya said as she took another look at the open door leading to the castle. At the dead bodies lining the entrance. "Because we have a whole castle labyrinth to get out from underneath of. And the number of wandering guards and Destroyers is not to my liking." She grimaced as we heard loud steps right above our heads. "Well, let's go."

We walked fast, though very cautiously. The castle was now well lit, decorated with beautiful tapestry and statues signaling wealth, yet my heart only focused on two things.

Make it out alive and find Gideon.

I followed each of Priya's steps as we crept up at a quick pace along the walls, occasionally stopping still behind the large, rich curtains when guards rushed past us. Yet when we passed yet another corridor, I realized that we were just going around the castle blind. Each one of these doors could be another prison, another trap.

"We need to find a wide staircase with large Sunflower art, there is a secret passage behind that," I whispered to Priya as she paused, calculating which door to use.

"Stairs in a giant castle and a painting leading to a secret passage? Well, that's helpful, *not*." She rolled her eyes, pausing, carefully listening for any indication of approaching guards. "I'll get us out of this, Freckles, no need to go full Rebel on me with secret passages and conspired works. I think they've done enough harm for the day." She gestured me to follow her, and I obediently did. "Just past this door and we will be good to go," she said, opening the door, leading down yet another long hallway.

This one was so simple. Servants' quarters, I realized. The walls were now just decorated wood, the rich statues replaced by tall flower vases.

There was nowhere to hide. Nowhere to run as the narrow hall only had two doors at each end. Though the hall had lots of windows, none of them were big enough to crawl out of. Priya realized that too, yet she continued walking until the doors opened. Ten worn out guards full of adrenaline and anger poured in. They saw us as soon as we saw them.

All of us halted to a complete stop.

My mind calculated our chances. Two assassins versus ten well trained guards double our size. Priya could take on five, I didn't doubt that, but could I? Sleep powder on one. Poisons for the rest, I just had to live long enough for them to kick in.

Both of us had to make it out of there.

Dagger, pins, and anger were my ammunition.

The guards pulled their swords out.

"Who are you?" one of them asked, as we stared each other down.

"Your mamma's boyfriends, that's who." Priya grimaced in annoyance, pulling her own daggers out. "Ready, Freckles?" she asked, without turning her head to me, assessing the enemy in front of us. I pulled Heart Piercer out as well.

"As ready as I'll ever be," I said, dipping the end of my dagger in the small vial of poison.

"Good," Priya said, throwing her own dagger without giving a guard so much as a chance to blink. She jumped on them like a leopard on a gazelle. I followed. The clash of metal and daggers filled the air, poisons and powders coming out to play.

Quiet numbness took me over. It was comforting. Slash, slice, pierce. Wound all of them first, let the poison work, then finish killing them one by one. Staying alive was the next step of the plan as I dodged another sword. Gods, I was fast, but Priya? She was Death

Incarnate. Grunting, she stabbed one after another and another, as vicious and precise as a livid viper.

I winced as a sharp blade brushed over my arm. Six down, four more to go, I mentally tallied up the bodies. I could go a little longer. In fact, I welcomed it. The adrenaline, the sweat, the noise, my body fueled by everything but fear. I rushed and moved until another body thumped on the floor and then another and another.

We finally paused, our breathing rapid, sweat dripping down our brows. We both launched our daggers at the same time straight through the last fleeing guard. Our daggers both hit their mark as he dropped, gasping for air on his knees. Priya strolled to him, kicking him down with her boots, narrowing her eyes slightly at the sight of Heart Piercer wedged deep inside his body.

"Not so fast you rotten piece of shit," she said, turning him to the side as he gagged on the white foam coming out of his mouth. She paused, staring deep into his eyes. For a minute I nervously glanced over the two exits. Whatever Priya was doing this was not the time to do it.

"We should really go." I nudged her, pulling my dagger out of the now still body. She sneered but pulled her dagger, sheathing it as well.

But we were too slow.

Another group of guards rushed past the doors, this time I didn't bother counting. There were more than ten, probably double. I calmed the sliver of panic running through me. The pins and poisons were almost gone and the three daggers between the two of us against twenty guards? My mind didn't bother calculating our odds.

Exhausted, I gripped my dagger tighter.

The guards stared at the piled bodies around us, pointing their loaded crossbows at us.

Crossbows, not swords.

We could try and run. Terrible idea but in this case, our best option. Maybe if we were fast enough, we could find somewhere to hide. I nudged Priya a bit, as if asking her, telling her to be ready to run. She ignored me. Mentally I gave Priya one more second and then I'd drag her through the castle myself if she didn't move right then.

"Priya," I uttered her name with a demand. It had to be now. We had seconds now that the soldiers shifted their fingers closer to the triggers.

"Oh, for fucks sake. I am *so over* today," Priya said loudly. Not scared or afraid, not even remotely tense, but more annoyed than anything. Some of the guards shifted on their feet. Uneasy, unsure of who of them would pull the trigger first.

Leaderless. I realized.

Being shot with an arrow in the back tonight was not a part of my plan. My eyes jerked between the guards and us.

"Priya. This is not the time," I said cautiously.

If she thought we could take them on she was insane. Ten guards were almost too much, but we still had a slim chance. But more than twenty with depleted resources? We would die. Maybe not without taking a life or two first, but we would die.

She glared at the guards without speaking a word.

I gasped. Instead of firing their crossbows they all—*all* two dozen or so of them—dropped to the ground, squirming and screaming in complete agony as they grabbed their heads, blood rushing from their ears and noses.

Shocked, I stood still watching them all die. Every single one of them. Until the very last screams went out and their blood pooled together. The exit to the hall was now lined with dead bodies.

Priya moved then, stepping across each lifeless man. She was no longer sneaky or cautious. She walked as if she owned the castle. I carefully followed her. She opened the doors, slamming them loudly. Another two guards went down in the same agonizing torturous death within seconds as she cast her eyes on them.

I silenced the familiar shock.

Later. I will deal with this later, I told myself, as I threw my dagger straight through another guard emerging on my left.

Priya no longer hid as she strode open through the castle, no longer doubting which direction to take until we were by the Royal Stables. Two servants screamed in pain, grasping their heads, pulling their own hair out. Blood pooled out of their ears and noses just the same as all the guards in the castle.

Later, I reminded myself.

I saddled a horse.

"Please tell me you know how to ride?" were the only words Priya spoke to me as she jumped on the back of the black mare in the stall next to me. I nodded.

It's not like I had any other choice as Priya had already galloped across the perfectly cut green lawns of the Royal Castle. The loud screaming of guards followed her, but it wasn't the guards I froze from. No, it was the smell of the fire, the smoke, as the burning arrows slashed across the black sky, burning bright with the silver Cleansing Fire—*Destroyer's* fire.

I stiffened completely, yet my brown mare followed Priya's as if it knew that my life depended on her. Slashing through the cold air, I begged her to keep going faster and faster, as another arrow landed just a few feet away from where we were seconds before.

We were approaching the large stone wall that encircled the whole estate.

Jump.

The thought came before I could realize what was happening.

Jump.

Ignoring the screaming doubts and any reason, my body obediently followed the command, launching myself off the galloping horse to the top of the bright tall white wall, quickly climbing up and then jumping off into the flower beds below, well hidden by the darkness of the night.

46

Tremendous crowds were gathered around. Some came to celebrate Death Day, some came out to see the explosion and what was left of the ballroom hall. We snuck below the shadow of the wall until we were far enough from the gates that we could mingle with the crowd. Slowly squeezing in between the gawking, gossiping people, only occasionally glancing over our shoulder to make sure we weren't followed.

The crowds slowly thinned out as we went further into the city. The well-taken-care-of shops and the neat townhomes were completely dark and only the tall streetlights lit up the curved cobbled streets.

I could no longer hear the noisy masses; now almost completely alone, Priya and I walked hastily down the streets of Svitar. I tensed, passing another group of drunk out-of-their-mind patrons. They were so blissfully unaware of the two assassins amidst them, so oblivious to the tight grip on our half-drawn daggers.

First, I heard the click of hooves; next Priya roughly shoved me through the door to the previously locked shop. The dark room encompassed us as we were plastered against the floor, hidden by the night.

I watched as a couple of Destroyers, dressed in their dark silver armor searched the street. My Basalt Glass dagger singing to my blood, turning it to lava. Fear mixed with wild anger caressed my veins.

"Calm down, Freckles. We've had enough drama for the day, don't you think?" Priya whispered, rolling off me and now laying still next to me.

You think? I wanted to say to her but didn't. Calmness, patience and restraint were much more useful tools than fear and anger. They were tools of precision and skill. Tools that I knew how to wield.

The two Destroyer soldiers were gone from my view, but we didn't risk getting up just yet. I turned my head to Priya. Our eyes met for the first time after all the chaos.

She glanced away first.

"Who are you?"

"*Really?* You are going to ask me that? *Now?*" she said, getting off the floor.

"Who are you?" I asked again, sitting up, determined to get an answer.

Though deep inside, I already knew.

I knew the answer but desperately wanted it not to be true.

Priya turned around the room. I kept my eyes on her.

"How convenient," she said, coming up to the shelf. We were in a bakery. Though the shelves lay empty, there were a few well packaged bags of rolls in the cupboards. Priya ripped into one. "I am starving. Are you? You would think the Royals would have better food, wouldn't you?" she said, stuffing a roll into her mouth. Her tone was so careless and upbeat like we hadn't just walked out of the Royal Castle murdering people left and right. With *her* killing them with just a thought.

"Priya. I need you to answer," I stated. My tone stern, though quiet.

"Why? Why would it matter? I told you I'd save your skinny ass and I kept my promise. I think that's plenty of answers for you. Maybe you should try and be grateful."

I was.

I was grateful. I knew full well that if it wasn't for Priya, my fate would have been altered today, the same way it was altered when she found me exhausted on the riverbanks of the Dniar river.

"You are a Truth Teller." My heart sank as I said those words out loud. Tuluma didn't teach me much about the Magic Wielders, yet she warned me about Truth Tellers. They weren't magic, no. It was a skill. A mind talent. Ability to read your thoughts, alter them. Human or mage, or even elven. Anyone could be a Truth Teller, yet they were so rare and dangerous. *Very dangerous.*

"And if I were, what is it to you?" she angrily spat.

My heart twisted as feelings of betrayal sunk in.

"Why didn't you tell me?"

"Why would I?" Priya glared at me.

"So, I wouldn't have to question what was true and what wasn't during these past months," I blurted out.

"You give yourself too much credit, Freckles. I wouldn't waste my energy altering your rather pathetic memories of life. You were already obedient and pitiful all on your own." She had drawn on those words on purpose, aware of their sting. I clenched my jaw.

"How often?" I asked, unsure if I even wanted to know. "How often have you read my thoughts, mingled in my memories? My feelings?"

"Well…" she casually said, as if we were discussing a play playing in the theaters and not her invading and potentially altering my inner being, betraying any kind of trust I had for her. "There were a few times," she said, taking another bite of the roll.

"I listened to you, I obeyed you, I heeded your every command. I *trusted* you. That day by the river, you promised me that I would have my freedom and yet all I've had was just a better master and a nicer cage?" Hurt poured like hail bruising my soul.

"Oh, don't go all righteous on me now, Freckles, you have not been the perfect little pet you portray yourself to be."

"Which ones, Priya?" I asked her while devastation and complete defeat settled deep within me. She frustratingly glared at me. Those eyes though, sharp as her blades, warning me; one wrong word and it would be me who was bloodied up, grasping my head on the ground. "Gods, are you reading my mind now?"

"Relax. It requires a lot more to read someone else's mind than glaring at them. It's also rather exhausting, always leaves me so damn hungry and the headaches afterwards are really not worth it." She rubbed her temples. "So, believe me when I say that when I have done it, I've only done it out of necessity," she said, stuffing another roll.

Necessity.

Her necessity.

Her choice.

Never *mine*.

She would never answer me, I realized. She would never tell me, and I would never know. I would have to spend the rest of my life questioning it all and just accept it as is.

Maybe that was the price I had to pay for the comfortable life I lived in the past few months.

I was ignorant and unaware.

Anger rose within me but not at Priya. At myself. I knew better. I had seen the red flags. I should've connected the dots, but instead I was so focused on everything else.

I was a starved little mouse for so long that I didn't realize I set my foot in a trap while chasing cheese.

No, she would never tell me. Not now, not later, not ever.

But this ignorance?

I was done with it now.

No more.

"What did you do to those guards?" I asked, sitting up on the ground, staring at my dust covered boots. Descending deep into the numb within me, while my world got torn apart in twisted realities.

"Oh them? Their brain just forgot how to function for a little bit. You'd be surprised how painful it is when your brain turns to mush," Priya said feeling smug.

"I thought most Truth Tellers could only read thoughts, and skilled ones could alter memories. I don't remember hearing about them turning brains to liquid," I said, hiding my feelings, hiding my thoughts far behind the wall of anger. The creature awoke within me rattling its chain.

She threw her half empty bag of rolls on the floor, now scavenging the rest of the cupboards. I stood up, tugging on the ends of my ripped dress.

"Well turns out if you are any good at it, you can do a lot more than that. And I..." She pulled out a pack of cookies. "I am really, *really* good at it."

A truth and a threat all in one.

The shattered heart within me ached. Not because she'd broken my trust, though that too hurt, but because I gave her that trust to begin with.

I cared for her.

Priya, twisted in her ways, was the closest thing to family that I had and maybe it was dishonest and even a little cruel, but she had saved me, she had given me a haven when I needed it the most.

I took a long breath, watching her shove cookies into her mouth one after another.

I cared for her.

"Come with me to find the Rebels, Priya," I softly asked.

A lifeline.

One I deeply hoped she would take.

A chance for us to fix what was broken.

"I need to find the Rebels. Come with me. We could make a difference. We could make something good from all those killings." I looked outside to an empty street, the Royal Castle far on the horizon. "Come with me, Priya. *Please.*"

Priya laughed. Gutturally. Wickedly. Her laugh landed like a knife, stabbing me.

"Oh *Freckles,* Truth Tellers were hunted long before Magic Wielders were. Maybe for once we enjoy not being the center of attention. Plus, I have no desire to become some Rebel tool of war until I get my throat sliced in my sleep."

"Priya. You have *a gift.* You could do so much good with it!"

"*A gift?* You think Truth Telling is *a gift?!*" She raised her voice as she turned to me sharply, her brows bunched up and eyes narrowed. "Do you know how one becomes a Truth Teller? How one can obtain such a *gift* to be in someone else's mind? Do you know?!"

I stayed quiet, watching hatred rise within her darkened eyes.

"No? Yeah, that's what I thought. Somehow people conveniently forget about the most important detail. You have to be *tortured*, but not *one time* kind of torture, but *continual, daily torture for years* so that eventually your mind and body are so exhausted, wanting to die so bad yet unable, so you make the jump."

My eyes slightly widened.

I didn't know.

Priya scowled but turned her eyes to the empty streets covered by the darkness.

"You have to be so painfully close to death yet so strikingly craving for survival that one day your mind just can't go on anymore, so it jumps into someone else's body. Dissociates so far from reality that you find yourself free of pain yet drowned in someone else's thoughts. But do you know what happens next, Finn?"

She paused, twisting her neck and scoffing at me.

"Even if you made the jump, you were now being completely choked out by foreign thoughts, their memories, their feelings, and you have to claw yourself out of the quickly suffocating swamp. Did you know that many make the jump, but not many come back? It's a torture of its own. And each time you make the jump it's still painful. Your mind and body being ripped apart."

"I am sorry, Priya." My heart ached for her. With her.

"So no, don't tell me it's a fucking gift. Because it's not. Would you like to know how *I* got this *gift*? I'll tell you since you always wanted to know. I was a child sex slave. My family was brutally murdered, and my sister and I were sold and trafficked for years. My baby sister didn't make the jump. She died within her second year. A relief, I suppose, because she didn't have to endure it any longer. I on the other hand? I wanted to. Everyday fucking day I begged for it, prayed and begged each time they showed up and ripped me to shreds. I begged to die. Until I realized that my will to survive triumphed over it all. So, I stopped begging and stayed alive. Raped and tortured multiple times a day for years, ever since I was five until I made my first jump at thirteen.

Have you ever been in a psychotic pedophile's rotten mind as he was raping you, high from torturing you? No? Well, I have. I practiced jumping every time the men ravaged my little body. I willed my mind to stay there, to accept the waves of their foul feelings and thoughts. To wander their memories. To surround myself with their foul desires as if it was my cozy blanket. I willed myself to give in into their horror and…soon enough I learned that once you stop flopping like you are drowning, you can try and swim. So I did.

They were always so unaware. Until one day, I pulled on that little thread I knew would end him. And I watched him choke and die in his own blood as his mind became *nothing*. As *I* made him *nothing*. I ran away that day, living on my own ever since.

So no, it is no gift. I will not use it for anything or anyone but what it is created for. *Me*. My survival. I think I've paid a high enough price. I've lost my family, my sister, my childhood, my sanity and innocence to the bloodlust of men. I will never. *Never*. Be someone's toy to handle when they need it."

Our eyes met as she continued.

"The Rebels, the war, the Royals, it is all the same, Freckles, don't you see? Hungry men hoping to get more power."

I stood still, unsure of what to say. The air in the room felt even colder than before.

It all made sense to me then, the bitterness, the never-ending violence, the complete lack of sympathy, the constant craving for control, the sarcastic humor and that scar. Branded as an animal for everyone to know that she is a slave.

A child slave.

My heart broke in more pieces than I knew it could.

I knew the world was evil but the realization of how evil would never stop breaking me. "I am so sorry, Priya," I said, knowing full well that those words were nothing, though I meant them with the entirety of my soul.

"I don't need your pity," she grumped back.

"The baker...he was one of them?" The words came out loud as I started piecing everything together.

She chuckled.

"Oh, the baker? Nah, he was just that. A baker. He used to bring me extra slices of cake and treats to our compound." She paused, taking a look at the cookie she was devouring. "Ironic, isn't it?"

She took another bite. "I killed them all, Freckles. Today, all of them are gone." She paused as she stared at the wall, unsure of herself what to feel. "Ten years of me hunting and now the Baroness was the last one." Priya lifted her hand, showing the exquisite ring on her finger. A Royal ring. "She orchestrated it all. I guess when your son is a pedophile and you have the means, you provide the perfect environment for the kidnapped pretty kids to indulge his needs." She sadly chuckled. "All of them are gone. Each one of them. Even the staff that cooked us meals, the ones that ironed our cutesy dresses, that brought the toys and gifts for us."

"They brought you gifts?"

"Don't be so surprised. They kept us 'happy.' Broken in. Rape you in the morning, make you cake and bring you a new doll at lunch time. Rape and cut and choke you in the afternoon, a new dress and nice care by the nurse two hours later." She smiled tensely. "Messed up fucks are gone, but I wish I could say that justice was served. But scars never go away..."

She chucked a cookie at me, and I caught it, though I couldn't bring myself to take a bite as bile rose high in my throat burning me from within.

"You know," she said, taking another look outside as another group of drunks passed. "I came back after a while to the compound where they kept us. A nice little manor it was, secluded, away from anyone. It was run down since my first kill but a few girls were still there." She took another bite. "I murdered them all there that day. I did what I hoped someone would do for me and set me free; so they would never have to figure out how to live their lives so broken. I left everyone to rot, except those girls. Them, I buried in my overgrown garden."

I was going to throw up. Nausea held me as a prisoner as I thought of those young girls enduring so much only to be brutally killed by their *savior*. Shoved into the cold ground to never see the world again. My eyes filled with tears, and I blinked faster to stop them from pouring down my cheeks.

"Oh yeah, I used to have a garden there. If I had any time, I used to go to the garden. My keepers would get so mad since the dirt would get under my little nails, and we were to be kept pristine." Priya smiled at that memory. "Then I asked the baker to bring me gloves, and he did. And so, I gardened every single day. That book you've read? *'Plants and Poisons around the world?'* I asked for it as a gift from the Baronesses' son. I was his favorite to take, and he almost thought we had a connection. It was the last birthday of mine that I remember or chose to remember."

My chest ached as I tried to take a long breath. So many questions lingered within me. Why? Why would the gods allow this to happen?! Screw the gods, why were there so many people aware of it and yet not saving those girls? How many people were okay with the wrong, knowing that they should've done something yet closed their eyes and choose to not intervene.

"You know, at first, I asked for the book to learn about poisons so I could kill myself or at least learn which plants would get me the highest of highs enough to numb myself or let me have a nightmare free sleep once in a while." She smirked. "Isn't it funny how things turn out in the end? All of them dead with poison in their blood from me? I outlasted them all. *I killed them all.*"

"Why me?" I asked her.

"Why not? I needed laundry done and you seemed fit for the job." She shrugged, finishing up another cookie.

I ignored that deflective answer.

"That day, by that river. Why me, Priya? Why did you help me?" I knew it wasn't sympathy, I was sure she didn't feel those emotions. I wasn't sure why I needed to know that answer. Why I cared, but something inside of me did. Maybe it was the last thread connecting me with her, begging me to stay with her.

Priya snarled but replied.

"Because that day on that beach, I looked at your memories. I looked deep inside of you, and you know what I saw? I saw the same craving for survival and the same wish for Death I had. I also saw the kindness and love that I could never feel, and it reminded me of her. And I thought, what would it be like if my baby sister had survived? If we both went along and killed our enemies, if I made you into a perfect little assassin of mine. And for once I could have the family I wanted."

My heart broke once more with realization.

"The Royal sailor...You orchestrated that Royal sailor to rape me that day in the Port City, didn't you," I stated, my chest squeezing tighter.

Priya rolled her eyes at me.

"He was never going to rape you, Freckles. But I think you would agree that you needed a little push."

My mouth opened then closed, unable to say the things I needed.

"You are going to leave me, aren't you?" Priya said, turning to me. "You are going to leave. Me," she said, her voice filled with betrayal and sadness.

"I have to find them, Priya. I promised."

Priya's face slashed with bitterness.

"Oh, just like you promised Viyak that you'll come back for him? Or just like you've promised to kill the Destroyer General? Or how would your dead elven maid feel about your promise to live a better life when you are signing off on your own death by joining the Rebels? And for what? *A hope for a better world*? There is no such thing!" she snarled. Each word filled with poison.

Like a whip, her words ripped the pieces of my soul. I didn't bother asking how she knew all about those promises. About things I never told her, things I never told anyone.

Things that haunted my soul every day.

"That is exactly why I am doing that," I fought back. I was broken and beaten. So damned defeated, but I would fight back for the only thing I had left. "The world might not be a better world. But *hope*; hope is what I am fighting for. I've lived my life ignorant, unaware, on the sidelines for too damn long, and now I have a chance to make a difference. You have a chance too, Priya."

"Leave," Priya commanded as she pointed to the door, her face flashed with anger and hate. "Leave and *never* come back." I didn't move until she pulled both of her daggers out. I pulled mine but I wouldn't fight her. No, I couldn't do it.

She closed the space between us, and I tightened the grip on my dagger. Now just a few inches away from my face, she uttered.

"I cared for you, Finn. Despite it all, I really *really* cared for you. I thought we were meant to be sisters. I thought we would be a family. But now...Now, I see that I was wrong. I could never be sisters with some elven raised trash. I could never be family with someone who doesn't even know what that means. I did everything for you, but it turns out you are just an ungrateful pig." She narrowed her eyes on me. "Go and never come back because if I see you again, I will not just alter your memories but make your life a living nightmare and you will wish you'd never escaped from the Destroyers."

My mind was silent, as if it had completely abandoned me today. Maybe it made me a coward, but I wasn't going to question Priya's intentions. I wasn't going to wait for her to deliver on her threat. I pushed the door open. The freezing cold air should've frosted my lungs, but all I felt was numb.

I stopped in the door frame to give her a last glance.

My friend, my family, and yet also my oppressor and captor.

"Priya," I whispered. My only goodbye.

"Goodbye, Freckles."

47

The heavy silver clouds bathed in the moonlight above me. My hands were freezing in the winter air. I ran.

I ran towards the familiar golden gates; towards the house I called home for so long.

Priya's goodbye still rang in my mind loud and clear with each step I took. The ball, explosions, Kahors, Rebels, Inadios, capture, escape, Priya, and so, so much death. It felt as if my soul couldn't take it anymore. Yet I ran on, biting my cheek occasionally to stop tears from flowing.

The warm house and the welcoming lights embraced me as I walked up familiar stairs. I fought the urge to fall down on the couch, to close my eyes and hope that today was just one of my dreams, my nightmares, to rest just for a minute from the complete exhaustion I was debilitated with, but I had to go, and I had to go now.

I scrubbed my frozen blood-covered hands until they were almost raw, washing off the mix of make-up and blood off my face and rinsing off my hair from the Kahor's stench, tying my hair into a tight ponytail.

I quickly changed into the leathers, grabbed all the money I had and threw on my winter cloak. I zipped up my leather boots, putting the daggers and pins into them. I threw my shoulder bag on, stuffing in a few provisions. I put Kaius's ring on the same chain holding Tuluma's amulet and hid it well under my leathers. Heart Piercer was now securely stored within reach and a large Basalt Glass arrow hid well under my cloak.

I took the little present I got for Priya and left it in the laboratory with a note. A note that said to come find me when she was ready to talk.

I would welcome her back. I would forgive her.

You choose forgiveness over justice, and it really shows.

Priya's voice rung in my mind as I quickly wiped a tear sliding down my cheek.

The scars she ripped opened bled deep.

With poisons and all matter of weaponry packed on me, I stood in the entrance hall still, glancing over it as I said my silent goodbye to the sleeping Ratika, to the beautiful art I stared at so much each day, to the stacks of books and fairytales I read each day, to the clean bandages folded neatly, awaiting the next sparring match to be used.

I knew I wouldn't miss the luxury or the comfort, though I genuinely enjoyed it, but I would miss the safe haven this place had become for me. A place that gave me a moment to rest, to breathe, to process and to grow. A place that reminded me that I am capable of more.

At last, I glanced far to the corner that led to the laundry room. My own kind of solace.

"Goodbye," I whispered sadly and slipped into the dark.

48

I paced past the town square leading to the Queen's Palace, glancing just occasionally behind my back, watching for any approaching guards or Destroyers. The streets had quieted down, though a certain level of uneasiness still chilled in the air.

I tugged on the handle. The familiar alley door was locked.

"Shit," I mumbled in frustration. Lights far above me shone bright from the tall windows. I was in no mood to climb but as I looked around, I was left with no choice.

I tugged on the nearby vines, pulling myself up. I just had to make it high enough to reach the fire escape ladder above me.

My face flashed with pain while my cold hands gripped the metal, almost pulling off my skin with each grab. I climbed until I was close enough to the small balcony.

I tried not to think, just act. I ignored the fact that I would splatter against the cold cobblestone alley with one wrong move, or the fact that the balcony door too could be locked, or the fact that I was breaking into the most well-known drug Lord's place. I disregarded it all.

I had to jump before I convinced myself that this was idiotic.

"Sorry," I whispered to my bag as I threw it across the gap to the balcony first. Then, taking a long breath, I threw myself at the marbled railing. I jumped far enough to grab one of the curved pillars on the balcony's edge. *Good enough,* I thought, as I pulled myself up, my shoulders burning. My bag luckily was still intact as I pulled it over my shoulder and went for the tall glass doors. I pulled quietly on the handle, and the door slid to the side. A little shiver the only sign of relief that went through me.

I walked into the well-lit corridor leading to two doors, the smell of the strong familiar cologne eased the heavy tension. I knocked on one of the doors.

"Come in," Florian sounded from the other side of the door. I quietly slipped in.

"Finn, is that you?" He raised his eyebrows in surprise, as I lowered the furry hood of my cloak.

"Hi Florian," I softly said and approached his bed. He was laying down on his bed, propped up by large pillows, his leg and arm now in a cast, his face and the rest of his body bandaged up.

"Finn, hey, what are you doing here?" he asked, his voice laced with concern as he took another look at the door behind me, at my cloak and the peeking daggers.

"I wanted to make sure you were okay," I said, accepting his gesture to sit next to him on the bed. Though his face still showed concern, he smiled.

"Sure-sure...*Or* did you just want to come see me half naked?" He winked at me, and I smiled. I didn't neglect to notice that he was in fact half-naked, sitting just in his briefs. I noticed his other tattoos, covering his upper arms and legs, none of them as exquisite as the large floral tattoo across his chest contrasting against his ivory skin.

"I am sorry, Florian." I grimaced looking at a large bandage on his face. That would leave a large scar.

"Oh gorgeous, I am already working on a great story to go along with it too. Honestly, I should've gotten it a long time ago. Such a wasted opportunity. Women are going to get drenched, once they see my newly upgraded face." He chuckled, though I could see a little bit of grief behind it. "What a night, huh?" He glanced over me, pausing on my stuffed bag. "Is Priya okay?"

"Um, yes." I wasn't sure what to say. Okay seemed like such a small word for what she was. "We found each other and made a run for it. She is...she will be okay, I think," I said, unsure of where to even begin to explain what happened when I left him in the ruins of the ballroom.

"So, what's wrong?" he asked gently, grabbing my hand. "Why does this feel like you are here to say a goodbye?" he asked, taking a deep look into my eyes.

"I am leaving, Florian." I looked away from him, a part of me regretting even coming here.

"So, we had one bad date and you're running away from me already? Oh, come on,

give me another chance, Finn. I promise to find something a little less *explosive* next time." He smirked at his own joke.

My heart tightened but I smiled back at him, hoping that somehow that smile would make the next few words to come out less painful.

"I've come to say goodbye, Florian. I am leaving tonight. Right now. I... I don't know for how long, but I know it's going to be a while. And before you object," I said, seeing his mouth open. "I have to do it. I have already promised," I said, avoiding his persistent stare, worrying that those kind eyes would convince me to stay.

Knowing full well that a part of me begged them to.

"What happened, Finn? Did Priya find my amazing drawings of her? Is it because of those horns? And now she's upset? I'll send her a sorry card then."

He rubbed my hand with his thumb in comforting strokes. Gods, this was so much harder than I thought it would be.

I turned my head to face a wall. Such a simple room for the heir of the drug empire.

"Seriously though, is it Priya?" he asked again, his tone picking up a bit; the only sign of desperation creeping in. "To hell with her, to hell with them all. Come live here. If it's money, I have plenty, you can live here, and I can give you money and whatever else you need and before you say no…No, you wouldn't have to sleep with me for it, unless you really want to." His tone was upbeat, yet his face filled with heartbreak.

I put on a smile, choking on the lump stuck in my throat. Florian was my friend.

A friend that I didn't deserve.

"Finn, you have to say something." He squeezed my hand, unwilling to let go.

"Florian, I am sorry, I wish I could explain everything and tell you everything, but I can't. There is no point in it. I have to leave, but I do need you to do something for me."

Florian just opened his mouth to object, yet a small meow sounded from my bag. I reached my hand into it, pulling out a small orange and white striped kitten. Florian raised his eyebrows in astonishment.

"Okay, when I wrote *pussy* on my drawing, I meant something completely different, but now in retrospect I see that I should've clarified," Florian mumbled as he moved his hand to pet the cat.

"Meet Ray, like a ray of sunshine, Ray. I found him abandoned under the bridge in the Central market. Priya doesn't allow any animals in the house, so I've kept coming back to him and feeding him or paying a maid at the Butcher's shop to feed him if I was gone, but now I am leaving for a long time and with the winter…." My voice broke for a second. This hurt so much. I took a large breath calming my broken heart.

Later. I will deal with the heartbreak later.

"I need him to have a home, Florian. I need to know that he is going to be okay."

Even if I am not. Unspoken words flowed in my mind.

But the reality was that I was never okay. Not from the moment I was born, not now. I took another look at my little kitty cat, my friend. He too, was abandoned at birth, left alone in the world to make it. Perhaps, he wasn't okay before, but he would be now. One of us had to be.

"You brought me a cat?" he said, taking another look at the small ball of sunshine in my hands, now purring as he rubbed his head against my chest. "He is a boob man, I can relate," Florian said, petting his belly. I laughed through watery eyes, blinking fast as if that somehow would help stop the tears building up.

"Please take good care of him. He was the only friend I had until I met you, and now it's only fitting that two of my friends unite. You can even create a little red head club together and talk crap about me." Even through my soft smile, tears slipped past me as I handed off my little Ray to Florian. With soft paws, he climbed onto Florian's chest and purred as he rubbed his head against Florian's chin.

"Finn, please tell me what I can do to stop this?" Florian dropped the boyish tone, his voice somber. "Whatever it is I can help, I am the freaking Casteol heir, that has to mean something. I have connections, I have influence. Whatever it is, I bet a few smiles from me, and we can figure it out."

"I wish it was that simple," I said sadly, smiling while discreetly wiping the salty tear away. I stood up, putting my cloak back on.

A part of me knew that if I offered to have him to come with me, he would. That if I told him that I was a runaway slave, and the truth about everything that had happened with me he would be there for me through it all.

A part of me wanted to tell him everything.

But I was selfish.

Selfish, because it was my burden to carry. Selfish, because for once I wanted to do it myself. It was *my* promise to fulfill.

It was selfish of me to deny him even that chance to help. I knew that.

But I had to do this alone.

When you were burned enough times, you tend to stay away from the fire no matter how cold you get.

"Finn, please. What can I do to help? Talk to me," he asked again, letting me see the anguish and the heartache. I was glad the fur shaded my eyes away from him.

"I am going far north, past the Cursed Forest, do you know how I can get there?" I asked, adjusting the strap of my bag across my shoulder.

Florian hesitated as if trying to find an argument to make me stay. He rubbed his forehead with his hand.

"No boat will carry you to the Cursed Lands. But I know a man that will get you very close. Find him at the docks by the fishermen's shack. Tell him Florian Casteol sent you. The key word is Crest. He can't talk since his tongue is cut out but tell him the location and he will take you there." He exhaled slowly in defeat. "Finn, I'll cover the fare so do whatever you need to but keep him there so he can bring you home. As long as it takes, Finn." He looked at me then, with his eyes filled with those words, as if shouting at me that he meant it.

"Thank you," I said, hiding the wince at word *home*. Truth was, I didn't have a home. Not then, not now. Not anymore. At times I started to believe I was never meant to have a home. Maybe I didn't even know what that word meant. Not truly.

Maybe I was meant to stumble across the world. To be displaced. Dislodged.

A young nurse stumbled in the room with a new case of bandages and medicine, and she stopped, shocked to see me.

"Oh, I am sorry, I didn't realize you had guests, I will come back later," she mumbled, turning back.

"Oh, I am leaving," I said and adjusted the hood over my face. "Goodbye, Florian."

Florian didn't reply as he watched my figure cross his room towards the door.

"Finn?"

"Yeah?" I turned my head just slightly, to take my last look at his banged-up body. Ray, as if sensing my goodbye, lifted his head and whined at me.

"The Cursed Lands are called *cursed* for a reason. Please be careful."

"Take good care of yourselves, you two," I said, marching out of the Queen's Palace. Traitorous tears slid down my throat, mixed with blood from a bit lip, as I swallowed once more, trying to keep the rising sobs down.

I had to be strong. I had to be sharp. I had to be brutal. Life had been cruel but so could I. I would bring the information to the Rebels.

But I wouldn't give it to them for free. No, I would trade it. I would trade it for Viyak.

They'd blown up the Royal castle...they could surely free the slaves.

I clenched my teeth. Ruthless. I had to be ruthless.

Cold air caressed my lungs. No, I wouldn't cry anymore. I'd save those tears, I'd save that hurt; let it fuel me, let it dwell with my anger within me.

I waved to the nearest carriage not too far from downtown.

"To the dock, please."

49

The rivers this far north were calm. *Too calm*. Not a single ripple. The waters, clear and pristine, opened to the utter blackness. As if the water itself was not water but pure black ink.

I dipped my hand to ensure that it was indeed just water. My mind still expecting my hand to come out black, yet only ice-cold water dripped off my hand.

A large, mill-like wheel securely stationed behind our boat propelled us quietly further. We'd been traveling for a week now, taking river routes I didn't even know existed. Some of them so shallow that a thin ice was covering them, yet the boat kept on going.

It was just the two of us on board. The captain was in his fifties, his gray beard neatly trimmed, his skin permanently red from the salt and water of the oceans and rivers. He wore a large, round hat, rubber boots, and a heavy, double layered coat. His pants and shirt were clean but heavily worn, with patches and worn-out streaks seen here and there.

The boat was small, just a single room cabin that we shared. We slept in two neatly hung hammocks that were put away during the day to allow for more room. One old oil lamp served as the only source of light within. Days got so much shorter here, sun only peeking through for a bleak few hours.

It snowed on day two. I walked out one morning to specks of white landing on my cheeks. My very first snow. So enchanting, so beautiful yet, instead of excitement, I welcomed my grief.

Somehow, I expected snow to be different, clumpy and fluffy. Instead, it was more like crystalized crumbs of dust that melted the moment they touched my skin, evaporating as if they never were there.

It hadn't stopped snowing ever since. Large, dark clouds followed our boat, even as the shores became emptier each day. No longer could I see any docks or little towns spread alongside the riverbanks. We stopped seeing even fishermen's boats as we made our way up the river further north.

So tranquil.

I finished my dinner of canned beets, stale bread and smoked cheese, sitting on a small box. Our wooden, mill-like boat casually cruised on the line between the opaque blue sky and the dark water. I watched Cap as he watched the horizon, holding on tight to the steering wheel. I pulled out a pen and paper.

"What's beyond the Cursed Forest?" I questioned, eyeing the small map he occasionally stared at. The world looked as if it ended past the Cursed Forest.

He shrugged, but still took my paper and pen. Our only way of communication. He was mute, barely literate.

All go, all die. Nobody come back, nobody speak.

I took a long breath, wrapping my cloak tighter around myself.

The answer seemed to be the same no matter who I asked. The girl we bought provisions from in the last village went pale and said that I should be cursed for even asking those questions. The fishermen I asked were a little less dramatic, just telling me only those who have a death wish go to the Cursed Lands and that nobody could ever pay them enough to sail their boat there.

The Captain handed me back the pen and paper.

"It's okay. Go eat," I said, gesturing to the small bag hanging on the door filled with whatever remaining food we had. We would arrive tomorrow, in the last known small village on the border to the Cursed Lands. When he hesitated, I smiled, pointing with my chin to each of the river shores so far apart.

"I promise I won't crash the boat," I smiled. The river was wide, so surprisingly wide, it was odd for me to see no large boat, no sea barge coming through. Surely this black ink water was deep enough for them to pass.

Cap paused, debating. He raised his finger to gesture one minute and went off to grab some food and relieve himself off the side of the boat.

I grabbed the steering wheel, coming to the conclusion that I would much rather be a man and pee off the side of the boat, than having to squat over a stupid bucket every time.

50

I woke from the light thud of our boat. The quiet steam engine was completely still. I glanced over to Cap's empty hammock. Bright morning sun blinded me as I walked outside. Everything around us was white, covered in a thick layer of snow. My boots sunk deep; the snow high above my calf as I took a step off the dock. So much snow.

Cap was tying his rope around a metal pole on the wobbly dock.

Looking around I could see a small village on the horizon. Smoke from chimneys mixed with the translucent clouds. The village was on top of a tall hill, connected to the docks only by a small, snowed in path.

My bag was already across my shoulder, my weapons all strapped in and hidden well underneath my thick fur cloak.

Cap paused, looking at me and gesturing to me with his hand. I handed him some paper and pen.

Cursed Lands there. He pointed to the horizon beyond the village. I nodded in understanding.

My legs burned as we approached the village. The hill was much steeper than my eyes led me to believe, and thick heavy snow felt like a swamp, sucking you in with each step. Though cold air bit my cheeks, big streams of sweat rolled down my neck and my back. White snow blinded me as it reflected the bright daylight sun.

The town was small. Houses were just big log cabins, placed close to each other, with circling streets going spiral. Only a few vendors had their tents out, selling picked veggies and smoked salmon. I waited as Cap bought a few provisions for his journey back.

We finally made it to a small tavern. Warm air and a delicious smell kissed my nose. My stomach grumbled in excitement for a warm, hearty meal. There were only three round tables inside with a few chairs right next to them. All the furniture was quite simple, yet you couldn't miss the craftsmanship of each piece, each detail of the carpenter. I pulled the chair quietly, trying not to disturb the heavy layer of hay on the floor soaking up the melting snow off our boots. Cap sat next to me.

I pulled my leather gloves off. Though it was warm, too warm, I kept my cloak on, not wanting the extra looks from the few people that already glanced over us on the way in.

"Oy aye, lass, here I come." I heard a trudging woman's voice behind the thick door. Her thick accent was not one I'd heard before. "Oy ye strengers ovr her, I see. What is it you want, lass?" Her big mouth stretched in a welcoming smile. She was in her mid-thirties, well dressed and well nourished. Her long, two braids were bright red and her face full of sun-kissed freckles. Her cheeks were all red, either from the heat or make up, I wasn't sure. But she was adorable. I smiled at her.

"Some warm food, miss, if you have any," I replied.

"Oh ye, warm food it is. Bright morning innit today." She chatted as she ran her towel across our table and tucked it back into her apron. "We got rabbit stew and salmon eggs," she said. "And of course, some good ol' ale to keep ya warm." She winked at the Cap. He nodded in agreement. "It'll be a min, but I be back with ya nourishment." She quickly disappeared behind the door, her two long braids swaying behind her.

I scribbled a few things on the paper.

"Please give this to Florian when you get back." I handed it off to

Cap, who without questioning, nodded and put my little note in his pocket.

The tall woman was back just as quickly as she promised with a tray full of steaming hot food. My mouth watered just by the sight of it.

"Her ya go." She handed off the hot plates from the tray and poured ale into the wooden cups.

"So, where is it ya going?" she asked curiously as we stuffed our faces, a few prideful notes filled her face as she watched us devouring the food, even as we burned out throats.

Curiously, I replied.

"Cursed Forest." Keeping a tight look on her face, I noted every slight change. A part of me hoped to uncover the truth here. Villagers lived across from the forest; she would surely know something.

I wasn't wrong. Her face changed at my words, now quickly sharper and poignant.

"Dead ye wanna be? What ye be going to the forest for?" Her brows raised in suspicion; her voice laced with concern.

A lie it is, I made my next call.

"I am looking for my friend."

I knew she saw through my lie the moment I said it. Tuluma always told me I wasn't a good liar unless my life depended on it, but the woman didn't question it.

"A friend, ye say? Nobody comes back from the Cursed Forest alive, lassie. I've lived here long enough to tell you that I've seen enough of half-eaten dead bodies flowing down that river for a lifetime."

I paused. Dead, I knew that... but *eaten*?

"What lives out there? Do you know what's beyond the forest?" I asked, poking and probing. Just as I knew she sensed my lie, I could bet my life on the fact that she was hiding something.

I couldn't blame her for it though. Both of us were.

She paused, pursing her lips together. Considering.

"Terrible things, *necromantia*." She whispered that third word, her eyes warily glancing over me. "Any other villager will tell ya to go home lassie. Kep ye life. Sorry abut your friend, but no need to lose another soul for 'im."

"'Any other villager', but not you?" I asked, a corner of my mouth turning upward. She smirked back, though her eyes narrowed.

"Who am I to kep ya all away. You die, mor friends will come to look for ya. More customers for me. Stupidity might be bad for ya, but good for ma business."

I chuckled at that, raising my cup and nodding at her. She nodded and departed back.

I wish I could say I was scared or worried about dying, but I wasn't. What I feared the most wasn't death, but failure.

I could deal with the monsters, I could deal with the terrible fate, but the unknown... The unlimited possibilities of failure truly terrified me. My mind spiraled down quickly, and I took another sip.

I wouldn't fail, I repeated to myself, even as I looked outside and saw the never-ending white fields around me. Quickly, I was becoming much less of a fan of the never-ending snow.

Cap finished drinking his stew and huffed, putting his fur coat on. At last, he raised his brows at me as if questioning for the last time if I was sure; sure to let him go. Sure to leave it all and go into the unknown.

"Oh, don't give me that look." I smiled back kindly at him. "I'll be fine. Just make sure you take that vacation we talked about since Florian is already paying for this trip." I winked at him, and he chuckled back, waving an awkward goodbye at me as he walked out of the tavern.

I rested on my chair hesitating, my body feeling groggy as if all that warm food was lead, making my legs heavy and my eyes droopy. I chewed on the fresh piece of bread, watching two men across me playing rocks, one of them clearly cheating. I pulled my hood on as another group of a few people walked in, a couple of women and their children. The owner welcomed them with a kiss and pointed to a table near me. Silent words were exchanged between them as they eyed me in question, looking back at the owner as she shrugged.

The door opened once more. A tall figure walked in. He had a simple, dark green wool cloak on, black leather pants tucked into his tall black boots. My eyes stopped on the small hilt of the dagger slightly peeking just above his boot. It was expensive, decorated with gemstones.

Unusual and yet discreet. I pulled my hood on slightly more. He lowered his.

My heart stopped when I saw his face.

Him.

I would recognize him even in a crowd of millions.

Him.

I forced myself to take a casual breath. I was suddenly too alert. The hairs on my back rose, knowing that though dressed in civil clothing and without his armies, the Destroyer General stood in front of me.

As he lowered his hood, I saw the two familiar hilts of his swords, stationed on his back, blood rubies shining dull with condensation.

He was *here.*

Here.

I had no doubt both of us were here for one purpose.

Rebels.

Anger stirred within me.

I watched him approach the door to what I assumed was the kitchen. He knocked on it softly. I held back a snarl as he ran his fingers through his dark hair, shaking off the bits of snow.

A wolf in sheep's clothing, and unaware sheep around me.

I quickly glanced at the women beside me. Gods, their children. The village. I should tell them to run, to hide. Tell them who was here before this entire village collapsed in flames.

But then another thought crawled in and rooted deep within me.

A chance.

A chance to kill him.

There were no armies around him and I for once had a way to stop him for good.

I silently moved my leg closer to me, lowering my arm, preparing to grab Heart Piercer.

"Well look who the cat dragged in." The woman opened the door and smiled wide at him. I froze, my fingers just inches away from my dagger.

He smirked and followed her behind the door.

I scratched my calf and eased my body back in the chair.

Unsure.

I should've stabbed him right there, before he killed off the village, before he burned the town to the ground. I clenched my jaw tight in disappointment, though I didn't dwell on it long as the door opened again and both of them walked out. She quickly returned to the customers patiently awaiting her. Pulling his hood on, he walked out of the tavern.

My breath was ragged, hands clammy as I watched him through the window walk towards the edge of the village.

Doubts crept in within my mind. I could die and then Kaius's death was in vain, mine was too if I didn't succeed.

I grinded my teeth.

I should let it go.

I should find the Rebels and warn them about him.

And yet I should've killed him the first time around but instead I ran.

I wouldn't make the same mistake twice.

My anger already roaring within me, blinding me more than the snow. I left a few coins on the table and followed his trail.

Though I didn't see him, I had no doubt a set of the large footprints in the snow were his. They continued even beyond the village, down the hill leading straight to the Cursed Forest.

I looked at the horizon, a small strip of trees stretching for miles. A black divider between the blue sky and the white snow. I looked down the steep hill into the empty valley, looking for him amidst the low settled clouds. A second later, I saw him; his dark cloak a beacon against the white snow even in the fog.

A rush of thrill went through me.

I wasn't prey anymore. I was the hunter.

I reached for the longbow hidden well behind my cloak.

My fingers were frozen and my palms damp, but I felt for the glass arrow in my quiver. As I touched it, it sung to me—to my blood—as if calling to me.

I watched him take each step. The further he walked, the faster my heart raced against my chest. The distance was far, and I had to be precise.

Act, damn it. Act! I yelled at myself. But I stood still, my fingers aching but unwaveringly stretching the string, aiming the heavy arrow.

One shot is all I had. *You are a terrible shot.* Priya's little voice ran wild in my head. A gust of cold wind sang around me, as I aimed at his heart.

One chance.

One shot.

One promise.

His body was now barely visible hidden by the thick fog in the valley.

"For a better life," I whispered to the arrow as I let it free. The black arrow flew quickly, cutting through the cold air. He turned to face me just as the arrow pierced him. I didn't look away as our eyes locked. His face was full of disbelief. Mine full of determination. He fell a second later, swallowed by the heavy fog, sending ripples through the mingling air. I quickly slid down the hill, the snow rolling around me.

Slowing down my steps as I saw the blood trail where his body was. My crossbow was already loaded and my Basalt Glass dagger ready to land a killing blow. I moved deliberately, watchful of each movement of the thick fog around me.

I locked my jaw. He should've been dead. There was enough poison on that arrow that anyone should have been dead within seconds. Yet his body wasn't there.

I stopped, just fast enough to pull the trigger at his approaching figure. One and then another. He groaned from pain. My lip curled in disgust and satisfaction.

I was the fucking predator.

Rage roared within me in triumph.

Fog separated as I saw him limp, his sword pointed at me. With a quick glance I knew that my arrows hit the target; one wedged deep in his right thigh and the glass arrow halfway through his shoulder, only ever slightly above his heart.

I shot another arrow at him. He fell to his knees as it wedged in his other leg.

"*You*," he said, shocked. His voice made my bones shiver.

"Surprised to see me, *Destroyer*?" I said back with as much disgust and hate I could summon in my tone.

I twisted Heart Piercer tight in my hand.

"Where did you get the Basalt Glass?" he asked, his voice laced with unpleasantness that brought a smile to my face. Priya was right. This was satisfying. This was rewarding.

Pure revenge was never the death of your enemy, but pain.

It was seeing your offender hurt, defenseless, and in pure agony that gave that thrill unlike any other.

"It's not the glass you should be afraid of, Destroyer, it's the poison on it," I sneered, loading up another arrow in my crossbow, hiding my quickly raising concern with a smirk. He had four arrows within him, all laced with deadly poisons. Poisons that should've killed him the moment they broke his skin and yet he was still breathing. Holding a sword, though his arm was now shaking.

"You're searching for the Rebels, aren't you?" he asked. If he was scared of the poison, he didn't show it. His voice was cool, collected. "I will make a bargain with you. I shall take you to them. I know precisely where they are. What do you say? My life for a path to the Rebels?" He clenched his jaw shut, though I could see the sweat beads rolling down his face.

I smiled cruelly. Poison had to be making its way to his rotten heart.

"You see, Destroyer, your death is worth more to me than your life," I said, taking a step closer as his sword dropped on the ground. He grunted. Pain. He was feeling the pain. But not enough. Never enough.

"My death, though satisfying, will bring you no joy, *mage*. But even so, you could trade me to the Rebels. They would love the information I have on what Mad Queen wants to do with the Rock Quarries' slaves."

My heart dropped.

"What do you know of the Rock Quarry slaves?" Taking another step, I was close to him now. Too close.

I pointed Heart Piercer at his throat.

"Speak," I commanded.

"Do we have a deal, *mage*?" he countered, and I could hear agony in his words.

"Tell me what you know of the Rock Quarry slaves and I shall decide then."

"I will take you to the Rebels and tell them everything I know of the Rock Quarry slaves and what's been happening to them. You have my word. I know where and what she is doing with them. Give me the antidote and you have my word; I shall do no harm to you."

My heart dropped. Viyak's face flashed as I tried to blink. Praying, hoping that he was still alive.

The Destroyer plummeted to the ground. He clenched his teeth tight until the white foam was now spilling through. Hesitation ran through me.

But it didn't matter now.

"I have no antidote, Destroyer. Let Fate decide. Survive the poison and we have a deal. You die and I hope you burn in Hell for eternities." I said to him bitterly. "I'll see you on the other side," I spat as I kicked his sword away.

"You..." He withered through clenched teeth. "I... D-D-deal," he rumbled, closing his eyes shut and letting the white drool pool beside his mouth.

51

I stood there staring at his motionless body, at the glass arrow piercing his skin. I wished for that hate to fill my blood, for that anger that I felt the day I escaped from him, but it wasn't there. Now I just felt disgust and pity.

A well-known ruthless Destroyer General now laid dead in the middle of nowhere, taken down by not even a mage, but by a human, a runaway slave.

Fate was indeed a funny thing. I picked up his sword and dropped it immediately. It burned, yet my hand was not even red. The sword was heavy; I could feel its power from within, as if the sword itself captured all the souls it slayed, keeping them locked in.

The fog was getting thicker by the minute, and the sun was making its way towards the horizon. I glanced around again and again, realizing that I wasn't sure which way to go. I was so preoccupied with vengeance that I refused to pay attention to anything else.

I growled in frustration, though refusing to feel regret for my decision.

I killed a Destroyer General. Surely, I could find my way to the damned forest.

CHAPTER 51

I wasn't sure how long I stared at his lifeless body until I finally tugged on the arrows from his thighs, snow turning bright red with his blood. I reached for the Basalt arrow when I saw a slight twitch of his arm.

He was alive.

Alive.

Somehow, he was still breathing. Barely. His lungs raised so very little that my eyes couldn't catch it. I lowered my ear to his chest. A small thud thud thud ran through me. I shuddered and took a few steps back.

No, it couldn't be.

That poison was deadly, and the arrows were covered in it.

Deadly.

Yet there was no doubt as I watched his chest rise subtly. He was indeed alive.

I pulled my dagger out. I could end it. Right now, right here. Slice his throat. End it all for good.

His words came back to me as if a parasite poisoned my mind. Rock Quarry slaves, Rebels… were they all more important than my vengeance, than vengeance for all those tortured kids?

I felt nauseous.

A defeated chuckle erupted from me. *Live a better life.* This was a twisted way of doing that.

I pulled a thick rope and started tying his hands together. One of his palms was covered in brutal scars, burn marks. Scars he didn't have the last time I saw him.

My heart winced as I broke the glass arrow, until just a little piece of it was buried inside of his wound, even if he tried, he wouldn't be able to get that shard of glass out of him without help.

I made a deal with a monster, and I would honor it.

His life for his knowledge.

I shot another arrow at him, this time at his other shoulder, disabling his other arm.

But life can be very very painful sometimes.

I patted down his muscled body, taking away every single piece of weaponry he had. Resting against my small bedroll, I waited for my enemy to wake up.

52

I woke up to the voice rumbling near me in anger.

"You shot me again?" he frustratingly growled. "What happened to letting Fate decide?" he asked, slowly sitting up, wincing as he tried to move his arms. I quickly got up to my feet. He was awake and alert.

Alive, godsdamnit. *Alive.*

My face filled with annoyance and disappointment as he stood up. A tiny hope that he would indeed die through the night vanished at last.

"No harm was part of your deal, Destroyer. Mine was to allow you to live." I glared at him, sizing his rising body. After a while, I bandaged his wounds to stop the bleeding last night. A pathetic move I now regretted, as he cautiously eyed the bandages. He moved his hand and I flinched at that gesture. A fire summoning gesture I recognized. And to my ease and satisfaction, nothing happened, not even a single spark.

"You've wasted enough of my time. Now take me to the Rebels before I disagree with Fate's decision," I commanded.

He took another look at me, at Heart Piercer now visibly strapped on my thigh. Our eyes locked, and I growled. "Move it."

Though annoyance was rising with each of his breaths, a part of me calmed at the knowledge that now I had not one but two bargaining chips.

The Destroyer General with the intel to sell, and Kaius's papers; all of which I could trade for freeing Viyak.

"You are the one who shot me in both of my legs. How quickly do you think I'll walk?" he said, tugging on his roped hands, though he started walking. "Did you wield my swords?" he asked intrigued, glancing at the swords wrapped in my blanket. I didn't reply, but the corner of his mouth rose. "How did it feel?" he asked, now smirking wide.

"It felt like you have a tiny dick and are overcompensating with two swords for it. Now move or I'll chop it even shorter."

He smiled wickedly and I debated ending the bargain right there, but he moved, taking a limping step ahead. I followed him close behind. My crossbow, ready to fire at any moment, aimed at his heart. He paused only after a few steps, turning to take another look at me from head to toe, considering; something primal in him shifted as if he sized me up like a predator sizing their prey before an attack.

No, not anymore.

"I missed the first time, but I won't miss the second," I said, narrowing my eyes. "Or should I demonstrate that I am a better shot now?" I lowered my crossbow until it pointed straight at his manhood. He raised his brow as if daring me to do it. I almost pulled the trigger just to wipe off the roguish smirk of his face, but I paused, realizing I would have to bandage him *there* and I would rather let him bleed out and die. "Move." I glared at him and gestured with my eyes to the distance.

"As you wish." He sarcastically bowed. We started walking towards the unknown horizon.

"How do you know where the forest is?" I finally asked after following his steps in the deep snow for hours, lost amidst the fog.

"I sense it. Don't you?" He kept walking but I could sense smugness in his tone as my silence confirmed that I didn't. "Ah, so that's why you didn't kill me," he said out loud, snickering. "And here I thought it was your honor."

This was a mistake. I knew it. But Viyak's starved figure crossed my mind. For him I would do this. But after?

No, after this, no more promises. No bargains. Never again.

I wasn't sure if I could even keep this one. Luckily for me, the General stayed silent most of the way. We didn't stop all day, though I could see his limp getting heavier by the hour, his pace slowing down to an unbearably sluggish crawl.

I felt it then. The little tug of damp air laced with just a bit of something I couldn't wrap my mind around. It dawned on me then.... Magic. Cursed magic, I realized as we stepped onto the threshold of the forest.

"Welcome to the Cursed Forest," he said, carefully crossing the definitive line between the deep snow and thick yellow leaves rotting on the ground. I followed him hesitantly. Glancing back only once to the valley still covered in a thick fog. The forest wasn't foggy, and it was also surprisingly dry, I realized. Looking around, only thick trees and shrubbery were spotted around us as we stepped through it all. The trees were large, their roots twisted and wide, but it was the heights of those trees that left me breathless. They were the largest trees I'd ever seen. Their highest tops reached so high, they seemed to touch the sun itself.

I looked up just enough to see that almost no sky was visible through those large, heavily intertwined branches, as if they all were connected with one another. Though it was dry, the air was cold; so cold that even as we walked, I couldn't stop shivering. Ice was filling my lungs, quickly sucking the life out of me.

We hiked, crossing the wilted leaves and stepping over broken branches.

I kept my eyes on the General most of the day, allowing myself only quick glances to my surroundings. Even with his legs wounded and his left shoulder bandage bleeding through his cloak, the Destroyer moved with grace. I might have stumbled a few times, but he walked as if the whole world was under his feet, and he was the king of it. He might have been my prisoner now, but I had not forgotten even for a second had that he was the Mad Queen's brutal General. A cruel, wicked General. A Destroyer.

No, he wouldn't let me forget. His pristinely cut hair, his muscled body, his sharp cheekbones, his strong jaw, his calloused hands and those sharp ancient eyes; everything about him painted the picture of a bloodthirsty monster and his attractiveness was just more proof. A tool to lure you in, to frazzle you, to let your guard down.

I should be scared of him. I knew I should.

And maybe in a way, I was. Though I didn't want to dwell on it. My body was in complete overdrive around him from stress. Grimacing, I reminded myself that he was just a man, and I should pity him. I despised him for what he was. A truly rotten human, with power and skill to change the world, yet power that was used only to terrorize and hurt people...*children.*

And now, only good for the answers he had.

No, I wouldn't be afraid of him.

I watched him pause, taking a breath, slowing down to almost a crawl. I should feel pity, but instead I imagined Heart Piercer slicing through his large back.

I would kill him.

Once I knew what was happening with the Rock Quarries' slaves, I would sink my dagger straight into his rotten heart, bargain or not.

No, vengeance wasn't pretty. Vengeance wasn't meek. Vengeance wasn't kind.

And neither was I.

I readjusted his wrapped-up swords. I could feel the heat even as my skin just slightly grazed over it. He took a few steps and paused again. I stopped, highly alerted as I looked around, searching for anything that made him stop so abruptly. His eyes narrowed. He too was on high alert.

He was cautious, too aware, and it irked me that it wasn't because of me. Whatever was in this forest made him pause. Whatever it was, I realized, it was a much bigger threat than the poisoned crossbow arrow pointed at his back, or the sharp Basalt Glass dagger strapped to my thigh.

I listened with him, and I heard nothing. Absolutely *nothing,* I realized.

Not a cricket, or a bird, nor a deer or a hopping rabbit. I grew up in forests and fields, they were noisy, so loud, but here...Here, I heard nothing, not even the wind.

Only cold, frozen, stale air and deathly silence.

"We camp here for the night. It's not safe to keep going," he said, taking a look around and finally resting against the bottom of a large, twisted tree. My face laced with unpleasantry, but I didn't object as I sat down on the fallen tree across from him.

"How long until we arrive?" I asked, pulling a bag of provisions out.

"Another three days or so. Unless you decide to shoot me again then probably a week or more." He smirked with arrogance.

"Don't tempt me, Destroyer," I snarled back as I threw a piece of bread at him.

He nodded in appreciation.

I sliced a large piece of smoked salmon to make a sandwich for myself and drank just a sip of my water. I didn't think that it would've been a concern with all the snow around, but this forest was dry, and each sip counted if we were going on a three-day journey with only one day's worth of water supply.

Dinner was quiet and scarce. The tiny rays of sun that snuck past the tall trees were gone. Replaced by darkness and cold. My body shivered nonstop now, a pointless attempt at keeping me warm.

"You should start a fire," the Destroyer mumbled, resting against the tree with his eyes closed.

"And you should keep your mouth shut or I'll cut your tongue out," I spat back. He chuckled.

"If I keep my mouth shut, how shall I give you all the intel you want me for, *mage?*" He kept his eyes closed still, though a corner of his mouth tugged upright. It irked me that he called me mage. Not the word itself, but his tone. Like he too knew that I wasn't one.

"You can write." I clenched my teeth to stop them from shattering.

My toes were numb, and my nose now covered with the large scarf was runny. Each breath froze my wet lip, but I would rather freeze to death than risk a fire with the Destroyer in my midst.

The swords clanged against each other as I dropped them on the ground, wrapping myself in the warmed-up blanket. Though still shivering, I sighed in relief as my body slowly warmed up thanks to the thick wool.

I kept my eyes open, staring at him and each of his slow breaths.

"If you keep staring at me like that I might turn into ashes." He smirked, opening his eyes, locking with mine. There was something different about him this time, I realized. Still arrogant and still deadly, yet his gaze was so unlike the day we met.

I raised my eyebrow at him and curled my lip.

"I keep hoping for that and yet you are still here. *Talking.*" I adjusted my blanket and bags, settling in the cocoon of warmth.

"You know you can sleep. I won't hurt you," he said, looking at me. Reassuring. My eyes narrowed at that look.

"Says the person who incinerated a Royal guard within seconds. Yeah, I think I'll put my trust in someone else."

"Says the person who shot me even when I was unconscious."

"You deserved it."

"Didn't he?"

He did, but I didn't reply.

We both stayed quiet for the rest of the night. I wasn't sure if he was asleep as I fought exhaustion until my eyes couldn't stay open anymore. Just an hour, I promised myself.

53

I woke up from a sudden sensation of falling. One blink and I was no longer buried in the light clouds far in the sky, deep within my dream. Instead, I was slumped against the ground. One glance and I realized the Destroyer was gone. His spot by the tree empty. My eyes raced through my surroundings.

Not a single trace of him.

Anger flooded me but not even at him. Gods, I would do the same. I *did* the same.

No, I was pissed at myself. I took another look; he couldn't have gotten far…unless he walked all night.

Gods. I had to have been out for hours. I bit my lip in frustration.

No amount of Fate or luck could make up for this lack of competence.

"Shit," I angrily mumbled. I was alive, so there was some upside to this but now I was stranded deep in the forest with no sense of where to go. "Shit!" This time I yelled kicking the frosted leaves around me.

"Good morning, *mage*." I jumped at his voice, which sounded as though it were just a step behind me. He snuck up so quickly. *Too* quickly.

"Where the fuck were you?" I asked, choking out the anger within me, suspiciously assessing him. My dagger was already out. My eyes instinctively scanned his shoulder, analyzing the bandage. Still intact with the same bloodied knot that I tied. Basalt Glass still deep inside the wound. Good.

"I needed to use the bathroom, or shall I relieve myself in front of you?" he asked, raising his brow, tilting his head slightly to the side as he leaned against the large tree.

"Actually yes, do that. I will kill you if you leave my sight again."

He raised his brows in amusement just for a second, and then narrowed his eyes with a challenge. He lowered his body until his nose almost touched mine. My drawn dagger pressed into his chest. He lowered his voice until it was a sultry whisper. "Swear it?"

I didn't back down, my eyes confidently staring back at him. He was just a man, I reminded myself. A part of me was unaware that instead of fear and panic, my mind was distracted with his strong pine and campfire smell.

He moved then, walking past me, leaving me standing there, dumbfounded, still rifled by a complete mix of feelings within me. I turned to follow him.

We continued our journey for hours. Quietly.

I thought about asking so many things, saying so many things. Telling him just how much I despised him, telling him how I would kill him for everything he had done. Carve him up into pieces. But I realized that no words would express my feelings enough for him to understand because no matter how long the dog barked, the cat wouldn't understand it.

He stayed quiet too. His limp was getting better, I realized, when he didn't take as long to overstep a fallen young tree. Priya mentioned that Destroyers healed faster but it had been barely two days. I thought about shooting him again and though my crossbow was now always loaded, I didn't pull the trigger. Maybe tomorrow.

The loud raven's screech yanked me into the present, away from the abyss of my thoughts. Both of our heads turned as we saw a large black bird flying over us. A little note of excitement ran through me as I watched the bird fly away. We had to be approaching the end of the forest now. Maybe we would see more animals or life.

I turned my head back just as the Destroyer General slammed into me with full force of his body. My dagger fell a few feet away from me. Even with his hands tied, the sheer mass of his body was suffocating me underneath. I didn't even have the chance blink as a cloud of black shadows and bones appeared out of nowhere and sunk claws into his back.

He groaned from the pain as the creature took a chunk of his flesh, ripping his cloak apart. The creature shrieked and recoiled only after a minute. I pushed the General off and rolled to the side, quickly getting up to my feet. The shadow moved again, this time shaping, becoming more of a physical creature. I shot my arrow at it, but it went through it like a cloud, landing far behind it. The creature screeched again, almost busting my ear drums. Adrenaline shot through my veins.

"Give me the sword!" the Destroyer yelled, his eyes still on the creature.

"No!" I shouted back. Whatever this was, I knew the true monster was the one right next to me.

The creature lunged for me again. I jumped, but the being was faster. The Destroyer shoved me back again, shielding me with his body. Both the creature and the Destroyer roared as his chest was shredded with claws.

"Burn it!" he yelled at me from the ground. A General commanding his soldier. The creature within me tugged on its leash, eager to be freed but I willed myself to not panic.

Breathe.

But that breath cost me. The creature, as if feeding on the Destroyer's flesh, became more visible. Its claws became more deadly as it lunged for my chest, I twisted but not fast enough as the curved claws scraped my chest, ripping to shreds my leathers until they were nothing but ribbons.

"BURN IT!" he yelled at me again. I dodged the creature again as it leapt for us.

"I would rather die than let you summon fire!" I yelled back as I dodged another claw.

"We will both die, if you don't burn him right now!" He turned to face me just for a second as he yanked my body to the ground, letting the creature tear into him again. He dropped to his knees in agony. His back soaked in blood; the remaining threads of his cloak mixed with his flesh. "Use the sword," he roared, as I glanced at the platinum piece of metal shining against the darkness.

I lost whatever control I had over my panic. Immobile, I watched the creature gather its shadows and lunge for another attack.

"The SWORD, FINN!" he yelled at me again. The creature, now as if on wings, flew down to me with its bear-like claws opened wide. "GRAB THE FUCKING SWORD, FINN!" The General shouted.

Those words. My name…it was as if a bucket of ice water poured over me, pulling me out of the sheer terror. I grabbed the sword and sunk it deep into the creature, but I was too slow. The creature sunk its claws into my leg, shredding it to pieces. I screamed in agony. My eyes darkened just a bit, but I didn't let go of the sword, holding it tight with both of my arms, twisting it deeper.

Another large sword went through the creature, decapitating it, slicing it to pieces, until there was nothing left. The being dissolved into thin air just as quickly as it had appeared.

I dropped my head to the ground, panting. Still clenching tight to the sword. I glanced at the Destroyer. He was on his feet, warily looking around us, his sword out as if expecting another attack. When it didn't happen, he lowered his sword, resting against it just for a blink. His body was covered in blood. Soaked. His breaths were long and inconsistent. But it wasn't the blood or the gore that made my heart plummet. It was anger.

Rage laced his face.

I glanced over to the loose ropes on the ground, too far from my reach.

I attempted to rise but winced from pain. My leg was grated. Just as shredded as my leathers, exposing my chest down to my bra.

Though the monster was gone, another was freed and now stood in front of me, sword in his hand. Rage didn't leave his face, though he dropped the sword. His eyes stuck on my wounded leg.

"Where are the bandages?" he asked, dropping to his knees beside me. I wasn't sure how he was still moving. His wounds were much worse than mine. And mine hurt like hell.

"You are hurt, where are the bandages, Finn." Not a question, but a command.

"I am fine. What was that?" I asked, pulling on those last threads of adrenaline blocking away the pool of tears ready to spill.

He ignored my words as he ripped the leg of my pants open.

"*Do not touch me* or I will kill you." I glared at him, aware of just how empty the threat was. The muscles at his temples twitched, but he moved his hands off my bleeding leg.

His eyes moved up from my leg, scanning each inch of my body, pausing on my chest, on the ripped leathers, and the bloodied up exposed skin.

"What is that?" he asked, staring straight at my breasts, his tone changing completely.

"Take a step away, *Destroyer*." But this time he didn't move; his eyes didn't move. I clenched my jaw. "*Move back*," I commanded, standing up, wincing as pain shot through my body. He still didn't move. My blood boiled at his defiance.

"Where did you get that ring?" he asked, his tone low, guttural. Only now it dawned on me that Tuluma's amulet and Kaius's ring were no longer hidden, hanging between my barely covered breasts. "You only have one chance to answer me and you better make it count, *mage*. Where. Did. You. Get. That. Ring?" He no longer had the smirk or the mocking tone.

No. Now stood the General I remembered. The bloodthirsty, death loving devil.

He might not have been able to summon fire, but his eyes, gods, they burned. I snarled like a wounded animal.

"I found it."

"*Liar.*"

He moved faster than a panther in the night, closing the distance between us within a blink, shoving me against a tree. I slapped him hard against his cheek. He flinched, grabbing my wrist tight. Muscles in his jaw tensed. "Let me ask you one *last* time. Where did you get this ring?"

"I'll tell you once we get to the Rebels."

He grumbled, not liking my answer.

Pitted against the tree, my feet dangled in the air. I tried kneeing him in his groin with my other leg, but he just pinned me harder until I couldn't move at all.

I had run out of moves or any kind of options.

This was it.

"It's time we stopped playing games, don't you think, *mage*?" he whispered in my ear.

Then he headbutted me so hard that I blacked out.

54

I was alive, I realized as I opened my eyes. Warm, welcoming air filled my lungs, even as small rays of sunshine kissed my cheeks. I was alive.

Stitched up and well bandaged too, I noticed, looking at my chest and my leg.

Yet the concern came crashing in as I took in my surroundings. I was in a large, circled tent, tall and spacious, decorated with well-maintained furniture. But it wasn't the lamps or the pillows or the neat desk that made my heart stop. It was the dark armor in the corner and the large black cape behind it.

I winced as I jerked my body up. Limping to the small window not too far from my bed, hoping, praying, begging for one simple truth.

My wrists were sore from the thick rope that tied them together. I pulled on a small flap to peek behind the tent window.

It couldn't be.

My heart raced as I beheld a large camp. So many tents, and those black and silver flags. *Destroyer* Flags. I turned away from the window as a group of Destroyer soldiers walked by laughing, their laughter like poison, making me instantly nauseous.

No.

It couldn't be.

But reality slipped through.

Somehow, the twisted threads of Fate brought me to the one place I was so desperately trying to escape.

Dread sunk deep in my soul as if it were an anchor on a ship, pulling me to a complete halt.

I was in the belly of the beast. Surrounded by Destroyer soldiers. My daggers were gone. My knives were, too. Intuitively, my hands quickly ran through my hair. In the matted, blood and dirt covered hair, I pulled out a pin. The only one left in my almost completely unbraided hair. I looked at my prized possession.

I only needed one.

* * *

I LIMPED OUT OF THE TENT. TWO DESTROYER SOLDIERS—THE General's guard dogs—startled by my sudden appearance cleared their throats.

"Please, follow us," one of them said as he pointed to a tent that was larger than the rest. I didn't reply as I clenched my fists and followed them.

"Here." The soldier raised the tent flap to the entrance.

The room was spacious; bright, thick rugs lined the floor. A large, circular table took up most of the space surrounded by many chairs. There were only three people in the room.

I recognized Orest immediately. He wore his dark silvered armor, though without his helm. The burgundy curls on his head were longer now since I saw him last. He nodded to me in recognition.

A petite, almost too short of a woman, stared me down as I walked in. She was leaning against the table. Her loosely fitted tunic cut off at her shoulders exposing her very toned tan arms. Her shiny, charcoal-black hair was in a high bun with two steel spikes poking through it. Sides of her head were shaved down and a large tattoo covered her left side, starting at the top of her face and extending deep down her neck.

She stopped fidgeting with what I realized was Kaius's ring, as her thin pointy eyes narrowed in on me, her already harsh features becoming even more piercing as she slowly let out a loud breath and clenched the ring in her small hand.

And then there was *him*.

The General was the only one sitting, resting his elbows on the glass tabletop. He was shirtless, I realized, though most of his body was covered with bandages, exposing only his well sculpted arms.

The soldiers behind me stayed outside the tent as I took another heavy step in.

"Free me," I demanded clenching my fists tighter, trying to keep the anger at bay, though failing. "We had a deal."

"Yes, about that…" He looked back at me and readjusted in his seat, stiffening a bit.

"Where is Kaius?" the woman interrupted him. Her tone, her face so intimidating. Menacing.

Dead.

But I wouldn't delight them in that knowledge.

"Oh, it seems I am late to the party." A seductive male voice sounded at my back. I turned just in time to see a giant of a man come in. He was breathtaking. His skin was as black as the abyss. His eyes shimmered with gold. His hair, braided in long, thick braids, with gold trinkets decorating them. And his face…there were no words to describe the complexity of his utter beauty. Whoever he was, he was *a god*.

"Commander." His perfect lips stretched in a welcoming smile at the woman near me. The god of a man exchanged a small greeting with Orest too and then looked at the General. "So, we finally get to meet her." Amusement lit his face as he pulled a chair out and lazily sat on it, his gold eyes studying me.

"So did you really bite him?" he asked to taunt me, his face full of delight.

But I didn't answer his question either. Instead, I took a step closer and spat at his face. The Commander raised her brows in angry shock and sharply turned to the General.

But the god of a man slowly wiped the spit off his face, taking a long breath, then he turned to face the General and Orest.

"I am sorry, but you two imbeciles thought that she was a *Creator*? She reeks of defiance." Orest lowered his eyes, hiding an upbeat smile. The General just ignored his jab. The man lowered his eyes to my tied wrists, his face filled with concern.

"Did she not agree to join us?" He turned to the General.

But those words struck me harder than any whip.

"Join you? *Join. You?* Even if I am not a mage... I will *never* join you. I would rather give up my soul than join *you*. The day will come soon when I'll dance on your bones and watch each one of you be brutally slaughtered by the Rebels. Justice will come for you, and I for one hope you all choke on your own ashes for eternity," I angrily hissed.

"Rebels?" Xentar now turned again to the General. "Oh Gideon... you haven't told her?" He rubbed his face with both of his hands.

"Between her proactively attempting to murder me, the glide attacking us and finding Kaius's ring, I haven't had a chance, but was about to before somebody interrupted me." He looked at Zora.

She folded her arms tight. "I still think it's a bad idea to tell her *anything* before she gives us answers first, Gideon." She narrowed her eyes at him.

Gideon?

Gideon.

Gideon.

My face widened in shock as my mind frantically connected the dots. My heart slowed to an almost nonexistent beat.

"*Tell me what?*"

"We *are* the Rebels, princess." Xentar smiled at me.

"*No.*" My head shook in denial. My eyes instinctively turned to Orest. He just nodded in confirmation.

"It can't be. But you are all Destroyers."

"Oh, please. Do I look like a Destroyer to you?" Xentar laughed as he twisted his hand and vines filled with flowers appeared out of thin air.

A Creator.

No. My mind crumbled like a sandcastle against a large ocean wave.

"There is one more thing, Finn." The General. No, Gideon.

Gideon said, looking up at me sensibly.

But my mind was already numb from shock, unable to process the words that came out of him next.

"You, Finn, are a Destroyer."

THE END

AFTERWORD

Thank you so much for taking a chance and reading my debut novel! I hope you enjoyed it!

For a new indie author reviews are **crucial** so please consider leaving a review on Amazon and/or Goodreads and sharing with your friends and family your new find!

Also, if you are interested in joining my ARC team please register at bakumovka.com.

A Simple Truth, Book Two is coming out February 2024! So make sure to sign up for my newsletter for updates!

ACKNOWLEDGMENTS

It feels a bit surreal writing this. My debut novel is written, edited, and now officially published.

To be honest I am still amazed that I even made it to this point.

A written story.

A published book.

And now you – an actual reader!

The countless hours and late nights spent on creating this wouldn't be the same if it wasn't for you – my readers. For taking on a new book, for accepting this adventure, for trusting a new author and for giving it shot. Thank you! Thank you! Thank you!

As a reader I always read authors acknowledgements but now that I am writing one I feel like I could write an entire book about all the people that made this possible. But here are a few that have altered my life.

To Kassidy Griffin, for being the best beta reader and my very first fan. You have changed the course of my life forever and I will be eternally grateful for your feedback and support.

A special thank you my sisters in law, Katie, Kayla and Lexi for being the best sisters in law. For always listening to my never-ending book ideas and being excited for me. For being my very first readers! You guys are the best book club I could ever dream of! Thank you for supporting all my crazy adventures and being the best ACOTAR cosplay team there is ;)

To my dear father and mother in-law, Bud and Kris, while you are not allowed to read these series haha, I am forever grateful for your unwavering support and love, for watching my kids so I could have a break, for always providing the best snacks, and for taking me in as a young Ukrainian girl and loving me unconditionally.

To my sister, Yelena. There are not enough words to describe how much I love our relationship. Thank you for being my creative director, my confidant, my best friend and for taking that one picture of me writing my first novel at 13 just prove to mom that I was keeping you up (picture is on the www.bakumovka.com) I might have hated your guts growing up but turns out you are not too bad after all :P

But most importantly, I could never have done it without Bud, my husband, my very best friend and my soulmate. Thank you for all those countless hours of making dinners and putting kids to bed everyday so I could focus on my book. For listening to me ramble on and on about books, Booktok and AuthorTok drama, for reading ACOTAR just so you could understand why Suriel videos are funny, for watching TV shows on silent so I could write alongside you. Thank you for pushing me to publish my stories even when my doubts crept in. Thank you for always being there for me through the bad and the good, and for showing me what true love is. I love you forever and always.

Book 2 of the Freckled Fate series coming to you soon!

ABOUT THE AUTHOR

 Tetyana was born and raised in Kyiv, Ukraine. In 2012, she moved to Utah, USA to attend Ensign college and pursue a degree in business. She is now a proud wife and a mother with a successful career in software sales.

Tetyana has had a strong passion for reading ever since she was a kid. But her world completely changed when she read Harry Potter series at the age of 8 and discovered the world of fantasy. She hasn't looked back since. Now, as a self-published fantasy-romance author, Tetyana looks forward to helping other authors on their journey. She named her publishing company after a tiny rural Ukrainian village in Kyivska Oblast' where she spent her summers growing up. With no internet or cell service or even indoor plumbing, Tetyana spent her summer days helping her grandparents take care of their small farm while spending any free time outside reading. "Bakumovka stands for more than a small village to me. It stands for a place of peace and magic. A place where imagination runs wild and free. A place of comfort and love." Tetyana says.

Made in United States
Orlando, FL
21 October 2024

53001898R00195